D0275948

Snowbooks

First Edition
Copyright © Sarah Bryant 2006

Sarah Bryant has asserted her right under the Copyright, Designs
and Patents Act 1988 to be identified as the author of this work.
This book is sold subject to the condition that it shall not, by
way of trade or otherwise, be lent, resold, hired out, or otherwise
circulated without the publisher's prior consent in any form of
binding or cover other than that in which it is published and
without a similar condition including this condition being
imposed on the subsequent purchaser

Proudly published in 2006 by
Snowbooks Ltd.
120 Pentonville Road
London N1 9JN
www.snowbooks.com

A CIP catalogue record for this book
is available from the British Library

ISBN 1 905005 22 9
ISBN-13 9 781905 005 22 2

By kind permission of Saqi books, English translation of "The
Crusades Through Arab Eyes" © 1984, 2004. from original
edition by Amin Maalouf 1983

The donation from the author's profits will help UNICEF to
provide children in the Middle East with better health care and
education, safe water and sanitation, as well as protecting children
from exploitation.

SAND DAUGHTER

SARAH BRYANT

For an end to crusades.

snowbooks

LONDON

Acye
Al-Quds
An-Nashah
Hadhbat al-Jaulan
Damascus
Eiq
Busrah
Amman
Kerak
Jebal Habis (mountain)
Al-Bitra
Nahr al-Urdun river
Ayla
Wadi Hiwil
Dijlah river
Euphrates river
Baghdad
JAZIRAH
Zagros Mountains
PE
Yazd
Domat al-Jandal
An-Nafud Desert
Shatt al-Arab
Basra
OULTREJOURDAIN
Mecca
KINGDOM OF JERUSALEM
ANTIOCH
KINGDOM OF AMENIA

MAP OF THE MIDDLE EAST c. 1187

Samarqand
Shomali Plain
Shebar pass
Bamiyan
Kabul
Hindu Kush
KHORASAN
Zabol
Hirmand river

PROLOGUE

"There is Kerak Castle," said Yazid, pointing to a low mountain
in the middle distance, topped by fortress walls. "That is the
home of Brins Arnat."

Rahil clutched her grandfather's hand more tightly. Like all
Muslim children in Oultrejourdain, she had been brought up on
tales of the Franj prince's savagery, but she had more reason than
most to dread this place. It had haunted her dreams for as long as
she could remember, for it was Kerak that had killed her parents.
They had been taken prisoner in one of Arnat's many raids as
they made their own pilgrimage when she was two years old. And
so, although Rahil had never laid eyes on the castle before, she
nevertheless knew it by the intimacy of fear, just as she knew her
parents' faces in her nightmares, though she had long forgotten
them by day.

Now the only family left to Rahil was Yazid, but though she
loved him devotedly, she would have given anything to have been
left at home. She had even asked him if she could stay with a
neighboring family; but in the end, her grandfather had felt that
it was wrong to impose on others for so long. The trip to Mecca
was long and unpredictable and besides, he had said, it would
be good for Rahil to make the *hajj* now, while she was young,

instead of leaving it until the end of her life, as he had.

They drew closer to the hilltop fortress. Danger radiated from its walls like the miasmic shimmer of heat on a noontime desert. Rahil tried to convince herself that what she felt was merely fear, not foresight. She tried to concentrate on the caravan's size and the strength of its defenses. She counted it down from the front, where the *Amir al-Hajj* rode on a magnificent bay stallion. He was personally responsible for the safety of the travelers; it was a matter of honor. Spreading out behind him was a troop of soldiers led by a phalanx of officers. There were also all the officials of a town: a judge, his notaries and secretary, officials to oversee the care of the animals and the distribution of provisions, a saddler, a staff of cooks, even an inspector of weights and measures. Then there were the pilgrims themselves, grouped according to their point of origin and marching with the discipline of soldiers.

Surely, thought Rahil, even Brins Arnat would think twice before attacking a group of such size and might; and if he did, he would surely be interested in the wealthy pilgrims, with their rich trappings and their high ransom potential. Surely he would not touch an old man and a ten-year-old child in nondescript clothing, carrying only enough money to pay their way at the caravanserais. Surely…and yet as the castle loomed closer, Rahil found that she was sure of nothing but her own terror.

*

As Rahil looked up at the castle, Brins Arnat looked down, watching the caravan approach with a quickening of his pulse that was all too rare since his wife began locking her door at night and then, to spite him, those of the serving wenches. He did not, of course, think of himself as Brins Arnat, though at least, in their club-tongued way, the Saracens had the sense to refer to him as "Prince". In fact, he had been born Reynald de Châtillon, but he preferred to think of himself as the Prince of Oultrejourdain, and forced all of his underlings to refer to him as such. The other nobles and the king simply called him "Kerak" after the mighty focal-point of his southern domain. Though he would have preferred for them to call him "Prince" as well, Kerak was acceptable when laid alongside de Châtillon, for the latter name was the only thread still connecting him to the tiny blot of a lordship in the Champagne where he had been born, and Kerak preferred to forget it.

Now, in his sixty-first year, he could hardly remember Europe at all, and it was more a conscious act of forgetting than not. For Kerak had been his father's second son, with no birthright but the name and an ambition that soared well beyond any reasonable expectations. As an adolescent he railed against his filial insignificance, never imagining that in the uneasy territories of Outremer, his destiny was already forming. The challenge came in the shape of an upstart Syrian *atabeg* called Imad ad Din Zengi. Zengi was a brutal warrior with a deep conviction of the wrong done his people at the hands of the Frankish invaders and a consuming ambition to take back the holy city they had conquered half a century earlier. Not a man to waste time, he began by attacking the weakest of the Franks' territories, the northern County of Edessa, which fell like a ripe peach to his *mujahiddin*.

The outraged Pope Eugenius III responded by calling for a second Holy War. For de Châtillon and all the other second sons of Europe, it was a golden opportunity. In 1146 he took the cross and marched south under the banner of Louis VII of France, ostensibly to avenge Edessa, but driven mainly by the ambition to wrestle some kind of significance from the slipshod society of Outremer. Though the holy war failed, he had acquitted himself favorably in the battles, and so he won the hand of a wealthy widow.

Even then, securing his place had not been simple. Some would say that he'd orchestrated his own trouble. The razing of Cyprus had landed him in the Aleppo dungeon for sixteen years, an experience he had used to hone his hatred of all things Arabic. His wife died three years into his incarceration and upon his release de Châtillon married another widow, this one far wealthier than the last. Among the many assets Stephanie de Milly brought to their marriage, none charmed de Châtillon quite so well as the dusty piece of property at the extreme south of the Frankish kingdom, known as Oultrejourdain.

In the years since his marriage to Stephanie had soured, de Châtillon – now known as Kerak – had mastered that wild county. Franks and Saracens alike quivered in his iron grip; even the king dared not defy him. In fact, in all of that wide land there was only one man who did not respect Kerak's will. The would-be prince was determined to break his him, and there below his castle walls, practically within spitting distance, was his opportunity.

"You have a leery look in your eye, *Messire*," spoke a voice behind Kerak. "What is it you are thinking of?"

Kerak turned from the caravan to face Gerard de Ridefort. The Templar Grand Master stood looking back at him calmly, white tunic fluttering in the morning breeze. His face was properly obsequious, but there was a glimmer of derision in his blue eyes which sent a hot spike of anger rising in Kerak. Though allies by necessity, Kerak and de Ridefort bore little love for one another. Perhaps they were too much alike: for de Ridefort, too, had risen to his position from humble beginnings. The younger son of a minor Flemish lord, he, like Kerak, had unwittingly possessed all the prerequisites to rise to the top of the Holy Land's frontier society: flexible ethics, a way with a sword, a faculty for sycophancy and a handsome face.

But while Kerak had chosen the sword to hack out a name for himself, de Ridefort had slithered his way to the top by political maneuvering. While both had paid dearly for their present status, it wasn't immediately visible in de Ridefort's case. Age and bitterness had ground and warped Kerak into a plump, red-headed devil with a ruddy drunkard's face marred by a dead, milky eye, the remnant of a run-in with a Saracen blade during the razing of Cyprus. De Ridefort, while just as atrophied within by his own brand of bitterness, had clung to his bland, blonde looks and still presented a good approximation of most ladies' ideal knight – something that had stood him in good stead when it came to wrangling for his present position. Kerak hated him for this more than anything else.

"What do you want?" he snapped.

De Ridefort bowed slightly, the sun glinting on his long, gray-streaked golden hair. "*Messire* requested my presence."

Kerak was about to bluster when he recalled that this was true. He had called for de Ridefort as soon as he had spotted the caravan, before he allowed its possibilities to distract him. "Yes…" he said, then, "yes," again, with more conviction. "You see the heathen caravan passing below? It is armed, and it should not be. Take the garrison and teach them a lesson."

De Ridefort looked at Kerak as he might a fractious child bent on some disastrous amusement. "Forgive me, *Messire*, but are you certain that this is wise? We are currently bound by a truce to the Sultan Salah ad-Din –"

"That truce was none of my making!" Kerak cried, furious that this underling would challenge him.

"But if you break it," de Ridefort answered carefully, "the war that follows will be."

"Yes…and the Latin states will thank me for doing what their king is too spineless to do himself."

"Careful, Kerak," said the Master, with a twist of smirk in his voice, though his expression remained pious. "Remember who it is that keeps you."

Kerak eyed the caravan, framed now in sections between the crenels and merlons of the battlement. A few more minutes and it would be too late; and so, although he longed to check de Ridefort for his arrogance, he kept his temper. "Kill the guard," he said coldly, "and put the pilgrims in the dungeon. If the women protest, rape them. If the men do, kill them."

De Ridefort's expressions were like fine water-color drawings: delicate, perfectly schooled, never overt but always giving clear voice to his thoughts. Now, he wore a look of refined disgust. Observing this, Kerak approached him with a tender smile until they were close enough to kiss, and for a moment the Templar

Master wondered if Kerak was mad enough to do just that.

Instead, fixing his eyes on de Ridefort's, he said: "You are hesitating, *Messire*, which leads me to wonder whether there is there something to the rumors that you have…how shall we put it…a particular 'friend' among the Saracen tribes?"

De Ridefort shut his eyes against the cruel glint in Reynald's, but he could not shut out the words, nor the rush of guilty hatred that ensued.

"The king may be an idiot, *Messire*," Kerak continued, "but he is still the king. A word from me and the whispers about you might become a good deal more…"

"You think that he would take the word of a madman over that of the Master of the Temple?" de Ridefort snapped, his pastel composure finally succumbing to a bright flush of anger.

Kerak shrugged, looking once more at the caravan. "Madmen generally speak the truth, while politicians lie by profession."

De Ridefort looked at Kerak for a long time, wondering why, of all the nobles in Outremer, it had to be this one who formed the buttress of his plan. But of course, as both of them knew, he had no choice but to obey him. So, with the slightest of bows he said, "*Messire*," and turned to rouse the garrison before he had to witness the satisfied smirk on Kerak's face.

PART I

I

"Khalidah!" Zaynab called for the third time. "When I find you, girl, I'll have your hide!" She looked around, one hand on her hip, the other shading her eyes from the late morning glare. Then, muttering, she walked off toward the horses' grazing area.

From the sandstone cave high on the slope above the camp, Khalidah and Bilal watched her go. "I think I'd prefer a beating to what Numair and 'Abd al-Hadi are planning," Khalidah said.

"How do you know what they're planning?" Bilal asked, drawing circles in the dust with his finger.

"Don't pretend to be stupid, Bilal," she said, for he had watched with her that morning as her father's twin, with whom he had fought on and off for control of the tribe since their own father died, had arrived with a retinue of armed horsemen and a magnificent mare. The mare was, quite simply, the most perfect that Khalidah had ever seen: a golden chestnut, her wedge-shaped head high and proud, her tail flickering out behind her like lightning strike. But though she loved horses beyond almost anything, the sight had filled Khalidah with the blackest despair. Among the tribes, where horses were family and a good war mare worth more than a man's life, a horse like that one was beyond value. She could not be sold or traded, only given as a gift of the highest honor: not unlike a sheikh's only daughter.

Bilal gave her a long, hard look and said, "Most girls would swoon at the prospect of marrying a man like Numair."

The words stung like a slap. "You think I should be happy to be traded for a warhorse?" Khalidah asked coldly.

"Your words, not mine."

"Speak plainly!"

"Fine," the boy said defiantly. "Don't marry your cousin; marry me."

It wasn't the first time he had said it, but it was the first time Khalidah thought he might mean it. She looked at him more carefully than she had looked in a long time. Like her, Bilal was just shy of sixteen. He was still more child than man, smooth-cheeked and scruffy in a worn-out robe that showed too much of his wrists and ankles. Still, he was well-built, with a fine, open face, skin the color of parchment and black-fringed eyes of a startling blue unseen among the tribes, which he hated for exactly that reason. He would make the kind of man most girls dreamed of. Yet even if he had not been the fatherless son of her own father's servant, and therefore unworthy of her, Khalidah would not have considered his proposal seriously.

"We're all wrong, Bilal," she said, continuing the thought aloud. "You know that."

"I know only that you keep saying it. You are my best friend, Khalidah –"

"And you are mine," she interrupted, "and that is exactly the problem. We bicker like old women; we know each other too well. I think for a marriage to work, it is best not to know too much about one another." Bilal frowned, and Khalidah wondered whether she really believed this. "I mean, honestly," she continued more loudly, to cover her own doubts, "how could I act subservient to you when you're the little boy who used to pee the bed?"

"Khalidah!" he wailed.

"Well, you could say the same of me. And besides, do you really think that you could beat me?"

"You want a husband who beats you?" he asked incredulously.

"Of course not!" Khalidah cried, wondering how the conversation had come to this. She thought for a moment, then, deciding it was better to change the subject, she said, "As for beatings, I suppose Zaynab really is too soft on me. She always threatens, but she never does it."

"I wish I could say the same."

Khalidah looked at Bilal with a mixture of pity and envy. "She's your mother, and my nurse. That is why she beats you and only threatens to beat me."

"I would gladly trade places with you."

Khalidah did not trust herself to answer this kindly, so instead she looked down at the assembly of black tents fluttering in the late-winter breeze. Beyond the tents, the horses and camels and goats grazed the scrub; beyond them, the desert seared white to the mountains on the horizon. At that moment, Khalidah knew, somewhere between the desert and the cave, the men of her family were constructing her fate. Her throat tightened at the thought.

"Come on," she said aloud, and started down the hill without waiting for Bilal to answer.

When they arrived at the camp, Bilal wandered off in search of something to eat while Khalidah made her way to her father's tent. The *majlis* was silent when she reached it, its *ghata* rolled up to show the men's quarters bereft of all but empty coffee cups and a smoldering fire. Khalidah's heart sank further: they had already decided. She was about to walk on when a movement caught her eye. She peered into the *majlis*'s shadows and then leapt back again in alarm, for it wasn't quite empty after all. Far back in one corner a man was sitting, beckoning to her. He looked to be about the same age as her cousin Numair – that is, twenty – but he was otherwise unlike him. His face was open where Numair's was reticent; he had black, wide-spaced eyes over a straight nose and a mouth that looked ready to smile. His beard was trimmed close, his hair cut short under an embroidered skullcap and he wore a short robe over baggy trousers with an embroidered woolen waistcoat on top. Most intriguing of all, he held a *qanun* on his lap – the most difficult and beautiful of the traditional instruments.

Nevertheless he was a stranger, and no doubt one who belonged to 'Abd al-Hadi. Khalidah had no intention of entering the tent with him on her own. Apparently surmising this, the man set the *qanun* aside with a sigh and came toward her. Instinctively, Khalidah drew away, but he caught her arm. She was going to scream – she ought to have screamed – and yet something made her hold back. Even years later, she would come no closer to defining it than to say that it was a kind of recognition: that sudden, rare recognition one feels for a person who is about to alter the course of one's life irrevocably.

Into that pause, the man spoke: "There is no time, *Sayyida* – they will be back in a moment. But I must implore you to say yes."

"What?" Khalidah demanded, recovering herself enough to snatch her hand away from his.

His sigh was full of the inevitable, his voice low and full of music. "Please, *Sayyida*, there is no time. Only promise me that you will say yes to whatever they ask of you."

"Who are you?" she demanded, furious. "You are a madman!"

He smiled. There was sun in it, the kind that drives for a blinding moment through stormclouds. "I'm not, more's the pity. They are coming now. They must not see us speaking together. But please, *Sayyida*. Say yes, and buy me time to explain…"

And then he was gone, back in the tent's shadowy corner like a mouse into its hole. Khalidah blinked after him for a moment, but then, hearing her father's voice and her uncle's ricocheting laugh, she turned and fled to the *maharama*. She had been hoping for time to compose herself before she faced Zaynab, but her nurse was sitting at the front of the tent with the *ghata* half raised, a wedge of sunlight falling across a garment she was stitching.

"So kind of you to make an appearance," the nurse said dryly.

"Have you been looking for me?" Khalidah asked, trying to make her voice sound normal.

Zaynab looked up as she bit off a thread and gave her a wry smile. "As you and my no-good son must know very well." But she said it affectionately. "You have too little respect for your elders, Khalidah. Not everyone is as forgiving as I am."

Noticing the anxious furrow between her brows, Khalidah felt a pang of guilt. "I'm sorry to have worried you, Zaynab."

"Hmm." She raised one eyebrow, her face set to chastise further, but when she looked closely at Khalidah she changed her mind. "Are you all right? You look pale."

"I'm fine."

Zaynab did not look convinced, but as Khalidah had already pushed past her into the *maharama*, she only said, "Good, because the men have asked you to join them at the noonday meal. You must change your dress."

"Zaynab!"

"Yes, I know. You'd much prefer to wear rags and break your neck riding with Bilal. Inside, please. You look as though you've been rolling in a dung heap."

Grudgingly, Khalidah followed Zaynab into the *maharama*. It was unusually spacious, even for a sheikh's tent; or, more to the point, unusually empty. A *maharama* was intended to house a harem of wives and their female children, but 'Abd al-Aziz's was occupied only by Khalidah and Zaynab. Though Khalidah knew that this was a mark of shame on her father, she could not wish it otherwise. The living quarters of other girls were hot and crowded with squabbling women and crying children, thick with the smells of cooking from the adjacent kitchen and the babies' dirty swaddling. She knew that they pitied her for her solitary existence, but Khalidah never woke without being thankful for the silence and ordered calm.

Zaynab let the *ghata* fall. With an effort Khalidah pushed her strange conversation with the minstrel out of her mind and began to take off her clothes. A moment later, a serving girl came in with a basin of hot water and a towel. The steam rising from the bowl was heavy with the smell of roses.

"Where did we get perfume?" Khalidah demanded.

"A gift from your uncle and cousin," Zaynab answered, without meeting her eyes.

"Since when do they bring us gifts?" she grumbled. "Usually it's misery." When Zaynab said nothing, Khalidah realized that she had been hoping her nurse would contradict her. A lump rose in her throat.

"Your father will handle them," Zaynab said at last, "but in the meantime, I won't have you dishonor him in front of his brother."

To avoid Zaynab's eyes, Khalidah pulled her dirty dress over her head, dropped it onto her bed. As she began to wash, she asked with careful nonchalance, "Who is the man they brought with them?"

"They brought a number of retainers with them, as always."

"I do not think that he is a retainer. He looks like a musician."

"Ah, yes," Zaynab answered. "He's 'Abd al-Hadi's new minstrel. They say the sheikh has taken a shine to him, and brings him everywhere with him."

Khalidah nodded as though this information was of only perfunctory interest to her and continued her bath in silence. When she was finished, Zaynab approached her with the blue dress. It was a *thoub*, the traditional double-dress of the tribes, made of deep blue wool and heavy with Zaynab's own embroidery.

"It's so hot…" Khalidah began half-heartedly.

"It brings out the color of your eyes," Zaynab said in a tone that brooked no argument. This was her standard reply when Khalidah complained about clothing, but it made little sense to the girl. The color of her eyes – a deep, coppery gold – was not generally considered an asset. It reminded people of her mother, and most wanted to forget that Brekhna had ever existed.

Nevertheless, Khalidah stood obediently while Zaynab tied her sash, loaded her with jewelry and pinned up her red silk headscarf. When Zaynab was finally satisfied, she led Khalidah outside and made her wait while she brought tea from the kitchen in an elaborate silver pot. She handed the pot to the girl and gave her a gentle push in the direction of the *majlis*. Then, as Khalidah had hoped, she retreated back inside.

Though called Al-'Adil, "The Just", by his people, Sheikh 'Abd al-Aziz's reputation for eccentricity was nearly as widespread as his reputation for just dealings. Khalidah's unconventional education was generally agreed to be the primary example of this, along with the fact that he had married only once, despite that wife having died early on and her leaving him only a single, worthless daughter. A more acceptable madness was his passion for horses. Though many tribesmen shared it to the extent of bringing their best horses into their tents at night, none of the Hassani went as far as to give them a room of their own, decorated as richly as the sheik's *majlis*, complete with woven tapestries and filigreed lamps.

This stable lay between the *majlis* and the *maharama*. During the day it was empty, and long ago Khalidah had discovered its usefulness both as an escape route during tedious gatherings and for eavesdropping on the interesting ones to which she was not invited. Looking around to make certain that she was unwatched, Khalidah slipped inside the stable. She lifted her skirts out of habit, though the floor was pristine, having already been cleaned for the coming night. Setting the teapot down beside a copper watering pail, she put her ear to the cloth wall.

A man with an affable, expansive voice, like her father's but smoother, was saying: "I realize that this must seem abrupt to you, but the Franj have been testing the treaty of late, and I fear there may not be time for lengthy negotiations." This would be 'Abd al-Hadi.

"*One* Franji," her father answered, his own voice cool and meticulous. "Brins Arnat."

"Yes, and Arnat may well be more powerful than the rest of them put together, since their pathetic king appears to be his puppet and the Templars his lapdogs. Arnat flouted the truce when he attacked that caravan at midwinter, and as far as I have heard, none of his own people have done anything about it – least of all King Guy."

"Salah ad-Din is said to be negotiating the prisoners' release."

"Arnat does not negotiate," said 'Abd al-Hadi, his agitation more apparent against his brother's calm, "except with the point of his sword."

"Our swords, too, have points," 'Abd al-Aziz countered.

"I have no desire to fight the Franj," his brother said. "Don't look at me like that – as if I were a coward, worthy of your disdain! It is not cowardice, but wisdom. If that hot-headed Kurd challenges Arnat, it will be all the excuse the infidels need to begin another war. And since it seems unlikely that Arnat will suddenly decide to listen to his king or appease the Sultan, I would prefer to be as far from both of them as possible, as soon as possible."

"Then why this proposition?" asked 'Abd al-Aziz, his own voice neutral. "What do you think an alliance with me will be worth to you when my grazing lands are covered by Franj fortresses?"

"More than it will be if I'm skewered on a Franj sword."

"More, then, than Allah's rewards to a fallen warrior of the Faith."

There was a taut, bitter silence. Then 'Abd al-Hadi said, "The Franj are rash and impatient. They will overreach themselves one day, and these lands will be ours again. When I have lived to see that day, I will meet Allah gladly." After another long silence he continued, "Either way, we have strayed from the purpose of our conversation."

"Indeed," 'Abd al-Aziz answered slowly, and Khalidah could

almost see his face, narrow and intelligent with a faint wash of contempt, the black eyes bright with the thoughts he was not speaking. "I can see the wisdom in your suggestion; but Khalidah is not prepared for marriage."

And there it was: the word she had known she would hear. Presupposing it had made it no less bitter. She longed to think that her father was stalling out of love for her, that perhaps he would not really let this happen, but she could not quite deceive herself.

"She is nearly sixteen," countered 'Abd al-Hadi. "Most girls her age are married already."

"Khalidah is not like other girls. She has not had the benefit of a mother's guidance."

"Has her nurse not educated her?" her uncle demanded.

'Abd al-Aziz sighed. "Zaynab has little enough experience of marriage herself to pass along."

"Why then do you keep her?"

'Abd al-Aziz said nothing.

"I surmise from your reticence that there have been other offers."

Still, 'Abd al-Aziz didn't answer.

"Blood is weightier than gold, *Akhah*. You cannot tell me you would prefer Khalidah to marry outside the Hassani, especially when you have no heirs to carry on the bloodline…"

Khalidah turned away, disgusted. There had indeed been other offers of marriage. Not many, to be sure – she had her own outspokenness and her mother's mysterious ancestry to thank for that – but she was still a clan chief's daughter. She had listened to all of her suitors' petitions through this same woven wall and as always, the labyrinthine negotiations had reached their bottom line: the sum of her worth.

The offers had thus far been refused. Khalidah's father would not have been easily bought, even had he not been wealthy already. But 'Abd al-Aziz was human, and therefore not without a secret longing. Where other men lusted for gold or status, he longed for unity. The only thing he regretted more than the loss of his wife was the division of the Hassani. As far back as Khalidah could remember, her father had been trying to find a way to reunite with his brother, but 'Abd al-Hadi had never been willing to settle for less than his brother's complete abdication. Never — until now. Khalidah thought of the mare — the color of hope and longing — and knew that 'Abd al-Hadi had finally found her father's price. She picked up her teapot, hoping that it wasn't too late.

2

The *majlis* was full of men, mainly 'Abd al-Hadi's retainers. They were busy tearing at the roasted sheep on its massive platter of rice, which was laid out by the fire. Around the rugs were piles of cushions in brilliant jewel colors, and on the cushions the men reclined: Khalidah's father, thin and stern; 'Abd al-Hadi, with a similar face but the build of a well-fed king; her cousin Numair, who had been a petulant boy when she had seen him last and was now a tall, bearded man, handsome but just as sullen; and, finally, the minstrel, whose eyes bored into her from the shadows.

"It is not like you to await an invitation to sit," her father said dryly.

Realizing that she had been staring at the minstrel, Khalidah quickly inclined her head to her father and uncle and said her *salaams*. Then she poured a little of the now-tepid tea into the sand in the obligatory sacrifice, and set the pot down. "I'm sorry to have kept you waiting, *Abatah*," she said.

'Abd al-Aziz began to answer, but his brother interrupted, smiling, "Who would not wait a lifetime for such grace? Last time I saw you, you were a skinned-kneed child. Come, *Sayyida*, sit by me." 'Abd al-Hadi patted a cushion between himself and Numair. Reluctantly, Khalidah sat down, twitching her head-scarf forward to hide her expression.

"No, put it back," Numair said, pinning her with snake's eyes.

"Let me see your face."

Both the request and its manner put her back up. Khalidah glanced at her father, hoping that he would chastise her cousin, but he told her, "Do as he says," looking as though he would rather have said something quite different. Reluctantly, Khalidah pushed back her scarf, its decorative coins tinkling as they fell behind her shoulders. She could feel Numair's eyes burning into her right cheek and the minstrel's on her left, cool and appraising but no less intent. She sensed acutely the dark undercurrents battling beneath the placid scene.

"Try the mutton, Khalidah, it is superb," 'Abd al-Hadi said, reaching into the sheep's ribcage for a kidney.

Khalidah's stomach flopped over; a roasted carcass made her queasy at the best of times, and at the moment she was already feeling nauseous. "Thank you, *Ammah*, but I have eaten already." She poured herself a glass of cold tea and sipped to hide her discomfort.

Her father and uncle exchanged a look, then 'Abd al-Aziz cleared his throat. "Khalidah," he said, "you know that I have long wished to see the two branches of the Hassani united again, as they were under my father. Now my brother has come with a proposal which would achieve this, and end our constant warring." He paused, as if steeling himself. "He suggests that you and your cousin Numair marry."

Khalidah leveled her eyes at her father. "And how have you answered him, *Abatah*?"

"I haven't, yet."

"And why not?" she continued, not caring now whether the men thought her too bold.

After a long pause, her father said, "Last summer, when the Franj child-king died, he left their kingdom in chaos and his mother, Sibylla, to claim the crown. More importantly, though, he left her free to declare her new husband king; and so we are saddled with Guy de Lusignan, a weak, insipid man by all accounts, far too willing to listen to the loudest voice in a crowd and too stupid to remember anything but the last words it said."

Khalidah set her tea-glass down, but said nothing, for although none of this was news to her, her father seemed to want his guests to believe that it was.

"Unfortunately," he continued, frowning, "the loudest voice at present is that of Brins Arnat, and Arnat has no respect for Salah ad-Din's truce."

"What about Count Tripoli?" Khalidah asked, earning herself a raised eyebrow from the minstrel, an indulgent smile from 'Abd al-Hadi and a look of cold suspicion from Numair. "He may not be king, but he is respected by his people, and he himself has always respected Salah ad-Din."

'Abd al-Aziz indicated to Khalidah to pour him a glass of tea. When he recorded its temperature he gave her a pointed look, but rather than comment he set it aside and said, "This is precisely the problem. Tripoli was regent to the late king. Many think the crown should have passed to him, and he is far too concerned with asserting his rights to worry about the bigger picture. Meanwhile, Arnat sits in his wife's fortress at Kerak pulling Guy's puppet strings and calling for Saracen blood, with no one to exercise reason. In fact, they say he has the Templar Master in his thrall now. If that is true, then it is only a matter of time until he convinces Guy to act, and Salah ad-Din will be all too ready to meet him when he does."

'Abd al-Aziz lapsed into silence, staring at the tapestry that separated the *majlis* from the stable. Zaynab had woven it: an intricate pattern of indigo, crimson and green that always seemed about to resolve itself into an image, but never quite did. When Khalidah was certain that no one else was going to speak, she ventured:

"Forgive my ignorance, *Abatah*, but what does this have to do with my marriage?"

Again, an unfathomable look passed between the brothers. It was 'Abd al-Hadi who answered, "The Hassani are wealthy and powerful, but right now we are like a snake with two heads." He sighed. "Both my brother and I feel" – and Khalidah knew that she did not mistake the coldness in his tone – "that the time has come to stop spilling our own blood: to reunite the Hassani into a force that can withstand both the Franj and the Kurd."

Khalidah was well aware that there was more to this than either man was saying, more even than what she had overheard; yet what they *were* telling her was strange enough. That they would wish to unite against the Franj made sense, but she knew that her father respected Salah ad-Din, and the conversation she had overheard made it clear that he would willingly fight for him. Why then speak of withstanding him?

Finally, she said, "And when did you plan for us to marry?"

This time, when 'Abd al-Hadi looked toward his brother, 'Abd al-Aziz didn't look back. Attempting a smile, 'Abd al-Hadi said, "Given the situation, I would suggest we hold the *Laylat al-Henna* tonight."

It was only through love of her father that Khalidah didn't throw her tea in her uncle's face. The *Laylat al Henna* was the first ceremony in a series that would last a week, at the end of which she would be Numair's wife. It should have been preceded by two others: the *Koutha*, where 'Abd al-Hadi and his close relatives and friends would visit her father and formally ask for her hand, and the *Akhd*, where the marriage contract would be negotiated. What 'Abd al-Hadi was proposing was a disgrace, an indemnification of her own honor and her father's, as the only time a girl was married so quickly was when her purity was in question, or her father had some dire need of her bride-price.

Nobody moved. It was so quiet that the gentle creaking of the wooden tent poles in the breeze seemed like a storm in a forest. The minstrel had stopped fiddling with his *qanun* and sat staring at her over his master's shoulder, with a look in his eyes that was very like a plea. And she wanted nothing more than to scream, Why? Why should I trust you? Why should I do what any one of you asks of me?

Yet she could not shake that earlier feeling of recognition, or her sense, however unfounded, that the minstrel's was the only request she had heard that day apparently untainted by self-interest. So, in a small, cold voice Khalidah said:

"*Ammah*, you do me too great an honor. But as you have asked, I most humbly accept my cousin's proposal and look forward to joining your family as a daughter." And then, without waiting for a reply and with nothing like humility, she stood and left.

*

Khalidah didn't go back to the *maharama*, but walked away from camp toward the scrubland where the horses were grazing. She did not want to think about what she had just done, nor why. Instead she watched the new mare. Among the horse-breeding tribes, the Hassani line was considered the finest, but the gift horse blazed out among them like Al-Zuhra among lesser stars. *And yet*, Khalidah thought, *you too are only chattel.* She pictured the golden mare leading a whooping column into battle. No doubt she would throw herself among the spears and swords with a lion's courage, and Numair – for Khalidah had no doubt that Numair did not really intend to part with this horse – would only curse her when she fell. The mare danced, graceful despite her hobble, and Khalidah sighed.

"She is beautiful, isn't she," said a low, musical voice at her shoulder.

Khalidah whirled. 'Abd al-Hadi's minstrel stood behind her, looking, as she had looked, toward the new horse. "You!" she sputtered. "Why are you tormenting me?"

"This isn't the place to discuss it, *Sayyida*," he said softly.

"We shouldn't be discussing anything, anywhere," Khalidah said.

"No," he agreed. "I should be practicing dance tunes and you should be brushing your hair or bathing in lime juice or whatever women do to prepare for a henna ceremony." He smiled in a way that told Khalidah she had not imagined the irony in his tone. "Instead, we both stand contemplating Zahirah. No doubt this means something; but I am a musician, not a philosopher."

"Zahirah?"

"What else would you call a beast so bright?"

Khalidah glanced from the horse to the man. His skin was fairer than her own, the cast of his features softer than the tribes'. He looked a bit like the Persians they sometimes met along the caravan routes. There was also something regal in his bearing and a pride in his keen black eyes that set him in relief against the desert. He looked like a man others would die for; even as she thought it, the idea appalled her.

"If you have something to say to me," she said shortly, "then say it – preferably in plain terms."

"I have a good deal to say to you, but we must find somewhere safer. I have enough troubles without being caught alone with a sheikh's daughter."

Khalidah stared at him in the way she knew unnerved most people, but he just looked calmly back at her. Finally, against all her better judgment, she said, "Do you see those rocks above the camp?" She pointed, and his eyes followed her finger to the sandstone outcropping where she and Bilal had hidden from Zaynab that morning. He nodded.

"Pretend to be examining the horses. When you have walked once around the herd, go up there. On the eastern side, you'll find a small cave. I will be there." She turned to go, and then turned back. "Have you a name, minstrel?"

"Sulayman," he answered.

Khalidah nodded and hurried away. She rounded the camp and then made her way up the hill, keeping to the rocks when she could and hoping that no one was watching. She settled into the cave's shadow, watching a hawk wheeling in the deep blue sky until Sulayman appeared, backlit by the afternoon sun, his face momentarily in shadow and his head surrounded by a bright nimbus. For a second Khalidah felt she was looking at something more than human, and that he in turn was looking into her. Then he knelt beside her and the illusion was broken.

"Thank you for trusting me, *Sayyida*," he said.

"I do not claim to trust you," Khalidah answered.

"Well, then, for listening." Khalidah conceded this with a nod,

SAND DAUGHTER   29

then waited for him to go on. At last he said, "There is no easy
way to say this, so I will simply say it. You are in grave danger. I
did not mean to unsettle you earlier, but it was imperative that
you accepted Numair's proposal unconditionally."

"Why?"

"Because you wouldn't have survived the night if you had not.
He intends to have your tribe's lands at any cost."

"And so he would murder me in my bed?"

"Precisely."

"And how exactly would he do that with only a handful of
men, and me with all my tribe around me?"

Sulayman sighed. "Things are not quite as they seem. Several
miles to the west of here, there is another camp. A camp of your
uncle's *ghuzat*, substantially fleshed out with Franj mercenaries."

"Franj!" She paused, considering the possibilities, not least of
which was that Sulayman was mad. "How do you know this?"

His head gave an equivocal tilt. "A rich man's minstrel
hears things, many of which he'd rather not, most of which he
shouldn't. I will not endanger you by identifying my sources. But
rest assured, they are entirely trustworthy."

Of course he was lying; he *had* to be lying. Bedu *ghazawat*, or
raids, were first and foremost about honor. Surprise attacks were
honorable. Hiring Franj mercenaries was not.

"It's senseless," she said, more to herself than to Sulayman.
"Our lands are not worth his honor."

"Perhaps not now," Sulayman answered, "but they could be.
If, for instance, your cousin controlled a port city adjacent to
them."

"Well, he does not."

"Not yet. But I have heard he has wrangled a promise from
someone in a position to make it, that he will be given lordship
of Ayla, in exchange for certain services."

It was just strange enough to be true. At any rate, no matter
which angle she approached it from, Khalidah could not come
up with a compelling reason for Sulayman to be lying. "So what,
then?" she asked at last, bitterly. "I have no choice but to submit

to Numair and become Lady of Ayla? To live in a palace like a canary in a gilded cage, turning a blind eye while the Franj drown pilgrims and slaughter children? Or does my honorable cousin intend to throttle me on our wedding night?"

She had intended sarcasm, but as she spoke the words she found she could easily imagine Numair doing just that, with the same calm, predatory stare he had cast on her earlier. "He'll cut my father's throat after the wedding, I suppose," she said, her tone suddenly defeated. "Perhaps his own father's, too. He'll take our wealth and our horses, and what's left of the Hassani will wander the deserts like outcasts…" She shook her head. "There must be an alternative."

"Indeed…that is why I am here."

"You? Do you intend to fight off Numair's *ghuzat* yourself?"

"Hardly."

"Then I suppose you mean to run away and hide."

"Precisely," he answered. "And I intend to take you with me."

"Will I find then that you are a long-lost prince?" Khalidah laughed bitterly. "You must think I'm a fool! You could be working for anyone – for Numair himself."

He nodded, squinting into the afternoon glare. "I could be. But consider that we have sat here alone for the last ten minutes. If I had intended to kill you, I'd have done it already."

Khalidah smiled to herself, but she said nothing. It was better to let him believe this for the time being; if she needed to disabuse him of the idea of her vulnerability, surprise would work in her favor. "Even if I agree to go with you," she said at last, "I don't see how it's possible. They're bound to notice if I'm not at my own henna ceremony. Then my father will be after us, and he knows every sand grain of this desert…as do my uncle and cousin."

"You'll go to the ceremony and leave afterward. By the time your people are in a condition to follow, we'll be far enough away that it won't matter."

Khalidah wanted to take exception to the implicit command, but she couldn't. The fact was, despite what she had said – despite the pure, mad folly of it – she had known that she was going to go with Sulayman the moment he suggested it.

"What are you going to do to them?" she asked, still trying to sound equivocal.

"Don't worry about that. Just make sure you drink nothing but water tonight."

"Do you plan to poison the wine?"

He smiled. "Only to modify it."

Khalidah shook her head. "And so we ride away, and leave my father and Zaynab and Bilal and all the others to the mercy of Numair and his Franj."

Sulayman sighed. "I don't know much, *Sayyida*, but I do know that your cousin is essentially lazy. There is always a risk in battle, and if he can claim your lands without one, that is the option he will prefer. I intend to make it clear that you are still alive; as long as Numair believes that, then your people should be safe."

"Should be?"

He sighed with an infuriating note of tolerance and said, "This is the best I can do, *Sayyida*. It is this, or certain death. But of course, the decision is yours."

"Who do you think you are?" Khalidah demanded.

To her surprise, Sulayman smiled, his eyes creasing to half-moons, teeth flashing white against his dark skin. Again, Khalidah had the bewildering sensation that she was in the presence of someone who deserved reverence. "I'm afraid that's a question without an answer," he said. "But what you really mean is, who am I to you? As to that, I'm little more than a messenger from someone who does not wish to see you harmed. I can lead you to a safe place, where there are people who can help you. But first you have to trust me."

"In fact, I do not," Khalidah answered. "I need only agree to ride with you."

Sulayman shrugged. "As you like."

Khalidah looked at him, her eyes brighter and more golden than her head-scarf's coins. "Numair intends to keep Zahirah for himself, doesn't he?"

She thought she knew the answer, but Sulayman surprised her, saying, "No. She is a gift…or rather, a bribe."

"For a Franji?"

He nodded. Khalidah considered this, her eyes fixed on the grazing horses far below. Even at a distance, Zahirah's graceful form was unmistakable. "I'll go with you," she said. "But Zahirah is mine."

3

When Khalidah returned to the tent, Zaynab was waiting for her with another rose-scented basin of water. She had expected a scolding, but Zaynab didn't even ask her where she'd been; she simply helped her off with her dress and began to wash her hair. At last Khalidah couldn't stand it anymore.

"Say something, Zaynab," she implored.

Zaynab squeezed the water from Khalidah's hair and then sat down behind her to comb it out. "It's you, *Sayyida*, who are withholding words."

Cold water trickled down the inside of Khalidah's shift and she shivered, wondering how Zaynab could have found out so quickly. She was trying to decide how best to answer her, when the woman continued bitterly, "It isn't like you to submit so silently to so great a dishonor. To think, they haven't even given you time to gather a *jihaz*!"

Giddy with relief, Khalidah's words tumbled out, "What use is a *jihaz* anyway? I would never wear all those dresses, jewelry makes it difficult to play the *oud*, and the lot of it weighs down the pack camels needlessly when it's time to move."

"And what does this cousin of yours bring with him to sweeten the bargain?" Zaynab continued, ignoring Khalidah's argument. "No gold, no camels or goats, just a horse!"

"She *is* a very fine horse…" Khalidah ventured.

Zaynab snorted. "I might have known you'd say that. But you can neither wear nor eat a horse – unless you are a Franji, filthy creatures – and anyone can see that she is not intended as a broodmare. It is of little use to anyone else that your father will look fine riding her at the front of a caravan – or, as Allah wills it, to charge the Franj."

Little do you know, Khalidah thought sadly. "What would my mother have done?" she said aloud.

Zaynab frowned and came around to face Khalidah, holding a pot of kohl and a fine brush. Looking at her, Khalidah wondered why Zaynab had never re-married. She might not be wealthy, but she was certainly attractive, her skin still smooth, her thick black hair unmarked by gray, her eyes full of kindness. She was no doubt still fertile, too. Though Khalidah liked the romance of the possibility that she still loved Bilal's dead father, she doubted that this was the reason for Zaynab's persistent widowhood, partly because of Zaynab's intrinsic practicality, but mostly because of the hard look her face took on when Khalidah asked about him. Nor would she talk about him to her son: Bilal said that she refused even to tell him his father's name.

"If Brekhna had been here," Zaynab answered as she began lining the girl's eyes, "it would never have come to this. Look down, don't squint!" she admonished; then she sighed. "Your mother was my friend, but there was a good deal about her that she kept close. She was unpredictable, some said fickle. But one thing I can tell you, she never liked Numair's mother, and she saw right through 'Abd al-Hadi's bluster to his weakness. She would never have married you to their son."

"Who would she have chosen, then?"

"Ah, Khalidah, what's the use of speculating? Brekhna is not here, and there's nothing I can do to stop this farce."

Khalidah heard the apology in the words and she leant forward to kiss Zaynab's cheek. "It is not your responsibility to stop it. If it buys peace for the tribe, then it is worthwhile and in the end…well, I'd have been married one way or another. What difference is there between husbands?"

Zaynab's look turned shrewd and slightly pitying. "I think you would find that there can be a very great difference; but that doesn't signify now. At any rate, I will be with you in your new home, which I hope will be a comfort to you."

"You intend to come with me?"

"Of course I do, if Numair will have me. What use will your father have for me once you are gone?"

"What about Bilal?"

Zaynab sighed. "Bilal is not a child any longer, and for all I love him I cannot show him how to be a man. I leave that to your father, just as he has left it to me to show you how to be a woman. Besides, Bilal and I have never brought each other much joy. Perhaps we will love each other more for the separation." She paused, shook her head. "Anyhow, you will have children of your own soon, and then you will need my help as you never have."

Khalidah had a sudden image of a long line of little boys, all looking up at her with cold, reptilian eyes. To hide her horror, she turned toward the front of the tent. "Do you hear that?" she asked.

Someone had taken up a *tabla*, playing a fast beat. A *na'ay* joined in with a reedy syncopation. The next moment, Khalidah's frayed attention was snared by a rippling, reverberant trill that grew in volume until it plunged like a cliff bird into skimming flight. She had heard a *qanun* played once or twice before, but never like this.

"You're still in your shift!" Zaynab called sharply.

With a start, Khalidah dropped the tent flap she had been about to lift. "I'm sorry. It's just that music..."

Zaynab gave her a keen, appraising look. "Indeed. Put on your dress, and then you can go see."

It was then Khalidah noticed the dress spread out on her bed: silk the color of heart's-blood, the yoke and hems covered with Zaynab's colorful embroidery, which always suggested birds and beasts without ever quite breaking the laws against idolatry. Zaynab must have been working on it for a long time; she had no doubt intended it for a happier occasion than this. Tears pricked Khalidah's eyes as she touched the soft fabric.

"At least you won't be married in rags," Zaynab said, pretending not to notice. "We can make others once you have gone to – "

She bit off the rest of the thought and busied herself with helping Khalidah to dress. When she was finished, Khalidah and Zaynab stepped outside. In the space of a half hour, the camp had been transformed. The short desert twilight had deepened to night, and a full moon was cresting the sandstone hills. The camp itself was alight with fires and lanterns, and the stars had retreated from the competition. Despite the evening chill, the *ghata* had been turned back from the front of the sheikh's *majlis*, and people were spilling out from the bright interior into the flickering shadows.

With Zaynab in her wake, Khalidah made her way through the crowd toward the fabulous music. They parted for her, wishing her good luck and happiness. She saw both men and women, which was strange. Normally the henna night was segregated, the women and men celebrating separately. But then, Khalidah reminded herself, nothing about this wedding was right, and by the next morning none of it would matter anyway.

In the *majlis*, a group of women sat in a tight circle by the stable wall. They were women she had known all her life, and yet when they looked at her now she saw wariness beneath their smiles, and she burned with shame for what they must be thinking. Sulayman glanced up from his *qanun* and for a moment their eyes met; then he looked back at his flashing plectra. Numair watched her with predator's eyes, while Bilal sat in his shadow with a brooding look. Her father and his brother were deep in conversation and did not notice her at all.

Looking from one to the next, Khalidah felt suddenly lightheaded. Well aware that fainting now would only add credence to everyone's suspicions, she greeted the men quickly and then went to sit among the women. She barely heard as they began to sing the traditional songs extolling her beauty and virtues. She held out her hands obediently for Zaynab and sat

staring at them while her nurse applied eucalyptus and olive oil,
then began to draw intricate patterns with the tube of henna
paste. Khalidah had of course attended many henna ceremonies
before her own, and normally she fidgeted until the unfortunate
artist sent her away, usually with her tattoos only half-finished
and admonitions not to touch the paste until it had dried (which
she invariably ignored). Now, Khalidah's stillness was such that
Zaynab asked her repeatedly if she were well.

In fact, Khalidah was wondering the same thing herself.
Dizziness had become dislocation: it was as if a fine muslin scrim
had come down between herself and the world and nothing
looked quite real. She watched as if dreaming while the men drank
wine and passed the hookah, growing loud with false merriness,
and the people outside the tents danced and the women painted
their hands and sang words they didn't seem to hear. From deep
in the shadows Bilal watched her, and Sulayman played a melody
that seemed to grow ever more intricate, mirroring the latticed
paintings on her skin.

When she thought that Zaynab wasn't looking, Khalidah stole
glances at the minstrel. The lamplight flickered golden against his
cheek and his fingers moved like river reeds, the plectra's metal
rings flashing. Then, as she watched, a figure emerged from the
shifting light and shadow of the tent wall behind him, hovering
against the corporeal scene like an image from a fever dream. She
was a woman, her white robe richly embroidered at the collar,
cuffs and hem, as was her headscarf. She wore no veil, and her
dark hair hung down her back in long plaits beneath the scarf,
wound with beads and cowry shells. Her face was fair-skinned,
marked at the forehead and cheeks with some kind of patterns,
and her features had a fierceness that reminded Khalidah of a
hunting hawk. Her eyes were as golden as Khalidah's own.

Abruptly, the music stopped. The woman faded back into the
white-and-gold tapestry behind Sulayman and Khalidah realized
that she was standing, her patterned hand reaching toward the
place where the woman had been, where now Sulayman sat
alone, his hand resting on the *qanun*'s strings as another man's

might on the belly of his lover.

"Khalidah!" Zaynab hissed. Khalidah sat, and Zaynab leaned toward her, whispering, "Say that you recognized the song...say anything, Khalidah, or the minstrel is dead!"

Khalidah looked at her father, who looked back with cold eyes. She could think of nothing to say but the truth and so, though she knew that it was nearly as bad as their suspicion, she said, "I am sorry, *Abatah*. The music the minstrel was playing...it seemed as if...that is to say, it put me in mind of my mother, and it seemed for a moment that she was here with us again..."

Her father continued to look at her, though now his expression was inscrutable, and Khalidah's heart sank. All at once 'Abd al-Hadi roared with laughter. "Ah, the look on your face, girl!" he said. "Truly, you have seen little of the world if Sulayman's pandering can capture your imagination so. Now, if they're finished with you, how about a song?"

Khalidah looked around in confusion. She still wasn't entirely certain how she had come to be standing in her father's tent, with so many suspicious eyes on her and her heart scurrying like a hare in a hawk's shadow. She hated singing to an audience at the best of times; now, it was unthinkable. So she offered up her hands, covered with intricate pipings of sticky, green-brown henna paste.

"I cannot play my *oud* with these hands."

"From what I have heard, your voice needs no accompaniment," her uncle answered without missing a beat.

She took a deep breath, said, "As you wish, *Ammah*," and stepped toward the fire. She settled herself between her father and 'Abd al-Hadi, with her back firmly to Sulayman and said, "What would you have me sing?"

'Abd al-Hadi seemed already to be losing interest in his own idea. "Oh, anything," he said, pulling a piece of meat from the roasted goat at the center of the gathering and contemplating it. "Perhaps a love story. 'Layla and Majnun'?"

He rolled the meat with a bit of rice and tossed them into his mouth. Khalidah swallowed around the lump in her throat.

Though it was indeed a love story, she could think of few less befitting a marriage celebration than that ballad of star-crossed lovers driven to madness and death. But, as with the rest, she had no choice but to obey her uncle's order.

A few lines into the ballad, a silence fell over the guests. Khalidah's voice was a spear that pierced and pinned them, made them listen; and, listening, they felt the faint stirrings of a profound remembrance, as if they had wept with Layla, or raved with Majnun among the wild beasts. At last it was over. Khalidah fell silent as the last notes spun out into the night and were lost on the wind. For a moment no one moved, and no sound was heard but the half-remembered echo of Khalidah's song. More than a few people, not realizing it, were silently weeping. Then the murmuring began and time resumed. Khalidah tried not to notice the strange look some of the people gave her, a mixture of awe and fear.

"Wonderful!" roared 'Abd al-Hadi. "Your Khalidah is truly a jewel among women – eh, Numair?"

He nudged his son and Numair looked up, his eyes like caves in his sandstone face. "Indeed," he answered. "A voice so extraordinary almost makes one wonder if the stories about her mother are true." He looked at Khalidah for a moment with detached intensity before he smiled. 'Abd al-Hadi laughed again, too loudly, and 'Abd al-Aziz took a sip from his cup to hide an expression Khalidah could imagine only too well.

Khalidah herself was exhausted. If she had not known it to be impossible, she would have said that while she sang she had been with Layla, walking every step of her tragic road. If she closed her eyes she could even see her: slight, frail-skinned, unremarkable except for her eyes, wide and deep as the night sky above a half-smile of recognition. She reeled, and the room darkened. She knew that she had to get out, away from this celebration of her purchase, from the duplicitous smiles and the lamplight's flickers of illusion. She was unaware of having reached out for support until Zaynab's arm came around her, wiry and warm. At that moment she could have wept, and Zaynab seemed to know it.

"You must excuse Khalidah now," she said to the men. "This has been a long and exciting day for her" – this she said with a distinct irony – "and she needs to rest."

She stood up, still firmly supporting Khalidah without appearing to, and when they had been dismissed, she led her out of the *majlis* toward their own quarters.

4

The walk back to the *maharama* seemed to last forever, though it was only a few steps. Finally they were inside, and Zaynab was pinning the *ghata* into place. Khalidah sank gratefully onto her bed, unpinned her headscarf and jewelry and laid it aside, then began unwinding her sash.

"Let me do it," Zaynab said.

Khalidah shook her head. "I'm not a child anymore."

It seemed to Khalidah that there were many things Zaynab wanted to say to that, but instead she watched silently, looking oddly helpless, as Khalidah undressed and combed her hair and climbed under her quilt. It occurred to Khalidah then that she had no idea how she would know when it was time to meet Sulayman. From there worry widened into panic. After all, she had no reason to trust him, no reason anymore to trust anything…and yet she knew with mounting clarity that she could not possibly remain where she was.

Sighing, she turned over. The hanging lamp was trimmed low. Across the room in her own bed, Zaynab was a dark bulk with a faint glint of open eyes. "You are thinking of the boy with the *qanun*," she said softly.

Again, Khalidah wondered if Zaynab could have found out about their plan; then she realized that the woman had drawn an entirely different conclusion. "Why would I think of him?" she answered.

"I saw how you looked at him, Khalidah."

"Well, it wasn't what you think. Zaynab..." Khalidah faltered among the first lies that came to hand, but in the end she discarded them all. "What I said to my father was the truth. When he began to play, I saw my mother. *Saw* her – not just a memory."

Zaynab said nothing. Khalidah listened to the guttural patter of the drums, the low warble of the reed flute that seemed to have replaced Sulayman and his *qanun*. The filigreed lid of the lantern threw golden constellations across the dark cloth of the roof. They wavered gently as the tent swayed in the breeze.

At last Zaynab said, "I never knew that you remembered her."

Khalidah sighed. "Neither did I. But the woman I saw...I'd have known her anywhere."

Zaynab was silent again for a time; then, slowly, she said, "I suppose it's little wonder that the boy's music brought her back to you. Your mother played the *qanun* too."

A flash of white cloth and golden eyes, a faint drift of music: a memory. Khalidah sat on a high dune looking out across a universe of sand. A woman in white sat beside her. Her headscarf had slipped back, revealing four plaits of dark hair with deep red lights, like fire beyond a nighttime horizon. She held a *qanun* on her lap, but she did not play it. The wind blew across the strings, pulling faint harmonics from them and whipping them away again.

"She used to take me out," Khalidah said tremulously, "away from camp, into the desert."

"That's right," Zaynab agreed, "though I'm surprised that you remember. You were barely walking then. Brekhna had a hunger for open spaces and solitude. She never liked life in the camp, though she bore it for your father's sake and for yours. What else do you remember?"

"Not much. A feeling...a look. The color of her hair. Inside it looked black, but in the sun it was like the coat of a dark bay horse. The way she smiled, as if it was meant to cover something that it couldn't, quite. And then...and then, she was gone. I cried for her, but she never came. And then you came into our tent, and after a while I stopped missing her so much. I forgot her face...I thought I did..."

"She was a caged bird," Zaynab said in an odd, dreamy tone. "Your father is a good man and a good leader but – Allah forgive me my boldness – your mother should not have married him. She could never belong to him, as a wife must belong to her husband. I saw it in her at once, as she must have seen – " She faltered, and Khalidah had just time to wonder what words Zaynab had suppressed, before she was speaking again. "She couldn't forget the ways of her people," she said, her voice even softer, more laconic than before, "and though she never said it, I always thought that she had loved someone else, once." Zaynab sighed. "But we are women. Our feelings don't matter in the world of men. You and Brekhna and I, we're all alike, except that in the end she had the strength to look truth in the eye. That's why she left. Perhaps there was Jinn blood in her after all..."

Zaynab's words slurred into sleepy silence, but Khalidah was wide awake. "Left?" she whispered. "What do you mean, left?"

Zaynab said nothing.

"My mother died!"

Zaynab answered with a snore. All at once, Khalidah realized that the camp had fallen silent. It was far too soon: a henna night celebration often lasted until dawn, as hers had had every appearance of doing when she had left. Khalidah pulled on a simple woolen dress and wrapped a shawl around her head, then lifted the *ghata*.

In the flickering light of the fires people lay sprawled and curled. She crept outside and nudged the first person she saw, a plump old gossip called Rusa. The woman mumbled something unintelligible and then settled back to sleep. There was a cup in her hand, with a little wine still left in it. Khalidah pried it from her grasp and tasted the dregs. The bitter-sweet tang of poppy sap was subtle but to her – thanks to a long bout with a wasting cough as a child – unmistakable.

She was looking down at Rusa, wondering where Sulayman

could have acquired enough opium to drug an entire wedding party, when a hand closed over her shoulder and whipped her around. The man who held her was one of Numair's retainers, though she could not recall his name. He had thin features, and the light of the dying fires sharpened them and hollowed his eyes, which fixed on her with a greedy look not unlike his master's.

"Take your filthy hands off of me!" Khalidah hissed, struggling against him; but he had caught her off guard, and he was too big for her to throw him.

"Unlike these fools," he said, while she fought his hands like a netted butterfly, "I never touch wine. It's too easily adulterated... as you have proven."

"How dare you speak to me this way!" Khalidah said. She had chosen outrage, hoping to stifle her fear, but his words chilled her to the bone. The suggestion of complicity was bad enough, but what really worried her was the fact that he would challenge her at all. Where he ought to show deference to a better who could, at a word, have him executed, he displayed only contempt, as if, to him, she were already dead.

"*Sayyida.*" He inclined his head with nothing like concession. "Your cousin would be very disappointed to find that you had a hand in this – " He gestured to the sleeping guests. "But you must admit that it looks suspicious. After all, you're the only one still awake – "

"Other than you."

He regarded her with cold amusement. "I haven't seen the minstrel since you left your father's tent so dramatically."

If all things were as they should be, the suggestion couldn't be more blatantly insulting to her, nor to him more dangerous. Khalidah tried again to pull free, but the man wrenched her around, slamming her against the pole supporting the stable wall. She cried out, but the night returned only silence.

"How dare you?" she spat, wavering between fear and fury.

"I?" the man laughed. "How dare *I*, you ask, after your scene tonight? Numair is a fool! Another man would have stoned his wife for such behavior!"

"I am *not* his wife," Khalidah cried, "and I never will be!"

She knew even as she said it that it was a mistake, but she couldn't stop herself: the insult of his hands on her drove the words out. As she watched them disappear into the sinkholes of his eyes, she knew that he was going to kill her. And then someone called her name.

She turned toward the sound and saw Bilal. She had barely time to register him running toward them before the retainer caught him on the head with a club-like arm and sent him sprawling. He lay where he fell, ominously still.

"Bilal!" Khalidah cried, but the man had turned back to her now; she was pinned, helpless against his rocklike strength. Time seemed to stretch as he drew the knife from his sash, to wash like slow water over stone. Nothing seemed real but the cruel sickle of the knife as he raised it to her throat. Yet as it touched her skin, Khalidah snapped from her torpor. Forcing a smile and a seductive tone, she looked up at the man from beneath her eyelashes and said, "Isn't there anything I can do to change your mind?"

He paused, momentarily relaxing in his surprise. It wasn't much, but it was enough. Khalidah pulled her arm free, grabbed his knife hand and twisted it away. With a grunt, he kicked her legs out from under her. She fell, winded, and he pinned her to the ground. She fought him, managing to keep the knife away from her face and neck, but she couldn't shift him off of her.

"If you kill me," she said desperately, "Numair's plans will come to nothing."

"What do you know about that?" he snarled, but once again he had been thrown, giving Khalidah time to wriggle free. He reached for her, grabbing the hem of her dress. She jerked it away, and as he struggled to his feet, she tripped him. He fell forward heavily. Khalidah brought her knee down hard on the wrist of his knife hand and felt something snap. The man screamed such that she thought he must wake the camp, but the supine figures around her didn't stir. She snatched the knife and as he tried to throw her off, she plunged it into his back. He flailed for a moment, trying to reach the knife with his useless hand, then he fell forward again with a grunt and lay twitching.

Khalidah sank to her knees, shaking. For some reason, all she could think of was her shawl, which had slipped away during the fight: her head felt light and strange without it. But after a moment she remembered Bilal and turned, only to find Sulayman standing behind her, her shawl in his hands and, in his eyes, cautious respect.

"How long have you –" she began,

"Long enough."

"Bilal! He –"

"– will be fine, aside from a few days' headache. I already checked. He's a brave one. So are you." He considered the dead man for a moment, then said, "I can't say I'm sorry for the loss, but this will make more work for us. We'll have to move quickly."

"What are we going to do with him?" Khalidah asked, re-wrapping her shawl.

Sulayman smiled, and from the breast of his waistcoat he drew a folded sheet of vellum stamped with a broken red seal. He handed it to Khalidah. She opened it and found a page of writing. Like the rest of her tribe, Khalidah couldn't read, but she knew enough to recognize that this was not Arabic script.

"Is it Franj writing?"

"It is," he said, taking it back.

"Can you read it?" she asked, impressed despite herself.

"I wrote it," he answered, and seeing her puzzled look, he flipped the letter closed, matching up the halves of the broken seal. It showed two knights riding a single horse.

"The Templar seal?" Khalidah said, more puzzled than before.

Sulayman nodded. "Your alibi – and hopefully, it will buy us enough time to get away. It doesn't say much – it's allegedly a letter from a holy brother staying at Kerak to the Grand Master, discussing trouble with the local tribes and asking for help to subdue them. It doesn't mention you, but it's enough – that is, if anyone in this camp can even read it."

"A Bedu has no need of written language," Khalidah bristled.

"Yes, well, I wanted to cover your tribe harbored one who could; but it doesn't matter much. When your father sees the seal, he'll assume that the Templars killed him" – he prodded the dead man with a toe – "and kidnapped you as a barter piece. With any luck, they'll all race off toward Kerak…" He considered the dead man for a moment, then added, "Unfortunately, it makes *him* look like a hero." He thought for another moment, then smiled. "Unless, of course, I make him a conspirator." Sulayman took a small pouch from his sash and tucked it into the dead man's.

"What was that?" Khalidah asked.

"The rest of the opium," he answered, then pulled the knife from the dead man's back, laid the letter over the wound and drove the blade through the parchment and back into the flesh. Khalidah didn't flinch. "This isn't the first time you've killed a man," he said, observing her composure.

In fact, it was; but Khalidah still preferred that Sulayman not know too much about that aspect of her education. Rather than answer, she asked, "What about you? If you're gone, won't they think you were a traitor, too?"

"What does it matter?" he asked with a shrug. Khalidah had a feeling that it might well come to matter a great deal, but there was little to be done now about any of it, and still less to say. "We need to leave," he continued. "We've already waited too long."

Khalidah nodded and turned to the stable. Sure enough, Zahirah stood inside with her father's favorites, looking at her with wide, calm eyes and long ears pitched forward. Khalidah picked up the nearest saddle and began to ready the horse for riding. She stood as docile as a lamb while Khalidah tightened the girth and slipped on the nose-chain and reins, but underneath the stillness she could sense the horse's taut energy. When Zahirah was ready she looked up to find that Sulayman had tacked Numair's own horse, a gray mare called 'Aasifa. In contrast to Zahirah's calm, she was dancing and tossing her head against the reins and her dark eyes showed a rim of white.

"Are you sure about her?" Khalidah asked. "She looks like a handful."

"A horse is only a handful when her master doesn't know how to hold her." He laid a hand on the mare's shoulder and her movements became less frantic, though she still quivered with fear.

"You hate him," Khalidah said as she handed him a water bag and parcels of cracked wheat and dates and dried camel's milk.

Sulayman's face hardened for a moment as he stored the provisions in a saddle-bag. "Hatred is a base emotion; but it's difficult to think of a better one to attach to a man who rapes his retainers' wives and then has them stoned for adultery."

Khalidah looked at him in shocked silence, then away. They said nothing more until the horses were loaded and they'd led them outside, beyond the tents.

"Are you ready?" Sulayman asked then.

Khalidah nodded and climbed onto Zahirah's back. Now the red mare began to dance like the gray. Khalidah took one last look around the sleeping camp and then she touched her heels to Zahirah's sides. The horse leapt forward like an arrow from a bow, picking up speed as she reached even ground, but Khalidah held her to a canter. She looked over her shoulder. 'Aasifa was there on Zahirah's heels, throwing her head about, fighting the reins. Khalidah turned back to the empty desert unrolling before her and gave the mare her head. Zahirah looked around at her, as if to make sure she meant it, then she hurtled off across the sand toward the starlit horizon like a spent night's memory of flame, shadowed by the storm gray mare.

Hidden in the shadows at the edge of camp, Bilal watched them go.

5

Under the full moon the desert was almost as bright as morning, and for a long time they let the horses run. When at last
they began to flag the moon was nearing the far horizon, and
Khalidah too was beginning to feel the effects of the tumultuous
day and sleepless night. She loosened her hold on the reins and
let Zahirah stretch her neck, then looked across at Sulayman,
whose eyes were on the east.

"Are you expecting someone?" she asked.

"No one, in fact," he answered. "But I need to be certain the
expectation is justified."

"Where are we going, Sulayman?"

"There is a cave south-east of here, with a spring nearby. We'll
reach it by daybreak."

Khalidah shook her head in exasperation. "And then what?
We will live in this cave until my father forgets that he ever had
a daughter?"

"All in good time, *Sayyida*."

Khalidah sighed. Part of her wanted to push him for the truth,
the rest couldn't bear to hear it. So she let the silence carry them
over the streaming sand and past towers of stone, windhewn
and mutable, her thoughts drifting from her mother's ghost to
Zaynab's words to Bilal's motionless body. At last they fetched up
against the snap of bone, the viscid resistance of flesh to metal.

This troubled her mainly in how little it seemed to matter. She suspected that she ought to be appalled at having killed a man, but she felt only relief that he could not follow her. Likewise, when she thought of all that she had left behind she felt not a loss but an opening, as if her heart had split to blossom. She watched the constellations turn on their slow wheel across the sky, and she could find no space in them for grief, only the offer of a wild, glorious freedom.

At last the sky ahead began to brighten, then to glow with light-streaks the color of butter and spring grass. 'Aasifa and Sulayman had taken the lead and Khalidah, half-asleep in the saddle, nearly tumbled when Zahirah drew up short behind them. They stood at the top of a long, gentle slope, the bank of a shallow wadi. At the bottom a slender stream trickled with the remnant of the winter rains. Sulayman dismounted and led 'Aasifa down to the water. When all of them had drunk, he pointed upstream.

"The cave is there."

"Surely this stream is known to the tribes in the area, and the cave too."

Sulayman said nothing, only smiled and led his tired horse off toward a cluster of rocks. Sighing, Khalidah followed him. When they reached the rocks she expected to find them cracked and fissured, as rocks were in that desert when they concealed caves, but instead they walked along a smooth wall almost twice her height. Khalidah could see nothing in it that looked like an opening, and with a sinking heart she realized that Sulayman had been mistaken. Well, she asked herself, what did you expect? Obviously he was a madman, and she must be mad herself to have followed him.

As Sulayman studied the recalcitrant stone, she leaned miserably on Zahirah's shoulder, burying her face for a moment in the horse's coppery mane. Rather than shy or toss her head, Zahirah stood still and blew softly onto Khalidah's neck. The familiar, sweet smell of horse and the warmth of her breath were comforting. *At least I have her*, Khalidah thought; *I have her and the Franji doesn't*. She looked up again, and then blinked. Sulayman

was gone. She tugged Zahirah forward, her heart quickening
with fear. She had nearly passed a stand of dead tamarisk trees
when a whistle stopped her. Looking more closely at the trees,
she saw what had seemed before to be a snip of shadow; except
that now, Sulayman's grinning face was peering out of it. She
thrashed angrily through the trees. She found him standing
within an envelope of rock just wide enough to accommodate a
saddled horse. Behind him, it led into darkness.

"This is no time for games!" she snapped.

"Of course not," Sulayman said demurely. "I am sorry,
Sayyida."

Though she suspected that his contrition was an act, Khalidah
was too tired to protest. Leading Zahirah, she followed him along
the stone passage and into a rough chamber just big enough for
the four of them to lie down. The crevice narrowed again above
their heads, but it ran right up through the rock. High above, she
could see a strip of brightening blue.

"We must eat," said Sulayman, "and then sleep. We'll ride all
night again."

Khalidah pulled off Zahirah's saddle and bridle, spreading the
saddle-blanket on the sand to dry. She gave both horses barley
and dates and a measure of dried camel's milk, taking some of
each for herself and Sulayman. They ate in silence, then lay down
on their blankets with their backs to each other.

"I truly am sorry if I frightened you," said Sulayman.

Sighing, Khalidah pulled her blanket over her head and fell
into deep, exhausted sleep.

*

She opened her eyes on a mist like a fine veil, full of half-formed
faces that shifted as soon as she tried to make them out. The air
she breathed was cool and damp and thin, the ground beneath
her feet thick with grass. Nearby a figure stood, dressed in a long,
white robe with embroidery at the hems and beneath it, loose

trousers like a man's. But she was a woman, of that Khalidah had no doubt, nor of her identity. She turned, revealing golden eyes as deep as wells, dark patterns on her forehead and cheeks, a smile full of tears, and it was no wonder then to Khalidah that they said she had gathered hearts like wildflowers, though she was no beauty.

"I thought I had forgotten you," Khalidah told her, admitting her most shameful secret. "I didn't remember your face, I didn't even dream of you anymore…" But that wasn't quite right, because she recalled a tapestry from which this same face had emerged not so long ago, to the bidding of a plucked string. Time pitched and whirled, flagged with images: vines on her hands, blood on parchment, the snap of bone, a smile in a sunlit nimbus. "Were you there? Are you here?"

Little girl…life of my soul…

The words brushed Khalidah's mind with the insubstantial delicacy of the ghost-ridden mist. "*Ummah*, please," she whispered. Brekhna smiled again, but she was fading, and Khalidah had the sensation of duality that comes at the end of a vivid dream, when the dream world and the visceral one run momentarily parallel. "Wait!" she cried. "Tell me where to find you!"

Again the sad smile, the words like phantom fingers stroking her mind: *First find Qaf…*

Qaf. At the sound of the word, fragments of the *imam*'s teachings toppled through her mind: the end of the world, land of the Jinn, mountains of emeralds and beings of smokeless fire…and while she paused to capture them, her mother slipped away like sand through spread fingers.

In her wake, though, the mist cleared. Khalidah stood on a hill above a valley ringed by mountains, the nearer ones green with grass and trees, the farther blue and violet and tipped with snow. On the valley floor a river flowed clear over golden stone and a herd of horses grazed the lush grass of its banks: fine horses, perhaps even finer than the tribes'. There were rows of buildings on a hill to her right – dwellings, she thought, made of wood and stone, each a perfection of carving and care, stacked so that the

roof of one formed the terrace of the one above. At the far end
of the valley, at the foot of a hill, was a larger building with what
seemed to be a minaret rising at its center. A gallery ran along
the upper storey, and tucked back into its shadows was a seated
figure, also dressed in white. The figure looked up and seemed
to see Khalidah, seemed about to gesture. Then the mist closed
down again, and the dream disintegrated.

*

At first, Khalidah couldn't remember where she was. Above her
was a jagged strip of blue-green twilight, behind her the solid
warmth of a sleeping horse. She sat up. Zahirah whickered softly
and nibbled the ends of her hair, and everything came flood-
ing back. She looked across at Sulayman, who was still sleeping
soundly. 'Aasifa was standing near the passageway, her head
stretched toward freedom.

"All right, let's go," Khalidah said. Grabbing her saddle-bags,
she led the horses outside to drink.

As they sucked greedily at the little stream, Khalidah did her
best to wash her face, wiping it dry it on the inside of her dress,
which was still relatively clean. Then she knelt and performed the
Salatu-l-Fajr, the dawn prayer, wondering whether Allah was still
listening to a woman who had done as much wickedness as she
had in the past night. She looked down at her broken reflection
in the last of the twilight to see if it had changed her face, but
she found herself searching instead for her mother in her own
features. She didn't find much beyond the golden eyes. Her skin
was darker than Brekhna's, her hair resolutely black, and her face
was softer, heart-shaped, with her father's open features.

All at once another face wavered beside hers. She jumped,
then whirled angrily on Sulayman. "Don't do that!"

He smiled benignly and knelt beside her, cupping his hands to
drink before he answered, "I'm sorry if I startled you."

"No, you aren't," Khalidah said. "It's just like earlier – you
were trying."

"Honestly, I wasn't. It's the force of habit."

"What kind of habit requires you to move so silently?"

He tilted his head, looking at her reflection rather than her face. "That is a story in itself, and right now we must be going. Here, put these on."

He laid a bundle of pale fabric beside her. She picked it up and shook it out. It was a man's short, linen robe and baggy trousers, like Sulayman's own. A red sash and *kufiyya* fluttered to the ground. She saw then that he had changed his embroidered cap for a similar headdress, but his was blue.

"Where are we going that I am required to dress as a man?" Khalidah asked warily.

"It's not the destination that requires it, but the journey. We'll keep to the desert as we can, but sooner or later we're going to meet other people. Believe me, it's better that they think you a boy."

Sulayman tactfully walked downstream toward the horses while she stripped off her gown and shift and replaced them with the trousers and robe. She plaited her hair and dropped it down inside the robe, then tied on the *kufiyya*. With her dress and shift under her arm, she went down to Sulayman, who had already tacked Zahirah and was working on 'Aasifa. Khalidah thought that the gray mare looked less skittish than she had the previous night. Sulayman's hands on her were as delicate as they had been on his *qanun*, and though she danced while he tightened the girth and shied when he approached her head with the bridle, the horse no longer trembled. All the time he spoke to her in a low, gentle voice.

"You have a way with a horse," Khalidah observed.

"And you with a pair of trousers. You make a very convincing boy." She scowled at him and he added, "Though an uncommonly pretty one. I wouldn't like to answer for your fate if we meet a troop of lonely soldiers. Better say you're studying to be a *darwish*."

Her scowl deepened. "Will that really stop a rapist?"

"No. But it will deter him long enough for you to draw your

knife." Sulayman laughed at her expression. "Have no fear, *Sayyida*. I won't let anyone touch you."

She let him give her a leg up into the saddle, but she couldn't repress a smile of satisfaction as she nudged Zahirah's sides and the golden mare shot off, leaving the gray far behind.

6

A bald sun rose over Wadi Tawil, bringing wind with it, a Sirocco full of grit and heat from the Sahara. Its blasts and lulls rattled the tents like husks, foretelling a dry season. *To add insult to injury*, thought Bilal, looking toward the grazing land where the tender shoots of the new season's grass were already withering. He felt as if he were one of them. His head pounded and his eyes still wouldn't focus properly, though he couldn't tell whether this was a result of the drug or the retainer's fist; not that it mattered much.

"All right, Bilal," 'Abd al-Aziz sighed at last. "Let us hear this one more time."

Bilal regarded the solemn group gathered in the *majlis* in stark contrast to the reveling crowd of the previous evening: 'Abd al-Aziz, looking gray-faced and ill; his brother, pinched and for once, contrite; Numair, whose stony circumspection was now tainted by wounded pride; his mother Zaynab, whose eyes above her half-veil were oddly serene; and at the centre, the blood-stained letter, the presence that subdued them all with its implications.

"I've told you everything I know," the boy answered.

"What you have told us is primarily conjecture," the sheikh corrected mildly. "And I am trying to ascertain the facts."

"The facts!" cried Bilal, whose anger had had time enough to grow an offshoot of doubt which fed right back into it, stoking it higher than ever. "What fact is there, but that Khalidah ran away with that rogue like a –"

"Bilal!" Zaynab interrupted sharply.

Bilal shut his eyes for a moment, wishing that he could as easily shut out his memories of the past night; for whatever the letter with the Templar seal might mean, it did not change the fact that Khalidah had abandoned family and honor to run away with a man no better than a servant. No better, Bilal's heart whispered to him, than you are. He had tried to tell himself that it changed nothing – that Khalidah would never have been his anyway, that he had always known that she didn't love him – but it didn't lessen his pain. For though she would have been another man's wife had she stayed, it would not have been her choice, and would have taken nothing from him. This, though, was different: this left him not even the sanctity of his impossible love for her, to sustain him in her absence.

Still, Bilal agreed with 'Abd al-Aziz: it was the facts that were important and the facts were, in his mind, incontrovertible. Drawing a breath, he said, "I was asleep, drugged like the rest of you, though not so heavily. I'd only had a part of a cup of wine, since my mother forbade me to have more."

"Wise woman," 'Abd al-Hadi muttered. The others remained pointedly silent. Zaynab had, after all, slept through the entire incident.

"Something wakened me," Bilal continued. "A woman screaming. When I went to look, I saw Khalidah speaking with 'Abd al-Hadi's retainer – the dead man. She was saying that she would never marry *Sayyid* her cousin." His eyes flickered apprehensively to Numair, whose own look remained impassive. "The retainer saw me then, and he hit me. When I wakened again, it was just in time to see Khalidah and that – the minstrel, riding away. I followed them to the edge of camp, but when the horses began to run…well, what could I do?"

There was a moment of taut silence, then Numair spoke, his voice as grave as his uncle's but devoid of empathy. "You could have roused someone who might have been able to catch them."

Bilal looked as though he had been struck. "I tried to, *Sayyid*," he answered tremulously, "but no one would wake."

'Abd al-Aziz fingered his beard contemplatively. "And the letter? You have no idea where it came from?"

Bilal shook his head. "The first I knew of it was this morning, when it was found."

"Ah, what I would give for a man in this camp who knows his letters," the sheikh said in a bitter undertone.

"It would not help," Zaynab said dryly, "unless he knew Franj letters too. Besides, what does it matter? The seal tells us everything." She glanced significantly at 'Abd al-Hadi as she said this. 'Abd al-Aziz, too, was looking at his brother.

"You cannot blame me if one of my men had defected to the Franj!" he cried.

'Abd al-Aziz gave him a long look full of conjecture, but in the end he said only, "What we need to determine is whether or not the Templars had a hand in my daughter's disappearance, or if she left simply because…"

Here, for the first time, the sheikh's composure failed him. Though the question had been addressed to Bilal he looked at Zaynab, who looked back with unflinching eyes. Her silence had a distinct cast of indictment.

"Therefore," 'Abd al-Aziz continued at last, "although I would never normally ask anyone to betray a confidence, I ask you now, Bilal, whether Khalidah ever said anything to you that might give a clue, a reason why she might have wanted to run away. Something, perhaps, about the Templars?"

The sheikh could not keep the hope out of his voice with the last statement, which irritated Bilal. He answered shortly, "The only thing she said to me was that she did not wish to marry her cousin."

'Abd al-Aziz scrutinized him for another long moment. Then he said, "Thank you, Bilal. Your faithfulness will not go unrewarded. You are dismissed."

"But…" Bilal began.

"You have something else to tell us?"

Bilal shook his head and retreated, avoiding his mother's eyes.

Once outside he circled the tent, ducked past the kitchen with its sharp-eyed serving girls and then slipped into the stable from the back. When he put his ear to the tapestry, he heard his mother's voice, low and angry: "...don't know any more than you do!"

"Forgive me, Zaynab, if I find that difficult to believe," 'Abd al-Aziz answered.

Zaynab snorted. "Which is precisely why you are sitting here wondering what to do."

"Meaning?"

"You fail to accept what you *do* know."

"What is there to accept?" interjected 'Abd al-Hadi. "If you ask me, the two events are un-related. My retainer was deceiving me, and my niece ran off with my good-for-nothing minstrel. The former seems to me to be a closed case, as the man is dead. As for the latter, your daughter's intentions are obvious, particularly in light of her scene last night. No father should be asked to accept such dishonor."

"As I recall, Khalidah offered a legitimate explanation for that 'scene'," said Zaynab.

"What," scoffed 'Abd al-Hadi, "that silly story about her mother?"

The silence stretched and sagged. At last 'Abd al-Aziz broke it. "I would like to believe that Khalidah has gone to look for her mother," he said wearily. "I would rather believe that she was kidnapped by Brins Arnat and the Templars than what appears to be the case. But I do not think that either Arnat or the Templars could have much interest in a Bedu's daughter, and a sudden longing for Brekhna does not explain the drugged wine, the murdered retainer, the stolen horses, and least of all the presence of the man with the *qanun* in all three." 'Abd al-Aziz's voice had risen toward the end of this speech, its frayed edges betraying his struggle to resist anger. "Particularly when my wife is long since dead."

"Dead to *you*," Zaynab said stonily, and on the other side of the tapestry Bilal found himself suddenly attending her words.

"What are you saying?" asked 'Abd al-Hadi, warily.

"Tell them, *Sayyid*," Zaynab said, in a tone Bilal could not believe his mother would take with the sheikh, and still less that the sheikh would endure. "Tell them that you have lied to your daughter – to all of them – about her mother's fate."

"Don't tell me that you told her so," 'Abd al-Aziz replied, the anger flowing forth now.

"I told her no more than she had already guessed – which is that her mother is still alive."

"And why did she guess that, Zaynab?" 'Abd al-Aziz's tone was cold, mocking, not unlike Numair's. "What clues did you let slip, out of spite for me?"

"Spite for you?" she answered, equally furious. "Ah, *Sayyid*, I would never have taken you for so great a fool! Do you not realize that this is your own doing? You might have been able to banish Brekhna from your own heart, but the living cannot be buried. Khalidah could not stop being half her mother's, just because it hurt you; and yet she tried out of love for you, and is it any wonder that you don't like the results? Did you really think that Brekhna's daughter could submit to a marriage of convenience? She tried to tell you – even last night she tried – but the only one who listened was the minstrel. So follow her if you like, but do not underestimate her."

A sweep of fabric, a tinkle of coined anklets followed by hush. Bilal sat as stunned as he knew the men on the other side of the tapestry must be, his mother's words echoing through the long silence. Once again it was 'Abd al-Aziz who broke it, and though the fury in his voice was gone, it remained cold and sardonic.

"You have said very little about any of this, Numair. She was, after all, your betrothed. What, in your opinion, should we do?"

"Let her go," Numair answered without pause or emotion. "She is no longer worth the sweat of our horses."

"And if the letter is not a coincidence? If the Templars had some hand in this?" It was difficult for Bilal to tell from his tone whether 'Abd al-Aziz himself was advocating the idea.

Numair shrugged. "I will go into Oultrejourdain if you like, and see if I can find her."

"You do not sound particularly keen."

"That is because I do not believe that I will succeed," Numair answered.

"Very well," the sheikh answered, "but I am not so quick to dismiss my daughter. Therefore, I will accept your offer and I will send my own men east."

Numair smiled wryly. "Do not bother, *Ammah*. I have already sent my own men east."

"You are very certain of her guilt," said 'Abd al-Aziz, his voice frigid.

A pause, during which Bilal would have given anything to see the expressions on the three men's faces. Then Numair answered with distinct irony, "Allah metes out justice in the few places you cannot reach, *Ammah*. And now, if you'll excuse me, I will choose two of your horses to replace the ones your daughter has stolen – no, make it three, as I have never seen the horse that could match Zahirah – and then I will be on my way to Oultrejourdain...if that's really what you wish."

But his non-question was to remain forever unanswered, for there was a sudden clamor of hooves, a horse galloping up to the sheikh's tent.

"Forgive my interruption, *Sidi*," gasped a man's voice, which, after a moment, Bilal matched to 'Abdu'llah, one of 'Abd al-Aziz's retainers. "I thought that you would want to know immediately – the Sultan has declared war upon the Franj!"

Exclamations of surprise from the adjoining room, and then 'Abd al-Aziz's voice cut through the commotion like a cool blade: "Please, be seated and explain your message. You, girl – bring the man a drink."

Another pause and shuffle, and then the messenger spoke again, hardly less breathlessly for sitting. "I have just heard it from one of the Sultan's official messengers. No doubt you were aware that the Sultan had appealed to King Guy for the release of the prisoners Arnat has been holding from the caravan. Well, when the king petitioned Arnat, he refused to let them go. And when the prisoners reminded Arnat of the truce, and demanded their release upon its terms, he said to them, 'Let your Muhammad come and save you!'"

There was a moment of silence while this sank in, which extended as the serving girl returned with a drink for the messenger and he slurped and gulped. At last he continued, "When he heard Arnat's words, they say the Sultan swore to kill the infidel with his own hands. His army is already mustering in Damascus."

"And so, the time has come at last," said 'Abd al-Aziz, with what seemed to Bilal to be a cast of anticipation.

"Indeed," 'Abd al-Hadi answered faintly.

"Will we go to join the army, *Sidi*?" 'Abdu'llah asked, with barely-suppressed excitement.

There was a pause, then the sheikh answered, "Let it be known, 'Abdu'llah, that any man of this tribe who wishes to join the Sultan's army is free to go; and may Allah go with them."

"You cannot speak for the tribe!" 'Abd al-Hadi gasped in disbelief.

"The terms of our agreement, *Akhah*," 'Abd al-Aziz answered coldly, "state that the two branches of the Hassani remain autonomous until such time as our children should marry. Based upon your reaction to this decree, I cannot help but view my daughter's disappearance as partly propitious."

"This is outrageous – " 'Abd al-Hadi began, but Numair cut him off, his voice silky-smooth, apparently unperturbed.

"No, *Abatah*," he said. "It may be, as my uncle suggests, for the best. And perhaps, after all, we should not be too quick to dismiss the Sultan's call to arms."

"But – but you cannot mean – "

"Come, *Abatah*. We can discuss it later, at our leisure. There is no reason to stay here any longer."

As the men bid their stilted farewells, Bilal sat back against a tent-post to consider all he had overheard. He had just begun to relax when the stable's *ghata* opened. A barb of light struck the darkness. Numair stood within it, gesturing to Bilal, who approached reluctantly.

"I suppose you have been listening all this time?"

Bilal nodded, waiting for the reprimand, but instead Numair gave him a faint, reptilian smile.

"Good. I need not go through all of that tedium again." He paused, then said, "Tell me – do you love your mother?"

Bilal was so surprised by the question he thought he must have imagined it. But Numair was looking at him expectantly, so at last he said, "Of course I do."

"There was a 'but' in that statement," Numair observed.

Bilal sighed. "There is not much upon which she and I see eye to eye. There has never been."

Numair nodded as if none of this surprised him. "And your father?"

"I never knew my father," Bilal answered, unable now to meet Numair's eyes. "He died before I was born."

"What if I told you that he did not – that your mother has lied to you all these years, as Khalidah's father lied to her about her mother's death?" Bilal could only stare at him, stunned. Numair smiled. "It's true, Bilal. Your father is alive and well and a mere day's ride from here. Do you wish to meet him?"

Bilal finally found his voice. "Even if this is true – " he began.

"Do you doubt my word?"

"No, *Sayyid*, of course not…only, it is so strange. Who is my father, that he might be so near and I do not know him?"

Numair's eyebrows flew upward in surprise. "Do you mean that your mother denied you even that knowledge?"

"Tell me, *Sayyid*," Bilal answered softly.

Numair studied him for a long moment and then said, "No. It is far too dangerous to speak of him here. But I will say that he is a man of high position, and he may well see fit to do something for you. If you can be ready in half an hour, I will take you to him. Pack your essentials and meet me at the edge of camp; I'll have a horse ready for you. Tell no one what you are doing."

Bilal was reeling; he half-shook his head. "But my mother – "

All at once, Numair's calm turned to an intensity that bordered on menace. He stepped even closer to Bilal and took him by the shoulders. "Usually I do not make an offer twice; but because you are young, Bilal, and because I understand that this news must come as a shock, I will put it to you again in the clearest possible terms. I am leaving in half an hour, to keep a meeting with your father. You can come with me and have a chance at significance, or stay here and rot in oblivion. Those are your choices."

Even then, Bilal knew that this was not quite true, that there were in fact a number of choices before him then and that Numair's offer could not be without strings. However, Khalidah's cousin was correct about one thing: to remain in Wadi Tawil would be to consign himself to a life of oblivion. After a moment he nodded, and Numair smiled.

"Good," he said. "You will not regret this."

7

As on the previous night, they let the horses run as long as the ground was good and they had the energy. Khalidah found that she enjoyed this ride much more than the last, whether for sleep or acceptance of the situation or the dreamed reassurance, or all of them. When at last the horses slowed, she drew Zahirah back to walk beside 'Aasifa. The red mare reached out to sniff the gray's nose. 'Aasifa snorted, but her ears stayed forward. Sulayman took a packet of almonds from his saddle bag, poured out a handful, then handed the bag to Khalidah. She looked across at him as they chewed. His face was placid in the moonlight, but his eyes showed a mind intricately at work.

"It's time to tell me where we are going, Sulayman."

He rode on in silence for a time before he said, "Qaf."

"What did you say?" she demanded.

"You heard me. And I would have thought that you, of all people, would not give me that look."

"What look?"

"As if I were mad. I have heard the stories about your mother, Khalidah: that she fought like a man and had an uncanny eye for a horse. That she was no beauty, but she conquered hearts as easily as the Queen of Sheba. That your father's good fortune began when he married her, and ended when she died. That she did not come from the tribes, but called herself a Jinni."

Little girl... Khalidah bit her lip against tears. The next moment, though, bitterness blazed to anger. "If you believe that rumor, then perhaps you should heed the others: that she was a succubus with eyes of fire and a voice like honeyed poison, sent to destroy my tribe. That she bewitched him such that he would never marry again, never produce a son to succeed him. That she left him with nothing more than a witch-child, no better than a curse. Did you think I didn't know? Every jealous slave girl and superstitious old man has whispered it behind my back since I was old enough to realize that they meant me to hear." She looked at him with sharp defiance. "If that is why you wanted me, then I prefer Numair as a fate!"

Sulayman sighed with a note of tolerance that would have riled her further, if it had been possible. "Did I say that I wanted you, *Sayyida*? I've told you, I came to help you, but if you choose to believe otherwise, there is little I can do."

They rode in silence for a long time, until at last Khalidah's curiosity got the better of her anger. "You spoke of Qaf," she said, "as if it were a real place."

"It *is* a real place," he answered with good grace, "which I have witnessed with my own eyes. Like most legends, Qaf has its roots in truth. Its mountains are not made of emerald, nor do they lie at the end of the world, but they are both greener and more distant than you can imagine." He sighed. "I know that this must sound like madness to you; in time, *Insha'Allah*, you will accept that it is not. For now, all you need to know is that Qaf is real, as are the Jinn. They are neither demons nor fallen angels, however, but a tribe of flesh-and-blood warriors. In fact, they are quite possibly the best warriors in the world, and your mother, Brekhna, was at one time in succession to lead them."

"A woman, heiress to a tribe of *ghuzat*?" Khalidah said dryly. "Now *that* is madness."

Sulayman shrugged. "You will understand when you meet them."

"When I meet them," she repeated dazedly. "And that will be...?"

"The moon will wax twice more at least before we reach Qaf."

Khalidah looked up at the sky: the moon was just waning from full. She wanted to laugh, but instead she said, "Who are you, Sulayman?"

He sighed. "I told you already, I don't know."

"You're a grown man. You didn't spring into being as 'Abd al-Hadi's minstrel. Somebody fed you and raised you. Somebody taught you music, and French, and how to move like a thief."

"Many different people, actually," he said, then paused, looking off over the moon-tinged sand. "But that's something different. I cannot tell you who fathered me, nor what woman carried me, nor even where I was born."

There was bitterness in the words. Khalidah wondered what it was for: plenty of people knew as little about their origins, but did not live in the shadow of that ignorance.

"Then tell me what you *do* know," she said.

Sulayman sighed again. "Well...the first place I recall is Cairo. I lived there with a stonemason and his wife, who were in essence my parents. They had no children of their own, and by the time they found me wandering in their street they were too old to hope for any. Luckily for me, they were also soft-hearted and devout. They accepted me as a gift from Allah.

"I was happy with them. They weren't wealthy, but we were never hungry, and they loved me. My father began to teach me his trade. Then, when I was seven, he and my mother died in a plague. They had no relatives to take me in, so I went back to the streets. But I had forgotten how to survive there. I was starving by the time I found the troupe. They were traveling musicians, and one had a *qanun*. I had never heard anything like it before; it called to me. I tagged along with them while they were in the city, and they ignored me. I became more difficult to ignore, though, when I followed them back onto the road.

"Once again, I was lucky. Rather than send me away, their leader, 'Umar, gave me a drum and asked me to repeat a string of rhythms. I can only imagine that the result pleased him, because the drum became mine and I became his apprentice. One by one, the musicians taught me to play their instruments, beginning with the *tabla* and culminating in the *qanun*. I grew up with them, traveling the lands of the Prophet (peace and blessings be upon him). By the end of it I had mastered every instrument they owned, and learned to read and write in several tongues. I'd learned also to move like a thief, as you say."

"Why?" Khalidah asked, fascinated despite herself.

Sulayman shrugged. "The life of a traveling musician is a string of obstacles. Sometimes to stay alive we had to take advantage of our wealthier patrons, and the dangerous jobs usually fell to me, being the youngest and the quickest. And then of course a musician, by nature of his work, sometimes hears and sees things his employer would rather he hadn't. Then his survival is a matter of outwitting his host…"

"So the troupe took you to Qaf?" she asked.

"No; by then I had left the troupe. I was tired of the danger and uncertainty of that life. I bought a *qanun* of my own and set off to find a permanent patron. As to why I went east, it was mere practicality. The Persians are by far the most generous benefactors of the arts, so that was where I went. But once there, I could not find a place I wanted to settle in. Something drove me onward…eastward."

He shook his head and smiled ruefully. "It was only an idea when it began, little more than a daydream. I never imagined how it would take hold of me. Before I knew it I wanted to go further east than I had ever gone before; than anyone had ever gone. By the time I saw the mountains of Khorasan, it had become an obsession. I could not stop. My daydream had been burned away by a compulsion I didn't understand, to keep moving east, always east.

"Winter closed in as I moved from village to village, growing colder and hungrier all the time. At some point I became ill, but still I pushed onward. When I finally collapsed I was days from the last village, deep in a mountain pass in heavy snow. I knew then that I had been bewitched, that some evil jinni had led me to die in that bleak place." Again he smiled, and again there was more regret to it than humor. "I was right about the jinni, if not about his intention. For I lay down in the snow, hoping that death would be quick and painless, and awakened in Qaf."

"How did you know that it was Qaf?" Khalidah asked carefully.

"At first, I didn't. I thought that I had died, and awakened in the interworld. That delusion didn't last long, though. I was all too obviously connected to my body, which ached and burned with fever, and rejected the broth that some patient soul kept trying to feed me, and made me wish that I had died in the snow rather than suffer this version of living.

"For many days I lay like that. Delirium reached and receded like a tide. People came to me now and again, to feed me or make me drink infusions of herbs or to change the bedding. Some were men, some were women. The women had marks on their faces – tattoos – and they all dressed strangely, in heavy woolen clothing with thick embroidery, as if it were very cold. I couldn't understand this: it seemed to me as hot as a summer desert. That is why, on the morning I awakened shivering, I knew that I was getting better."

Sulayman lapsed into silence, and Khalidah waited impatiently for him to continue. At last, when she thought he had said all that he meant to, he began again. "A woman was kneeling on the ground beside me, watching me. She had strange eyes – golden, like yours. Her hair, too, was golden." He paused. "When she saw that I was awake, she got up and came back with a bowl of soup. She put it down beside me and helped me to sit up. I asked her where I was, and she told me, 'Qaf.'

"Of course I thought that she was lying, or mad, or perhaps the fever had burned away my senses and my own damaged mind had supplied the word, and for all I knew the speaker too. It didn't much matter. She helped me to eat the soup, saying nothing the whole time, and by the end of it I was exhausted again. I went back to sleep and didn't awaken again until the next morning.

"For a long time, that was my life. Sometimes that woman fed me, sometimes one of several girls. All of them had golden eyes, and they spoke a language I had never heard before. I began to pick up pieces of it, but even when I could ask them questions, their answers told me little. Perhaps it was only that I didn't understand." He shook his head. "I began to walk again, though only within the house. The area where I had lain ill seemed to be a kind of common living area, with several closed doors leading off of it, and a large one that I knew led outside. I couldn't try the doors – I was always watched – and the windows were high up in the walls by the ceiling. A gallery ran around the top of the room, with more doors opening off of it in between the windows.

"When I asked to go outdoors, they looked at each other in a way that I had seen certain patrons look in my days with the troupe, a look that meant they did not intend to allow me to leave. Then one morning when my requests to go out had become more habit than anything else, Batoor – that was the name of the man of the house – gave a nod and told me to follow him. I wondered if it would be to my death; but by that time I was so sick of that single room, I hardly cared.

"He handed me a coat like the one he was wearing, a pair of thick felt boots and a rolled woolen hat. I suppose this made me feel better: why would he bother giving me warm clothing if he only meant to kill me? Then he opened that big door, and it was as if I had seen paradise. Of course I knew that it couldn't be paradise, any more than it could be Qaf…but at the same time, I could see the bones of the legend in it." Sulayman's voice had taken on a wistful tone, and Khalidah knew what she was going to hear next. "There before me was a wide valley covered in grass greener than you can imagine. It was ringed by mountains, the nearer ones green – like emeralds, I suppose – and the farther ones blue with distance and snow. And along the valley floor – "

"Runs a river," Khalidah interrupted, "clear as glass over the stones at its bed. Beautiful horses graze there, and at the far side of the valley, under a mountain, is a wooden building, a mosque I think, with someone in a white robe sitting on the gallery."

Sulayman was staring at her in incredulity. "How did you know?"

Khalidah sighed. "While we slept, I dreamed. My mother came to me, and showed me this place you're describing. She called it Qaf."

"It seems, then, that it was more than a dream," he said after a moment's reflection. "Did she say anything else to you?"

Life of my soul, Khalidah thought, and to hide the looming tears she said, "Not really." Sulayman's disappointment was obvious, and Khalidah told herself guiltily that the words she withheld could mean nothing to him. "Well," she asked, "did you go into the mosque? Did you meet the man in the white robe?"

"Yes," he said slowly, "but it is not a mosque. It is a hermitage of sorts, but the Jinn are not Muslims."

Khalidah turned to him in surprise. "They are Christians?"

He laughed. "Hardly. They follow a religion that was already ancient when Christianity was founded. It is…" He stopped, shook his head. "I do not think that I can do it justice. Let it suffice to say that it is a religion of great beauty. As for the person in the white robe, he is your grandfather, Tor Gul Khan, and he is the Jinn's spiritual leader as well as their chief. I suppose he is a kind of a Sufi."

"A Sufi is chief of a tribe of *ghuzat*?" Khalidah asked. "A tribe of *kafir* demon *ghuzat*, no less!"

"I've already told you, the Jinn are not demons. They are perfectly human, though they have skills and talents that might make them seem more than that at times. And if they are *kuffar*, well, they still manage to conduct their lives in a manner far more worthy of respect than those of many Muslims I have known."

The moon slipped behind a cloud, rimming it with silver. "Well," Khalidah sighed, "what did you do there for a month?"

"Listened to Tor Gul Khan, mostly. He is a great teacher as well as a great thinker. He gave me peace and purpose while my body healed. When I was strong enough, he sent me to exercise with the warriors. He wanted me to learn their skills, but I fear that I failed him miserably, for just as the roots of the mythical Qaf were there in its reality, it was clear, watching the Jinn's mock-battles, why they are called demons. They move with a grace and

silence that would be the envy of any thief. They seem to come
from nowhere: a whirlwind, a blur, and suddenly the straw man
is headless, with no swordsman in sight. Even on horseback it's
like that. Their horses obey them entirely. They can stand so still
they seem to fade into the landscape, and a moment later they're
off like comets."

He shook his head, sighed. "Those days passed like minutes,
and at night I slept soundly on the floor of the house of Batoor
and his wife Warda. The girls who had tended me were their
daughters. There were six of them, and once they knew that Tor
Gul Khan had accepted me, they treated me as one of them. I
wanted nothing but to stay there forever, but on the evening that
marked a month from our meeting, Tor Gul Khan called me to
him. We sat on the hermitage gallery, and he spoke the words I
had been dreading all along.

"I begged to be allowed to stay, to serve him, and he smiled – a
kind smile, like yours – and told me that I would serve him best
by leaving Qaf. He told me then about his daughter, Brekhna.
She had been his pride and joy, one of those charmed creatures
who excel at anything she turns her hand to. She had been set to
succeed him – 'to be our salvation', those were his words."

"Salvation from what?" Khalidah asked.

"I don't know. The Jinn did not seem to me to need saving,
but he did not explain his statement, nor what it was that went
wrong between himself and his daughter. I know only what you
know yourself – that she left the tribe and never came back.
But he must have known more than he said, for he knew about
you."

"About me," Khalidah repeated. It gave her an odd, disjointed
feeling.

Sulayman nodded. "And that, he said, was why he was sending
me away – to find you."

"But what does he want with me?"

"Again, I did not ask, and he did not say; but it seems likely
that he intends for you to replace your mother."

Khalidah gave him an incredulous look. "And lead a tribe I

know nothing of, except that they are *kuffar*?"

Sulayman shrugged. "He was adamant that I find you. It was the only way I would return to Qaf, he said – and that was the last thing he said to me. He embraced me and gave me a glass of wine. Next I knew it was morning, and I was asleep under a cannabis bush at the edge of a village. I got up and started walking west."

"And now we are going back to Qaf, as you always wanted."

"It was what I wanted then."

"And now?"

Sulayman sighed. "Part of me wants nothing so much as to see that place again. Another part of me dreads it, because I know that I am not one of them, and so it can never be mine."

He looked at Khalidah, and this time she understood his bitterness. She wished that she could offer him some consolation, but she couldn't think of anything adequate. So they rode on in silence until dawn streaked the sky ahead, and they stopped to say their prayers, and Sulayman located another hiding place where they would wait out another day.

8

Gerard de Ridefort had not come to Outremer with the intention of leading an order of holy knights. Like Reynald de Châtillon before him, he had banked on a good marriage to secure his fortunes in the Latin kingdom, and at one time it had seemed that he was well on his way to achieving it. He quickly landed the modest but respectable office of Marshal of the Kingdom of Jerusalem, and soon afterward, he caught the eye of Raymond III, count of Tripoli. Tripoli took the young knight under his wing, and for a time the two were the closest of friends, a relationship that culminated in Tripoli promising his protégé the titled wife he longed for in the form of the heiress Lucia de Botrun. But after a time de Ridefort's cocksure attitude began to irritate Tripoli, and when a Pisan merchant offered him Lucia's weight in gold for her hand in marriage, he accepted.

De Ridefort promptly left his service, which the count had expected, and joined the Order of the Temple, which he had not. The intervening years had done nothing to shift the grudge de Ridefort held against his erstwhile patron, despite the fact that he had gained far more power as Master of the Templars than he ever could have done as Lucia's husband. If anything, his bitterness had grown more potent with time, making him into the kind of man who could not tolerate equivocation. In the current political climate of Outremer this posed a problem, for de Ridefort knew that if the Latin states went to war with Salah ad-Din in their present riven condition, they would be destroyed. More to the point, as the Templars were a particularly troublesome thorn in Salah ad-Din's side, de Ridefort would be first in line for extermination.

Most would have called his solution treason. He preferred to think of it as hedging his bets.

*

Bilal, of course, knew none of this, and in fact he was hardly thinking of Numair as they rode toward Kerak. For Bilal, the castle was a nightmare come true. As the Hassani's seasonal migration took them close to Brins Arnat's stronghold, their children grew up on stories of his brutality and their mothers' congruent threats: "If you slap your sister again, I'll leave you at Kerak the next time we pass!" Or: "Quiet down, or you'll wake Arnat, and I hear he is looking for meat for his spit!"

Zaynab's threats had been particularly grim, possessing a chill ring of truth in that she offered them only as a rebuttal to others. For instance, when Khalidah, aged six, told Bilal that he'd better give back her toy horse because Brins Arnat came in the night and took bad children away to be roasted for dinner like game birds, Zaynab replied, "Nonsense! But he *has* been known to take them from his dungeons and throw them from the battlements to entertain his dinner guests." This put a decided end to their squabbling.

Likewise, when Bilal, aged nine, told Khalidah that Arnat cut out the tongues of children who contradicted their mothers, Zaynab informed him calmly that she had never heard anything of the sort. "However," she continued, arresting Khalidah's incipient gloat, "once, when a man refused to give him money, he sliced up his bald head, smeared it with honey, and tied him up on the roof of a tower until the swarms of insects drove him mad."

Bilal had not forgotten any of these stories, and the only thing that kept him moving toward that dreaded castle now was Numair's promise that his father was to be found within – though the prospect looked rather different in the bleak light of the desert dawn than it had in 'Abd al-Aziz's stable the previous day. Numair had refused to tell Bilal anything more about the man they went to meet than that he was to be found at Kerak. He had also admonished the boy to let him do all the talking, and to keep his eyes down. Therefore, Bilal didn't look at the knights who guarded the gate at the mouth of the wadi that led up to the castle, nor at the grooms who took their horses in the forecourt. However, he stole glances when Numair was not looking, and they did little to bolster his confidence, for all the people he passed wore the same pinched, haunted expression.

Bilal followed Numair into the keep, where Numair stopped to speak in broken French to a man in a red-crossed white tunic. Following the man's directions, he led Bilal to a chamber no bigger than a closet and nearly filled by a wooden table. At the table a man sat writing in a ledger. As he looked up, Bilal's heart bloomed with sudden hope, for if this was the father Numair had promised, he was worth all that Bilal had forsaken to meet him. He wore a knight's mail and a plain, dark mantle. He looked to be in his thirties, with short auburn hair, a neatly trimmed beard and warm brown eyes that seemed to see something beyond the paltry room in which he sat. His features were softened by that rare natural kindness that shines from a man like a light, and makes others want to befriend and submit to him at once.

"Are you – " Bilal began, in French, but Numair interrupted him with a sharp Arabic "Shut up!" followed by a glower.

Bilal's burgeoning hope disintegrated, and the knight, seeing his look if not understanding it, gave him a brief, sympathetic smile. When he looked at Numair it was with a good deal more circumspection. "We had not expected you again so soon, al-Hassani," the knight said to him in Arabic. His grasp of the language was excellent, and his accent made it into a song full of rests and cadences, further charming Bilal, and adding to his disappointment.

"I must see your master at once," Numair said curtly.

"It is very early," the knight answered. "The Master is not yet awake."

"Then wake him," Numair growled. "This cannot wait."

The young knight sighed. "And what shall I say is your business?"

Numair looked speculatively at Bilal for a moment, then said, "Tell him that I have brought someone to meet him, who will interest him greatly."

With a curious glance at Bilal, the knight closed his ledger and left the room. As soon as he was gone, Bilal said, "Who was that man?"

"Jakelin de Mailly," Numair answered tersely. "Marshal of the Order of the Temple, and no concern of yours."

As they waited for de Mailly to return, Bilal mulled over Numair's reference to de Mailly's "master" and his own mother's apparently intimate knowledge of Brins Arnat's personal habits, and a terrible suspicion began to take shape. By the time de Mailly returned and told them that his master would see them, it had solidified almost to certainty. They followed de Mailly through the corridors in a daze, and when the knight stopped at the iron-studded door, Bilal was shaking uncontrollably. De Mailly nodded and left them. Numair rapped on the door.

"*Entrez*," a man called from within.

Numair pushed the door open. Inside, a man sat by a brazier poking gloomily at the coals. He looked up when Numair and Bilal entered. The light from the window behind him obscured his face, but there was no mistaking the hostility in his voice when he said, "Shut the door." Numair ignored him, so Bilal shut it.

The man leaned toward them. Bilal had a quick impression of pale eyes in a golden face before the man spat: "I thought I told you never to bring anyone with you!"

Numair was smiling again – his hard, glittering smile. "Forgive me, Master, only I thought you would want to meet your son. Gerard de Ridefort, may I introduce Bilal ibn Zaynab al-Qabbani. Bilal, stop gaping and greet your father as befits the Grand Master of the Order of the Temple."

*

Bilal's relief at finding himself absolved of Arnat's paternity was short lived, for it took him only a few moments to realize that as a potential father, Gerard de Ridefort was hardly more desirable. True, he was handsome, but the quality of his features was a kind of afterthought to their intimidating cast. Besides, they were marred now by a great twisted tree-root of a vein which had come out on his forehead when he learned Bilal's identity. Worst of all, though, were his eyes. They were the vibrant blue of the sea seen through heat-shimmer, the kind of eyes that mark men unequivocally as kin; the very eyes that Bilal had hated all his life as the advertisement of his foreign blood.

"What," de Ridefort asked, apparently stifling a rampant fury, "is the meaning of this?" He spoke Arabic as confidently as de Mailly, but with a very different accent: harsh and choppy and overly-full of vowels.

"I would think that that would be obvious," Numair answered coolly, taking a seat he had not been offered, next to a writing desk. "You and I were at an impasse in our negotiations; I have, unless I am greatly mistaken, discovered its antidote."

De Ridefort smiled coldly. "Blackmail," he said. "How original. But unfortunately for you, I have no son."

Numair leaned his elbow on the desk, rested his cheek languidly on his palm and studied de Ridefort. If it was an attempt at intimidation, it failed, for the Master met his eyes squarely as he said, "A number of years ago – I'd say about seventeen – you spent some time in Antioch. While you were there, the Sultan Salah ad-Din gave his niece – a girl who had been raised in his

household, and of whom he was very fond – in marriage to one
of his *umara*. She was fourteen years old, and by all accounts, a
beauty. Her name was Zaynab bint Ibrahim al-Ayyubi."

De Ridefort could not quite hide his flinch. Numair smiled.
"I see you remember her. You will recall as well that Zaynab's
marriage was a troubled one. Her husband was much older
than she was, and he beat her out of jealousy, as old husbands
of young wives will. I hear he was rather merciless. Well, she was
crying over her bruises one day in her garden when she chanced
to look up and see a Franj knight watching her. He had come to
her home for a meeting with her husband, he told her, and had
lost his way in the corridors. He asked her why she was crying,
and she was so miserable that she found herself telling him. To
make a long story short, when he offered to rescue her from her
predicament, she accepted.

"She wasn't stupid, Zaynab. She knew what the knight's white
mantle meant. But she *was* young, and I suppose like any young
girl she thought that love would win the day. She was wrong.
Within a week her knight had left her with a bag of silver and
an admonition never to speak of their affair or come looking for
him. If she did, he said, he would immediately have her returned
to her husband, who would of course have her stoned to death."

Numair stopped to observe the effect of his story on the
listeners. De Ridefort was staring at him with unguarded
loathing. Bilal, on the other hand, was white with shock and
disgust, hostility bristling from him like spears from a martyr.

"Zaynab did just about the only thing she could do," Numair
continued at last. "She disappeared: went south to the wilds of
Oultrejourdain, and lost herself in a tribe of nomads with whom
she passed herself off as a widow. Her son was born nine months
later, and the two of them have lived with the Hassani ever
since."

De Ridefort looked at Numair for a long time, then said, "And
I suppose your Sultan has been calling for the head of this errant
knight?"

"Oh, no doubt he's long since forgotten about the affair,"

Numair answered. "But that's not to say he couldn't be reminded. I am certain he would find the information quite interesting in light of your recent dealings with him. And as for your Order – "

De Ridefort laughed wryly. "The Sultan I will grant you, but the brothers would never accept the word of a Saracen against mine."

"Probably not," Numair agreed, "which is why it's so very fortunate that your son has inherited your most striking feature." He pulled the still-stunned Bilal into the light. Startled, the boy looked up at the Master. "Even among the Franj, one seldom sees eyes of quite that shade of blue. But for a Bedu, it is unheard of."

The Master gave Bilal a long, inscrutable look, then he turned back to Numair. "What do you want, al-Hassani?"

On any other face, Numair's smile would have been beatific. On his, it was diabolical. "I want twice what you're paying me now to carry your information," he said. "And you can forget Ayla. If the Sultan wins, I want Kerak."

*

What Bilal learned as the men bickered over the next few hours was enough to make the discovery that he was the son of the Master of an order of celibate Franj monks seem almost prosaic. De Ridefort had decided several months earlier to pave his way with the Sultan against what he considered the likely event of the Muslims winning the coming war, by supplying him with the kind of information to which few others in the Latin kingdom had access. But since a man of his position could not be seen to be consorting with the enemy, de Ridefort had hired what he considered a suitably insignificant go-between to carry his information: Numair al-Hassani.

De Ridefort's reward for his efforts was the principality of Oultrejourdain – or it would be, Salah ad-Din promised, as soon as Jerusalem was back in Muslim hands. Numair, in turn, was well paid by de Ridefort out of the Templar coffers for carrying his information to the Sultan. At first, this arrangement had suited Numair well enough. But when his father began to speak of his marrying his cousin and consolidating the tribal lands, Numair in turn began to consider power as well as money. To rise, he needed more than a nomad's tent. He needed something permanent, something that signaled his significance to anybody who passed. He told de Ridefort that he would no longer work for him unless he could expect a town after the Muslim victory. To his surprise and delight, the Master had promised him Ayla.

But informing was dangerous and difficult business, requiring long hours of travel, and Numair was essentially lazy. After a run-in with a group of Templars on the way back from one of his missions, he demanded more money. This time, de Ridefort refused, and threatened to cut him out of the deal altogether if he continued his demands. So Numair went looking for something he could use to coerce de Ridefort, and he found Bilal.

Now, as the men debated the borders of countries that did not yet exist, Bilal's mind drifted. He knew that he was embroiled now in this strange business, and as such, he felt a pang of sympathy for Khalidah. It was clear to him that she had only ever been fodder to Numair's insatiable lust for significance, as he was now, and he wondered if she had known it. Perhaps it was the reason why she had run away – and at that, Bilal felt a pang of guilt that he had not tried to help her, even if it was only to deflect everyone's suspicion for a little while.

All at once, Bilal realized that the two men had stopped talking. Both were looking at him with similarly cold surmise. For a moment he wondered if they were about to kill him. But of course, that made no sense: whatever de Ridefort's thoughts on the subject, Numair still needed him as a barter piece.

"No," said de Ridefort at last, as if in response to a question of Numair's that Bilal had not heard, "I think I will send him north, where he cannot cause trouble." His eyes lit with a sudden inspiration. "Indeed, yes – I will send him north, into the Sultan's army, where he can perhaps be useful to me as an *informateur*. For of course, it is to my advantage to know what the Sultan is up to, as long as he knows what we are…"

Informateur. Bilal understood the word well enough; he understood a good deal of the Franj tongue, if it was spoken slowly and clearly. It seemed ludicrous to him that nobody asked him whether or not he wished to be a spy, but then, he supposed, it was better than a knife in the back.

"He has no military training to speak of, beyond a *ghazi*'s spear," Numair said.

"That must be remedied, if he is to have any hope of getting close to the Sultan," de Ridefort answered. "I will send him to one of our garrisons to train. We will tell them he is to spy for us in the Sultan's army; nobody will question it, if the order comes from me."

"Do you really think that I intend to let him out of my sight?" Numair scoffed.

De Ridefort gave him a cold smile. "Pack your sword then, al-Hassani. You're about to become the Sultan's newest *mujahid*."

"But – "

"No buts!" de Ridefort roared. "You're useful to me, but you're not irreplaceable, and right now a word from me would land you in Kerak's dungeon. You do know what Kerak does with his prisoners?"

Numair looked contrite, Bilal faint. De Ridefort smiled. "It appears then that we have terms."

9

As the days passed, Khalidah grew used to traveling at night. The cold no longer bit so sharply, her eyes accustomed to the dark. On the third day they crossed out of the rocky Syrian Desert and into the beginnings of the Nafud, the great sand desert of northern Arabia. Khalidah had traveled the western edge of the Nafud many times with her tribe, but they had never crossed it. No one crossed it, given the choice.

She and Sulayman stopped their horses by the last of the rocky mounds on the shore of the great sand sea. The cold wind of the coming night pulled at their *kufiyyas* and the horses' tails, and their sunset shadows reached eastward across sand like a shimmering expanse of apricot silk. But Khalidah knew that morning would change the soft ripples to a white-hot iron, easily capable of killing them.

"We will not be able to hide out there," she said, turning to look at Sulayman.

He squinted into the east wind with its scouring sand, still as the stones beside them. A herd of Oryx crossed the sunset like revenants, pursued by something too far off to see, and were gone as quickly. At last Sulayman turned to her, face inscrutable, eyes hidden in shadow.

"We will not have to," he said. "An-Nafud keeps its secrets."

With that, he kicked 'Aasifa forward. Khalidah couldn't help

feeling that this was the moment of truth: once Zahirah's delicate
feet touched the sand of the great desert, her last ties to her home
and her old life would snap. A pang went through her, of regret
or nostalgia or simple fear, she didn't know. But Sulayman was
looking back, a dark stone in a nimbus of sunset linen, his face
erased by the last sear of light; and then Zahirah was moving
forward.

*

They rode through the night and the early part of the next
morning. When the sun grew too fierce they rigged a shelter with
their blankets, and crawled inside to wait out the heat. Though
Khalidah was tired from the riding, she couldn't sleep. Her mind
kept leaping from one fruitless thought to the next. Finally she
sat up, and a moment later Sulayman joined her. He opened the
bag of dates and set it down between them. They sat there chewing on the fruit in silence, watching the horses doze in the sliver
of shade cast by the makeshift tent. The animals stood nose-to-
tail, a haze of wind-lifted sand swirling like smoke around their
ankles, reminding Khalidah of a question that had haunted her
since Sulayman first told her about Qaf.

"If the Jinn are human," she said at last, "then where have all
the stories come from? The shape-changing, the bottles of smoke
that take the form of giants when they're unstopped, and all the
rest?"

"I never asked," Sulayman answered, "but I assume that they
came from the Jinn themselves."

"What – they just invented their own legends and spread them
through the bazaars?"

"I don't imagine that they had to. If you came on one of them
here, for instance – that is, if you survived the encounter, since
you'd be unlikely to come on one unless he intended to kill you
– then the most you'd know of it would be a cloud of dust about
the height of a man on horseback. By the time it settled, he'd be

gone; and by the time you made it to the next town, memory might well have made him into a demon of smoke, which would grow with the telling. And who would disabuse you of this idea? Certainly not the Jinn themselves: they prefer that people shun them."

"Why?"

Sulayman shrugged. "Why do your father's people keep to their clans and their traditional lands?"

Khalidah sighed. "I suppose what I meant is, what do they do with their solitude? You say they're great warriors, but to what end? Whom, or what, do they fight for? Surely not for the protection of Qaf, if it's as remote as you say it is."

Sulayman shook his head. "Qaf is their refuge, and they have made certain that it will stay that way. No, the Jinn are essentially *mujahiddin*."

"But they are *kuffar*!"

"*Kuffar*, perhaps; but they are faithful to their own gods, and they fight only those battles which they believe their gods require of them." Seeing Khalidah's dubious look, he sighed. "It is difficult to explain to someone who has not met them. All I can say is that in their way, they are devout, and whom or whatever they fight for, it generally ends up being for the good."

"What good?" Sulayman's eyes shifted away, but Khalidah looked at him levelly. "Whose good is it serving to bring me to them?"

"Whose good was it serving for you to submit to marriage to your cousin?"

"That is an evasion, if ever I heard one."

Sulayman looked at her with eyes that were tired and a little sad. "In all that's happened to me since I first saw Qaf," he answered at last, "there has been much possibility and very little certainty. I too find this very strange, Khalidah; and in the end, I know little more than you do. But what I *do* know is that your grandfather is a good and kind man, and he is desperate to find you."

Khalidah sighed. "Very well." She paused for a moment, then said, "How did you know that I would listen to you?"

"What?"

"The other morning, when you told me to say yes – how did you know that I would do what you asked, instead of accusing you of harassing me?"

He smiled and shook his head. "I didn't. It was, at best, a guess; at worst, pure idiocy. After all, you might have accused me…or screamed, or fainted."

"I don't scream," Khalidah said, appalled. "And I've only fainted once, and then only because Bilal and I bet each other that we couldn't walk all day without a drink…"

Sulayman laughed. "Well then, you might have cried witchery and demanded my head on a platter."

"So, why did you try?"

"As I told you, it was life or death."

And if I had died, you'd have lost Qaf, Khalidah thought, with a trace of disappointment she couldn't quite account for. She was annoyed with herself, and him, feeling that she'd been fishing for an answer from him that he had not provided. To take her mind off of it, she said, "Sulayman, I would like to ask you a favor."

He raised his eyebrows, with the faintest quirk of a smile. "Anything for you, *Sayyida*, if it is in my power."

Khalidah scowled at him, but she continued, "I would like you to teach me to read."

Sulayman looked at her in surprise. "Now, that is not what I expected."

Wondering what he had expected, but unwilling to ask, Khalidah said, "Well? Will you teach me?"

"If you like."

Khalidah waited for him to begin. When he didn't, she sighed, exasperated, and gestured to the blazing desert. "Did you have other plans for the afternoon?"

Sulayman's eyes rested thoughtfully on her face. "All right," he said at last, and broke two sticks from a desiccated bush. He kept one, handed the other to her, then settled himself cross-legged beside her. He smoothed the sand in front of them with his hand,

and then, with his stick, he drew a symbol. "That is *'alif*," he drew another, "and this is *ba'a*."

He made her draw them several times, repeating their names and the sounds they made. In this way, they went through the entire alphabet, and then again, twice more. At the end of it Khalidah's mind was jumbled and reeling, and she was quite certain that she would never make sense of all the symbols and sounds.

As if sensing her discouragement, Sulayman smoothed the sand again, then wrote the symbols for "Khalidah". "That is your name."

Khalidah looked at her name in the sand for a long moment. It was a strange feeling, to see herself marked on the surface of the earth, even if only temporarily. She copied out the characters again, sounding out each one as she went.

"And you?" she asked, when she'd finished.

Sulayman wrote in the sand again, this time his own name. Khalidah copied those, too. "Sulayman," she said. "Khalidah, Sulayman." She looked up at him, beaming. In return, Sulayman's ghost-smile lit his face. The sun was behind him, well down the afternoon sky. She had not realized how much time had passed.

"What about 'Zahirah'? 'Aasifa'? And 'Bilal' and 'Zaynab' and ' 'Abd al-Aziz'…"

Sulayman laughed. "I need to rest now, Khalidah, even if you do not. Teaching is hard work!" Seeing her crestfallen look, he said, "Don't worry. You are a natural. By the time we reach Domat al-Jandal, I promise you, you'll be able to spell it."

"The fortress city?" she asked. "Do you plan to stop there?"

"We'll need water by then, and other supplies for Jazirah."

At any other time, Khalidah would have inundated him with questions, for she had never been to Jazirah, though she had always longed to see Baghdad, the seat of the Caliph. But at the moment, the wonder of her name in the sand precluded anything else.

"Thank you, Sulayman," she said, gesturing to their names.

"You don't know how much this means to me."

Sulayman's smile blossomed, and Khalidah found that she could not look at him.

*

She dreamed she slept in Sulayman's arms. In her mind they clung to each other, not like lovers so much as twins in the womb: two souls that belonged to one another beyond desire, beyond need. For a moment between sleeping and waking, Khalidah felt a peace unlike any she had ever known. Then she opened her eyes. Through the slate-blue twilight, she saw Sulayman looking back at her. He didn't say a word, but she knew that he read that dream on her face as if it were an open book. For a moment they looked at each other, Sulayman's eyes wide with possibility, Khalidah's with shock. Then she rolled away from him.

Shaking from head to foot, Khalidah went blindly to Zahirah, poured her some water and mixed in dried camel's milk, then leaned with her face in the mare's mane as she drank, wondering what the dream meant. They had not touched each other, but she could not have felt more humiliation if they had. Her head swam with rote-learned recriminations, and in her guts was a deep, deep ache, as if she had torn herself when she turned from him. She wanted to say something to him, but there were no words. So they saddled their horses in silence, and in silence, rode toward the night. It was only much later that Khalidah realized she had forgotten to pray.

10

Bilal looked up at the crumbling façade of a pagan god's palace. All around him the red cliffs rose, their improbable carved columns and porticoes fading into the weirder handiwork of wind and water. Even before the late Leper King had extended Franj influence to encompass Oultrejourdain, the tribes had avoided the ruined city of Petra. They believed it haunted by the spirits of the infidels who had cut it from the rock in a past so distant their name was lost.

Turning from the empty-eyed ruins, Bilal's gaze settled on the back of the man who rode ahead of him, and his sense of unreality deepened further. Less than a week ago Bilal had been a boy certain of, if beset by, his lot in life. Now he followed a man who ought to have been a mortal enemy toward a destiny he had never imagined in his wildest dreams. Strangest of all was the fact that he felt no discomfort with this Franj knight, but rather an unnerving affection, and a desire to please him.

As if he'd heard Bilal's thoughts the Franji turned, his warrior's face softening when his eyes lit on the boy. "Not much further now," de Mailly said in his beautiful Arabic. "You have done well."

Bilal flushed with pride at the praise, and his eyes flickered shyly away from the knight's as they left the ruined city and headed toward a high sandstone hill. To its right was a lower hill, its smooth face pitted by the vacuous cavities of looted tombs. Around the top ran a modern wall, encircling a keep and a tower that reached into the dazzling morning sky.

"Jebal Habis," said De Mailly, pointing to it. "Your home, until your master summons you."

Bilal wanted to answer him, but the words would not come: the mention of Numair, reminding him of their terrible duplicity, had silenced him. De Mailly believed he was bringing Bilal to Jebal Habis to teach him to spy for the Franj, and while this was nominally true, in the end, of course, he would in fact be helping de Ridefort to undermine the Franj. Bilal's unease wasn't for the Franj as a whole – they were the invaders, after all – but the thought that he was deceiving de Mailly bothered him more than he could account for.

The horses broke into a canter as they reached the hill, momentarily scattering his obsessive ruminations. Bilal had to admit that Numair had given him a good horse. She was a dark bay with four white socks and a white star on her forehead, plus three little star-like marks on her right flank, for which she had been named Anjum. She was a tribesman's horse, far better suited to the desert than de Mailly's. Bilal felt somewhat disloyal thinking it, and held the mare tightly to keep her from flying past the knight's heavy Destrier. They entered the castle's forecourt through a gate guarded by two armored knights, who gave Bilal no more than a cursory glance, but greeted the Marshal warmly as he rode past. Once inside, de Mailly dismounted and handed his reins to a waiting groom. Bilal followed suit.

"Come," the Marshal said.

Bilal could hear in his voice that de Mailly was already thinking of something else. He tried to stifle his disappointment. After all, he told himself, he had never been more than a chore assigned to the Marshal. He tried to focus on the castle he was going to. Unfortunately, it wasn't much of a distraction. Jebal Habis was little more than an afterthought, a poor frontier fortress serving little purpose beyond its signal tower. After Kerak, it seemed tenuous: a child's toy perched on a sand-hill. Bilal followed de

Mailly through another gate and down a flight of stone steps
into a wide yard. The signal tower stood just ahead, its beacon
smoldering, ready to be stoked at a moment's notice. To the left,
an inner wall enclosed the keep, a mute block of stone with slit
windows and faded banners fluttering from the roof.

Early as it was, the castle was already buzzing with activity.
Servants ran back and forth on their errands and knights called
to one another on their way to their morning exercise, followed
by little squires struggling under their armloads of gear. The few
women carried bundles of linen or pails of water; the servants,
slops to be emptied somewhere away from the living quarters. De
Mailly strode across the yard with an air of authority, nodding to
those who stopped to greet him. Most of them bowed to him,
and all called him "*Messire.*"

They descended another set of stairs into a smaller yard with
a stone cistern at the far side, half-filled with murky water. To
the left, a narrow doorway opened in the inner wall, guarded by
two more knights, both wearing Kerak's black and red livery. De
Mailly ducked through the doorway, Bilal doggedly following.
He stopped, gave Bilal a brief, intense look.

"Remember, you represent the Templars here," he said.

If only you knew, Bilal thought; but he said nothing, only
stood meekly looking at his feet as de Mailly turned to one of
the knights and began speaking to him in French too rapid for
Bilal to follow.

"*Oui, Messire,*" the knight answered when de Mailly finally
finished.

De Mailly looked at Bilal with a shade of pity and a fugitive
smile. "This is Thibaut," he said in Arabic. "He will help you to
settle in."

"Will I see you again?" Bilal asked, trying to keep his voice
neutral.

Again the pity, and the smile. "I will do what I can."

The young knight, Thibaut, regarded Bilal as de Mailly
disappeared into the keep. Thibaut said something to him in
French, to which Bilal replied with a shrug: de Ridefort had told

him before he left Kerak that it would be better to be seen not to understand much of the language.

Thibaut tried again in broken Arabic: "You Kerak's new *informateur*?" Bilal said nothing, only stared at the man. After a moment, the Franji shrugged his mailed shoulders and turned back toward the stairway. "Come. I to show where sleeps."

He walked off across the dusty courtyard, his armor rattling and clanking like a camp kitchen at mealtime. Sighing, Bilal followed the young man into a ramshackle timber building that leaned against the far wall, his spirits sinking further with every step. He ducked through the low doorway into a dark room that stank of unwashed bedding and forgotten chamber pots. The long row of narrow bunks was empty, but the rank smell of the inhabitants' sweat lingered like a presence. Thibaut seemed to have exhausted his knowledge of Arabic, and was speaking to Bilal in a long, impenetrable flow of French. At last Bilal discerned that the man was directing him to an unmade bunk. He nodded and said, "*Merci*," though he could not bring himself to smile.

The knight studied him for a moment with a cold eye, then said in French: "I hope that you will be quite miserable here, you filthy little infidel. I'd give my horse to know whose bastard you are."

Bilal had to smile. "It would cost you more than your horse," he answered in Arabic, "and even then, you would not believe it."

The knight couldn't have understood, but he was clearly shaken by the idea that Bilal might have. He left quickly, his armor percussing away into the half-silence of the morning.

Bilal lay back on the stale straw mattress, thinking about the vagaries of love. He wondered whether it ever kept its promise: the examples in his own life certainly suggested otherwise. He counted them off, beginning with his parents, of whom love had made traitors. Then there were Brekhna and 'Abd al-Aziz, whose marriage had ended in inexplicable heartbreak. Of course he thought of his own erstwhile love for Khalidah, but even that shed no more light on the matter, for with its passing a disturbing idea had suggested itself: that it had never been any more than a figment of his imagination.

In fact, when Bilal thought of love now, a single image came to mind – that of Jakelin de Mailly. The idea of a Muslim boy falling in love with a Christian knight was as ridiculous as it was blasphemous and yet, when he was perfectly honest with himself, Bilal knew that it was no more of a moral or philosophical irregularity than his other examples. Perhaps less so, for like learning the identity of his father, once the shock had passed, it seemed that this aspect of himself had always been there in plain sight, and the realization had only ever been a matter of time.

*

Informateur. The word had a ring of sordid significance, but Bilal quickly found that the reality was merely sordid. The men with whom he shared the stinking barracks were ordinary foot soldiers, a rough and ragged lot as universally despised as their Muslim counterparts. De Mailly had gone back to Kerak the day after delivering Bilal, and when the other knights looked at him at all, it was with much the same expression worn by the servants emptying the morning chamber-pots.

And so Bilal's life became one of populated exile. In the mornings he joined the infantry in their exercises, as it had been made clear he was meant to do, though Numair had told him that he would ride with the light cavalry when they joined the Sultan's army. He imagined that it was meant to keep him busy while he waited – for what, he didn't know and couldn't ask. But the drills were tedious, and the unmitigated company of the big, stupid men left him far too much time to second-guess his situation. Day after tedious day on that scorched hilltop in Petra, Bilal labored the convolutions of his situation in his mind, trying to make sense of them and inevitably failing. Most of all, he wished to see de Mailly again, though he knew that this was as likely as a private audience with the king.

Then, when he had nearly succeeded in driving himself mad, his wish came true. Bilal had returned to the barracks while the soldiers went to their midday meal, too tired and dispirited to think of food. He was sitting on his bunk staring at nothing when the light from the doorway suddenly died. Bilal turned, his heart already beating in anticipation of reprimand, but the man filling the doorway was not the drillmaster or any of his soldiers.

"It's you!" he cried, to his instant mortification.

De Mailly smiled and said, "Come," then turned on his heel and strode out across the bright yard. He turned to see whether Bilal was following. The boy, still half-stunned, leapt from the bunk and ran after him.

As they mounted the steps to the upper yard, de Mailly said, "How have you enjoyed your infantry training?"

Bilal drew a breath. "It has been...informative."

De Mailly gave him an odd, sideways glance and then, abruptly, burst into laughter. "You Arabs are natural diplomats. Sometimes I wonder why we are still at war."

Bilal saw then that they were headed for the stables. Anjum and de Mailly's horse were outside, tacked and ready, their reins held by an Arab groom who would not meet Bilal's eyes.

"Am I finished, then?" Bilal asked, trying not to show too much eagerness. "Are we leaving?"

"We're leaving," de Mailly said equivocally, vaulting into the saddle, "but you are not finished."

"Where are we going?"

"Kerak," De Mailly said.

"Why there?" Bilal asked, unable to disguise his apprehension.

De Mailly sighed. "Because de Ridefort is asking for you."

"De Ridefort?" Bilal repeated, with a slight tremor in his voice. "Why?"

De Mailly's face cracked into a bitter smile. "For good or ill, my Master keeps his own council."

The contempt in his voice was so clear that Bilal looked around to see if anyone else had heard. Except for the dour groom, they were alone in the courtyard. He could feel de Mailly's eyes on him, heavy as tombstones.

"Bilal," the knight said, scorn turned suddenly to supplication, "forgive me if I am speaking out of turn, but I think that I understand your situation, at least a little, and…well, I want you to know that you are not alone. You are very young to be involved with men so powerful. If ever you find yourself in need of help, please know that you can call on me."

"Thank you," Bilal said softly, wishing with all his heart that he could wrap his arms around the knight with the saint's face. Instead, he put his hand over his heart and bowed.

"In working with us, you work God's will," de Mailly said at last, his voice tremulous. "Remember that."

Bilal smiled, thinking bitterly that he could hardly remember whose will he was working anymore, and wondering if he would ever really know. He also wondered what de Mailly thought he knew, for it certainly wasn't the truth. He felt a sudden sharp pity for the Templar Marshal, and a strong urge to reach out and touch the white skin of his face. Impossible, he reminded himself, and mounted his horse in a fluid motion. But when she started to move he sat rigid in the saddle, reins clenched in white fists, frozen by an overwhelming surge of despair that grew blacker still as they reached the valley floor, and turned east toward the hazy borders of Oultrejourdain.

11

On the third day after her disturbing dream, Khalidah spotted turrets on the horizon, shimmering in the afternoon heat.

"Qasr Marid," Sulayman said when she pointed them out. "The fortress at Domat al-Jandal. We should reach the town by evening."

The fortress grew larger by increments as the afternoon wore on, and soon Khalidah could see the smaller buildings of the town around it, as well as a pointed stone tower, not quite a minaret, which Sulayman told her belonged to the Mosque of Omar.

"It looks old," she said.

"Seven hundred years old," he replied, "and it began as a Christian church."

Khalidah reflected on this. It was easy to forget that Islam and Christianity had shared the same cradle; that they had, for a time, shared it in peace. Seven hundred years seemed much less when it measured the time it took for a religion founded on love and compassion to become a viper gnawing its own tail.

The guards at the gates barely glanced at them as they rode through. Once inside, the town lost the monastical air afforded by the high walls and sandstone hill, its stately solitude dissolving into the manic flurry of an isolated trading post. After so many days in the desert's vast silence, Khalidah found the sudden bustle of tight-packed humanity slightly unreal.

"We'll need to find an inn," Sulayman said, casting a critical eye over her. "You should pass, as long as you keep your mouth shut. Let me do the negotiating." Khalidah nodded.

They rode slowly through the streets. Domat al-Jandal seemed, at first, like any town of its kind. The houses were small and neat. Veiled women in dark gowns collected dried laundry from walls and bushes, children and animals played in the streets, groups of men sat smoking in dooryards and tea-houses. And yet it seemed to Khalidah that there was an extra note to the town's purposeful song, like an *oud* with one string too many. This feeling intensified as Sulayman was turned away at inn after inn, all of them filled to capacity.

"Why are they all full?"

He shook his head. "I don't know, but I suspect something significant has happened since we left."

"Why?"

"Because they aren't just full – they're full of soldiers," he said. "Or those who would be. Men from southern Arabia and Jazirah – some even from Persia."

"They would come so far to fight for the Sultan?"

"If you met him, you wouldn't be surprised."

This startled Khalidah into meeting his eyes for the first time since her unsettling dream. In them, as she had known she would, she saw the awareness of it. Taking a deep breath, she pushed past it: "Do you mean to say that *you* have met him?"

Sulayman's eyes moved back to the space between 'Aasifa's ears. "On my way back from Qaf," he said, "I stumbled onto a soldiers' camp and was taken to their *amir*. I didn't realize who he was until afterwards."

"What was he like?"

Sulayman smiled briefly. "Plain, quiet, entirely undistinguished. If the others had not so clearly deferred to him, I would have taken him for a servant. He asked me a few questions which all seemed irrelevant, then he asked me to play for him. In the morning he gave me a few coins and sent me on my way. It was only later that I realized whom I had played for – and how much I had told him, without having been aware of it."

"That doesn't inspire my confidence."

Sulayman shrugged. "On the contrary. I would have *every* confidence in a man like that – as long as we draw swords for the same side. You could see it in his men: they loved and respected him, yet at the same time they weren't distanced by that respect. He found a way to make each of them feel equal to him, even as they aspired to be like him. That's a rare quality in a leader." Khalidah wondered whether he realized he was describing the very quality of which she kept seeing glimmers and flashes in himself.

By the time they found a room, night had fallen, and the horses were hanging their heads in exhaustion. The inn was on the outskirts of town, where the houses were poorer, the streets shadowed and seedy. It was clean, though, and the innkeeper seemed honest.

"The rooms have all been taken," he said, leading them around the back of the house, then across a small courtyard littered with broken bricks and rubbish from the collapsing building next door. A veiled woman sat by a fire, humming tunelessly and stirring something in a large pot. Khalidah twitched her *kufiyya* across her face as she passed, fearful that another woman would see through her disguise more easily than a man.

"But you can sleep here," the innkeeper said, opening a door onto what seemed to be a disused animal shed. There was a single small window high up on the wall and a couple of old straw mats on the floor. Khalidah heard the whine of mosquitoes, and resigned herself to a sleepless night. "And the horses – "

"Will stay with us," Sulayman said firmly. Khalidah could see the man looking over their dusty clothes and sand-crusted shoes, and knew what he was thinking. She had long been aware of the contempt with which city dwellers viewed the nomadic tribes. It would be no different if this man knew that she was the daughter of one of the wealthiest sheikhs in Arabia. But to his credit, the innkeeper only nodded and, after collecting his money, handed them a bucket of water and a towel and left them alone.

After washing off some of the dust and letting the horses drink, they went back out to the courtyard, where the old woman handed them steaming bowls of curried beans and one small flatbread between them. Taking these, they went to join a group of men seated on the rubble from the ruined house. The men were dressed for colder weather, in heavy woolens woven in somber colors. A big man with creases around his eyes and a smattering of white in his beard gestured to Khalidah and Sulayman to sit down with them.

"As-salaamu 'alaikum," Sulayman said.

"*Wa 'alaikum as-salaam,*" the man answered in a heavy Kurdish accent.

Tearing the bread in half, Sulayman gave a piece to Khalidah along with a warning look. "You are far from home," he said to the man who had invited them. "You must be on your way to join Salah ad-Din?"

The man looked warily at him. "Who's asking?"

"I'm sorry," Sulayman said, casting his eyes demurely downward, "I didn't mean to presume. It does seem, though, that all the men of Islam are migrating west at the moment...and unfortunately for us, they've all chosen to stop here for the night." He gave a self-deprecating smile. "That is why my cousin and I have the honor of sleeping in a goat shed. I suppose it's little enough hardship for him, though," he added, gesturing to Khalidah.

"How so?" asked the man, looking at Khalidah, interest glimmering through the suspicion.

"Well," said Sulayman with a conversational shrug, "he will endure worse hardships than the smell of musty goat in his quest for divinity."

"A *darwish*?" The man's tone had softened and he looked more closely at Khalidah. "He's young for it."

She kept her eyes resolutely on her food, but she couldn't help noticing Sulayman's smile, the one she had begun to think of as his thief's smile – slight as the moon's first waxing sliver and as covert, more of a dare than a promise. Inwardly she cursed him, hoping that he knew some Persian prayers, because she certainly didn't.

"Oh no, he's not a *darwish* yet," Sulayman answered. "But he was our *imam*'s top student. The man has run out of things to teach him, so he is sending the boy to a group of holy brothers to continue his education. My uncle asked me to escort him. He is, after all, very young, and the roads aren't safe for a boy so delicate…" Sulayman raised his eyebrows at the man with pointed significance. Khalidah rolled her eyes at her beans.

"Nor are most monasteries," the man said dryly. "I hope that you are not headed to Persia – it is said that the Sufis there take on beardless boys for no other purpose than – "

"We are not going to Persia," Sulayman interrupted quickly, to Khalidah's disappointment. "Our destination is Jazirah – an-Najaf." He said this with studied nonchalance, and as if on cue, the older man's look changed from sympathy to rapture.

"An-Najaf! Oh, you are blessed indeed! There is no more beautiful city in Jazirah – no, nor in all the lands of the followers of the Prophet (peace and blessings be upon him)!"

Sulayman raised his eyebrows as if in surprise. "You aren't from an-Najaf?"

"Near as," said another man, whose reticence appeared to have dropped away as quickly as his companion's at the idea of somebody seeking religious enlightenment in their home town.

The older man shook his head. "Not so near – we are from the mountains – but we do go regularly to the city to trade. And to answer your original question, yes, we are indeed going to join Salah ad-Din. Ours may be a small village of no consequence, but the news does reach us. When we heard about the incident, we knew that we could no longer lie like dogs for the invaders to kick as they please."

"So we go to fight for Allah," another man said.

"And Salah ad-Din. Who better to lead the *jihad* than a fellow Kurd? My wife's cousin saw him once, and he said…"

Sulayman allowed them to chatter on for a few minutes before he interrupted, with apparently little interest, "This incident you speak of – you refer to the business with Arnat?"

"What else?" said the older man, whose name, he had informed them, was Birzu Yalik.

"We have been in the desert a long time," Sulayman said. "We heard rumors, of course, but perhaps you could give us an accurate version of events…?"

Birzu nodded vigorously. "Surely you know about the caravan that he attacked?"

"Yes, we heard just before we left…to think of all those poor pilgrims taken prisoner."

Birzu put his plate aside, lit a small pipe of *banj* and drew on it, shrugging. "I suppose it would tempt a better man than Arnat, all that unguarded wealth passing right under his nose…but it doesn't excuse what he did." He shook his head, expelling smoke through his nostrils like a dragon and passed the pipe to his son. "Yes, he went too far this time. The guards were killed, the pilgrims and merchants imprisoned in the dungeon at Kerak. Some say the Sultan's aunt was among them –"

"His sister," Birzu's son interrupted.

"My guess is, neither of them was within sight of that caravan, but they have been added to the story for effect. Either way, that wasn't the true offense." Raising his eyebrows and his voice, Birzu quoted, "'Let your Muhammad come and save you.' That's what he said when the prisoners reminded him of the treaty. Can you imagine it?" He spat, and the others followed suit, then lapsed into darkly brooding silence as the pipe made its way around the circle.

"And so, Salah ad-Din heard about it," Sulayman prompted.

Birzu shrugged. "Of course. And now he's sworn to kill Arnat with his own hands…and we intend to help him do it, *Insha'Allah.*"

"How long ago was this?" Sulayman asked.

"A week, more or less."

Sulayman nodded and drew contemplatively on the pipe as it came to him. Khalidah watched with interest to see whether he would pass it to her, but he handed it over her head to the next man, saying apologetically to Birzu, "My cousin has foresworn smoke as well as wine, as part of his devotions." Birzu shrugged again. "Tell me," Sulayman continued after a moment, "where is the army gathering?"

"Damascus. That's where we are headed, at any rate. You ought to join us, once you have delivered your cousin to the brothers."

"Perhaps I will. Do you have any idea when the Sultan plans to attack?"

"No," Birzu answered, "but it will take him some time to assemble his army, and of course, the battle season is still a few months off…"

Sulayman's eyes had lost no intensity to the drug, making Khalidah wonder if he had actually taken any at all. They glittered with thought for a few moments before he said, "Thank you, Birzu Yalik. Your story has inspired me, as it should inspire all men of faith, to resist the infidel. I hope that we will meet again; but my cousin and I have a long way to travel yet, and if I am to return in time to join the Sultan's *jihad*, then we must make an early start. Good night, and may Allah have mercy upon you."

The men wished Sulayman and Khalidah farewell, and the two of them returned to their goat shed for the night.

12

The traces were quite discernable, if one knew what to look for. Still, finding the trail so easily hadn't given Daqaq much pleasure. Tracking his master's faithless fiancée across the desert was the last way he would have chosen to spend his time, but Numair had insisted. Daqaq wasn't sure what Numair hoped to achieve by finding her; he only knew that he had been instructed to bring her back alive.

Late in the afternoon of the first day, the trail turned abruptly toward an outcropping of sandstone by a little spring, and then disappeared. Daqaq got down from his camel while the others waited in the sliver of shade cast by the rocks. He crawled like a lizard over the ground, studying the area around the rocks, but for all the evidence he found, Khalidah, her lover and their horses might as well have been swallowed whole by the earth. If he had been a superstitious man, or even a religious one, he might have believed just that. But Daqaq was eminently practical, his faith cursory, and so he came to the correct conclusion.

"They camped here yesterday, and they left last night. They are headed for Domat al-Jandal."

There were groans from the men, who knew that Domat al-Jandal meant crossing the Nafud. One of them, Ja'far, a whining fourteen-year-old who should never have been here except that he was one of 'Abd al-Hadi's bastards, even went so far as to question him: "There is no trail from here. How can you know that is where they went?"

"A lesson for you, boy," Daqaq answered, his tone calm and cold. "A desert is like the sea. Against its vastness, a single ship may seem like your proverbial needle in a haystack, but no ship can survive the open sea forever. Sooner or later it must put into port. An-Nafud is a sea, and Domat al-Jandal is the port."

He climbed back into the saddle, and his kneeling camel lurched to its feet. He turned its head east once again. Ja'far began to say something else, but Daqaq's patience for him had reached its limit. He gave his camel a smack with his crop, and pretended not to hear when Ja'far yelled his protest as his own broke into a gallop, hoping against hope that the boy would lose his seat and break his neck.

*

It took them five days to reach the town. All through the bleak monotony of the desert crossing, Daqaq held onto the idea of catching Khalidah as a kind of guiding beacon. He imagined the shock on her face when he came upon them, the wild pleas, the horror when he ignored them and skewered her lover on his sword. But when they finally reached the town, his assurance disintegrated. Domat al-Jandal was in upheaval, and it didn't take long to figure out why. The news of Arnat's challenge had arrived ahead of them, and though there had yet been no official decree, the *muttawiyah* were already flocking to Damascus from all parts of the empire. All of the inns were full of these religious volunteers, and more to the point, full of foreigners. Khalidah and the minstrel wouldn't even need to try, to lose themselves in such a crowd. But Daqaq didn't dare return to his master without at least an attempt to find her. He sent the men off in opposite directions, instructing them to inquire after a *qanun* player at all of the inns and gathering places, and to meet back by nightfall at an address he gave them.

The other retainers rode off obediently, but Ja'far said haughtily, "I will not waste my time on a goose-chase."

"Meaning?" Daqaq snapped.

"Only a fool would have performed here and called attention to himself after less than a week on the run."

"They left in haste," Daqaq answered through clenched teeth, "and took almost nothing with them. How else would they keep themselves, if not by his trade?"

Ja'far shook his head. "You have no idea what you are doing, do you?"

Daqaq reached out and grabbed him by the neck of his robe, twisting it as he pulled him close, nearly unseating him. "You listen to me, boy," he hissed. "The blood you share with the sheikh might protect you in his camp, but out here, it's worth nothing. I have friends here. One word from me, and your head will roll."

"You wouldn't dare," Ja'far said. "If something happens to me, the sheikh will have you executed." But he could not hide the fear in his eyes.

Daqaq chuckled. "You have a much-inflated view of your own importance, boy. Believe me, if you lose your head in an unfortunate accident, it will be little loss to your father. But, if you care to put it to the test…"

With eyes full of cold hatred, Ja'far turned his camel and rode off into the crowded streets. Daqaq breathed a sigh of relief as the boy disappeared. Despite what he had said, Ja'far's words had rung all too true. He had convinced himself that Khalidah couldn't elude him, but what he had taken for certainty was actually the beginning of this same blind panic. Numair had told him not to come back without her, and so he must not; yet he doubted that anyone could find her in this heaving town, if indeed she was here at all. But he still had a card to play. Gathering himself together, he turned his camel east.

*

Musa was a small, wrinkled old man with a cruel mouth bent by a crueler past. His first language was Persian, and there was Hazara blood somewhere in his ancestry, which showed in his round face and slanted eyes. It hadn't stopped him from slaughtering Shi'ites by the dozens in the service of several Persian *umara*. He hated his native Khorasan, hated its people more, and he could not understand why his young friend would go to such lengths for a woman of Khorasani blood.

"I am a retainer to a rich and powerful sheikh," Daqaq said as they sat outside of Musa's junk shop in the deepening afternoon. "I do as I am told."

"But what can your Numair want with her?" Musa asked, passing him the mouth-piece of the hookah. "Why marry a girl who will hate him and make his life a misery when he could simply kill her father and take these lands he so desires? Isn't that what your people have done for centuries?"

"I imagine there is more to it than I know," Daqaq answered, narrowing eyes already heavy with *banj*. "That is usually the case with my master."

"Mmm. Then perhaps it is time to find yourself a new master. Stay here – I will find you work."

Daqaq only smiled and shook his head. No matter the tribulations, he knew that he could never live any but a nomad's life.

"Tell me," Musa said after a few moments, "what tribe did this girl's mother come from?"

Daqaq scrutinized him for a moment, then answered, "I know only that she called herself al-Jinni."

Musa burst out laughing, sending gusts of smoke into the stagnant air.

"I am only repeating what I have been told," Daqaq said coldly.

Musa waved a deprecative hand. "Of course you are," he said, "and so she was al-Jinni. The Jinn are real, all right, but they hardly live up to the legends. They're little more than a bunch of hill bandits with delusions of grandeur. Their women, by the way, are intractable." Fixing Daqaq with the trenchant look of the very old, he said, "Tell me, have you ever met a Jinni?"

"I met Khalidah's mother, once."

"And did she bring her husband happiness? Or, for that matter, anything beyond misery?"

"She gave him only one daughter before she died. He has never remarried."

"Precisely." Musa sighed. "I do not think that any good will come of your search for this girl; certainly no good for your master. But I will help you catch her, if you are intent upon it."

Daqaq glowered at him. "I thought that you had no news of her."

"I haven't. But that is not to say I don't have the means of finding some."

Daqaq was contemplating a response when he saw a camel trotting up the street toward them. Its rider was 'Ali, and he had scoured the entire western quarter of the town, to no avail. Ja'far arrived some time later, leading his own camel and equally bereft. It was dark by the time Mahmoud returned, and the others were sitting in the tiny yard behind Musa's shop, eating the supper of pilau and yogurt his wife had laid out. Daqaq could tell at once by Mahmoud's face that he had been successful.

"You have word of her?" he demanded.

Mahmoud nodded as he sat down to eat. "Two riders were seen today at an inn not far from here. A young man and a boy, both on fine horses, a chestnut and a grey. It's a poor place, unlikely to be guarded."

"Praise the most merciful Allah!" Daqaq said, his taciturn face breaking into a grin. "We will take them easily." If he noticed Musa's dubious look, he ignored it. "You have served our master well today," he said to Mahmoud, "and I will make sure you are rewarded when we return home."

They proceeded to work out a plan for the capture while the old man looked on in contemptuous silence. They would wait

until the early hours when everyone was asleep, then break into
the inn and locate the runaways. They would kill the minstrel,
and take Khalidah alive.

*

Musa showed little surprise when the men returned near dawn,
empty-handed. "We checked every room," Daqaq explained.
"They were not there."

"And the innkeeper?" Musa asked. "Did you not think to
question him?"

"We could not afford to be seen."

"And the yard? Were there outbuildings?"

The retainers looked at each other. "We will return
immediately," said Daqaq.

"You cannot." Musa pointed to the sky through the shop
window. The horizon was already the color of lapis stone; soon
it would be time for the dawn prayers. In the ensuing silence,
Daqaq looked at Musa, who looked vaguely amused.

"You were right, old man," he said at last, grudgingly. "Now,
will you help me?"

Musa's twisted mouth stretched into a grin.

13

Khalidah and Sulayman rose early the next morning, and were given bread and tiny cups of thick, murderous coffee by the veiled woman at the fire, who seemed not to have moved since the previous night.

"Thank you," Khalidah said to her as they made ready to leave.

"Take care," the woman said in a voice like wind among sandstone canyons. "The sand-cat is close."

"What?" Khalidah asked, turning cold.

"In the night his men came creeping." The woman nodded to herself and chuckled, showing a gap-toothed grin. "But they could not find the sand-daughter, for she too has a wildcat's heart." She began to sing:

> *"Though you might see me*
> *sun-beaten as a sand daughter,*
> *ragged, shoeless,*
> *with worn feet,*
>
> *Still am I the master of patience,*
> *wearing its armor*
> *over the heart of a sand cat,*

shod with resolution…"

They didn't wait to hear the rest, but rode quickly out of the courtyard. When at last the woman's song was lost in the winding of the alleys, Khalidah asked, "Do you think that we have been followed?"

"Quite possibly. But I also think the woman was mad."

"Still, to sing those words – "

"It was Shánfara," Sulayman said.

"I know that," Khalidah snapped. "The 'Ode in Lʹ."

"It's a common enough poem."

"But what brought it to her tongue? And the sand-cat… 'Numair' means 'panther'. Could she have meant – "

"She could have meant anything," Sulayman answered. "But there's little we can do about it, other than hope that she's only mad. We'll buy our provisions, then put this town far behind us. If what those men told us last night is true, then Numair is the least of our worries."

Khalidah considered this. "So you think that Salah ad-Din really means to attack the Franj?"

"I think he means to make a bid for Al-Quds."

Khalidah turned to him in surprise. "That would be madness! The Franj won't let that city go while a soul is left standing to defend it."

"I imagine the Sultan is well aware of that."

She considered this. "Is he really strong enough to defeat them?"

"If he's careful in his alliances, he will be."

They rode through the *suq*, which had been crowded with would-be soldiers the previous evening, and was now deserted but for a few eager merchants unlocking shop doors and unrolling awnings. Sulayman, producing money Khalidah hadn't known he carried, bought more dates and powdered camel's milk, plus dried meat, fruit and lentils. They stowed the packages with the water-bags they had filled at a well the previous day.

"This will do for now," said Sulayman, "but we'll need a pack-horse for the mountains."

"And where will we get a pack-horse?" Khalidah asked.

"Something will turn up," he answered with irritating assurance, and rode on toward the eastern gate.

Khalidah looked curiously into the shops they passed. Then, abruptly, she pulled Zahirah up. Sulayman saw at once what had caught her eye. In a dirty shop window, among tangles of cheap prayer beads, cracked hookahs and tarnished candle-sticks, was a sword. It wasn't particularly impressive to look at: just an unembellished blade, rather short, neither old nor new enough to be of much value, with a plain leather sheath and belt. There was, however, a stone set in the hilt, dull with dirt but still recognizably golden.

A twinge of foreboding went through Sulayman. "Khalidah – " he began, but she was already scrambling down from Zahirah's back and tying her reins to the window bars. Frowning, Sulayman dismounted and followed her into the shop.

As their eyes adjusted to the sudden dimness, they saw that the shop actually contained very little. There was some broken furniture, a pile of dented pots and pans, a few battered rugs hanging from the walls and at the center, on a pile of dingy cushions, a small, wizened man. His round face was like a walnut shell, inert and riddled with creases around black, slanted eyes. He looked at them with little interest, drawing contemplatively on a hookah. The mouth-piece was made of bone, carved into the shape of a serpent with garnets for eyes, and the smoke it exhaled had the sinuous sweetness of poppy.

"May I help you?" the shopkeeper asked in Arabic, though his accent was Persian.

"How much for the sword in the window?" Khalidah asked, uneasiness making her voice shrill.

The man studied her. "You do not come from here," he said at last. Khalidah did not answer. "You are at the beginning of a long journey."

Unease growing apace with the conviction that she needed that sword, Khalidah answered, "As is every man in this town. How much for the sword?"

The man set the pipe down, the snake still trailing smoke through its grinning mouth, and hobbled over to the window. He rummaged around, and finally returned with the sword. He laid it next to the pipe and resumed his seat on the cushions, studying it with an odd glint in his eyes. He rubbed his thumb over the stone on the hilt. "This could be topaz. And even if it's glass, it's a sturdy weapon, and will no doubt fetch a good price with so many *muttawiyah* traveling through town. All you young men running after a piece of glory…" The tone with which he said "young men" deepened Khalidah's unease. She waited, not daring to look at Sulayman.

"But you are traveling east, not west," the shopkeeper continued. Khalidah looked up at him in surprise, but his face told her nothing. He paused, still scrutinizing her, then said, "I do not have long left in this world, and a good story is worth as much to me as a few coins. Tell me where you plan to take the sword, and perhaps I will make you a deal." He sat back, arms crossed.

Khalidah looked at him through the smoke. Her head swam, and it was becoming more and more difficult to focus her eyes. She didn't mean to say it, but the words slipped out, as if the grinning snake had charmed them from her: "It goes with me to Qaf."

The little man smiled without pleasure or irony. "Unlikely," he said, and the room erupted. The hanging rugs fell, revealing three armed men. They wore Bedu robes with *kufiyyas* pulled up to their eyes, and they closed in on Khalidah and Sulayman as the shopkeeper melted back into the shadows. In one fluid move Khalidah had the sword in her hand, and perfunctorily slit the throat of one of the Bedu. Then she looked around. Sulayman had drawn his dagger and turned his back to Khalidah's as they faced the two remaining men.

The Bedu circled for a moment, then attacked. They were well-trained, but the space was tight and Khalidah's movements had taken on an almost preternatural quickness. She slashed the other Bedu across the face and as his *kufiyya* split, she recognized one of Numair's retainers. The skin of his right cheek hung open, and his left eye poured blood. He stumbled in pain and confusion, lurching into the other man, who lost his footing. As the Bedu struggled to disentangle themselves, Sulayman grabbed Khalidah's arm and pulled her out the door.

The uninjured Bedu freed himself and came after them. Sulayman wrenched the sword from Khalidah's hand and pushed his dagger into it, then turned, putting himself between Khalidah and the Bedu. He seemed very young, and above his *kufiyya*, his eyes were full of fear. His sword arm trembled, but Khalidah saw a brief nobility in his courage as he slashed out at Sulayman. He had little skill, though, and fear made him clumsy. He stepped too far forward, Sulayman raised his sword with a look of grim determination, and then the boy's head was rolling in the dust.

It fetched up at Khalidah's feet. She turned and vomited by the side of the wall. She had barely stopped heaving before Sulayman was shoving her into the saddle. He slapped Zahirah's flank with the flat of the sword and the horse took off at a gallop. Khalidah hadn't had time to get her feet into the stirrups, and her legs were still too weak with shock and sickness to have much grip, so she leaned over the horse's neck and clung to the reins for all she was worth, whispering to herself over and over again, "I will not fall off...*I will not*..."

At last the horses slowed, and Khalidah realized that they had reached the city gate. "Bedu raiders," Sulayman said to the guards, pointing in the direction they had come from. "They attacked us in a shop on the main road – the Hazara's. Go, before they escape!"

They left the guard staring stupidly after them as they kicked their horses into a gallop once again. They rode flat out for as long as the horses could keep it up. When at last they slowed to a walk, Sulayman turned to Khalidah with furious eyes.

"Was it worth it?" he demanded, waving the bloodstained sword at her.

"You can't begin to imagine," Khalidah said.

"Imagine!" he cried. "It was quite clearly bait, laid by your honorable cousin and his Franj allies!"

Khalidah looked at him coolly. "Maybe; but I could not leave without it."

"And why not?"

"Look at the blade," she said. "There, by the hilt."

Grudgingly, Sulayman looked at it. And then he looked more carefully. Underneath the dried blood, he could make out an inscription. Scratching at it, he uncovered the words: *Life of my Soul.* They echoed somewhere deep within him, and despite himself, his heart skipped. When he looked up, Khalidah's golden eyes were there already, waiting for him.

"So what?" he said at last, but without the outraged certainty. "It's a common endearment."

"It's what my mother called me," she answered stonily.

He sighed. "Khalidah, anyone could have had a soldier's sword inscribed…"

"That is no common soldier's sword. It was my mother's."

"You have decided this because of the inscription?" he asked incredulously.

"No," she answered, "because I remember it. She kept it under her bed, wrapped in old clothes. The only time she ever slapped me was the day she found me playing with it."

"You've only just remembered this?" he snapped.

"I don't think that's really why you're angry."

They rode on in silence that grew increasingly strained. Finally, Sulayman burst out, "All right then: when were you planning to tell me that you trained as a warrior?"

Khalidah's eyes flashed at him. "When you needed to know."

"I see. Well, is there anything else that I might need to know about you?"

"Well, what about *you?*" she demanded. "You never told me you could fight like a…like a – "

"Thief?"

In fact, the word that had tripped her was "archangel"; the one he supplied deflated her anger. Sighing, she said, "I didn't keep it from you out of spite, Sulayman. Remember my position. I have only known you for seven days, after all." He kept grimly silent. "All right, ask me anything – I promise you the truth."

He was silent for a while longer; then he said, "I want to hear it all."

"What?"

"You've had my life story. Let's have yours."

"I wouldn't know where to begin."

"Begin at the beginning. Where were you born?"

Khalidah paused, then said, "Wadi Tawil. The tribe had just arrived for the summer grazing when my mother's time came."

"Do you remember her?"

"Very little. She di– I mean, she left when I wasn't yet three."

"And your father?"

She paused, then said, "I suppose my father never recovered from losing her. He'd married her for love…and she too, I suppose. She must have: they brought each other little else."

"They had you."

Khalidah smiled ruefully. "Indeed. An only child, and a daughter."

"And yet, your father thought enough of you to raise you like a son."

"In some ways. At times, I question the wisdom of that decision."

"It just saved your life."

"That is true. Perhaps it was some kind of promise to my mother," Khalidah ventured. "Or perhaps it was despair of ever having a son."

"Does it matter?" he asked.

This time, Khalidah didn't answer.

"So you learned the sword and the scriptures, poetry and music. What else?"

"What else?" Khalidah shook her head. "I learned that while a tribe might forgive their chief for marrying a nameless foreigner, they will never forgive his child for bearing her blood. I learned that people don't trust a girl who has learned too much, or whose talents outshine their own. I learned that in the end, a father's primary concern for his daughter is to be rid of her…that the truest love is an animal's…that real freedom exists only on a horse's back…"

Sulayman waited for her to continue, and when she did not, he said, "Should I pity you?"

"That's your decision."

Sulayman thought for a while. Then he said, "And Zaynab? What is she to you?"

Khalidah sighed. "As a child, she was everything to me. Now, she's the only thing I regret. I suppose she is my true mother."

"Where did she come from?"

"How did you know that she wasn't al-Hassani?"

Sulayman shrugged. "Just a feeling. Well?"

"I don't know where she came from, nor when – only that it was sometime before my mother left."

"Haven't you asked her?"

"Of course. But she always put me off. She never talked about her past at all, or Bilal's father, or why she was no longer with him; but she used to cry sometimes, in the night, when she thought that I couldn't hear."

"And you love her," Sulayman said. "And she loves you."

"Yes," Khalidah said softly, and then again, "yes."

"And her son?"

"Bilal, too. We were brought up together, like twins. He was my best friend – my only friend, truth be told, given how the Bedu feel about foreign blood…"

"But?"

Khalidah sighed. "Bilal is complicated. Laughing and melancholy by turns, and you never know which it's going to be, or why. Discontented too, I think because he's ambitious, and yet he has nowhere to go with it. And lately…"

"Your relationship has become difficult," Sulayman filled in. "His love for you took on a shape that yours for him did not."

Khalidah nodded. After a moment she asked, "Why do you want to know about Zaynab and Bilal?"

But he only shook his head, lapsing into silence as the climbing sun slitted their eyes, and the fickle sands shifted, and their shadows reached for home as their bodies moved ever further away.

14

In the light of the morning sun, the town of Ras al-Mai' looked like an afterthought. Throughout its history it had languished in the shadow of Damascus, less than a day's ride away on a good horse, and would no doubt have continued to do so if the keen eye of Salah ad-Din had not fallen upon it. Where others saw arid plains and dust, the Sultan saw space for twelve-thousand cavalry to maneuver unimpeded in their mock-battles. Where his *umara* saw other towns with the same proximity to training grounds and more in the way of creature comforts, the Sultan saw a water supply that would withstand the demands of an army which he knew, despite the gloomy canting of his advisors, would soon be the largest ever raised against the Franj.

Volunteers began to arrive before half of the recruiting letters had even been delivered. The first were *muttawiyah*, religious volunteers with little or no military training, but soon they were joined by members of the cities' *ahdath* militias, and the baseborn *rajjalah* infantry. Then came the elite, slave-recruited *mamalik*, the *nafathin* fire-troops, the miners and masons and carpenters who built the siege engines and kept them running, and finally the nobles' heavy cavalry, the *tawashiyah*. They flowed in from every corner of the Sultan's empire and beyond, Muslims, Jews and Christians, men from every walk of life united by the dream of freeing their lands from the invaders, and their faith in the

Ayyubid Sultan's power to make the dream a reality.

From the beginning, Salah ad-Din was determined that this would be a *jihad* unlike any that had gone before. Famously pious and fair, he demanded the same qualities of his soldiers. Hundreds of cooks were brought in to assure that every soul in the army ate the same food; huge, clay-lined baths were dug for communal use; and while no man was allowed to keep a wife at camp, their absence was assuaged by the ministrations of a sub-army of prostitutes, available to anyone with money, and toward whom Salah ad-Din turned a charitable blind eye.

Everybody followed the same schedule as well. Trumpets and drums sounded at dawn, followed by the cry of the muezzin calling the faithful to the *Salatu-l-Fajr*, the morning prayer. Though the Christians and Jews were exempted from the prayers, the army rose as one body. Following prayer was breakfast, and then a visit to the latrines: long trenches dug for the purpose well outside the boundaries of the camp. The day was filled with training – sword fighting and archery, cavalry and infantry maneuvers – until the drums and trumpets declared an end to work and the beginning of the evening meal.

The Sultan's bid for solidarity worked. From bowing to Mecca as a body, dipping their bread into communal stew-pots, squatting over the same stinking latrines and sharing the same whores, the lines between *amir* and servant, followers of Jesus or Moses or Muhammad soon faded. The men of Salah ad-Din's army became, first and foremost, precisely that, and as such they treated each other as equals.

To the advisors who had told him it would never happen, the Sultan merely said, "You see, in *jihad*, all men become equal in the eyes of Allah; why not in each other's eyes, too? For every man of this army recognizes the Righteousness of the Faith." And smiling at the play he'd made on his own name, he threw his arms wide, as if to embrace as one all the men gathered to his beacon.

*

By the time Bilal and Numair arrived at the Sultan's camp, it dwarfed the town. Banners of every color slapped the lucid springtime sky, and below them ranged tents of every kind, from the *rajjalah*'s humble camel-skin shelters to the brilliant silk pavilions of the nobles, adorned with Qur'anic verses and classical poetry in flowing calligraphy.

Anyone looking at Bilal would have taken him for a nobleman himself: the younger brother or cousin of the Bedu cavalryman at his side. Like Numair, he wore a lamellar cuirass covered by a robe of fine linen and a peaked helmet wrapped in a silk turban. A bright new saber curved from his sash, and a long spear and round shield were lashed to Anjum's saddle. But whatever his appearance to others, Bilal couldn't fool himself. His guts were a twist of cold nausea, his head a bee-swarm of anxiety. He was terrified of making a mistake and giving away his true identity, or worse, his duplicitous position. He wished that Anjum would wheel and run, but his horse was well-bred and impeccably trained, and she carried him into camp with her tail high and her ears forward, as if the chaos of noise and color were a quiet green oasis.

When they arrived at the tent that had been set up by the servants sent on ahead, Numair leapt from his horse, thrust her reins at a groom and retreated inside without a backward glance at Bilal. After a moment the boy dismounted as well. "*Sidi*," said a servant at his elbow, with an obsequious nod of the head and, Bilal thought, a flash of mockery. But before he could be sure of it, the man was leading his horse away.

Inside the tent Bilal found a bright *sajjadah* rug laid out with platters of grilled meat and flatbread and fruit. Numair was already eating, tearing at the food with a ravenous appetite. Bilal was still surprised at the equanimity with which Numair had accepted Daqaq's failure to capture Khalidah, and the loss of three retainers. But of course, Bilal reminded himself, Numair had far brighter prospects now than the few *farsakhs* of desert which marriage to Khalidah had promised. *Soon he will be lord of Kerak*, Bilal thought – *all thanks to me*. He was still smiling

bitterly at this when another servant appeared at his elbow with
a basin and towel. He washed his hands and face, and the servant
retreated.

"I am surprised you did not starve to death at Petra," Numair
said, causing Bilal to glance nervously over his shoulder. "Oh,
don't worry; the men are paid to hear nothing, and too stupid
to know what it means if they did." Thinking of the groom's sly
irony, Bilal wondered whether Numair was as mistaken about
this as he suspected he was about de Ridefort's ability to keep
a promise; but he kept silent. The past weeks, aside from the
time he was with de Mailly, had been one long lesson in keeping
silent.

"How those fools could have conquered anybody," Numair
continued, "let alone a people as superior as ours, on such
appalling sustenance, is truly one of Allah's mysteries." He looked
up at Bilal's anxious face and frowned. "Stop fretting, and have
something decent to eat while you still can. We'll be on army
rations soon, and they are only slightly superior to Franj slops."

Sighing, Bilal sat down on the carpet with Numair. He was
chewing half-heartedly on a tough piece of meat when the servant
who had taken Anjum returned and said, "A messenger, *Sidi*."

"Who from?" Numair asked irritably.

"From the Sultan." Bilal jumped as if he'd been touched with a
hot poker. The servant gave him a disdainful glance, then turned
back to Numair. "Shall I show him in?"

Numair grunted. Taking this as an affirmative, the man
retreated, and in a moment returned with a boy of surpassing
beauty, dressed in a silk robe of the Sultan's deep yellow. He
was about Bilal's age, with delicate, even features, bright, dark
eyes, curling hair worn long in the Ayyubid style, and a slender
grace reminiscent of a Bedouin sight hound. The boy glanced at
Numair, seeming to appraise and dismiss him in a moment, and
then tuned to Bilal. He gave him a longer look. For a moment,
Bilal had the absurd notion that the other boy had seen straight
through him to his duplicity. Then that look broke open with
the abruptness of a desert sunrise, into the most beautiful smile

Bilal had ever seen: warm, enveloping, clearly intended to put its recipient at ease. It drove into him like a fist.

"*As-salaamu 'alaikum*," the boy said, inclining his head.

Instead of wishing him peace in return, Numair looked the boy over with a dubious eye and asked, "Who are you?"

"I am Maslamah 'Abd al-Rahman Salim ibn Yusuf al-Ayyubi," the boy answered mildly, but with a glimmer of derision in his eyes. "The Sultan's son."

He should have apologized and made some gesture of respect, but instead Numair demanded, "Why have I not heard of you?"

Bilal wanted to sink into the ground, but the prince did not appear to be offended. Instead, with a ghost of that wonderful smile, he said, "Most likely because I am not Al-Afdhal, the eldest; nor Al-Zahir, the favorite; nor even Al-Aziz who, despite an entire lack of humor or wit, makes a swordfight look like a dance. Hence I am my father's messenger, and as such, I am here to invite you to wait upon him tomorrow morning."

"For what purpose?" Numair asked, with slightly more interest.

"My father seldom takes me into his confidence," the prince evaded politely. *And if he did, you would not divulge it to the likes of us*, Bilal thought. "In the meantime, he has asked me to acquaint you with the layout of the camp."

Numair spat out a mouthful of gristle. "One army camp is the same as the next," he said.

Burning with shame and desperate to salvage something from his master's effrontery, Bilal said, "I am not as familiar with such things as my cousin. I would be grateful of a tour, Your Grace."

Numair gave him a black look, but the prince was smiling again, and the glimmer in his eyes now was one of complicity. To Bilal, after a lifetime of superfluity, this was irresistible. He smiled back.

"Very good, *Sayyid*…?"

"Bilal, Your Grace," he answered.

"Bilal. And please, call me Salim. I am not my father." He inclined his head again, then turned toward the door. "I shall return when you have finished eating."

"I'm finished now," Bilal said.

"Let us go, then." To Numair he said, "*Ma'as salaama.*" Numair only glowered.

Once outside, however, Bilal's confidence evaporated. He wondered suddenly what the Sultan could possibly want with them. In fact, he was surprised that Salah ad-Din was even aware of their presence in the camp. There was little to distinguish Numair from so many other petty lords who had come to lend their swords to the Sultan's cause, unless...he floundered in a sudden, cold wave of panic. He tried to tell himself that they were working for the Sultan, but given de Ridefort's instructions to observe and inform him of Salah ad-Din's movements, he knew that this was not entirely true. And if the Sultan suspected that they were here as much to inform on him as to provide him with information...

Stop it, he told himself, and turned to his companion. "I apologize for my cousin's rudeness," he said. "We have traveled a long way in a short time, and sometimes when he is tired he forgets himself."

To his surprise Salim burst out laughing: a sound like the morning desert, when all the birds wake at once. "Let me tell you what I have learned as the undistinguished sixth son of a great king," he said. "Apologize to no one but Allah: not for your own actions, certainly not for anybody else's. There is nothing to be gained from it but guilt, which is too often appropriated and always pointless."

Bilal wondered how anybody with such a smile, such an agile turn of phrase, could consider himself undistinguished. "Thank you," he said, glancing shyly at Salim.

"Do you know," the prince said suddenly, "you have the most extraordinary eyes I've ever seen?" Bilal looked away in confusion. "I'm sorry," Salim added quickly. "I did not mean to embarrass you."

"You didn't," Bilal answered. "It's only..." He flailed a hand uselessly, as if trying to capture the words to explain.

"Yes, I know," said Salim, and oddly, Bilal felt quite certain that he did. Then, with another inexplicable, golden laugh, the prince put an arm around Bilal's shoulders and said, "Come. Let me show you this stinking heap my father has raised to the glory of Allah."

Shocked and delighted by his words, Bilal followed him, and for a while he forgot his worries in the chaos of the camp and Salim's glib commentary: "There is the pavilion of our best Kurdish cavalry archer, I cannot fathom why he has allowed it to be erected so close to that group of *rajjalah*: they smell like a pack of swine…there are my father's racing camels; he houses them here better than he does my mother at home, I wonder what they do for him that she does not?…there is the pavilion of a paltry *amir* from Jazirah – purple silk, does he think that he is the caliph?…"

But slowly, as they wove in and out of the alleys of fluttering tents, Bilal's anxieties crept back. He found himself replaying his last meeting with de Ridefort, three nights earlier in a shallow, nameless wadi not far from Kerak. Bilal had camped there in the week before Numair came to take him to Ras al-Mai'. In the afternoons, the Templar Master had met him there, drilling him on the finer points of his duties. He had also drilled him in swordsmanship. On this he had insisted, despite Bilal's Bedu proficiency with the spear, saying that no son of his would go into battle without every means of surviving it. Bilal considered this a strange thing to say, given that his demise would solve a number of problems for de Ridefort; but having nothing better to do, he worked at the exercises until he was passable.

On the night Numair finally returned from his trip, de Ridefort had met them at the wadi. He'd given them armor and money and clothing and a jar of wine which Numair immediately commandeered, though he'd already consumed one of his own.

"To victory!" he had said, and raised the jar to the others before taking a swallow, wiping his mouth and passing it to Bilal. The boy had taken a perfunctory sip and handed it on to de Ridefort, who had taken none at all, only watched Numair with a hunting-hawk's glittering precision.

"Bilal, little cousin," Numair had continued, "you must drink with me to our future kingdom. Generations from now, the men of these lands will sing of us as – "

"Enough," de Ridefort had said with cold authority, causing Numair to look at him with surprise that would have quickly turned to anger, had he not been so drunk. Wine, contrary to what Bilal would have guessed, made Numair affable. "It is bad luck to speak of a victory that has not yet come to pass, and your young 'cousin' has not yet proven himself in any way that suggests he will be remembered as anything at all."

Numair had laughed and lit a pipe of *banj*. "Oh, he will."

Bilal had not liked the implications of that at all, nor the way the two men talked about him as though he were not there. He had retired to his tent, but sleep evaded him, and so he'd lain listening as the men bickered and plotted, thinking of Khalidah and trying not to. Memories of their shared childhood had kept surfacing like recriminations, the last scene lashing him like a whip: her words of defiance before the retainer's stunning blow; the sound of horses' hooves dispersing into the black silence of the desert; the disloyalty of his own heart as he listened to her disappear.

Bilal had awakened to a gray dawn, surprised that he had slept at all. De Ridefort was gone, the fire cold, and Numair lay by its remains, wrapped thickly in a drunken stupor. Bilal had felt inexplicably abandoned then, and for a few moments he had considered taking his horse and running, until he remembered Numair's threat, whispered to him as they left the castle after that first strange meeting with de Ridefort: "He may be your father, Bilal, but never forget that I am your master. You will do as I tell you to, or I'll make your mother's story known far and wide, and nothing will save her from the stones this time..."

"Watch!"

Bilal blinked, and Salim caught him just before he stumbled into the ditch in front of them. Looking up, he saw that they had reached the edge of the camp. Stretching before him were row upon row of trenches buzzing with flies.

"And here are the latrines," Salim said, lips twitching upward toward eyes already laughing, "with which you have very nearly become intimately acquainted. Are you a traitor?"

"What?" Bilal asked, horrified.

But Salim smiled, and Bilal saw that it was only another joke. "Shoveling the shit of the faithful is the particular commission of prisoners and lesser traitors." Salim nearly laughed, but a reflective look passed over his face instead, making it more beautiful still. "Or perhaps it belongs to all of us."

"What do you mean?" Bilal asked, still reeling.

Salim raised his eyebrows, graceful as birds' wings. "Ask me that again when we know each other better." And despite the cryptic portent of this remark, and the darkness of his previous thoughts, Bilal felt only elation at the prospect that Salim intended to know him better.

15

At first, Jazirah differed little from Arabia. Khalidah and Sulayman crossed a wide desert of monotonous regularity, its flat sands broken only by small settlements around the occasional well or oasis, and distant herds of ibex or gazelle, crawling like lines of ants across the horizon. They had abandoned their night-traveling after the incident at Domat al-Jandal, since it seemed to have made little difference. Now they rose with the first streaks of dawn, rested in the middle of the day and then rode again until they were too tired to go further.

After a few such days, green began to encroach on the unmitigated sand. First it was in the form of tough scrub grasses and plants around small, isolated pools or streams, but soon the air grew humid and the desert capitulated to wheat fields and orchards and great stands of date palms, irrigated by well-maintained canals running among neat farms and villages.

"We're in Mesopotamia now," Sulayman explained, when Khalidah commented on the change. "You can see why some scholars believe this was Eden." She looked at the fertile land in silence. Sulayman continued, "We'll reach Basrah tomorrow. We can cross the river there, if it hasn't burst its banks with the spring floods."

"What river?" Khalidah asked.

Sulayman gave her a strange look. "The Shatt al-Arab." Seeing that she still looked blank, he added, "The river that joins the Dijlah and Al-Furat."

Khalidah said nothing. Until that moment, Mesopotamia and its great delineating rivers had been as much a myth to her as Qaf, not because she did not believe in them, but because she had never imagined that she would witness them. But she would witness them; she would cross them, and leave them behind like the familiar deserts of Arabia. To hide her bewilderment she looked toward the indeterminate horizon, feeling every step of her distance from home.

*

Khalidah slept badly that night. They were camped in a grove of date palms by a small, silty pond. It wasn't hot, but the air was thick with moisture that clung to her skin and hair, making her long for the pure, dry cold of the desert. Flies plagued the horses, and they fidgeted, tails swishing; Khalidah sympathized, as she slapped yet another mosquito. She pulled her blanket more tightly around her, thinking of cool wind across sand.

When she finally slept, she had a strange dream. She was back at Wadi Tawil, standing at the top of the hill overlooking the camp. The sun had set, leaving a clear, lazuline sky stamped with a waxing crescent moon. A cloud lay on the horizon opposite the moon, bruised purple with edges of fire. As she watched, the cloud deepened to black and its edges flared crimson. It unfurled into the shape of a lion that leapt across the sky, strewing darkness in its wake, until at last it caught the moon in its jaws and swallowed it. As darkness closed in the world became a vacuum, and Khalidah felt her limbs freezing, her breath sucked from her lungs.

She awakened gasping and shivering. Several minutes of panic passed before she became aware of Sulayman's hand on her head, soothing without words. She was too grateful to protest. Soon afterward, she fell into a deep, dreamless sleep.

*

The sun rose red the next morning behind high, broken cloud, like bloodied arrowheads. Khalidah felt better, but Sulayman was acting strangely. His movements were sluggish and slow, and when she offered him food he declined, taking only a few sips of water, then went to 'Aasifa and fumbled with her bridle until at last Khalidah took it from him and fastened it herself.

"What is wrong with you?" she asked, searching his sallow face for clues. He only shook his head and hoisted himself into the saddle with far too much effort.

They found a narrow track running roughly east across marshy ground. When they had been riding for a while, Sulayman finally spoke. "What frightened you, last night?" His voice was thin and apprehensive.

Khalidah related the dream, then said, "Do you think it was like that dream of Brekhna? Does it mean something?"

Sulayman looked ill now as well as troubled. "I don't know. On the face of it, I'd say it was only a nightmare…but then, the images were telling – the Franj lion swallowing the crescent of Islam, perhaps."

"Or perhaps it was only my own fears taking form."

Sulayman said nothing. They rode on in silence, Khalidah leading on the straight path across land that became ever wetter. They forded irrigation canals, saw peasants working their fields with water buffalo or plying the waterways with long, graceful canoes they propelled with poles. The day grew greyer and hotter, threatening rain as the jagged lines of Basrah emerged beneath the low clouds.

"Stop, Khalidah," Sulayman said mid-way through the morning. "I think I must rest for a moment."

Khalidah looked over her shoulder at him, and then wished she'd looked sooner. His face had drained of color, leaving bruised rings under his eyes, and he slumped in the saddle as if he were in pain. She drew Zahirah to a halt and dismounted. Sulayman slid down to the ground and leaned against 'Aasifa's leg. "I'm sorry,

Khalidah…"

She reached out and laid her hand on his forehead. His skin burned like the deserts they had left behind. "How long have you been like this?" she demanded.

Sulayman shook his head. "I suppose it began last night. I thought it was only the change in the air…"

The clouds opened abruptly, pelting them with the heaviest rain Khalidah had ever seen. Sulayman huddled against 'Aasifa's flank, looking ill and miserable. Fighting down a wave of panic, Khalidah said, "We cannot stop here. It can't be far to Basrah – "

"No!" he said, and the insistence was clear even through the weakness. "It is not safe there. There is a place in the marshes on the other side of the city, where I have a friend…" He trailed off as though he'd forgotten what he meant to say, or the words he was speaking had suddenly lost their meaning.

"Can you make it that far?"

"Yes," he said, but he had begun to shake, his teeth chattering uncontrollably.

At that, something in Khalidah's mind clicked, and she knew what was wrong with Sulayman: quartan fever. She'd seen it often enough among the tribe, had even had it herself once. But with no medicine to give him and no choice other than to continue on, the knowledge did her little good. She forced water between his chattering teeth, then helped him back into the saddle. They rode side-by-side, Khalidah keeping a sharp eye on Sulayman's rapidly deteriorating condition, Sulayman himself apparently lost in the rhythmic suck-and-drag of the horses' hooves in the mud, the steady drench of rain, and the hypnotic quality of the watery landscape that unrolled mile after mile in shades of grey. His silence soon gave way to a rambling commentary that became less and less coherent: he spoke of a searing headache, of lights he claimed he could see beneath the water that encroached steadily on the fields around them, of someone called Ghassan.

As he cried out for help to this man, whoever he was, Khalidah finally allowed herself to realize what she had known since that morning: wherever they were headed, she was going to have to get them there alone. So, before Sulayman lost consciousness, she took him by the shoulders and forced him to focus his bloodshot eyes on her.

"Tell me how to get there," she said. "To your friend in the marshes."

"The river…" he gasped. "Must…cross the river…the *Ma'dan*…the floating village, ask for Ghassan. Ghassan…" And having uttered these dubious instructions, he slumped into her arms, unconscious.

"Most merciful Allah…" she began, but having no idea what to pray for, or indeed if Allah had forgiven her enough to hear it, she left the request unfinished. She managed to pull Sulayman from 'Aasifa's saddle onto hers, but when she tried to lead 'Aasifa the mare danced and pulled and refused to follow. Nearly weeping with exhaustion and frustration, Khalidah pushed and pulled herself and Sulayman onto 'Aasifa's back, and thanked Allah and all of his angels that the skittish mare did not throw them in the process. Tethering Zahirah to 'Aasifa's saddle, she started forward again, the horses stumbling on across the thickening mire until she saw the lights of a ramshackle settlement at the edge of a swift, swollen river.

The dialect the villagers spoke was so different from her own that she had to resort to pointing and acting to make herself understood, and even then her trial was not finished. Sulayman was shivering so violently that the ferryman was convinced that he was possessed by a jinni, and flat-out refused to carry him in his boat. It cost her both of the silver cheek-pieces from 'Aasifa's bridle to change his mind, and even then he would not touch the sick man or their horses. She had no choice but to dismount, lash Sulayman like a grain-sack to 'Aasifa's saddle, and then lead the horses aboard herself.

But the desert-bred mares had never seen so much water, let alone been expected to step onto a heaving platform atop it, and they thrashed and reared as if the boat contained an army of devils. Coaxing and shouting by turns, while the ferryman and

several of his friends looked balefully on, Khalidah managed at
last to drive the animals on board, and then stood holding them
as firmly as she could with hands that shook as violently now as
Sulayman's. At last the ferryman boarded and moved the boat
into the pitching stream.

By the time they regained dry land, Khalidah didn't have the
strength left to hold Sulayman in the saddle, so she left him lashed
to his horse and drove the frightened mare before her, praying
with the little will she had left that 'Aasifa wouldn't bolt. The
ferryman had understood the word "*ma'dan*" even if Khalidah
did not, and pointed to what might have been a path across the
boggy land, before he turned his boat and left her.

With no idea where she was headed, except that it might or
might not resemble a floating village, Khalidah pushed onward.
Sulayman drooped over 'Aasifa's back like a dead man, his face
grey, his breathing sharp and shallow. At least he is breathing,
she told herself, though it was little comfort. All the time the
rain poured down, and soon the day faded into darkness, so that
Khalidah had no idea whether she followed the path anymore, if
it had ever been a path at all.

When she had almost given up caring whether either of them
lived or died, she saw a glimmer of light. At first she wondered if
these were the phantom lights Sulayman had seen that morning,
if she too were growing ill. But as she rode toward it, it grew more
distinct, until she found herself looking across a short expanse of
water at a little domed house. Once again, she felt herself close
to weeping, but this time it was for relief, because the house was
floating.

It appeared to have been built on a thick layer of reed mats,
which floated like a boat on the water. The mats were tied off to
several palm trees with thick ropes. Other, similar houses spread
out behind it, their windows glowing with promised warmth,
some floating on similar reed mats, some sitting on islands
hardly bigger than the houses they supported. Each house had
a lithe canoe tied up outside, and some of the bigger ones had
outbuildings Khalidah assumed were for stabling animals.

She caught hold of 'Aasifa's bridle and guided the two horses through the shallow water to the nearest house. Summoning her courage, she rapped on the plaited-reed door. It opened almost immediately. A small, wiry man stood in relief against the warm glow. He was about her father's age, with a dark, weathered face, a beard like sheep's wool, and eyes that tended toward kindness, but were presently full of suspicion.

"Yes?" he said.

"I am looking for a man called Ghassan. I am sorry, I do not know his name beyond that, but I believe that he is acquainted with a friend of mine – a minstrel called Sulayman."

Now puzzlement joined the suspicion on the man's face. "In that case, you have found him – I am Ghassan ibn Anas al-Murabak. But who are you, and what brings you here on such a night, asking for me?"

Khalidah said nothing, only stepped aside, revealing 'Aasifa and her senseless burden. Ghassan's puzzlement deepened for a moment, and then shattered into fear.

"What have you done to him?" he cried. "*What have you done?*"

And Khalidah, to her intense mortification, burst into tears.

16

By the time Ghassan al-Murabak had untied Sulayman and brought him inside the reed house, Khalidah had managed to convince him that she was not responsible for Sulayman's condition. Ghassan laid him on a rug by a little glowing brazier.

"What happened?" he asked, pressing Sulayman's limp wrist for a pulse.

Bewildered and teary, Khalidah answered, "He got sick...I believe it began this morning, though it might have been sooner...but then, quartan fever can come on quickly."

Ghassan looked sharply at her. "What makes you think that it is quartan fever?"

"Do you believe it is something else?"

Ghassan sighed. "No; I believe that you are right. You did well to bring him here – whoever you are. But we will discuss that, and what is to be done with him, after I see to your horses. Take off his clothes and dry his hair." He tossed her a linen towel. "I will be back in a moment." Without waiting for a reply, he disappeared into the night.

Khalidah sat staring dumbly at the towel in her hands, and was sitting there still when Ghassan returned. His speculative look turned to one of anger.

"Are you an idiot, boy? Did I not tell you to undress him?"

"I..." Khalidah began and then, realizing that she was about to cry again, she did something she had not done since the first morning in the desert, when she put aside her dress: she pulled off her *kufiyya*. Her long, wet hair tumbled down her back.

"Ah," Ghassan said, frowning, but the anger had left his face. "Well, child, it seems you have a lot to tell me. Turn your back, and I will undress him while you explain…and please, be assured that I am a friend. You need not lie to me."

Khalidah chose to believe him. She handed him the towel, turned her back, and then, drawing a deep breath, she began, "My name is Khalidah bint 'Abd al-Aziz al-Hassani, and I first met Sulayman three weeks ago…"

As she told her story, she took stock of Ghassan's house. The walls were woven of reeds in latticed patterns, and riddled with shelves and compartments holding vials and jars and bowls, fishing equipment and drying herbs. The only furnishings were a low wooden table cluttered with more herbs and utensils for their preparation, the bright woolen rug by the brazier and a neat bed on the floor in one corner. Three cats – one black, one white and one patched various colors – were curled up on the bed.

When she finished her story, she looked toward Ghassan, who had moved to the table and was busy concocting something in a bowl. "Well?" she asked.

"Well, what?"

"Are you not going to tell me that I'm mad, to be talking of Qaf and the Jinn?"

He looked up at her with mild surprise. "Why should I? Do you not think that I have heard all of this already from Sulayman himself? The fact is, he stopped here on his way back from Qaf, to ask my advice about finding you."

She was too surprised to know what to say. Instead, she turned to Sulayman, who was wrapped now in a clean linen sheet and covered by a blanket, his hair drying rapidly in the warmth from the brazier.

"Can you save him?" she asked quietly.

Ghassan frowned at the pungent mess in the bowl and poured heated water into it. Then he folded his gnarled hands and looked up at her. "You do not seem like the kind of woman who asks a question hoping for a lie. Therefore, I can only say that I will try. But I can tell you that I have a good medicine on my side. It comes from the Orient, if you believe the trader who brings it. He certainly charges enough for the tale to be true. But in a village where the fever strikes so many, I suppose any price is justified."

"I will pay you back," Khalidah said.

"His life will be payment enough for me," Ghassan said grimly, strained the infusion, and picking up the bowl and a spoon, went to Sulayman and began the thankless task of trying to get the medicine into him.

Khalidah gave him a long look of her own, then said, "Who are you to him?"

Ghassan sighed. "Only he could tell you that. But as for who he is to me…well, I suppose that he is the son I never had."

"How did you meet him?"

There was a long pause, during which Khalidah knew that he was censoring his answer. At last he said, "I've known him since he was a child – the troupe he once traveled with stayed here when they crossed the marshes."

"And where is here?" she asked.

"The village of the Murabak tribe – one of many villages of the *Ma'dan*, the people of the marshes." He looked carefully at Khalidah's face. It was pallid even in the coals' warm glow, her eyes ringed with exhaustion. "I know that you have questions for me, Khalidah bint 'Abd al-Aziz, and I have as many for you. But our friend will get worse before he gets better; there will be time enough to ask and answer in the days ahead. Rest, now. Take my bed. And here, put this on. Your clothes are soaked through, and the last thing I need is for you to fall ill too." He handed her a long linen robe from a peg on the wall, which she accepted gratefully. "I'll wake you if there is any change."

Khalidah was too tired to protest. She dropped her wet clothes as soon as Ghassan turned his back, and put on the robe which, if far too large, was at least warm and dry. Clearing a space among the grudging cats, she lay down, and was asleep instantly.

*

The next day brought little change to Sulayman's condition, nor
to the weather. Ghassan patiently spooned infusions into his patient, and Khalidah mooned about, restless and desolate by turns.
In the clear light of day her situation seemed even stranger, and
the silence between herself and the healer became increasingly
awkward, as all of her attempts to draw him into conversation
met with monosyllabic rebuffs.

At last, driven by discomfort and frustration, she burst out:
"What is it that you are not telling me?"

She had expected another curt evasion, but instead Ghassan
set down his bowl and spoon, looked her in the eye and said, "I
knew his mother."

Khalidah could only stare at him in stunned silence, for
this was the last thing she had expected to hear. She said, "But
Sulayman told me that he knew nothing about his parents."

"And so he does not," Ghassan answered, passing a hand over
his weary eyes. "Nor does he know what I am about to tell you."

Khalidah shook her head. "Why...?"

"Because I realize now that I was wrong to have kept this from
him, though I did it to spare him grief...because he might very
well die here without knowing that he had a mother who loved
him, and though you have not told me what you and he are to
each other, I think that he would want you to know his story, if
he himself could not. So, Khalidah, do you have the strength to
bear it?"

Half-certain that he was mad, but curious now despite herself,
Khalidah nodded, and for the first time since her arrival, Ghassan
rewarded her with a faint smile. "Just over twenty years ago," he
began, without ceremony, "when Nur ad-Din was Sultan and
his nephew Salah ad-Din not yet more than a lackey to his uncle
Shirkuh, my father died. The foundations of our world may have

been quaking along with the Egyptian caliphate, but I hardly noticed. Certainly I regretted my father's death, but the true tragedy was that as a result, I was called home prematurely from Baghdad, where I had been studying medicine."

He paused, as if collecting his thoughts, then continued, "My father, you see, was a simple healer who was never satisfied with his lot in life, and so when his only son took an interest in his craft, he determined that I would be a 'real' physician. He saved all through my childhood to send me to Baghdad, depriving my mother and sisters of far more than I realized at the time, and stoking me with dreams of glory. Because of this, and because I was certain that my mother had called me home out of spite, I came back to the marshes in a wallow of self-obsessed misery, in which I was still firmly entrenched on the night that they found Haya.

"It was winter, a bitter evening alternating between sleet and rain. Radwan, the father of our current clan chief, was still our leader then, and we were gathered in his hall when two of his retainers brought her in. She sagged between them like a sack of wet flour, obviously ill and heavily pregnant, but so beautiful: hair like a rook's wing, eyes like spear heads, smooth skin the color of honey…"

There were bitterness and longing in his tone, and Khalidah realized that Ghassan had both loved this woman and lost her. She listened with deepening pity. "They had found her unconscious at the edge of the marsh. A young woman like that, with child, traveling alone so close to her time – there were few conclusions one could draw that left her honor intact. Many villages would have turned her away. Perhaps many already had. But Radwan had a great weakness for feminine beauty, and so he had the men bring her in.

"To her credit, she knelt before him with all the composure of a princess. He questioned her in Arabic, but she answered in Hebrew, no doubt believing that no one would understand her. She could not know that in Baghdad I had studied with a Jewish doctor who had taught me his tongue. Therefore, I learned a good deal more about her than I might otherwise have done. She was from Shiraz. The child was of course illegitimate, and had been conceived in Cairo. She would not tell me what she had been doing there, so far from home, nor why she was unable to apply to the child's father for help. In the end she had decided to go back to her family in Persia, but she had made it only this far when her pains began.

"Radwan asked me if I could do anything for her; even now, I'm not quite sure what he thought I *could* do. But I answered: 'Let her come back to my house. I will try to help her,' and then said the same to her in Hebrew. She looked at me, a look of such utter despair...I have never seen anything like it since and I hope I never do. No doubt she thought that I intended to take advantage of her." He shook his head.

"But she was in labor, she had little choice. She fought all that night and the next day to bring the child forth, and when he finally came, he wasn't breathing. She looked at me and said, 'Save the child, or cut my throat,' and I knew that she meant it. So I did something that I had heard about, but never quite believed was possible – I put my mouth over the child's and sucked the fluid from his lungs, then I breathed into them. Five times I gave him my breath, and then, the miracle: he screwed up his face and started to scream."

Ghassan paused, his eyes sunk deep in the past, then continued, "Haya had refused to tell me anything about the child's father, but when I gave the baby to her, I could see that she had loved him. She named the child Sulayman al-Mahdudh, for his preternatural luck." Ghassan paused to look at Sulayman's feverish face, and a shadow crossed his own. "She stayed for a week," he said, "and then she vanished. I looked for her, of course. Youth craves romance, and I imagined myself saving her from the streets and the child from illegitimacy, bringing them back to live in the marshes as my own wife and son." Ghassan smiled sadly. "I never found her, but I never forgot her either, nor that little boy I had brought back from the dead. I imagined him growing up somewhere, dirty and starving no doubt, but loved at least.

"I know what you must think, Khalidah. Sulayman is a common name, and a city the size of Cairo produces plenty of orphans. I don't suppose that I can ever prove it, but I was certain the very first time I laid eyes on him that Sulayman was Haya's son. He is the image of her."

"Why did you never tell him this?" Khalidah cried. "Do you know what it has cost him, to wonder who he is all these years?"

"Oh, yes," Ghassan answered, "I know. I have heard him speak the words himself."

"Then why did you keep silent?"

Ghassan looked at her, his eyes sad, but calm. "Because knowing would not have changed anything. Yes, I met his mother, but I never knew her. I do not know who she was or who she became. I do not know what man she loved to produce *him*, why she left him or why she returned to Cairo." He nodded at Sulayman, whose face rippled as if the words cast stones into the still of his feverish sleep. "As I said, I wish now that I had told him; but I still believe that telling him would not have brought him anything but grief."

Khalidah glared at Ghassan, but as his eyes remained steady on hers, gradually she began to forgive him. At last she sighed, and nodded, and Ghassan too seemed to release a breath he had been holding.

"You have a sweet voice," he said after a moment, and once again his own voice had turned speculative, "which could pass well enough for a young boy's...you sing?" Warily, Khalidah nodded. "And can you play?"

"On the *oud*, well enough," she answered.

"In that case," said Ghassan, "bind your hair again and come with me. We both need a break. The boy will be all right by himself for a few hours."

Reluctantly, Khalidah donned her *kufiyya* and followed him out into the rainy night.

17

In the end, it was several days before Bilal finally met Salah ad-Din. On the morning of their original appointment, the Sultan received word that his brother Al-'Adil had left Cairo with his army and was heading toward Syria to join the *jihad*. Lu'lu, commander of the navy, was also moving northward with his ships, and Salah ad-Din's nephew and favorite commander, Taqi ad-Din, had gone to Aleppo to watch the contentious border with Antioch. On top of it all, Count Tripoli – the only Franj the Sultan respected, and clearly the only one with any inkling of the intentions of the mighty force gathering outside of the city – was seeking an alliance.

Given this, the Sultan had as little time for Bedu nobles as he did for sixth sons, even if they were providing him with valuable information about the Franj. So Bilal was not surprised when Salim arrived at their pavilion the next morning with his father's apologies; he was, however, stunned by the prince's invitation to join him in exercising his horse. Bilal accepted, though his suspicion matched his pleasure. He had never in his life been courted as a friend, and despite what Salim had said to him the day before, he could not quite believe that there was not an ulterior motive to the prince's solicitude.

However, over the next few days Salim continued to extend gestures of friendship, and gradually Bilal's wariness dissipated.

His disbelief, however, was more tenacious. The only true friend he'd ever had was Khalidah, and though he had genuinely loved her, their relationship had been fraught from the beginning with inequalities that made it increasingly difficult to maintain. Yet it seemed never to occur to Salim, who was so much further separated from him by rank and experience, to treat him as anything but an equal. Bilal spent a good deal of the early days of their friendship puzzling over this. Much later, he would be equally puzzled that he'd ever wondered why the two of them found such easy respite in each other's company. Different as their lives might have been, both had been shaped by the burden of futile ambition.

Numair, meanwhile, gave himself over to the dissipation he had been unable to embrace under his father's watchful eye. On the afternoon appointed for their re-scheduled meeting with the Sultan, Bilal returned from a ride with Salim to find his "cousin" snoring beside an empty flagon of wine and a red-headed whore, both of them naked as newborns. Salim grinned, but Bilal trembled with shame. When he tried to rouse Numair, the man looked at him blearily and said, "Fuck off," then lapsed again into oblivion. So Salim led Bilal alone to a simple white tent half the size of Numair's, which bore more of a likeness to those he had left behind at Wadi Tawil than the bright pavilions of the nobility.

"Aren't you coming with me?" Bilal asked, alarmed, as Salim turned to leave.

Salim shrugged. "I was not invited."

"But – " Bilal began.

Salim put a long finger to his lips. "He may growl, Bilal, but he will not bite. Besides, I might still find a way inside." His smile flashed brighter than the afternoon sun, and then he was gone.

Bilal turned to face the tent. Two *mamluk* bodyguards barred the entrance, magnificent in their green brocade tunics and stiff, fur-lined *sharbush* caps. They kept their eyes fixed straight ahead, long spears at the ready, paying no apparent attention to Bilal.

He was wondering what he was meant to do next, when a little man emerged from beneath the tent flap. He was slight, almost frail, with skin as fair as Bilal's and small, intelligent eyes the color of strong tea. Though his long hair was streaked with grey, his beard was still full and dark. He wore no armor, just the plain black robe and turban of a scribe or holy man.

They exchanged *salaams*, and then, in a warm, cultured tenor, the man said, "You are not Numair al-Hassani."

"No," answered Bilal around the sudden lump in his throat, "I am his cousin, Bilal. My cousin humbly begs your pardon for his absence. He is…indisposed."

"Then I welcome you, Bilal ibn…?"

"Bakhir," Bilal answered, as Numair had instructed him to do. Bakhir had been the husband of one of 'Abd al-Hadi's sisters, and was the ideal fictitious father for Bilal in that both he and his wife had been dead for years.

"Bilal ibn Bakhir al-Hassani," the little man said, inclining his head. "Please," he added, holding back the tent flap with one arm and extending the other in a gesture of invitation.

Bilal entered the tent, the scribe at his heels. The interior was as spare as the exterior, with somber tapestries, sparse furnishings and a narrow soldier's bed just showing behind a curtain. The only marks of wealth were a large, finely-woven carpet covering the sand, and a pile of brilliantly-colored silk cushions. Reclining on the cushions was a large man dressed in fine yellow robes, with a jeweled brooch in his turban and the mouthpiece of an ornate hookah in his hand. Though he was clearly in his later years – his skin was creased and his beard liberally speckled with gray – he retained an air of great strength and vitality. Bilal was comforted to find the Sultan such an imposing figure, despite his austere surroundings.

He bowed low to him and said, "Your Grace, I am honored by your request for my humble presence."

To Bilal's consternation, both the Sultan and the scribe erupted into laughter. Flushing, he looked from one to the other, alternating between anger and uncertainty lest he had made some gross mistake in etiquette that would betray himself and Numair. And then he saw that the little scribe's face was lit with a smile that was a replica of Salim's, except that it did not quite erase the sadness in his eyes.

Bilal's face burned; he fell to his knees before the little man. "Forgive me, Your Highness, for my mistake."

Still smiling his wonderful smile, the Sultan took Bilal's hands and coaxed him upright. "No, you must forgive *us*." He placed a hand over his heart. "This is not, as it seems, a joke at your expense; only a joke on the pretensions of two old men. Your assumptions were entirely justified. But, so as to set the record straight, allow me to introduce my friend, the great chronicler and historian and my most trusted scribe, Imad ad-Din al-Isfahani. And I am Salah ad-Din ibn Yakkub al-Ayyubi, at your service."

"Sultan…" Bilal murmured, bowing again.

"Now, please, make yourself comfortable." Salah ad-Din indicated a few cushions that Imad ad-Din had extricated from his pile, and placed on the floor near him.

His head swimming, Bilal sat down. The Sultan sat directly on the carpet, his legs crossed and his back straight as a minaret. He seemed about to speak, when the tent flap opened again and Salim entered, bearing a silver tray with a teapot, glasses with gold-leaf filigree, and a plate of almond cakes. He flashed Bilal a wry look as he arranged the tea and cakes neatly on the carpet at the center of the seated men, bowed low to his father, and then turned to retreat.

Without looking at him, the Sultan said, "Stay." Obediently, the boy knelt at the edge of the silk carpet, directly across from Bilal. To Bilal, the Sultan said, "I understand that you have already met my son Salim. He has spoken highly of you." Though it should have been a compliment, the tone with which the Sultan said this left a good deal of doubt as to its meaning. "I hope that his presence at this meeting will not disturb you," he continued, "and that yours might teach him something." This time there was no mistaking the recrimination. Bilal wondered what Salim could have done to earn his father's displeasure; but the Sultan was speaking again, and reluctantly, Bilal turned his attention away from the other boy.

"I am honored that you have decided to join us," the Sultan said, pouring tea into the glasses. The steam curled up from the amber liquid, pungent with mint. Bilal accepted one, though his throat was so tight that he did not think that he could swallow it. "Of course, your cousin's services in relating certain delicate information to us has so far been invaluable, but his presence here, and yours, are valuable to me in other ways as well."

Salah ad-Din paused, indicating that Bilal was supposed to say something. But if he was meant to supply an answer, he was ignorant of its nature. "Your grace?"

The Sultan sipped his tea, apparently unperturbed. "As of yet, few of the Arab tribes have joined our numbers. But it is of your people we may well come to have the most need."

"You flatter us, Sire," said Bilal. "I do not think that the best of our horsemen can match the least of your *tawashiyah*."

"Incidentally, you are mistaken: I have often remarked that there is no match in speed or zeal for the Bedu *ghuzat*. But it was not to your horsemen that I referred. The men of my army are, for the most part, men of towns and cities. If our holy city of Al-Quds is to be won back at all, it will not be at its gates, but here in the desert, and nobody knows the desert as well as your people do."

Bilal sipped his tea automatically, then wished he hadn't. Forcing himself to swallow, he answered, "Again, you flatter us, Highness."

"How so?" the Sultan asked, his keen eyes steady on Bilal's face. Involuntarily, Bilal glanced at Imad ad-Din, who looked back with black eyes almost hidden in the folds of his heavy lids. His air was of preoccupation, even vacancy, but Bilal had the sense that the man was absorbing their words like a sponge, to be squeezed out later and considered at his leisure.

"My tribe seldom travels this far north," Bilal said cautiously. "Surely there are others who know this country better than we do."

Salah ad-Din shrugged with apparent nonchalance. "As a sailor knows the sea, the nomad knows the desert." He paused. "Do you know, several of your tribesmen have joined us already."

It was decidedly not a question. Bilal set his glass down, his mind whirling. "With all respect, Your Grace, you must be mistaken," he said. "When we left them, our tribe was preparing to move south. Our affairs being what they are following...some difficult family matters...none of 'Abd al-Hadi's men intended to enlist."

"Not 'Abd al-Hadi's," the Sultan said in the same affable, conversational tone, but Bilal knew by the taut pause that followed that he was being interrogated. "'Abd al-Aziz's. You will wish to meet with them, no doubt. I shall have them directed immediately to your tent."

There were questions in all of these statements, perhaps even accusations, and Bilal knew that he was far out of his depth. His mind had seized, and before he could stop himself, he had cried, "No!"

The Sultan regarded Bilal with interest rather than effrontery, and Imad ad-Din's eyes settled on him with the weight of stone. Even Salim frowned. "No?" The Sultan repeated.

Bilal tried to steady his whirling mind. He and Numair had never planned how to deal with 'Abd al-Aziz's men, should they find them here. In and of itself, it wasn't so strange that he, Bilal, would run away to join the army; but to do so with Numair was no better than treason. Even if they did not condemn him for that, they would certainly uncover his disguise. It had been a gross oversight...unless it had not been an oversight at all. Perhaps, whispered a small, dark voice inside of him, this had been de Ridefort's plan all along. It would certainly be an easy way to get rid of him.

"The two branches of the Hassan have long been at war," Bilal floundered at last, knowing that he had been silent too long. "Though we all hoped that this situation was soon to be rectified, the circumstances under which we last parted were...less than happy. Numair was to marry our cousin and unite our clan. But she saw fit to abandon him the night before their wedding, to run away with 'Abd al-Hadi's minstrel." He knew that he was acquitting himself well enough, if not brilliantly. Still, he wished that Salim were not there to hear him lie. Taking a deep breath, he continued: "You will understand that relations between our people and theirs are not entirely friendly at present."

"And yet here, you are all my men," the Sultan said, looking at Bilal with the same unruffled tranquility. "Does that count for nothing?"

"Your Highness, I can only speak for myself."

"He's right," Imad ad-Din said, the first word he had spoken during Bilal's interview. "Quite right, you know..." His voice was deep and rich, and he drew the final word out as though he were about to make it the beginning of a diatribe. Instead, he lapsed back into silence.

"Very well," Salah ad-Din said to Bilal, glancing at the scribe. "But tell me: what is the name of your errant cousin?"

"Khalidah bint 'Abd al-Aziz."

"And who is her mother?"

"She is dead," Bilal answered, "but she was called Brekhna."

The Sultan narrowed his eyes. "Of what tribe?"

"She was not of the Bedu tribes," he answered, reluctant to look ridiculous in front of this great man by repeating the rumors about Brekhna. "She was from the east – Khorasan, I believe."

But this seemed to be enough of an answer for the Sultan. He drew a breath and then let it slide away, the single indication of how much the information had been worth. "What was a woman from Khorasan doing in Arabia, I wonder..." he said to himself. He was silent for a long moment, his eyes somewhere far away. At last, recalling himself with a slight shake of the head, he said, "One more request, if you would, *Sayyid* Bilal. Do you happen to know the name of the minstrel with whom your cousin ran away?"

"I do not know his family name," he said at last, "but he called himself Sulayman."

"And his instrument?"

"The *qanun*," he said.

The Sultan and the scholar exchanged a look too complex for Bilal to decipher, then Salah ad-Din smiled at his young guest and said, "Thank you, Bilal ibn Bakhir al-Hassani. This has been a most interesting conversation. And fear not: I will respect your wishes with regard to meeting your rival tribesmen." He paused, then said, "But remember, we are one army here, gathered to serve Allah. Though I might respect your wishes, I cannot speak for Him."

The warning in the words was clear. Bilal was glad that etiquette required him to bow deeply, so that neither the Sultan nor his son could see his eyes.

18

The reed house, Khalidah had learned, was called a *mudhif*, but the *mudhif* of Radwan ibn Radwan al-Murabak was so large it seemed that it should bear a designation of its own. It was as beautiful as any palace Khalidah could imagine. The latticed walls had been woven in long, continuous strips of striking intricacy, no two the same. Huge pillars of bound reeds supported the walls, and small, round windows were set in a row under the eaves of the reed-matting roof. Even through the driving rain, she could hear animated chatter from inside, and someone playing a *na'ay*.

Pulling her *kufiyya* lower over her forehead, she followed Ghassan inside. The room was lit by flickering oil lamps and a few smoking braziers with coffee-pots warming on top. It appeared that most of the men of the village were gathered there. They sat on reed mats and woven rugs, some holding little earthenware cups of coffee, some sharing pipes of *banj*. Reclining on a pile of cushions against the far wall was a heavy, middle-aged man with deeply-lined skin, a prominent nose, thick, fleshy lips, and small eyes already heavy from the hookah. He glanced up at Khalidah with marked disinterest and said, "Who are you?"

"This is Khalid ibn 'Abd al-Aziz," Ghassan said with an ingratiating smile, "and he is a guest of mine. His traveling companion is ill, and they will be staying with me for a few days."

The chief grunted, "Young for it," and Khalidah was uncertain as to whether he was referring to the traveling, the ill companion, or her status as Ghassan's guest; nor could she see what his comment would mean by virtue of any of them. But he didn't seem to expect a reply, continuing, "Can he do anything?"

Khalidah looked apprehensively at Ghassan, who smiled at her and then answered, "He can sing, and play the *oud*."

"Well, let's hear him," Radwan said, as if he didn't expect to be impressed. He snapped his fingers and someone handed Khalidah an *oud*, then he settled back into his pile of cushions and apparently forgot about her.

Sighing, Khalidah sat down on a rug and began to tune the instrument, which was badly in need of it. When at last she had put it right, she settled it on her lap and ran through a series of scales, finding her fingers tight and clumsy from lack of practice and long hours wrapped in the reins. She widened the scales to arpeggios and finally felt the muscles begin to loosen. Almost unconsciously, the exercises diverged into a soft, haunting melody that had been germinating in her head since the morning they left Domat-al-Jandal.

Khalidah rarely composed, and never tried to: she had found long ago that it didn't work. When music came to her, it came by grace, a thousand dribbles filtering through her unconscious over weeks and months until they emerged almost whole. Even then, the new song remained a mystery until she touched finger to string, as a child is a mystery to its mother until the moment their bodies separate. And so, Khalidah had no formed idea of what would emerge that night in Radwan's *mudhif* until she found herself singing, the words fitting the music as if she had planned it meticulously:

> *"Thin as the new moon,*
> *ashen-faced, like arrow shafts*
> *rattling around*
> *in the hand of a gambler…*

He howls in the empty spaces,
they howl,
as if they and he were bereaved women
on the high ridge, wailing.
His eyelids sag. He grows silent.
They follow his lead.
They, he, forlorn,
take heart from one another…
surging, hard pressed,
keeping composure
over what they hide…"

She sang on, oblivious to the men who listened now with rapt attention as Shánfara's ancient words twined seamlessly with music that had begun as the chant of a half-mad old woman, endlessly stirring her stew-pot at the edge of a desert town. But when Khalidah reached the lines about the sand-daughter, she faltered.

"Nobody told you to stop," Radwan barked.

"Forgive me," she answered, unnecessarily re-tuning the instrument. "The *oud* does not like the rain."

The chief studied her from beneath his heavy lids. "You're no street-busker, and no mere child, either." Radwan raised the hookah's mouthpiece, sucked, and then lowered it again in a cloud of pungent smoke. "Come here, boy," he said in a low, rasping voice. "Let me look at you."

Many of the men had fallen silent against the music, and now they watched the scene with keen interest. Khalidah had the feeling that they all knew something that she didn't. Ghassan looked vaguely unnerved, but she had little choice other than to lay down the *oud* and approach the lumpish clan-chief of the Murabak. She knelt before him, her eyes on the floor, but he reached out and lifted her chin, forcing her to look at him.

"Such unusual eyes," he said speculatively, "and such smooth skin…almost like a girl's…" Her heart fluttered in panic, and

she thought, *He knows*. The thought seemed confirmed when
she saw the spark of lust in his eyes. "Tell me – where is it that
you are going?"

"Yazd," she whispered, barely aware of what she was saying,
and falling back by instinct onto the old story. "I am going to be
a *darwish*."

"A holy man, are you," Radwan said. "A pity."

She saw that the glint in his eyes had turned to one of
disappointment. All at once she understood, and was both relieved
and mortified. To her irritation, she saw out of the corner of her
eye that many of the men were laughing into their sleeves.

"And how long will you be staying with Ghassan?" he
continued.

"I do not know," she stammered. "My – my cousin has the
quartan fever, and I cannot leave until he recovers."

Radwan scrutinized her for a moment, and then sighed. "Ah,
well," he said resignedly, "at least your voice is sweet. You will
play for me every night that you remain in my village."

"As you wish, *Sayyid*," Khalidah said.

"I trust that you haven't foresworn *all* the pleasures of the
flesh?" Radwan asked, and Khalidah was confused, until she saw
that he was proffering her the mouthpiece of the hookah. She
looked at Ghassan, who only shrugged. Reluctantly, she accepted
the pipe. The chief watched as she drew on it, then exhaled in a
gasping cough. Apparently, this was a satisfactory response. He
gave her a bleary, gap-toothed smile, a whack on the shoulder
and then cried, "Now, boy, get back to your *oud* and play!"

*

The rain had slackened by the time Ghassan and Khalidah finally
stumbled back into his canoe. After her unwitting rebuff, Radwan
had warmed to Khalidah, demanding song after song and plying
her with harsh grain liquor and *banj*. The liquor she managed to
pour into the floor's matting when no one was looking, but the

mudhif's air was soon so thick with *banj* smoke that she could not have avoided its effects if she had ignored the passed pipe entirely.

Khalidah's prior experience with *banj* consisted of a single afternoon five years previous, spent with Bilal and a lump of cannabis resin which one of the retainers had dropped under Bilal's sharp gaze.

"Are you sure?" she had asked him, doubtfully examining the lump he held out on his palm, which resembled nothing so much as the petrified lumps of undigested rodent the hunting-hawks periodically vomited.

"It's *hashish*, all right," Bilal had said with a withering look that told her he was even more uncertain than she was, but determined not to show it. "Only, it does not look like very much…"

In fact, it was enough *hashish* to stun a horse. They'd smoked it with a will, neither having to tell the other that their honor depended on reducing the lot of it to ash, no matter what the consequences. The consequences were a brief euphoria followed by mind-crushing paranoia, which ended with them running to Zaynab in terror and tearfully confessing everything to her as they vomited their stomachs dry. Khalidah had not touched *banj* since that day, and as a result, she was now more stoned than she had ever imagined possible. She hoped that this would not become the norm of her stay with the Murabak. If it was, she had as little chance of surviving it as Sulayman.

But seeing Sulayman sobered her again. The coals in the brazier had burned down almost to nothing. She knelt by him as Ghassan added more, and low red tongues of flame lapped the edges of the new coals like the crimson lines around dark clouds. He felt Sulayman's forehead, gave him another dose of medicine, then turned to Khalidah.

"I am sorry about Radwan," Ghassan said. "I did not think he would take to you in quite so…immediate a fashion." Khalidah shot him a sharp look, but said nothing. "You did not tell me you could sing," he said in a different tone, one she recognized all too easily.

"In fact, I did – you asked me, and I answered, just before we left."

"Well, yes…but I didn't know that you could sing like…"

She left him struggling for words she knew by bitter experience he would never find. At last he said, "Well anyway, I am sorry."

She waved his apology aside and said, "I will stay up with him tonight."

But Ghassan was already shaking his head. "Sleep now," he said, "and let Sulayman sleep. The morning will bring change, one way or the other, and I'll need you rested."

Khalidah tried to protest, but she was too sapped to argue for long. She lay down with guilty gratitude on her blanket on the opposite side of the brazier from Sulayman, and fell asleep to the tide of his breathing.

*

Khalidah awakened the next morning to a stabbing brightness, feeling as if she'd been dragged for miles by a fast horse over hard ground. Her mind swam with the sound of lapping water and the sense that something was not as it should be. When she finally managed to turn over, she realized what it was: after so many days of unmitigated rain, the sun was shining. It shot like knife-strike through the chinks in the reed walls, sparked from the myriad vessels of glass and glazed pottery, and filled the doorway in a searing, sickening block. Slowly, she remembered: Ghassan, Radwan, the *oud* and the plangent sound of her own voice rendering Shánfara's words into something other than they had been. And then, strange dreams of an endless desert unrolling to the whine of mosquitoes that slowly became a voice hissing her name, a scorched wind that blasted her until she shook and burned with it by turns, a dark fissure in the earth full of red eyes and teeth like sabers, with which she fought for Sulayman's limp body. She sat up abruptly, gripped by the fear of the half-remembered nightmares as the room reeled around her.

And then her eyes caught on Sulayman's. They were open, and fixed on her.

The pitching room stilled. She leapt to her feet, crying, "You're better!"

"But still not well," Ghassan said from the shadows by his work table. "I imagine the two of you have things to say to each other – but Khalidah, don't tire him. I'll be back soon." He stood and disappeared through the bright doorway.

Sulayman pushed himself up slowly as Khalidah sat down by his bed, and then they sat looking at each other, neither knowing quite what to say. She wondered whether he was repressing a powerful urge to embrace her, as she was him. She felt near tears again, and fought them angrily.

"I'm sorry – " she began.

"*You're* sorry?" he interrupted. "The blame for this is mine. I've been so wrapped up in reaching Khorasan, I haven't thought about much else. I ignored the symptoms when I started to be ill, and so I left you to drag my carcass across half of Jazirah – "

"And I'd do it again, to save you," she said, with a level look.

He smiled weakly. "Brave words, *Sayyida*; let us hope you will never have to make good on them." Then the smile died, and he shook his head. "Quartan fever – honestly! I know better. The first thing the troupe taught me was never to camp in a damp place with bad air."

"There was a Berber herbalist who traveled with my tribe for a time," Khalidah said, "who claimed that quartan fever isn't caused by bad air, but by mosquitoes."

"Well then, he was a fraud."

Khalidah smiled. "That's what my father said when he dismissed him. Still, we have seen a lot of mosquitoes in the last few weeks…"

Sulayman shook his head. "If I am ill, it is because Allah wills it…and let us hope that he wills me a quick recovery too." They sat in the not-quite-silence of wind on reeds and water. Finally, he asked, "What do you think of Ghassan?"

"He is hard work."

Sulayman laughed. "Yes, he is; but name me something worthwhile that isn't." *You, most of the time*, Khalidah thought, but she said nothing. "Did he tell you how long it will be until we can leave?"

Khalidah sighed. "Ghassan tells me very little. I do not think that he likes me overly much."

"Ghassan does not suffer fools. If he didn't like you, you would not be here."

With eyes fixed on the sliver of bright water visible through the doorway, Khalidah said, "I think that he would suffer more than a fool, for you."

Sulayman considered this, his lips pressed into a ruminative line. "Did he tell you how we met?" he asked at last.

The image of a laboring woman flashed into Khalidah's mind. She stifled it quickly, but Sulayman had read the distress on her face. "What?" he asked, his voice suddenly tense and low. "What did he tell you?"

"He told me what you know already," she answered carefully, "and something else, which you do not. But Sulayman, you will have to ask him for that story yourself."

He looked at her with eyes stripped bare. When he nodded, she could not help feeling that it was less in agreement that in acquiescence to something he knew already.

*

Dusk came in a slow glide over the watery village. As the sun set in a quicksilver sky, mothers called their children home, water buffalo slopped heavily back to their stables, men plied canoes full of fish or fodder collected during the day, and the smoke of fifty cookfires drifted skyward. Sulayman and Khalidah sat outside with Ghassan before his own little fire as he cooked flatbread and grilled fish, then set the food down in front of them.

"Working cures sharpens the appetite," he said, tearing into the food and gesturing to his guests to join him.

Sulayman picked at a bit of bread, but Khalidah only gave Ghassan a long, incisive look. "Yes, I know that you want me to tell him," Ghassan replied, waving a hand dismissively. "All in good time."

"I do not like to have a secret divide us," she answered.

"And if you can keep to that, you're better off than most couples," he answered dryly.

Sulayman and Khalidah looked at each other, then away again, blushing. "You presume too much," she said in a low voice.

"Oh, I don't think so," Ghassan answered. His voice was curiously harsh, and cut by a resonant note of longing. He chewed reflectively for a long moment, then he said, "But, if you will..."

He proceeded to tell Sulayman the story he had told Khalidah the previous day. Sulayman listened to the whole of it with his eyes on his hands. The silence stretched out after Ghassan finished, until at last Sulayman asked, not quite bitterly, but without warmth: "Do you tell me this now because I am dying?"

And Khalidah found little comfort in Ghassan's answer: "I am telling you because you are mortal."

"That is no answer!" Sulayman retorted.

Ghassan looked at him calmly, then said, "We are all dying, Sulayman, from the day that we are born. I accept that I should not have kept Haya's secret as long as I did. Please, let the rest of it lie."

Sulayman looked at Khalidah. "And you? Do you believe I am this Jewish woman's son?"

Khalidah drew a breath of the watery air, then said, "I believe that what I believe does not matter. Just as I must construct the truth of my past from the pieces I am given, so must you."

Sulayman looked at her for a moment, then retreated back inside.

19

"Sanctimonious bastard," Numair grumbled, pulling his pillow over his head as the drums and trumpets shattered his stupor, followed by the high wail of the muezzin. Bilal made no attempt to rouse him. After the first few days he had learned that it was generally a futile effort, and his life was invariably more pleasant if his "cousin" was allowed to sleep late.

He dressed quickly and left the tent. The world around him was full of indistinct movement: dark figures with rolled prayer rugs over their shoulders shuffled toward the infantry's practice ground like a herd of small, misshapen pachyderms. For a moment he stood watching them. Overhead the sky was still dark and strewn with stars, but a rim of brightness ran along the horizon, as if night were a lid on the world and day fought to break the seal. For a moment he thought of the open desert, of other dawns when he and Khalidah had crept away from the sleeping camp to race her father's horses toward the rising sun. They'd generally been whipped for it later, but the prospect of punishment had never been enough to stop them. No pain could match the ecstasy of that moment when all four hooves left the ground, and two earthbound creatures grew the hearts of angels.

Bilal blinked. A solitary figure had broken from the herd and moved toward him. A smile materialized from the shifting wash of shadow, a slender hand touched him. *"As-salaamu 'alaikum,"*

Salim said, but Bilal could not answer him. He was too busy trying to stem the ensuing thought: that perhaps there *was* one feeling to match the divinity of flight, and it came in the shape of the five mortal fingers now resting on his arm. For if it was true, then there was no peace for him, no destiny but despair. He saw it stretched before him like his mother's loom lying warped and ready, the fabric not yet woven.

Stop it, he ordered himself, and forcing a smile he answered, *"Wa 'alaikum as-salaam wa rahmatu Allah."* Salim slipped his arm through the curve of Bilal's, and they walked together to the morning prayer, bowed to Mecca as the throngs spread out around them and, in the aftermath, the sun tore the heart out of night.

When the prayers were finished and the rugs rolled up, Salim sat back on his heels and said, "I have a secret."

With a flutter of anxiety, Bilal asked, "What is it?"

"If I told you, it would not be a secret." Salim laughed at Bilal's frown. "But I will show you," he relented, then paused, giving Bilal a long, speculative look. The rising sun turned his eyes the color of strong tea. "My father is leaving," he said at last.

"Is that the secret?"

Salim smiled. "Unlikely. He has given my brother Al-Afdhal command of the army, and Al-Afdhal will have wasted no time in letting everyone know it. I will not drill with you today," he added abruptly. "I am to sit with my father and observe a Sultan's preparations for war. Meet me after supper."

"I do not know whether my cousin – "

"I will send a whore with a bottle of wine," Salim interrupted, his eyes laughing. "Your cousin will not even realize you are missing. I will wait for you – don't be late." And he slipped away, a slight figure swallowed by the bright blood of day.

*

Salim had been correct in his prediction: by noon, every soul in

the army had heard of the Sultan's imminent departure. Rumors
flew about a private meeting with a Franj leader – Count Tripoli,
Gerard de Ridefort, even King Guy himself. The truth, as usual,
was a good deal more mundane. *Muharram*, the month when
the greatest number of *hajj* pilgrims was on the roads home from
Mecca, was nearly two weeks old. The first caravans would already have reached Oultrejourdain, and Salah ad-Din knew how
great the temptation to Brins Arnat would be. Fearing another
raid, he was leaving the gathering army in order to take his elite
guard to police the pilgrim road.

As the surge of excitement was dampened by the truth,
camp life returned to normal. After breakfast came the cavalry
drills, at which Bilal acquitted himself far better than he did at
the following exercises in swordsmanship. These were purely
voluntary on his part, for as a Bedu cavalryman, he was expected
to use the long spear, which he had been taught to wield since
he could sit a horse. He told himself that he practiced the sword
out of personal interest, but deep down he knew that he did it
for Salim. The prince, like all boys of his class, used a sword as
if it were an extension of himself, and Bilal could not bear for
his friend to see his own awkwardness. So he hacked away with
his unwieldy blade, pouring sweat into the ravenous sand, and
wondered about Salim's secret.

By the time he arrived back at the tent in the late afternoon,
mild curiosity had grown into a fever of anticipation, so it was
with a good deal of dismay that he found Numair neither drunk
nor tangled in the embrace of the promised whore, but washed
and sober and obviously waiting for him.

"Change your clothes," Numair said. "And arm yourself. I
have an errand for you."

Bilal shook his head. "What errand?"

"Do you question me?" Numair replied, giving Bilal the hard,
metallic look that he'd seen him cast on Khalidah during their
doomed henna ceremony. Bilal shivered, feeling a prickle of
empathy for her. "If I tell you I have an errand, you do it with a
smile on your face."

"This time, I cannot," Bilal heard himself say, with partial disbelief.

Numair stilled, that alien look sharpening. "You cannot?" He spoke in a tone of gentle mockery with an edge like a dagger's. "Have you forgotten why we are here? What is it, precisely, that would keep you from your duty?"

"A meeting," Bilal faltered, already regretting his defiance.

"With the Sultan's runt, no doubt," Numair answered. Bilal said nothing, but felt his face burning, with anger or with shame he no longer knew. "Did you think that I had not noticed all the time that you spend with him? What are you playing at, little cousin?"

Hating himself for the lie, but hating Numair more, Bilal answered coldly, "No, I have not forgotten why we are here. And given your master's desire for information on the Sultan's plans, I would have thought that you would be pleased that I have befriended his son."

"I did not take you for a schemer." Still those eyes glittered at him, dissecting his purpose. Bilal said nothing. "Watch your step, little cousin. Princes make dangerous lovers."

"What?" Bilal cried. "We are *not* – "

Numair cut him off with a chuckle. "Save your breath, Bilal. Fuck him, don't fuck him, I don't care – just don't fuck me. Remember that your mother's life is in my hands."

Of course he remembered. Remembering poisoned every moment of his own life. Numair watched him squirm, smiling faintly. Then he said, "Now listen carefully, and remember everything…"

*

De Mailly's face was like marble in the light of the full moon, the cross on his mantle like ash. He stood by his horse's withers, one hand absently toying with its mane as he listened to Bilal's message.

"Is it bad news?" Bilal ventured when, several moments after finishing, de Mailly had still said nothing.

De Mailly looked up at him with a weary smile. "I do not know. You say Salah ad-Din intends to send a detachment of troops to Tiberias, to bolster Count Tripoli's garrison there – are you absolutely certain that that is correct?"

"That is what I was told. Why, *Messire*? What does it mean?"

De Mailly looked closely at him, frowning. "Does your cousin explain nothing to you?"

"Only when it suits him," Bilal answered.

"Which, I take it, is not very often," de Mailly said, his contempt obvious. "Very well then: you will know that the Latin states are currently divided between supporters of King Guy and those of Count Tripoli. Tripoli believes that Guy was crowned unjustly. This is true, for when he named his sister's child as his successor, the former king also stated that should the child die before reaching seniority, the Pope should choose his successor. However, there are many who think that Tripoli's quarrel with Guy has more to do with his own desire for the crown, than any miscarriage of justice.

"Wherever the right of it lies, a divided kingdom cannot stand against Salah ad-Din, and just now the nobles of Jerusalem can talk of nothing but how to make Tripoli recognize Guy." De Mailly paused, sighed. "Kerak and my Master favor military action to force Tripoli's submission. The barons prefer diplomacy. But whichever they choose, if they fail, we stand to lose Jerusalem. And if Tripoli has the Sultan's help, as your information suggests he will, then they will quite likely fail."

"And what do you think, *Messire*?"

Again, de Mailly sighed. "It does not matter. Nobody asks the opinion of the Marshal of the Temple – only of its Master."

"I am asking."

De Mailly looked startled, then rewarded Bilal with a sweet smile. "Indeed, you are. Well then: I think that Tripoli is far and away the best statesman in Outremer, but he is also an idealist. His wish to reconcile with the Saracens is noble, but I believe that it is misguided."

Bilal looked at the knight's solicitous face, sick with the thought that this man didn't realize he was being double-crossed by the very Master he served so honestly. Softly, he said, "Do you think that it is impossible for our two races to live at peace with one another?"

De Mailly's smile saddened, and he touched Bilal's cheek. "Perhaps it is possible. But we must first learn to live in peace with our own kind. In that, your Sultan appears to have succeeded where our kings have so far failed. I only hope that we will not need to spill our own people's blood to achieve solidarity."

Bilal said, half to himself, "I wish it were not like this."

"I wish that too."

"If only there was something that I could do…"

De Mailly smiled, necessarily mistaking his meaning. "Brave boy…I fear this is beyond you. Your master, on the other hand, ought to have seen this truce coming and sent word. I hear that he failed to keep the meeting de Ridefort arranged for him with the Sultan. Tell me, what is distracting him?"

"What isn't?" Bilal muttered. Then, thinking that he had been too flippant, he added, "Perhaps I have not tried hard enough to keep him from temptation. I will do better."

"Do not blame yourself, *Petit*. You are not responsible for the failings of your master." He sighed. "And yet, I worry about you here, with only him to protect you. Perhaps I should apply to de Ridefort to find a better position for you."

"No!" Bilal said sharply.

"But why not?"

Bilal looked away. "It is complicated…"

He thought that de Mailly would push him, but the knight only said, "All right. But my offer still stands, Bilal: if ever you find yourself in need of help, do not hesitate to call on me."

Bilal nodded. "Is there a message to take back?"

"There wasn't," de Mailly said grimly, "but given what you have told me about your cousin's attitude, I think that you had better stress to him the importance of undermining the Sultan's mission to Tiberias. If he cannot stop it, then he must at least be among the forces that go to Tripoli's aid."

And your Master will tell him exactly the opposite, at the first opportunity, Bilal thought with disgust. "He will not like that," he said out loud.

This time, de Mailly's smile was cold. "I don't care."

*

Numair laughed when Bilal relayed de Mailly's message. Bilal waited, trying not to let his hatred show. "'Stress to him the importance of undermining the Sultan's mission to Tiberias,'" he quoted in a parody of de Mailly's accent. "They will not be rid of me so easily," he said to the flame of his oil lamp. "I have agreed to lend them my eyes and ears, but my blood is my own, to spill as I choose."

"I suppose de Ridefort wants you to remain where the Sultan is?" Bilal ventured.

"De Ridefort," Numair repeated contemptuously. "He does not call all the shots, you know." Bilal wondered how Numair could possibly have convinced himself of this, when both the Sultan and the King of Jerusalem were apparently de Ridefort's dupes.

"What will you do, then?" Bilal asked.

"I'll do nothing," Numair said, "until it's clear which way the winds will blow." He considered Bilal for a few moments, then said, "Don't look so anxious, little cousin. These Franj take themselves far too seriously. Most likely it will all come to nothing anyway."

But Bilal knew that it had already come to something, and he could only wonder how long he would hold out before it consumed him.

20

Though Sulayman continued to regain his strength, Ghassan still insisted on coming with them into the mountains. "Whatever he says to us, his health is still fragile," he told Khalidah in a tone that suggested there was a good deal more that he was not saying. "I'd like to keep an eye on him for a few more days. Besides, the Zagros are the fiercest mountains in Persia, and I know them well."

Khalidah left him sorting herbs and went to the stable to see to the horses. She found Sulayman there already, slumped against the wall with his head between his legs.

"All better, are you?" she said, looking down at him reprovingly.

He looked up, bleary-eyed. "Don't start," he said through clenched teeth. Khalidah said nothing else, just offered a hand and helped him to stand.

'Aasifa whinnied a greeting when she saw her master, looking up from the manger where she grazed between Zahirah and a water buffalo, who glanced balefully at her as she danced with two-weeks' pent-up energy. Despite the rest and the plentiful fodder, the horses still looked slightly out of condition. As she saddled Zahirah, Khalidah tried not to feel the nearness of rib to skin, nor to see the frequency of Sulayman's pauses in his own preparations.

As she was stowing her saddlebags, Khalidah looked up to see
Ghassan splashing across the marsh on a tall bay gelding, leading
a grey pony with a pack-saddle. The bay was a good hand higher
than Zahirah, with a long, straight nose and a rangy body that
gave him the look of a hunting hound.

"That's an Akhal-Teke," Khalidah said admiringly. "Who does
he belong to?"

"To me," Ghassan told her with a proud smile. "He stays in
Radwan's stable – mine is too small. He was a present from a
Turcoman noble whom I cured of an embarrassing condition a
few years ago. He'd heard of me in Basrah and came out here
to avoid gossip in the town...anyway, I believe that in Wasim,
I had the better end of the bargain. I do not know what Wasim
thinks."

He dismounted and handed Wasim's reins to Khalidah while
he loaded the rest of their gear onto the pack-pony. The horse
pranced and shook the fly-tassels on his bridle, looking playfully
around at his master with a smile in his eyes, and Khalidah knew
exactly what Wasim thought.

The weather was fair as they set out, so clear after the days
of rain that they could see the foothills of the Zagros on the
horizon. Ghassan knew the best routes through the marshes,
and the water seldom reached higher than Zahirah's knees. Still,
it meant a slow, steady gait, for which Sulayman was grateful.
As the sun moved across the sky, the marshes became shallower
and the grassy patches wider, until at last the water dispersed
into damp meadowland studded with well-tended orchards of
fruit trees and date-palms. At midday they stopped, and Ghassan
prepared a bowl of medicine for Sulayman. He drank it and
nibbled a piece of flatbread while Ghassan and Khalidah ate a
more substantial lunch, and the horses cropped the long grass.

"And now, Sulayman, you must rest," said Ghassan when
the younger man had drunk the last of the foul liquid from the
bowl.

"I don't need to rest," he protested.

"Yes, you do," the healer said sternly. "It will take all your strength to cross the mountains, and at the moment you have little to spare. Rest, now."

Sighing, Sulayman unrolled his blanket and lay down under a tree. He was asleep almost immediately. Looking at him, Khalidah wondered how he had managed to convince them that he was better. His face was sallow as parchment, and the fingers resting on the blanket by his cheek were slender as river-reeds with the weight he had lost over the last couple of weeks.

"He's not really recovered, is he," she said.

"Perceptive girl," Ghassan answered dryly.

Khalidah frowned at Ghassan, whose lined, almond-shaped face remained impassive. "Then what are we doing?"

"We are going to the Zagros."

"Of course – just the place for an invalid. Or do you have some plan that you aren't telling me?"

"If I do," he answered with an infuriating smile, "why would I tell you merely for asking?"

Khalidah gave him a long look, then said, "Why do you disapprove of me?"

Ghassan shook his head. "The arrogance of youth! My silence has nothing to do with you. But if it will save me two-days' dose of a young woman's petulance, then you might as well know that I have heard of someone in the mountains who might be able to help him…and perhaps you, too."

"Help me?" Khalidah demanded. "With what do I need help?"

"Tell me," he said, "what it is you hope to find in the wilds of Khorasan?"

Khalidah's mouth collapsed into an obstinate line, and Ghassan smiled wryly. "Very well, then; you keep your secrets and I'll keep mine." And with that, he lay back on Wasim's saddle, drew the end of his turban over his face and gave a pointed snore. Sighing, Khalidah leaned back against a palm trunk to wait.

*

It was late afternoon by the time they started off again, and the nap seemed to have erased their earlier altercation from Ghassan's mind. "Tell me, Khalidah," he said, "do the tribes intend to join the Sultan if he makes a move for Al-Quds?"

"I can only speak for my own," she said, "and even that has no straight answer, for we are a divided tribe, half following my father, and the other half my uncle. My father supports the Sultan, but my uncle…" Khalidah looked at Sulayman, passing the buck.

Sulayman smiled wryly. "'Abd al-Hadi wants little beyond a plateful of delicacies, a bedful of slave girls and a peaceful death in the shade of a palm tree…or so he would have you think. With him, it is often difficult to tell."

"Do you, too, intend to join the *jihad*?" Ghassan asked Sulayman.

"If you do not kill us in the mountains," Sulayman answered neutrally. "And if we return from Qaf in time."

Ghassan gave him a shrewd look. "Somehow, I do not think that will be a problem."

"What do you mean?" Khalidah asked.

"Does the timing of all of this strike neither of you as odd?" When they looked blank, he added, "The heiress to the greatest warriors of the Oriental world is called to their leader just as Islam is about to engage in one of the most important battles of its history. I think the two were meant to converge."

"It would be a neat theory," Sulayman answered, "except that the Jinn are not Muslims."

"That does not preclude a common cause."

"Perhaps not. But either way, Tor Gul Khan does not approve of Salah ad-Din."

"Does he know him?" Ghassan asked with interest.

"No, but he certainly knows of him. I believe he called the Sultan 'that arrogant, over-reaching son of a goat-herder.'"

Ghassan chuckled. "Well, it's hardly surprising – kings seldom have a high opinion of each other. But none of it convinces me that the Jinn have no place in Salah ad-Din's *jihad*." He paused, considering this, then turned to Khalidah and said, "You, child – what will you do once you've been to your people and Sulayman has ridden off to war?"

"Ride off with him," she retorted.

"For Sulayman's sake, or the Sultan's?"

Khalidah looked at him squarely. "Why not for my own?"

"I thought that your tribe was undecided about fighting the Franj."

"I have left my tribe. But I am still a Muslim, and I believe that all Muslims must quarrel with those who have taken our holy city from us. Therefore I will lend my sword like any who has learned to use one, to the man who bids for its return."

"You are so certain of your righteousness," Ghassan said. "Yet one must never forget that the Franj are here because they, too, believe in the righteousness of their cause. Like our *mujahiddin*, they believe that they are God's warriors, and for this they deserve our respect."

"The Franj slaughtered and ate Muslim children when they first took Jerusalem. I cannot see what is respectable in that."

"Do you think that the people of Islam have never committed atrocities?" Ghassan returned.

"Then you suggest giving the Franj free reign of our lands?"

"I suggest nothing of the sort! I said that they deserve respect, not compliance: the respect of well-matched adversaries, if need be; and yet, I am not sure that it does. We are all people of the Book...surely there must be a way for us to live together in peace?" Ghassan seemed to have lapsed into ruminating aloud, rather than speaking directly to them. Now he recalled himself. "I see that you doubt me," he said, looking from Khalidah to Sulayman. "Take Al-Quds as your example, then. Is our claim to it any better than theirs?" He didn't give them a chance to answer before he continued, "Who founded the city?"

"King David," Khalidah answered promptly, "one thousand years before the birth of the prophet Iesu."

"Someone's taught you well," Ghassan smiled, "but not the whole truth. Al-Quds was already two thousand years old when King David 'founded' it. He took it from the Jebusites, who had no doubt taken it from someone else. And after him it passed to the Assyrians, then the Babylonians, Alexander of Macedon, Ptolemy, the Seleucids, the Maccabees, the Romans, the Byzantines and then – only *then* – the Muslims. We are a mere scratch on the surface of that great city: a scratch no longer or deeper perhaps than the Franj, in Allah's grand scheme. For if Allah has willed our existence, then he has willed theirs too."

"What, then," Khalidah asked with somewhat dampened defiance, "do *you* think that we should do about the Franj?"

"First, consider them," he said, ignoring the dark look that passed between Khalidah and Sulayman. "As I said, they are part of Allah's plan; perhaps they are here to teach us something about ourselves."

"And what do you think the Franj have to teach us?" Sulayman asked, pre-empting Khalidah's retort, which promised to be sharp.

Ghassan shrugged. "I'm a physician, not a philosopher. But it seems to me that we ought to take heed of their mistakes. Their *jihad* has sown hatred and misery, not least among their own people. They have all but forgotten the word of Christ in their struggles for power. If we are to wage war in Allah's name, then perhaps, rather than acquisition and repression, its object should be to spread His word. After all, what place is there among peace, enlightenment and fulfillment, for avarice and greed?"

Sulayman shook his head. "You are describing the Sultan: a man devoted to Allah and to his people, whose generosity and mercy are an example to us all. Isn't it better to follow a man like him into battle, than to grovel at the feet of a race of invaders determined to subjugate us?"

Ghassan smiled sadly. "Do you think that the Sultan is really all that the rumors tell us he is? Chivalrous he may be, Sulayman, but he is a man nevertheless, subject to weakness like any other; and, more to the point, his army is made of men. They'll loot and rape despite him and call it Allah's will, and then not faith nor mercy, not our God nor the Franj's can save this land from the damnation of war."

"War may be inevitable," said Khalidah, her eyes fixed on the deepening sky, "but I don't think that it is necessarily damnation. As you say, you are a physician: you know that sometimes salvation can only be bought by violence. A suppurating limb must be removed to save the rest of the body from infection; a living child cut from the belly of its dying mother so that two lives are not lost. You do these things because you believe in the sanctity of life." At last she looked at him, and the softness of her eyes after her earlier anger surprised him. "Well, could this not be the same? Could a sword not be our salvation, if the one who wields it believes strongly enough in faith, or mercy, or God...believes beyond his own strength or weakness, for the good of all who will succeed him?"

Ghassan's face grew suddenly grave, showing his age. "Perhaps," he said, and then gave her a smile as abrupt as sun through a rain cloud. "And so may you raise you sword only in belief, Khalidah bint Brekhna al-Jinni; and I pray that you prove me wrong."

There was pain on his face, and he turned away from her look of surprise. They rode on in silence through the dying light, toward the purple mountains looming like fate.

21

Salim reclined in the shade of a fluttering pavilion at the edge of camp, eating a pomegranate, while Bilal watched him intently. The fruit was long out of season, but this wasn't the reason for his interest, for over the weeks of their friendship the prince's apparent command of the miraculous had come to seem more or less ordinary to Bilal. What fascinated him was Salim's method of eating it. Rather than pushing the leathery skin inward and consuming the fleshy seeds in greedy bites (as Bilal had done with his own half) he held it like a cup in his left hand, while with the right he picked out each individual red-cased seed with the delicacy of a musician plucking an *oud*'s strings.

Besides, watching Salim was preferable to acknowledging the column of horsemen snaking away from camp to the south-west, toward Tiberius. Tripoli's agreement with the Sultan was sure to tip the scales in favor of a military action against him, and ridiculous as he knew it to be, Bilal could not bear the thought of de Mailly going into battle. However, one distinct advantage to the situation was that de Ridefort had ordered Numair to volunteer for the detachment, and Bilal – whose relationship with Salim had not been lost on him – to remain behind. The possibility of his master being run through with a Templar lance was enough to bring a smile to Bilal's anxious face.

"What amuses you?" Salim asked, sucking a seed from his

fingers, inky eyes intent on his friend. Immediately, Bilal's smile leveled. "Ah – I would not have marked it, had I known that marking it would crush it! *Sayyid's* smiles are rare enough. Is civilization proving too comfortable? Does your nomad's heart pine for the bare, blowing sands?" Bilal could not help smiling again at that. "That's an improvement…and here is your reward."

A pomegranate seed balanced on the tip of Salim's outstretched finger. There was a hint of a smile in his eyes, a challenge perhaps, and in a moment of liminal radiance Bilal saw himself leaning forward, taking the seed with his tongue. The image was so vivid that he could even taste the salt of Salim's skin. He shut his eyes for a moment, and when he opened them the seed still quivered before him like a songbird's heart. Shaken to the core, he took it between his thumb and forefinger and crushed it; but he could not stop himself licking the juice, and its bright bitter-sweet spark mocked him.

Salim's eyes narrowed for a moment, showing perhaps a tinge of disappointment; then he went back to picking at the fruit. "You have not asked me, you know," he said with the shade of petulance that sometimes crept into his tone, the only affectation that ever belied his position.

"Asked you what?" Bilal asked, with ignorance as disingenuous as Salim's peevishness.

"What I was going to tell you the other night, when you did not come."

Bilal sighed. "I've told you I'm sorry about that. Numair wouldn't let me leave. My cousin has suddenly embraced sobriety, and it has not left me time to think of much beyond his demands."

Salim was looking down at the husk in his hand, his long hair half-obscuring his face. "So you have said." The petulance was more overt now, and with it the genuine disappointment.

"I am sorry…" Bilal repeated.

For a moment Salim kept his silence; then, crushing the empty husk in his hand, he looked up with one of his cloudburst smiles. "It doesn't matter. Soon you won't have to worry about your cousin, sober or not."

"What do you mean?" Bilal asked warily.

"It's what I wanted to tell you the other night. My father has asked me to go south with him, and he is giving me command of a *saqa*. Thirty horsemen of my choosing, to be used for reconnaissance. And he has told me to be certain to include you – as though I needed to be told!"

For a moment elation surged through Bilal. Then he recalled that the *hajj* road ran past Kerak, and de Ridefort's watchful eye, and he knew who had been behind this sudden rise in status. Neither the Sultan nor de Ridefort could be without his informer, after all. He watched as the last of the Tiberias detachment were subsumed in the dust of their departure, unable to find words to answer Salim.

"I had thought that you would be pleased," the prince said, and this time there was no petulance in his voice, only bewilderment and hurt.

"I *am* pleased," Bilal said. "It is only that…so much has changed so quickly. Two months ago I was nobody, and now I ride in a prince's *saqa*." He shook his head. "But please don't think that I am not grateful. I am, Salim – for everything."

"Do not thank me," Salim said, taking Bilal's hand in his, still sticky with red juice. "Allah looks after the faithful."

His smile flashed out like a flaying knife.

*

They left Ras al-Mai' at dawn, the Sultan solemnly entrusting his army to the eager Al-Afdhal – all pride and adolescent arrogance beneath his sparse black beard – before wrapping his heir in a fatherly embrace. Salim, watching from horseback at the fringes of the crowd, rolled his eyes, grinned at Bilal, then gave his mare a sharp kick. She reared and then plunged into a gallop, abruptly cutting short the ceremonial farewells. Salim and his advance guard were gone before his father's frown could catch him.

By mid-morning, however, even Salim's enthusiasm was flagging. The *hajj* road had been a caravan route long before the coming of the Prophet, but for all its history, it was only a wide, pale track on the dun-colored desert, thick with the dust of five-hundred years' worth of grinding feet. A Sirocco had risen with the light, filling the air with that powdery dust so that even those at the front found it difficult to breathe.

"Imad ad-Din would call this an omen," Salim said to Bilal, who rode at his side. Like the others, Salim had pulled a corner of his turban across his nose and mouth, but the bare parts of his face and the black waves of his hair were caked with the pale dust, making him into the parody of a Franji.

"And you?" Bilal asked.

Salim's eyes narrowed, and Bilal knew that under the dusty linen he was smiling. "I think that omens are the tools of old men who prefer wine and women to Allah's call."

"Don't let your father hear you say that," Bilal said.

"Do you think that I need the warning? And yet, I do not count the great chronicler amidst our company."

Which was true enough, though Salim knew as well as Bilal did that it had more to do with the Sultan's practicality than the scribe's preference for the comforts of home. Though Salah ad-Din was fond of his records, he also realized that he had little margin for error in this particular campaign. The pilgrims must be kept safe if only to keep order among the swelling ranks of the army and, if possible, Arnat's garrison must be contained. None of it, however, was worth the risk of Guy confronting the main body of the Islamic army while its commander was away to the south. The Sultan doubted that the Franj king was foolish enough to challenge the Muslims with Tripoli against him, but then again, he wouldn't have sworn to it. If the need arose, Salah ad-Din's division must be in a position to drop everything and return to the north. So: no scribes, no whores, not even a pretty serving boy who might distract the soldiers from their duty.

The men of this miniature army were professionals, *tawashiyah* and *mamluk* archers led by the Sultan's favorite *umara*. Bilal's guts ground in a now-familiar twist of anxiety when he imagined drawing his sword alongside them, and the only comfort he could offer himself was the very real possibility that he would die before it ever came to that. In fact, a timely death in Allah's name would solve most of his problems. Sighing, he nudged his horse alongside Salim's and tried to lose himself in the rhythm of her falling hooves.

At nightfall they reached the city of Busra, where they planned to camp. Lying on a fertile plain almost due south of Damascus, the town had been in existence for at least twenty-five centuries, when it had been known to the Egyptian pharaohs. Built by the Nabateans out of the local black basalt rock, it had survived occupation first by the Greeks and then by the Romans, who made it the capital city of Arabia. Under their influence it became a hub for caravans, a role that continued through the rise of Christianity, and then of Islam. An old story claimed that a Nestorian monk had met the young Muhammad here, passing through with his caravan, and predicted that he would be a great prophet. It was for this reason that Salah ad-Din had chosen the city as their outpost.

Bilal was too exhausted when they arrived to care about any of this. He could think of nothing but raising his tent and crawling into it. Salim, however, appeared to have left his weariness in the saddle. Bilal looked up from the jumble of ropes and pegs to see the prince walking toward him, carrying a lantern whose latticed sides threw stars on the sand.

"Leave that," Salim said. "There is something we must see."

Bilal looked wearily up at him. "The only thing I want to see is the backs of my eyelids, and I cannot do that until this tent is raised."

"Then share mine tonight, and tomorrow I'll send servants to raise yours…but only if you come with me now."

Bilal sighed. "What can we possibly see in the dark, anyway?"

Salim only smiled. Inwardly cursing his friend's cheerful energy, Bilal turned his back on the tangled tent and followed

Salim toward the town wall. At the gate, the prince slipped a gold coin to each of the guards, who let the boys pass without comment. They wandered the quiet streets, Salim seeming more or less assured of his direction, until at last they came to a high wall of black stone that arced against the star-tacked sky like the back of a huge and ancient creature.

"What is this?" Bilal asked.

"The citadel," Salim answered, and led him to a gate in the high wall, where he bribed another guard to let them inside. Once past the guard, Salim took Bilal's hand and led him into the shadows of an arched doorway, along corridors of closed doors lit by flickering torches, and finally out again into the open. They stood at the bottom of a half-moon of stone. Behind them, curved benches soared upward in widening arcs to the height of several houses. Before them spread a vast platform – a stage – with an elaborately linteled doorway at its center and columned galleries on either side.

Bilal looked around in pure amazement. "What is this?" he repeated, this time in a reverential whisper.

"A theater," Salim answered finally, setting his flickering lantern on the stone bench nearest him and sitting down, pulling his legs up underneath him.

"I thought you said this was the citadel."

"It is both," Salim answered. His face was rapt as he surveyed the structure. "The Romans built the theatre a thousand years ago, when this city was theirs. It could hold fifteen thousand spectators. The greatest actors of their time performed the greatest plays on that stage. Then, when the Umayyids had power, they built walls around it and made it into their stronghold, and that's what it's been ever since – a castle with a theatre at its heart. Can you imagine anything stranger?" Salim shook his head. "My father said that soon there will not be enough room for the garrison. He plans to enlarge it."

"You have been here before."

Salim looked at Bilal in surprise. "No. I have only heard and read about it. But I have always wanted to come, and I wanted you to see it with me."

The simple, straightforward kindness of the gesture overwhelmed Bilal. Much later, he would wonder why it was this, and not the countless previous kindnesses, that broke him. At the time he felt only a sudden, acute awareness of the ancient stonework hovering like a mountain slope above him, and the hopeless wish that it would let go and crush him in this moment when he was as near to happiness as he had ever been. But the stone held, offering neither judgment nor release, and Bilal collapsed beside Salim, head in his hands and shaking with sobs.

"But – what is the matter?" Salim asked in surprise.

"I don't..." Bilal faltered, "I cannot..." He paused, then looked up at Salim, who looked back, bewildered. "Why, *why*, Salim, did you choose me?"

Salim looked at him for a long moment, then answered, "Because my father is waiting for me to fail." His voice wavered, suddenly fragile. "He gave me this command to prove to me – and to himself perhaps – that I am incapable of it, and I, being selfish, and no doubt as weak as he supposes me, could not face the failure without a friend beside me. But if you would rather leave – "

"No!" Bilal cried, dismayed both by the confession and the thought of separation. "No, that isn't what I meant. I didn't know about this, about your father...I only wanted to know, why did you choose me as your friend?"

"Do you wish that I had not?" Salim asked.

"That's not what I mean either...Allah have mercy on me, I cannot seem to make right of anything!" Bilal looked miserably at Salim, who waited with soft, patient eyes for his explanation. Bilal knew that he could not continue to deceive him. "You have been the truest friend of my life," Bilal said, his voice like the ancient stone, "and yet I have not been true to you."

"You have accepted my friendship and given your own in return," Salim answered, puzzled. "I see nothing false in that."

"But if you could see into my heart, if you only knew – "

"Ah, but I think I do," Salim interrupted. To Bilal's bewilderment he had begun to smile, and beneath the smile was something beyond forgiveness, beyond affection or even affinity. "Why didn't you speak earlier?" Salim continued, reaching toward him with one tentative hand. "I cannot bear the thought of you suffering, thinking...well, I know well enough what you were thinking." There was steely defiance beneath the smile and the soft words.

"No..." Bilal whispered, but Salim's hand had come to rest on his cheek, and he could not deny the warmth that kindled in his cold heart in response.

"I know what the Bedu tribes believe, Bilal, but I cannot believe that love is a sin – not even when it looks like this."

Salim lifted Bilal's right hand and touched his lips to his palm, and then leaned forward to kiss his forehead, and finally his mouth, silencing the truth Bilal had not been able to speak. Bilal suspected then that he was damned, but he didn't care: everything he had ever worried or longed for had shattered against the sudden miracle of Salim's lips against his own. The world ebbed with their embrace. For a little while, all that mattered fit into the lantern's pool of stars.

22

Sulayman ate almost nothing the next morning, but all of Khalidah's inquiries about his health met with the same defiant glare. Before they left, Ghassan handed him another draught of medicine. He gulped it down and then paled, looking bilious; but he did not throw it back up.

They had camped in the Zagros foothills the night before, and they spent that day climbing. The long, plodding hours passed for Khalidah in a string of images that surfaced like islands from the abstraction of worry and aching muscles that had overtaken her: dry, rocky hills occasionally split by meadows of sparse grass, rivers quick with meltwater the color of stone, gullies and plateaus and a few white peaks in the somnolent distance. At last they reached a high, windy ridge, and for a moment Khalidah's mind cleared as she took in the magnitude of the scene before her. From the ridge the mountain plunged steeply into a valley of yellow-green grass spotted with wildflowers. At the far side of the valley the mountains rose again, their slopes cross-hatched with the remnants of ancient stone walls, the higher ones dusted with snow, on up to a ridge higher than the one on which they stood. Behind that was another higher still, and so on they marched to the horizon, their icy crowns bloodshot with the setting sun.

"These are the lands of Asag," said Ghassan in a low, reverent tone, "who took the mountains as brides and had boulders for

children, and was finally slain by Ninurta in the Battle of the
Gods..."

Sulayman smiled. "It is fortunate that nobody's here to hear
you, or your head would roll for blasphemy."

"What is it, really?" Khalidah asked. "This place?"

"The Zagros mountains are the territory of the *Lur Bozorg,*
the Grand Lur clan," Ghassan answered. "This part traditionally
belongs to the Bakhtiari."

"And who are they?"

"A tribe of nomads not unlike your own. They live in black
tents and migrate with the seasons over their traditional grazing
lands, but they keep goats rather than horses. At any rate, they
are not here now, and I doubt that they would grudge us a night
on their grasslands if they were. Come now, before the sun sets,
or make your bed on these stones." He nudged Wasim with his
heels, gripped the pony's lead-rein, and the horses began picking
their way downward through the gathering dark.

*

That night, Khalidah saw Sulayman's dreams. She did not look
for them, but they were there when she closed her eyes. A sword
of fire flayed him slowly; red wolves chased him through a labyrinth of dark volcanic stone. He screamed then, and she woke; he
screamed again when she and Ghassan tried to pull the blankets
from his burning body, for he saw them as leering Franj with
naked swords. By the next morning the delirium had passed,
but it took the last of his strength with it. He could not even
make himself swallow his medicine. As he shook on his blanket,
Khalidah asked Ghassan:

"How much longer until we reach this place we are going?"

"A day, if we can keep this pace and I can remember the
path."

"Will he last that long?"

He sighed. "It is in Allah's hands."

It took both of their strength to get Sulayman into the saddle, but 'Aasifa pitched him out again immediately, smelling sickness on him; or so Khalidah told herself, unwilling to face what else the animal might have sensed. So they put him on the stalwart pony, but when they tried to load the packs onto 'Aasifa she reared and screamed. In the end the pack-saddle went onto Zahirah, who bore it with a bemused look, while Khalidah rode 'Aasifa, who made her feelings about this known by shying and swerving at every blowing leaf. Khalidah clung grimly to the horse, wishing that she had insisted rather than suggested that Sulayman choose another.

They crossed the meadow and then began climbing again. Sulayman's instinct for the saddle went deeper than his illness, deeper apparently than consciousness, and he shifted his weight automatically with the shifting terrain, even when he did not see it. Khalidah was so intent upon him and the battling horse beneath her that she recalled no images from that day, just the sharpness of the wind, the searing brilliance of the sun, the air so thin and cold she felt that she could not make it fill her lungs. She heard Sulayman gasping, too. The sound seemed to come from far away.

In the afternoon he lost consciousness. Like that terrible rainy day when the fever first took him, he began to slump in the saddle, and finally to slide. Following a quick, curt negotiation, Ghassan and Khalidah agreed that if one of the horses was to bear the weight of a second rider, it had best be her slighter one. And so once again she found herself sitting behind Sulayman, holding his sloppy weight with one arm while she guided the patient pony with the other. Behind her, Ghassan struggled to hold on to both Zahirah and 'Aasifa as they picked their way up the stony path.

And Sulayman, trapped now in the deadly current of his dreams, clung to a thread of consciousness like a drowning man clings to a floating log. In his delirium he raved about it – a sound, disembodied, like the steady beat of a horse's hooves hitting sand. Somehow, Khalidah felt that she should know what he meant. It haunted her for hours before at last she realized that the sound he clung to was the beating of her own heart.

*

They forded the Pasitigris late in the afternoon, and stopped briefly to let the horses drink. A vast plain stretched out beyond the riverbank, rippling with long grass, but Khalidah looked past it to the place where the ground began to rise again. When Ghassan turned Wasim toward the mountains, Khalidah followed without protest. She knew that it was madness to go back into the mountains so close to nightfall, but she also knew that Sulayman might not live until morning. He shook and burned in her arms, and that alone would have driven her on.

As luck would have it, the moon was near full and the sky remained clear. It wasn't difficult to follow the paths once Ghassan found them, but finding them was something else again. The quick assurance with which he had led them previously was gone, and at each split in the track he paused, deliberating. Khalidah tried to keep her temper, but at last she burst out:

"Why do you hesitate, when he is dying?"

Ghassan gave her a bleak look. "Because his only chance – and, indeed, ours – is to find the right path. But if you'd prefer to go galloping off the nearest cliff and end all our misery – "

"All right," she conceded. "Just tell me one thing: have you ever actually been to this place you are taking us?"

Ghassan's look was all the reply she needed. Sighing, Khalidah nudged the exhausted pony forward again.

They climbed through the night, the air growing thinner and colder and the path ever more treacherous, until they were forced to dismount and lead the horses. With instinct born of exhaustion, Khalidah made Ghassan shift Sulayman onto Wasim's back, and the tall horse proved his worth. Although Sulayman slumped lifelessly over his neck, Wasim shifted his gait carefully with the terrain so that Khalidah only needed to help on the steepest slopes to keep Sulayman in the saddle. All the while the moon worked its way across the sky, and by the time it set they had reached another ridge, this one covered with a thin layer of snow. Glittering peaks stretched around them like waves on a frozen sea. Khalidah could no longer feel her hands and feet. The bitter wind cut through her clothes. And then she caught an incongruous whiff of wood smoke.

"There!" Ghassan cried.

With the last of the moonlight, Khalidah followed his pointing finger. At the very edge of the ridge, just before it fell away to nothingness, was what appeared to be a pile of stones, with a thin curl of smoke rising from it. They made their way toward this, and soon they could make out a dull flicker of light: a doorway, with just enough head room for the horses.

Inside, the stone hut was surprisingly spacious, encompassing a natural hollowing of the rock. In the center a fire burned, the smoke rising up through a hole in the roof, but the smell that permeated the room was of cultivated earth, for it was filled with living plants. They appeared to grow straight out of the rock, from the tiniest alpine flowers to huge tropical trees. The floor was strewn with rushes and sweet herbs, and the horses immediately fell to munching.

It took Khalidah a few moments to make out the tiny woman kneeling by the fire amidst this unexpected profusion of foliage. The woman gave the impression of beauty, though her features were in fact unremarkable, beyond a pair of clear green eyes. Likewise, she exuded a sense of youth and vitality, although her face was wrinkled and her long hair tangled and gray. When she smiled at them, Khalidah had the sudden and utter conviction that Sulayman would live.

Ghassan said, "*Sayyida*," and knelt before the old woman.

She smiled slightly, looking not at him but at Khalidah, then laid a hand on his head. Instantly, he fell asleep. She beckoned to Khalidah then with a gnarled hand. With the last of her strength, Khalidah dragged Sulayman toward the fire. The old woman smiled and nodded, and she laid him before her.

"Poor little thing, so lost," said the woman, in a voice like the wind among palm fronds, and though in fact Sulayman dwarfed the woman, the statement did not occur to Khalidah as odd. She laid a hand on Sulayman's burning forehead.

"Can you save him?" she asked.

The woman looked up at her again, her eyes deep with compassion. "I can divert death," she answered, with an equivocal look.

"Please, do it."

"In good time," the woman answered, and continued to stroke Sulayman's face as she might a favorite pet's. Her eyes were intent on Khalidah, boring deep into her. "What about you?" she asked. "Why have you come here?"

"I came for his sake," Khalidah answered resolutely.

"That is not all," the woman said, "and it will do you no good to deny it. Every longing means something, Khalidah. Would it comfort you to know a bit of your destiny?"

Khalidah looked at her, confused, anxious and desperately tired. "Should it?"

The woman gave her a smile of surprising sweetness. "You ask the right questions; in youth, that's rarer than gold. Very well then, I'll tell you only this: in choosing Shambhala, you chose correctly."

"Shambhala?"

"Shambhala...Eden...Qaf..." The woman shrugged. "But choosing correctly does not guarantee ease. Your road will have many turnings. Some lead to battles, others to peace; some to loss and some to joy. You will be mourned by many when you are gone." She paused, her green eyes glinting. "Are you certain that you do not want to know more?"

Khalidah shook her head. The woman smiled again, perhaps in approval. "You have carried him a long way," she said, "but he is safe now. Sleep."

Khalidah wanted to argue, but she found that she could no longer keep her eyes open. She lay down where she was, and it seemed there was a pillow beneath her head and a blanket covering her, though she was certain they had not been there a moment ago. The last thing she saw before sleep took her was the old woman crumbling herbs into a copper basin, as she hummed Khalidah's own tune to Shánfara's ode.

*

Khalidah dreamed that she fell through time, lighting now and then on scenes that flared with a crystalline clarity. She saw people in furs on a land of ice, then the young green of new gardens. Black-haired riders with slanted eyes galloped westward over vast plains of grass. Three little ships like walnut-shells, their sails crossed with red like the Templars' mantles, battled a wide, stormy sea. In one vision she stood in a sandstone room with a long window in one wall. Light poured through the window, and a woman sat haloed in its brightness, sewing. She had thick, black hair that nearly reached the floor, black eyes with a slight eastern tilt. She sang in a foreign tongue with a voice of such sweetness that it made Khalidah's eyes sting with tears.

The darkness opened beneath her, seared suddenly with light. Two armies faced each other, darkening the bright sands of a valley. On either side there were wooded hills, and far off in the distance, a vastness of water. Their standards waved in the morning breeze, on one side the red-crossed white of the Templars and white-crossed black of the Hospitallers, the colorful banners of the great houses of the Franj; on the other the warrior houses of Islam, yellow for the Ayyubids and *mamalik*, green and white for the Fatimids, black for the Seljuqs. The armies came together with a roar like thunder, the ground shook, and they were lost in the great clouds of dust they raised. Khalidah heard her own voice crying, "Now!" and then she pitched downward toward the storm of flesh and steel.

Just before she entered it, she jerked awake. Her pounding heart slowed gradually as she took in her surroundings, though at first she could not think where she was. She lay on an old reed mat on the floor of a cave, covered with her blanket. Beside her were the cold remains of a fire, touched here and there by sunlight streaming through chinks in the rocky roof. A battered copper bowl sat beside it, with what looked like the residue of an herbal decoction scumming the bottom.

Sulayman and Ghassan lay on the other side of the spent fire. Khalidah scrambled to Sulayman's side, fearing the worst, but found that he breathed easily. When she touched his cheek, it was cool. She sat back and looked around at the bare stone walls, her mind tumbling with confused images of flowers and foliage and a woman with an old face and a young voice who spoke in riddles, before sending her to sleep. But it all tangled up with her dreams, until she could not be sure that any of it had really happened.

She awakened Ghassan first. "Was she real?" she demanded. "Was any of it real?"

Ghassan nodded toward Sulayman. "You tell me."

Khalidah sighed, dropping her head into her hands. "Who was she?"

"Ameretat," Ghassan answered.

"Who?"

"Ameretat. One of the Amesha Spentas…a kind of goddess. She personifies immortality, and she is also the protector of plants."

Khalidah looked at him incredulously. "You expect me to believe that we've slept in the home of a Persian goddess?"

"I don't expect you to believe anything, except that we have slept in the home of someone called Ameretat, and she has saved the life of our friend."

Khalidah sighed again. "Well, what now?"

"Now," said Ghassan, reaching for Wasim's tack, "you must be on your way, and I on mine."

"Aren't you coming with us?"

Ghassan smiled and shook his head. "This is your journey, Khalidah; yours and his." He nodded to Sulayman. "But stop by my way when you return, if you can, and tell me how you have fared." He looked at her, and his eyes softened. "Say good-bye to him for me."

"Don't you want to wait and say it yourself?"

Ghassan shook his head. "He won't remember any of this, and that's probably just as well. Let him think that you left me in the marshes, and he recovered on his own."

Khalidah looked at the man; then she knelt before him, taking his hands in hers and touching them to her forehead. "Thank you, Ghassan. And I'm sorry – "

"Don't be sorry," Ghassan said. "Live truly." He kissed her forehead, then he led his horse toward the door, disappearing into the rising sun.

23

"Hush!" Bilal whispered, putting his hand over Salim's mouth. "You will be heard."

The prince lifted his hand away, lacing his fingers through Bilal's. "'The secret of love,'" he said, eyes glinting with mischief in the light of the hanging oil lamp, "'how can it be contained?'"

"I don't know, but you must learn to contain it, unless you'd like your guards to join us."

"Who knows? Perhaps that would be amusing."

"You're hopeless!" Bilal said, and rolled away from him.

But after a moment he felt Salim's fingers on his back, gentle as water, and when he spoke again he had lowered his voice. "'Beloved like a hart, with the heart of a panther…if you desire to slay, my heart is in your hand as clay.'"

"A poem?" asked Bilal, who could never maintain exasperation with Salim for long. "Is it yours?"

Salim laughed softly. "A poem. Certainly not mine." He kissed Bilal's shoulder. "'Beloved, like a scarlet cord his lips, burning like fire for they are his censer, and in them is the work of his signs…'"

"The poet is speaking of Allah."

"Yahweh, in fact. Isaac Ibn Abraham. He is a Jew from Al-Andalus."

Bilal said nothing, though inwardly he burned for his

ignorance.

"But what does it matter?" Salim continued, oblivious to Bilal's shame. "Don't the Sufis tell us that Allah resides in the love one being feels for another?"

"Do they?" Bilal asked quietly.

"'To watch and listen to those two is to understand how, as it's written, sometimes when two beings come together, Allah becomes visible.'"

Bilal shivered with the beauty of the words, of the passion with which Salim spoke them, wishing that he could match them. Sometimes it seemed that regret made up the better part of his love for Salim; regret that deepened when Salim misread it, as he did now.

"Do you still believe that what we do is wrong?" he asked.

"No," Bilal said, finally turning to face him. Salim's eyes were black wings in the lamplight, his mouth a split plum. "I never did. It's only that sometimes I am reminded that I'm unworthy of you."

"How can you say that?" Salim asked, genuinely incredulous.

If only you knew, Bilal thought, sighing. He said, "I do not know any poems, nor half of what you take for granted."

"You have only to ask. I'll send to Damascus for books – "

"Books I cannot read," Bilal said with quiet bitterness.

"Then I will teach you," Salim said, without hesitation.

If Bilal had not already loved him, he would have then for those words alone; and so he spoke before he thought: "Khalidah always said that one day she would ask her father for a tutor who could teach us to read – " He stopped abruptly, but it was too late.

"Khalidah?" Salim repeated with sudden interest. "Is she not the woman your cousin Numair was to marry?"

"She is," Bilal said after a pause.

"But if the clans of your tribe were at war, how is it that you were in a position to be taught by her tutors?"

There was no accusation in his tone, only curiosity. Bilal drew a deep breath, and answered: "Because I grew up in 'Abd al-Aziz's camp, not 'Abd al-Hadi's. My mother looked after Khalidah after her own mother died. I ended up with Numair because..." Bilal sighed, wondering how to lie without quite lying. At last he said, "I suppose, indirectly, because of Khalidah. When she disappeared, it confused everything. No one even knew whether or not we were still at war. Then word came that your father had called for *jihad*, and the debate about whether or not to go after Khalidah turned into a debate about whether or not to join the Sultan's army. I'd been thinking of leaving the tribe anyway, and so when Numair said that he was going north...well, I suppose events just threw us together."

It sounded ridiculous even to him, yet when he ventured a look at Salim he found the prince's eyes deep with thought, not suspicion. Salim said, "That's all very interesting – really, I had no idea Bedu politics were so complicated – but you must realize that what I really want to know is whether or not this woman, Khalidah, was your lover."

Bilal stared at him for a moment and then burst into laughter, as much for relief as for the absurdity of the idea. "Khalidah was my best friend – almost a sister, since we were the same age and brought up together. As for love..." He shook his head.

"What? Is she very ugly?"

Once again, Bilal laughed. "No, she is not ugly. But she was the sheikh's daughter, and I was only another boy from the tribe."

"You are *not* only another boy," Salim answered. "And besides, she ran away with a minstrel. Class can't have figured much into her choice of men." Bilal only shrugged, and after a moment Salim continued, clearly enjoying himself, "So, we have a headstrong desert princess who is not ugly, with a wild Khorasani mother...I suppose she can ride like the wind, fight like a warrior and look fetching covered in a day's sweat and dust?"

"Often all three at once," Bilal answered, grinning.

Salim rolled his eyes, shook his head. "You loved her. You cannot tell me you didn't."

"Yes, I loved her," Bilal said, suddenly serious, "but that is not what you asked. I loved her as a friend – as one lonely child loves another. We were both outcasts in our tribe, she because of her mother's blood and I...well, for my own reasons. Yes, there was a time when I thought that I wanted more from her than friendship..."

"But?"

"She did not want me." Bilal looked shyly up at Salim, his pale eyes prismatic in the lamplight. "And now, I am glad of it. Now I know that she never lived in my heart."

Salim blinked, then smiled in pleased surprise. He touched Bilal's cheek. Bolstered by this, and the courage of confession, Bilal put words to something he had kept close for a long time: "And you, Salim? Have there been others before me...others, I mean, like this?" He gestured to their shared bed, its storm of tumbled blankets.

Salim gave him an arch smile. "I did not think that the stoic nomad would succumb to jealousy." Bilal frowned, and he relented. "There have been girls like your Khalidah – and a couple of boys – whom I thought I loved and were far beyond my reach; and there have been others whom I knew I didn't, and who weren't." He paused, then said, "I may not have been a virgin when we met, Bilal, but what went before was merely the satisfaction of lust. You alone are the heart of my heart."

Bilal shivered at the words, both for their sweetness and their implicit challenge to all the impossibilities of this love. Salim, mistaking it for cold, slipped his arms around him, and Bilal shut his eyes, curled his fingers in Salim's hair, and let himself believe, for a little while, that love could vanquish threat as easily as it could the freezing desert night.

*

"A full week we have been here," Salah ad-Din said as he poured the tea, first into Bilal's glass, then into Salim's, and finally his own, "with all as quiet as a Franj monastery."

He paused, looking out at the camp's morning bustle with

narrowed eyes. The front of his pavilion had been rolled up and
the sunlight glinted on the ruby on his turban and the golden
embroidery on his red robes. Bilal wondered what had made him
decide to dress like a king here – which was more or less the
middle of nowhere – when his raiment had been so self-effacing
at the court-like Ras al-Mai'. But then, he had long since given
up trying to understand the Sultan's motivations, finding the
man's mind as labyrinthine as the sandstone wadis of his home.

"The men are getting fat," the Sultan concluded, frowning.

"I hardly think it likely, on our rations," Salim answered
dryly.

"Save your wit for the bedroom," the Sultan retorted, with
a pointed glance at Bilal, at which Bilal flushed. "I am telling
you that we must have action, before these men forget entirely
what the word means." He drank, then said, "That is why I am
sending you south: to find us someone who requires salvation,
protection, or whatever else might provide occupation for an
elite band of soldiers."

"Shall I go to Kerak?" Salim asked with palpable hope.

"Absolutely not," his father retorted.

"But it would be useful to know what Arnat is up to."

"I know what he is up to," said Salah ad-Din. "He is in Al-
Quds with the other nobles, trying to prod their king into some
kind of action against Raymond of Tripoli. They'll probably
succeed, too, and sooner rather than later…of course, they will
not be expecting Tripoli's new Muslim guard."

A shade of a smile crossed his face; then it faded, and he
focused his avid eyes once again on his son. "At any rate, as Arnat
is currently occupied, this is the ideal time for reconnaissance. If
possible, we must find out exactly how strong Kerak is – which
of his family are in residence, how many knights in the garrison,
the state of their supplies, water – "

"You intend to besiege them?" Salim asked, sipping his tea and
then setting the glass aside. Bilal could not help watching him;
the prince's grace was mesmerizing. The Sultan too was watching
his son, and Bilal thought that there was a glint of approval in

that look, however deeply buried. He wondered why the man wanted to hide it.

"I would rather it didn't come to that," Salah ad-Din said at last. "Not yet, anyway. I cannot waste the time or the men right now. But on the other hand, if Arnat's forces can be contained, then Jerusalem's army is significantly weakened. Let us leave further speculation until such time as we are equipped with facts."

Abruptly he turned to Bilal. "You say the clans of your tribe have a long-standing feud. Did you yourself ever take part in a *ghazw*?"

Surprised, Bilal answered, "Only as a scout, Your Highness."

The Sultan studied him for a moment, then he said, "The Bedu are without a doubt the finest *ghuzat* I have ever seen. I am hoping that you can teach my son something about their raiding tactics; as such, you will accompany him south." He turned back to Salim. "You will leave this evening. Go now and prepare your men."

The two boys bowed to the Sultan, and left him looking thoughtfully after them.

*

Salim laughed when Bilal asked him if he thought that his father suspected the nature of their relationship. "Do you think that my father does not know of everything that happens in his camp?" He laughed again at Bilal's look of horror. "I assure you, he knew the exact moment that you came to my bed, and he doesn't care. Why should he? You are not a maiden with a bride price or gold-digging father to threaten his honor; nor are you a married woman who could ruin mine. Besides, we are not the only lovers here. It is a part of life in a mobile army, when men are far from their wives and whores forbidden."

Daunted nevertheless by these revelations, Bilal threw himself gladly into the preparations for their departure. They rode out at dusk with little ceremony. The Sultan and his son nodded to each other, but exchanged no words. All that they might have said was gathered in the look they gave each other before Salim wheeled his horse, and his father turned back toward his tent: love tempered by disappointment, pride by doubt. Bilal knew that Salim ached with them. He had never lamented so bitterly that the nature of their love made it impossible to take Salim in his arms right then and hold him until the pain had passed.

Instead, he gave Anjum her head and tried to lose himself in the visceral perfection of her speed. The *saqa* rode throughout that night, and finally stopped in the lee of a low *tal* covered in the sand of many years' abandonment. They did not bother to set up tents, but lay down on their blankets wherever they could find a blank bit of sand and waited for dawn.

*

When Bilal awakened, Salim's blankets were already neatly rolled beside his. He looked around and saw the prince kneeling inside a low, open pavilion that had been set up against the rising wind. He was poring over a map with two of his *umara*. When he caught sight of Bilal he beckoned him over.

"We are here," he said, pointing to an area northeast of the village of Amman. "The town's garrison is small, and that makes it a good place to begin."

Instinctively, Bilal was calculating the distance between Amman and Kerak, though he had no idea whether his father was likely to be at one or the other, at the Temple in Jerusalem or, for that matter, marching north this very moment to deliver Tripoli an ultimatum. He wished that he had thought to learn more about the nature of de Ridefort's movements when he had the chance, for in the intervening months he had developed an overwhelming fear of meeting him somewhere unexpectedly. But until recently – until he met Salim, if he was honest with himself – it had never occurred to him that he could control any part of his destiny. When he thought about it now, Bilal was disgusted with himself.

"And what will we do there?" he asked, when it became clear that Salim and his men were waiting for a response.

To his dismay, the *umara* only continued in their expectant look, and Salim gave him a quizzical half-smile. "That is for you to tell us, *Sayyid*," he said.

"Me! But I know nothing about such things!"

"Did you not tell my father that you had participated in your tribe's *ghazawat*?"

Bilal sighed, running a hand over his short hair, which he had not yet covered. "Against other tribes, yes. But a Bedu camp is not a Franj garrison."

Despite this information, the *umara'* looks grew no less intent. Sighing again, Bilal sat down with them. "A Bedu *ghazw* is about stealth and speed: engaging the enemy when he does not expect it, killing him quickly, carrying away the prize before he even suspects that you desire it…" He realized with surprise that his heart beat quickly with the memory, and he ached with a sharp, unexpected nostalgia. "But this cannot interest you."

Salim's calm smile never shifted. "In fact, it interests me greatly," he said. "Though the prize here is information, not heads – not that my father would look askance at a few dead Franj – it can be won only by stealth and speed. So…" He handed Bilal the map. "I've showed you our camp, and Amman. These marks are wadis, these others hills and *tals*. Please, advise us."

For a long moment Bilal looked at Salim, searching for condescension, but there was none. So he looked down at the map, and drawing a deep breath he said, "We will begin here…"

24

Sulayman didn't ask any questions, either when he awakened in the cave or in the following days. Perhaps he knew the answers already, or else he was too grateful for his sudden, blooming health to question it. Either way, Khalidah was content to allow the story of their strange night in the cave to remain unspoken.

Ghassan had left them the pony, and they traveled more quickly now that the horses carried less weight, winding their way through the mountains on paths almost as familiar to Sulayman as they had been to Ghassan. At last the hills grew gentler and the air warmer. They descended toward a desert of searing brightness, patched in wide, white glittering mosaics of austere beauty. Khalidah was almost wild with joy at the thought of letting Zahirah run again, but when she said so to Sulayman, he shook his head grimly.

"What you see down there is not sand, but salt," he said. "It is a *kavir* – a salt desert. This part of Persia is covered with them. Once they were marshes, and beneath the salt crust there is still a layer of silt that would devour you like quicksand if you broke through. There are safe passages across them all, if you know how to find them, and there is one here that crosses near the mountain called Shir Kuh. But there will be no running."

"And once we cross it? What then?"

"We'll head south-east, past Yazd."

"We should stop there. We're running low on supplies."

"Yes, and we'll also need warmer clothes for Khorasan. But

we cannot stop at Yazd; we've told too many people that story.
We can make it a bit further on the supplies we have left, if we're
careful. Let's try for Ravar."

Khalidah had no idea where Ravar was. She sighed, resigning
herself to further days of subsistence on stale almonds and
camel's milk. Still, she was glad enough of Sulayman's health that
even these hardships didn't dampen her spirits for long. That
afternoon they descended into a sun-seared, rocky valley which
gradually gave way to the *kavir*, where a hot wind blasted across
the salt flats. Sulayman moved carefully along a tortuous path
among them, which to Khalidah was indiscernible.

However, any doubt she had in his judgment disappeared
when, in a moment of carelessness, she allowed the pony to step
to the left of the invisible path, and the animal plunged screaming
into the salty sand up to her shoulder. By dumb luck Khalidah
had kept hold of the lead rein. Sulayman eased the pack saddle
off of the struggling pony. Her rear end was free but floundering,
and it took all of them, humans and horses, to pull her free. It
was a long time before she was calm enough to accept the saddle
again, longer still before Khalidah stopped shaking.

After several more grueling hours the ground finally began to
rise again, and at last the treacherous sand became stone beneath
the horses' feet. They had come into a wide valley fenced on both
sides by jagged peaks. For the first time in days, the horses could
move with ease. Tossing her head, Zahirah broke into a canter,
but Khalidah, still shaken by their near miss, pulled her back to a
walk. As the sun sank behind them, a mountain emerged ahead,
its peak thrusting free of the others around it.

"Shir Kuh," said Sulayman, squinting through the horizontal
rays of the dying sun. "The Lion's Mountain. Time to stop."

They made camp in the brief twilight, in a wide, rocky cave
in the shadow of the great mountain, near a tiny, stony pool
that Sulayman had uncovered with what Khalidah was beginning
to believe to be a sixth sense for water. But when she lay down
on her blanket, despite the distance they had traveled that day,
Khalidah couldn't sleep.

"What are you thinking of?" Sulayman asked from the near-dark of the dying fire a few feet away.

"Home," she answered; but there was no wistfulness in her voice. After a moment she continued, "I wonder what has happened to the tribe – whether they have joined the Sultan as my father wished, or run like cowards with my uncle."

"I imagine the answer is a good deal more complicated than either one."

Khalidah was silent for a moment, then she said, "I can't stop thinking about what Ghassan said...that the timing of all of this is Allah's work. Do you think...I mean, could it be that the Jinn might fight for Salah ad-Din? That that is the purpose of our journey?"

Sulayman sighed. "Again, I think only that the answer will prove more complicated than that."

"If they did mean to join the *jihad*," Khalidah persisted, "would we even make it back in time?"

"Salah ad-Din keeps to the traditional battle season," Sulayman answered. "He won't challenge the Franj until summer. If we go on as we did today, we will make it to Qaf in time to be home by midsummer. But that assumes that we do not plan to stay there long."

If, Khalidah thought; but she didn't speak her doubts aloud. "Sulayman?"

"Yes?"

"Thank you."

"For what?"

She had intended a simple answer, a gesture of gratitude for all he had shown her she was capable of. But all that came was the memory of his fever, of the tremulous tide of his breathing. There were no words for that, but she thought that he had seen some of it in the look on her face. He extended his hand to her through the ember-red light. She met it with her own, clutched it as she had when she thought that he might be dying. It was only now, though, that she realized why.

Spreading her fingers like the petals of a lotus, he kissed her palm.

*

Just before dawn, the earth buckled. At first it was gentle, and Khalidah only half-awakened. Then rocks began falling like frozen rain, and Sulayman was dragging her out of the cave as its stones began to shift, and finally to topple. All around them the earth was tearing itself apart in screeches and groans, drowning out the terrified screams of the horses. They only managed to catch them because the animals were too afraid to know where to run; Khalidah wrapped her sash around Zahirah's neck and held on grimly as the horse reared and plunged. She knew well enough that if they lost the horses, they were finished.

The earthquake seemed to last forever, but in fact it could only have been a few seconds. When it was over, Khalidah stood shaking, trying to calm her horse and calling for Sulayman. "Here!" he cried at last, and leading Zahirah toward his voice, Khalidah found him far down the valley, holding the pony's rein with one hand and trying to soothe 'Aasifa with the other.

"Are you all right?" he asked.

"Yes," Khalidah said. They both stood for a moment, listening to the last falling pebbles settle. "Will it come back?"

"Not like that," Sulayman answered. "But sometimes there are smaller ones for a few days afterward."

"What will we do?"

He sighed. "Sleep in the open tonight. Even if the cave is not covered, it will not be safe. Tomorrow, we'll see if any of our things have survived."

When the horses were finally calm, they hobbled them and lay down in the lea of a boulder that sheltered them from the wind. Despite it, and Sulayman's body close against hers, Khalidah never shut her eyes again that night. When the sun rose and she looked at him, she knew that he hadn't either. He ran a hand over her rough hair, and then got up to check the horses.

'Aasifa and the pony were unscathed, though the mare had relapsed into her old skittishness, and she wouldn't let Sulayman touch her head. Zahirah had a long cut on her back right leg.

There was no heat in it, but it was deep.

"I would know what to do if I were back home," Khalidah said, "but here…"

"We can do nothing but wrap it and go on," Sulayman finished. "Come, let's see if there's anything left for bandages."

They picked their way through the rubble of shattered stone until they saw the corner of Sulayman's saddle-blanket protruding from a pile of sand and scree. Digging around, they gradually uncovered the rest of their belongings. Two of their three skins of water had burst, but miraculously, Sulayman's *qanun* had survived. Khalidah picked it up and plucked a string.

"Some angel watches over you, Sulayman," she said.

He smiled, but his eyes were sober. "Don't say that until we've made it to the next well on one skin of water."

As she handed the instrument back to him, she asked what she had been too shy to ask before: "Will you teach me to play it?"

The question didn't appear to surprise him. "If we find ourselves in favorable circumstances," he answered, wrapping it up again.

They re-buried what was damaged beyond repair, in case they were still being followed, then they bound Zahirah's leg and set off again. They hadn't ridden long, however, when they found their path blocked by two boulders apparently shifted by the earthquake. As Khalidah led Zahirah around them onto the slope where they had lain, she found herself walking on a monster's trail: five footprints stamped into the stone, the tracks of a three-toed beast, each as long as her fore-arm from toe to heel.

"Must we face dragons now, too?" she asked Sulayman, who had come up behind her.

He studied the prints thoughtfully for a moment, then he said, "Once in these mountains I broke a stone while trying to light a fire. When the two halves came apart I found between them the imprint of a fish's bones. I took it to Yazd to sell it, thinking that such a wonder would fetch a fortune, but I was promptly directed to a man in the marketplace with a table full of such stones. He paid me a pittance for mine, and told me that the mountains of

Persia yield many such wonders, and far greater ones too. He said these hills are the graveyard of creatures that roamed the earth before men – giant lizards and birds without feathers and long-toothed fishes such as we cannot imagine – and that time turned their bones to stone. Perhaps the same has happened to their footprints."

"The Qur'an says nothing of giant birds and lizards," Khalidah said skeptically.

"And the Qur'an tells us that the Jinn are made of fire."

Khalidah sighed. "A world ruled by monsters," she said, and a chilling image flashed through her mind: that on the other side of these mountains they would find not the city of Yazd or the town of Ravar, but a desolate plain where great scaled creatures roared and clashed. "I am tired of Persia," she said.

Sulayman laughed. "You have not seen Persia. Someday I hope to show it to you, for you would not find a more splendid country if you traveled the world from one end to the other."

"Not even Qaf?" Khalidah asked softly.

"Qaf…" Sulayman said after a pause. "Sometimes I think it is a world unto itself." He stood and led 'Aasifa forward, and they left the monster's trail to the mercy of time.

25

Amman was as old as Busra, with its own Roman amphitheatre and prehistoric ruins, and a history of modest significance under the early Islamic dynasties. But time had not treated it well. After its brief flowering under the Abbasids it was destroyed by earthquakes, and a long string of natural disasters foiled all attempts at rebuilding anything more than a village on the ancient site. No doubt it would finally have crumbled into oblivion if the Franj, in the course of their expansion, had not taken advantage of its situation at the edge of Oultrejourdain and built a minor fortress on the ruins of the citadel.

Even so, Amman was too far from Jerusalem or Damascus to merit much of an occupying force. Building had been hasty, and on the mild dawn when Salim's scouts went to study the fortifications, they found themselves looking at a squat hill-tower ringed by a ditch and castrum, surrounded by the crumbling remains of far older and more impressive structures. At full strength it could not have housed more than thirty men, but the scouts estimated the garrison currently numbered half that.

"And they do not look like knights to me," Salim concluded, moving away from the window of the ruined house from which he was watching the fortress. Reluctantly, Bilal took his place. Though he was no expert, de Ridefort had taught him enough to recognize the two guards stationed at the gate as infantry. Though logic had told him that this paltry outpost would never be manned by Templars, he could not contain a sigh as anxiety temporarily released him.

"Indeed," Salim said, misreading it, "they should not give us too much trouble, assuming we can lure them out…though I wonder if it is even worth the effort. Those men do not look the sort to possess the kind of information that would interest us. Perhaps we should try further south."

He pulled absently on a tendril of hair, his eyes fixed on the window in speculation. Bilal knew Salim well enough by now to realize that he was soliciting affirmation rather than opinion, but they were already closer than he had ever wanted to be to the castle his father frequented. And so he said, "I would not be too quick to dismiss it."

"I'm listening," Salim said, turning to him with a quick, birdlike intensity.

Bilal continued, "Going south is full of risk. The castles down there are some of the strongest in the Franj kingdom, and the land around them is terrible for reconnaissance – barren desert, flat as a platter. If we were to be spotted, there would be nowhere to run to. But this garrison," he gestured to the window, "looks to be made up of infantry. They'd make easy prisoners; in fact, if it came to it, we'd probably have a good chance of taking the entire fortress."

"Do you think so?" Salim asked, a sparkle of inspiration beginning in his eyes.

"I did not mean to suggest that we *should*," Bilal said quickly, "only that we might."

Salim's look went to the window. "Think what my father would say if I won him a Franj castle."

"Salim."

"Bilal?" Salim's mouth twitched into the beginnings of the smile Bilal had come to fear, for in the face of it, he could not deny Salim anything. "What is there to lose? We can only fail, and my father expects that already. So, are you with me?"

He touched his fingers to Bilal's own. The contact was slight, but like lightning grazing a tent pole, it seared straight through Bilal. He closed his fingers briefly around Salim's, and as Salim's smile blossomed, sweet with love, with trust, Bilal wondered if there would ever be a day when he did not despise himself.

*

Bilal had hoped that the *umara* would talk Salim out of his plan to capture the fortress, but he had underestimated the effects of so many months of boredom. They had supported the idea unanimously, gathering in his tent that evening to devise a plan of attack.

"I have no doubt that we can cut them down like so many stalks of wheat," Salim said, "if we can only draw them out. This, you see, is our problem."

"I have seen the Sultan use a *tal* or a sand hill to hide a band of cavalry," said a Kurdish *amir*, a short, solid man called al-Khani, "then lure the enemy into a fight with what they believe to be an inferior force. Perhaps something similar would work here."

"I know this tactic that you speak of," Salim answered, "but I've only ever seen my father use it when engaging a force far from its home territory. Here, we are cavalry against foot soldiers, which is no real contest. Even if we were fairly matched, the Franj would still be fools to leave the safety of their fortress without good reason."

"We could give them reason," said a tall, mournful Turk universally known by the nickname Al-'Aboos, "the frowner". "There are, after all, women and children in the town."

Salim resolutely shook his head. "I will not use the weak and the innocent to reach my ends; such intimidation is for the likes of Arnat. Besides, you know what my father would say to it, and my father must not find fault with this mission."

They nodded agreement, even Al-'Aboos, but Bilal knew that they didn't begin to understand. Of all of them, he was the only one who knew exactly what hung for Salim in the balance of his father's approval. Moreover, the answer to the prince's dilemma had been painfully obvious to Bilal all along. He was still uncertain about the plan, but he could not bear to see the doubt creeping across Salim's face.

"I know a way to draw them out," he said, "one that endangers none but those who raise their swords against us." Immediately, he had the *umara'* attention. He took a deep breath and continued, "Though the Franj see 'Saracens' as infidels, they respect us in their way, because we adhere to codes of honor which they recognize. But to them, Bedu are not Saracens. In their eyes, nomad tribes are lawless devils who cannot be trusted, allies one day and raiders the next, pillaging their towns and farms without mercy or honor…and perhaps in some ways their view is justified, for a band of Bedu *ghuzat* would not be here now, discussing how best to draw the soldiers forth and spare the women. To a *ghazi,* the women would be part of the prize. So if the men of the garrison can be made to believe that we are *ghuzat*…"

Bilal stopped, confounded by the weight of all the eyes on him. Many of them were cold with jealousy, but Salim paid them no attention.

"Tell me," he said, "how many *ghuzat* would be required to rouse the garrison?"

Bilal shrugged. "If we time it right, then only enough to be identified as such. Just before dawn, for instance, the soldiers will be sleepy and confused, unable to assess our numbers properly. If we are very lucky, and enough of them are drawn into the fight, we might even take the fortress before they realize what has happened…"

Bilal broke off again, still not quite believing that this idea was his. But Salim's delighted smile convinced him.

*

Before daybreak the next morning they were all in position. Salim and the main body of the *saqa* hid behind a *tal* at the back of the fortress. They took all the precautions of stealth, wearing dark tunics and the minimum of metal, securing all the parts of the horses' tack that might clash or creak. Bilal and four other horsemen, dressed in their best approximation of nomads' robes, waited in the desert bordering the most populated portion of the town. They watched the sky for Salim's naphtha flare, their signal to move, and at last it came, the flaming arrow burning white against the gray dawn.

"Ready?" Bilal said to his companions. They nodded. He gave a wordless cry, and Anjum leapt into the darkness like a shooting star. They swept through the straggling town like revenants, the horses' shoes striking sparks from the paving stones, their torches streaming comet tails behind, leaving flames and tattered screams in their wake. Though they touched no woman or child – Salim had been clear from the beginning that anyone who broke this rule would pay with his life – more than one townsman tried to engage them, and more than one fell. They were old men and boys, unsuitable for service in the fortress or the king's army, and none of them should have been out of their beds, let alone engaging professional cavalry. In his heart, Bilal cursed them for fighting; but they did fight, and so he had no choice but to cut them down.

It didn't take long to reach the fortress against such slight resistance, but still the news of their presence had preceded them. The garrison poured from the open gates as Bilal's band approached, the Franj soldiers half-dressed and wild-eyed and numbering not more than a dozen. They realized their mistake almost immediately, but it was too late. As if by magic, the little band of Bedu raiders had become a ring of *tawashiyah*, closing in on them from all sides. For a moment there was total, taut silence; then, with an anonymous cry, the cavalry and the foot-soldiers fell upon each other.

Bilal hovered at the edge of the fray, watching with morbid fascination as Salim's horsemen decimated the Franj with apparent effortlessness. He had always felt that a pitched battle had a certain bleak integrity to it, but this was not a battle: it didn't even have a *ghazw*'s structure of honor to rationalize it. The Franj had never had a chance, yet they fought bravely, and

Bilal could not help feeling for them, as he always felt for the vanquished. He caught a glimpse of Salim as his horse reared, yellow tunic lashed with blood and face ablaze with violent rapture. For a moment he hated him for his very righteousness; and then he looked down.

By his knee was a Franji, one of a few civilians who had come to the aid of the floundering garrison. He was about Bilal's age, with colorless hair and a pockmarked face that was almost nondescript, except for the conviction that shone from it with the brilliance of a sunrise. Bilal faltered, and nearly paid with his life. But Anjum was not troubled by human sentiment, and with her breed's innate good sense and her own meticulous training, she wheeled as the little Franji raised his sword and struck, taking the blow on her own flank and saving her master. In that moment, Bilal felt himself surface from the torpor that had subsumed him when Numair and de Ridefort co-opted him for their plot. He was filled with a sudden, overwhelming rage at the Franj – for forcing his lies, for daring to fight them, for being here at all. He turned Anjum back then and dropped the boy with a slash to the neck, and felt nothing but triumph as he watched him die.

*

"So Amman surrendered," the Sultan said as they sat in his tent that evening, looking at his son with eyes in which speculation had replaced censure. "You took no prisoners?"

Salim shook his head. "There were none to take. But there was this." He reached into his bloodstained tunic and pulled out a piece of parchment with a broken red seal, which depicted a running wolf. He could not conceal the flush of pride as he handed it to his father, and beneath it was a vulnerability that made Bilal wish he could tell Salim how well he understood him in that moment. Instead he kept his eyes cast down, but he stole glances at the Sultan as he read the letter.

"So, it is as I had hoped," Salah ad-Din said at last, his thin lips now curved in a faint smile of his own. "Better, even – every one of the southern lords in Jerusalem trying to bend the king's ear on the issue of Tripoli, and a frontier town taken from under their noses…indeed, it could not be better. You have done well, my son." The prince flushed more deeply still, and smiled at his hands.

"And you, al-Hassani." The Sultan turned to Bilal. "I hear that this success is due in large part to your inspiration." He paused, fixing Bilal with his golden-brown eyes, more intent than ever. "I admit that I had my doubts about you and your cousin when you joined us. I had heard rumors to suggest…" He trailed off, his look turning inward. "At any rate, I am glad to find that you have vindicated yourself." It was not lost on Bilal that he said nothing about Numair. "I hope that you will join us in our next venture."

Bilal inclined his head, wishing that etiquette allowed him to ask what that would be. But the next moment Salim voiced the thought for him.

The Sultan raised a quizzical eyebrow. "You tell me."

"Kerak!" Salim answered, his eyes bright with anticipation.

This time, the cloudbreak smile. "Good boy. Now go and tell your men we ride at dawn."

26

On the sixth day after the earthquake Sulayman and Khalidah finally saw the minarets of Yazd thrusting into the hazy morning sky. But their food ran out well before Ravar, and they were forced to stop at a nameless town in the foothills preceding the Dasht-e-Lut, the vast salt desert at Persia's heart. The town was inhabited by a flock of fat-tailed sheep and their minders, a tribe of semi-nomads with bright, finely-woven clothing and cutthroats' eyes. They did, however, have a well, plus ample stores of dried meat and apricots, and they were willing to trade. They spoke a quick, guttural dialect of Persian, and since Khalidah's grasp of the language had been gleaned from classical poetry, she let Sulayman do the bartering. But she understood well enough when the tribe's chief demanded Zahirah's silver bridle-pendant as payment.

"It seems a lot for a few bits of desiccated mutton," she said to Sulayman.

"On the contrary, it is a bargain," he answered. When she opened her mouth to answer, he said, "A useless scrap of metal in exchange for a chance of surviving the Dasht-e-Lut – or do you prefer to eat sand tonight?"

She pulled the pendant off of the bridle and handed it to the chief, who looked at it, tested its authenticity with teeth the color of dried palm leaves, and then pocketed it. Negotiations

complete, the people turned suddenly hospitable, urging
Khalidah and Sulayman to spend the night with them. Sulayman
finally managed to decline, but they did sit down for a glass of tea
in a black tent very like those of Khalidah's tribe. She sipped the
strong brew in a wallow of homesickness, then helped Sulayman
fill the water skins and load the new supplies onto the pony, and
they set off again.

That night they reached the fringes of the Dasht-e-Lut. It was
an eerie place, gray and empty, the sand a strange, coarse mixture
of grit and salt and pebbles that ran before a fierce north wind.
The upper layers visibly undulated like ocean waves, shattering
against dunes as high as the foothills Khalidah and Sulayman had
just left behind. They stopped in the lea of one of these great hills.
There was no fuel for a fire, nothing for them to do but huddle
together against the stinging wind and listen to its keening as the
sky grew dark.

"I'm afraid that the *qanun* lesson will have to wait again,"
Sulayman said at last. "We can't even work on your reading in
this wind."

"It's all right," Khalidah answered. "There's time for both."

There was a long pause. Then he reached out, took her hand
and said, "Khalidah, there is something I have wanted to say to
you for many days."

Her skin tingled where their palms met. She could just make
out the features of his face in the last of the twilight. "What is it?"
she asked, working to keep her voice steady.

He drew a breath. "When we reach Qaf," he said, "I intend to
ask your grandfather to marry us. If you consent to it, that is – I
would rather have no wife at all than a dutiful one."

Khalidah sat for a moment in stunned silence. At last she said,
"I cannot agree to marry you at Qaf."

Though it was too dark now to see him, Khalidah could feel
Sulayman recoil, and then bristle. "I suppose it was presumptuous
to imagine that a sheikh's daughter would have a worthless
minstrel," he said bitterly, letting go of her hand, "but I am sure
you can see why I thought you felt differently."

His sudden coldness stung her like the wind-flung pebbles. "What fools you men can be!" she cried. "If you had listened beyond your pride, you would have heard me say *not* that I do not wish to marry you, only that I do not wish to do so at Qaf."

"Why not, then?" he said, chastened.

She sighed, the quick anger dissipating. "Because I know nothing of it, nor of what path my life or yours will take when we reach it. Because, however many moral laws I have broken by coming with you, I am still a Muslim, and if I am to marry I do not intend to do it among *kuffar*. But mostly because, if we were to lie together, we might start a child, and I do not intend to bring a child into the world unless I can offer him – or her – a secure place in it. My actions have made me an outcast among the only people I know, and you – forgive me for saying it, Sulayman, but it is the truth – have no people at all. Where would we live? How would we keep ourselves and our children?" She shook her head. "No – I will not marry you nor anyone until I know where I stand myself."

Khalidah lapsed into silence that grew more painful with every moment that Sulayman did not break it. She wondered if she had damaged their friendship irreparably. Then he said, "You are right, Khalidah – I am a fool." He touched her cheek with the tips of his fingers. "No promises, then. But if – when – we find solid ground, perhaps then I may hope for an answer?"

Khalidah took his face between her hands, glad that he could not see the tears in her eyes, and said, "I have answered already." And with a boldness gleaned from the fireless dark, she kissed him.

As always, they lay down at a chaste distance from one another, but they awakened at dawn to find their limbs tangled and Sulayman's desire quite obvious. Khalidah lay for a moment barely breathing, knowing that for all the clothing between them, she was as bare to him then as she would ever be to anyone. Then, recalling herself, she pulled away and sat up, shedding the sand that had drifted over them in the night. The dunes were the color of an old wound, the rising sun cauterized by a wind full of salt and the dust of dead armies. She bowed her head and felt Sulayman behind her, but she didn't know whether it was his fingers in her hair or the wind, moving with the inexorable hunger of a vine toward the light.

✦

Water determines the course of life, and in the vast central waste of Persia they saw none of either. They rode for days across the shifting dunes, and except for the steady course of the sun from their faces to their backs, they might never have moved at all. Near dark on one of the first days, they came to the ruins of what must once have been an oasis. There was a single, shallow pool of water in the parched stream-bed, which the horses drank dry in minutes.

"What happened here?" Khalidah asked, looking around at the dilapidated wooden shelters and a series of curious walls, also made of wood, with the wasted remains of shrubs and vines and a few twisted fruit-trees still clinging to the sand behind them.

"Wind," Sulayman said, trying the door of one of the huts, which promptly came away in his hands. "The oases in the Dasht-e-Lut are fickle. For a few years the spring meltwater or a *qanat* keeps one going, and people are able to grow a bit, to graze their animals. Then a sandstorm fills the stream or the source of the aqueduct and overnight, the oasis dies."

"And the people?" Khalidah asked.

Sulayman shrugged. "They move on. That's why they don't build to last." He nudged the fallen door with his foot and then, sighing, he put the horses in the most solid-looking shelter and chose the next best for himself and Khalidah. Its wood was bone-dry, and had shrunk so much that large gaps showed between the boards of the walls. The whole thing shuddered in each gust of wind. "At least there is a good supply of firewood," he said, dropping an armful of wind-blasted boards on the sand floor. "Listen – the wind is rising."

Khalidah listened and shivered, longing for a goat hair tent. She hated this dead place, and she knew that if the wind thrashed itself into a full sandstorm, they might be here for days. At least the horses had shelter, she reflected, and they were doing reasonably well for provisions.

Sulayman managed to light the fire, and they boiled water for tea. "This is a good night for the *qanun*," he said and so, when they had eaten, he unwrapped the instrument from its blankets. He tuned it, explained the rudiments of the technique, showed her how to place the plectra, and then set her some exercises. She repeated them dutifully, glad of the distraction from the shrieking gale outside, until Sulayman – who turned out to be a strict teacher – declared them passable.

"Will you play something now?" she asked.

Sulayman took the instrument and held it for a moment. Then, as on the night of her doomed henna ceremony, he began to pluck the strings in a kind of musical rumination that seemed to be his path into the music. After a time a melody emerged, slow and wistful, turning and twisting around one note like a banner its staff in a fluctuating breeze. Sulayman's music had previously been characterized by a bright, soaring virtuosity. This time the mastery was in the nuance, the delicate shifts of the variations, and the words, when he began to sing, mirrored the pattern of the music: no linear narrative but a series of scenes, joined like jewels by a repeated phrase which gradually disclosed the story of a tragic love.

> *"Even now,*
> *My thought is all of this gold-tinted king's daughter*
> *With garlands, tissue and golden buds,*
> *Smoke tangles of her hair, and sleeping or waking*
> *Feet trembling in love, full of pale languor;*
> *My thought is clinging as to a lost learning*
> *Slipped down out of the minds of men,*
> *Laboring to bring her back into my soul…*

"*Even now,*
When all my heavy heart is broken up
I seem to see my prison walls breaking
And then a light, and in that light a girl
Her fingers busied about her hair, her cool white arms
Faint rosy at the elbows, raised in the sunlight,
And temperate eyes that wander far away…"

The wind raged through the darkness, seeking the walls' disparity, and the words drove into Khalidah like a burning arrow bearing an image: a woman hardly beyond girlhood, fluttering silk the color of young leaves, tawny skin and a sweep of black hair that looked too heavy for her slender frame. She raised her arms in a flash and tumble of glass bangles, with a smile as sudden as desire.

"*Even now,*
Though I am so far separate, a flight of birds
Swinging from side to side over the valley trees,
Passing my prison with their calling and crying,
Bring me to see my girl…

"*Even now,*
Only one dawn shall rise for me. The stars
Revolve tomorrow's night and I not heed…"

The bright girl faded to a guttering lamp on a prison wall. The *qanun* exalted, Sulayman's voice mourned on and on, each line more beautiful than the last.

"*…Upon a day*
I saw strange eyes and hands like butterflies;
For me at morning larks flew from the thyme

And children came to bathe in little streams…

"Even now,
I know that I have savored the hot taste of life
Lifting green cups and gold at the great feast.
Just for a small and a forgotten time
I have had full in my eyes from off my girl
The whitest pouring of eternal light…"

The music trailed off into a half-cadence, faded into the moaning of the wind. Sulayman sat with his head bowed over his instrument, his forefingers still ringed by the plectra and hands resting on the strings. Khalidah watched him silently, tears streaming down her cheeks. At last he raised his head and set the *qanun* aside.

"Did you write it?" she asked.

"The music, yes; the words, I think, are Allah's."

"He spoke them to you?"

He smiled ruefully, shaking his head. "It's a very old poem. I first heard it from a blind bard from Hindustan, with whom I shared a room at a Kurdish inn for several nights. We were caught by snow, and passed the time exchanging poems. I am no scholar of Sanskrit, but the little I understood of this poem caught at me. I hounded him until he agreed to help me write it out. It was no easy task. Persian was our only common tongue, and neither of us fluent in it. But I put down the bones of it, and over the years it has become a bit of an obsession. I have sought out other versions, and gradually pieced together an Arabic translation, though I don't think that I have done the original any justice."

"And who wrote the original?"

Sulayman began to wrap the *qanun* carefully in its blanket again. "A poet called Chauras, or sometimes Bilhana," he said, "though that tells us little. By some accounts he was Brahman, by others Kashmiri. Likewise, he was engaged as court poet of different kings, depending on the teller, from Kashmir to Kerala, one hundred years ago or one thousand. But the heart of the story is always the same: he fell in love with the king's daughter, Vidya, and when their affair was discovered Chauras was sentenced to death. In the last few hours of his life he composed the poem, and when he was called upon before his execution to account for his actions, he recited it as his answer. Some say that the execution was carried out anyway; others, that the king was moved by the poet's words and spared him, marrying him to his daughter."

"Which do you believe?" asked Khalidah.

Sulayman sighed. "I would like to believe the latter, but I have known too many kings."

And no doubt some wanton princesses whom you've wooed with this sad story, Khalidah thought dismally, never imagining that Sulayman had not sung that poem aloud from the day he wrote down the blind man's translation until this night; still less that he had intended never to do so.

"Anyway, does it matter?" he continued. "Life is fragile, but truth is immortal. Chauras' words tell a truth that time can never erode. Few men can claim that."

"Perhaps one day you will teach it to me," she said.

In the dying firelight her eyes were a dark tide, her heart-shaped face a cipher. Sulayman knew that the poet's words rendered in her siren's voice would very likely flay him. He said, "We will start tomorrow."

27

Late afternoon, and the black king was faltering. The white knight's path ran clear to the black knight; taking him would open the black king to checkmate, and Bilal's first victory in the three days since Salim had taught him to play chess. They'd spent those days trapped by a violent wind in a narrow, nameless wadi in the wastes between Amman and Kerak. It had been long enough for Bilal to get a good sense of the nuances of the game, but not long enough for him to be able to beat Salim so completely.

He looked up at his friend. Salim leaned on hip and elbow, legs bent like a knight's hooked path behind him, face flitting in and out of shadow as tattered cloud tore the sky above. He wore a look of calm surmise, and a hint of the smile that had been there on the afternoon he offered Bilal his heart in the shape of a pomegranate seed. For a moment Bilal hesitated; then he took a black fortress with a pawn.

"I've taught you better than that," Salim said.

"You were letting me win."

"You don't know that."

Bilal didn't answer. For a moment the sun carved a fickle script of shadow on the wadi's sandstone walls, then it retreated again. Salim sat up and cleared the board with a sweep of his hand. "Tell me why you fear Kerak," he demanded.

"What?"

"You heard me. And please, spare me the denial: there's been nothing but trouble in your eyes these last three days, and I do not think that it comes from my beating you at chess."

Bilal paused, then said, "Kerak is very near to Wadi Tawil."

"So?" Salim answered. "If we meet any of your tribe – which at any rate seems unlikely – do you really think they would still blame you for leaving? Even if they did, you're my father's soldier now; he would never let them harm you."

"It's not that," Bilal said slowly, "but the thought of being there again...it reminds me of all that I am not, and what I cannot be to you."

Salim's face set, his lips thinned to a ruthless line. Bilal had never seen him angry before; it gave his face an unnerving look of his father's. He watched silently as Salim collected the chess pieces, laying each of them in their box with cold precision.

At last he said, "You keep telling me this, and yet it tells me nothing but that when you lie with me, you lie indeed."

The words hit Bilal like the flat of a hand. "How can you say that?" he cried.

"How can I not?" Salim answered bleakly; and then, in a motion of violent despair, he hurled the box of chess pieces into the tent where they burst and scattered. But more shocking than this were the tears in his eyes. For all that had passed between them, Bilal had never quite believed that he'd touched Salim in any lasting way, and the proof of it stunned him.

As if to drive home this miserable epiphany, Salim continued, "Do you think that I feel only lust for you? Do you know that I stay awake to watch you when you sleep, just to see your face without the doubt?" His hands clutched convulsively, but the sand they met slipped through his fingers. "When you touch me, Bilal, you touch the quick of me. There is nothing that I would not do for you...and yet you don't even consider me worthy of the truth."

"As if it were so simple!" Bilal cried, glad now of the wind that tore their words away, shattered them before they could reach other ears. "You've never known a brutal truth."

"Oh yes, I have," Salim answered bitterly. "I know it every time I let you fuck me, knowing that you don't love me."

Bilal was appalled, not by the ugliness of the words but by the knowledge that he had earned them. In the wake of their devastation he looked truly at Salim for the first time. Instead of grace and beauty he saw a stained robe and a face smeared with grit and tears; instead of king's son, a boy trying to be a man in a world that didn't need him.

Sick to the soul, Bilal said, "All right." He paused, trying to still his whirling thoughts, and then he said, "The truth, Salim, is that I am not Numair's cousin – "

"You've told me that already."

"I know; but I have not told you that I'm no blood kin to the Hassani at all. I'm the bastard son of a serving woman and a Templar knight...no, not just any Templar knight, but their Master, Gerard de Ridefort." He stopped, waiting for a reaction.

Salim wiped a filthy sleeve across his face, drew a shuddering breath and said, "Is that all?"

Bilal uttered something between a laugh and a sob. "I would give my soul that it was. My father is a traitor, Salim, and so am I. I am here as an *informateur* – a spy."

Salim looked at him incredulously. "As my father knows very well. I did not think it was a secret."

Bilal shook his head. "You do not understand. Yes, Numair and I carry de Ridefort's information to your father; but we also carry information about your father to de Ridefort. I do not know for sure, but I believe that he does not intend to keep the deal he has made with your father; he cares only to ensure his success no matter who wins the war for Al-Quds." He'd intended to leave it there, but he found that having begun to unburden himself, he could not stop. "And you're wrong, you know, though I hardly blame you for it. I *do* love you, and I've lied to you only because I wanted to love you for a little while longer. And now you can take me to your father, it's what I deserve, but please, Salim, if you ever cared for me at all, then tell him to be quick – "

He broke off then because Salim had begun to laugh. But

there wasn't much joy in it, and when Salim reached for him Bilal didn't know whether it was to throttle or embrace him, until he found himself enfolded. "I am taking you nowhere," Salim said, "except perhaps to bed, if you'll still have me after the things I said."

Bilal pushed him away with a look of abject incredulity. "I've betrayed you, Salim!"

"And who but yourself accuses you of it?"

"Didn't I just tell you – "

"Yes," he said, "and once was enough." He sighed. "I do not doubt what you have told me, Bilal, but nor can I deny the witness of my eyes. You have fought by my side for my father's cause and Allah's, and it is by this that I choose to judge you, if you will make me judge."

"I have carried information intended to betray your father to his enemies!"

"And did you supply it?" Salim asked. "Or was it fed to you by your 'cousin'?"

Bilal shrugged, but Salim took his meaning.

"Very well then: you have done nothing but transport words from one man to another. That makes you a pawn, but not a traitor." He studied Bilal for a moment, then said, "And that is what I do not understand. If you bear no love for your father or Numair, then why is it that you do their bidding at all? If you fear that you would be implicated by accusing them, then I could speak to my father – "

"No," Bilal said wearily, "it is not that, nor anything to do with me at all. The two of them hold something terrible over someone close to me – "

"And they've threatened to reveal it if you defy them – hardly original. Are you certain that it's true?"

Bilal nodded miserably. "But Salim, I cannot ask you to endanger your own father for my sake. You must tell him what I have told you."

Salim rested his chin on his knee. "And if I tell you that my father has never trusted Numair, and suspects de Ridefort's duplicity, will it clear your conscience?"

Bilal sighed. "For the moment, perhaps. But it does not change the basic problem."

"Ah, Bilal," said Salim, smiling sadly, "are you not content with the trouble you are given, that you must seek out more?" He shook his head. "Even the Templars charge with the conviction that it is God's will; well, so is this. However you came to be here, Allah's hand was behind it. And now you *are* here, and Numair and de Ridefort are not. You answer to no one but the Sultan. So ride with me to Kerak, and fight for your people. If we live through that battle, then we'll worry about the next. And if we live through them all, then I think we'll have earned the right to live unbeholden to anybody."

Dusk had fallen, sinking Salim's eyes into shadow, but Bilal could imagine their expression of gentleness and wisdom and, however inexplicable, love. "Salim," he said, "how can I possibly – "

"By not finishing that sentence," Salim interrupted, "not ever. I do not want gratitude from you, Bilal. I do not want to question your worth. I only want to love you for the length of God's patience."

Insha'Allah, Bilal thought, reaching for him as the first stars pierced the night.

*

Much later, Bilal lay awake listening as the wind screamed around the tent like a damned soul, his few hours' tenuous peace in tatters. For in the intermittent lulls of the storm, he heard something that he could not have heard: the whistling cry of a desert peregrine. It was a sound that snaked back to his time in the wadi by Kerak, where it had been his father's secret summons. At last he gave up trying to ignore it, and slipped from Salim's arms: a murmur, a crease of the forehead like a hand across water, and fingers that clutched once at nothing before capitulating to sleep. Expelling a breath he had not known he held, Bilal tucked the covers around Salim, then pulled on a tunic, picked up the lamp left burning by the door and went out into the night.

A few steps into the darkness he found him, standing like a tombstone while the storm broke around him, his white mantle a whipping flag. They stood looking at each other like strange hounds, neither quite certain whether to attack or submit. At last de Ridefort turned and began to walk toward a black stand of rock, where his horse waited in a shallow cave beyond the reach of the wind. Bilal followed at a wary distance.

"You have grown," de Ridefort said speculatively, as soon as he could make himself heard.

"I have grown?" Bilal repeated, incredulous. "You came here to tell me that? Do you not know that this is the Sultan's own camp? His guard never sleeps, and if they had found you – "

"What, Bilal? Do you forget that I am the Sultan's ally? Or do you know something that I do not?"

Every word of the Master's was barbed with irony and challenge. Bilal opened his mouth to answer, then closed it again and shook his head. They passed a few moments in silence. De Ridefort was ruminating once again on his son's face, and Bilal had the disquieting feeling that there was something specific he looked for.

Abruptly, the knight said, "Why do you share the prince's tent?"

"How do you know about that?" Bilal demanded, and immediately wished that he hadn't. But there was no taking the words back.

De Ridefort smiled derisively. "I 'know about that' because I have had your detachment followed for many days…and I must say that what I have heard about your conduct worries me, not least your relationship with the Sultan's son."

"If you know about it already, then why did you ask?"

"To hear what you would answer."

"And what do you make of my answer?" Bilal asked, with a defiant courage he had not realized he possessed until that day.

"That you are treading on dangerous ground. What, exactly, is Salim to you?"

Bilal's first instinct was to tell him that it was none of his business; but somehow that answer felt like a slight to Salim, as if he, Bilal, were ashamed of the truth. So he answered with Salim's own words: "He is the heart of my heart."

The look on de Ridefort's face was enough to make a brave man blanch, but Bilal stood before him unflinching. "Filthy infidel," de Ridefort muttered at last, at which Bilal smiled.

"If you think so, *Abatah*, I will happily take your leave, and we can both pretend that we never laid eyes on each other."

De Ridefort laughed wryly. "And leave you free to poison the Sultan against me? Do you really think so great a fool would have risen as high as I have done?" He shook his head. "No, Bilal, I am not here to sever ties with you. 'Keep your friends close, hold your enemies closer' – that is an Arab proverb, is it not? Well, you have become a liability here, and it cannot continue. I do not intend to let you out of my sight again. I have not yet decided exactly what to do with you, but I think some time with a holy order – a *Christian* order – would be beneficial. Once you have learned the error of your ways, you may yet be of some use to me."

It was clear that de Ridefort expected anger and defiance, but Bilal nodded calmly, his eyes never leaving his father's, and said, "Perhaps you are right. Perhaps it *is* time that I repent of my…many sins." As Bilal had intended, de Ridefort was entirely unbalanced by this response, and while the knight stared at him, trying to find the trick in his words, Bilal's hand flashed out and whipped the sword from his father's belt.

De Ridefort was furious, but he was also a military man, and he knew when he was beaten. He looked at his son down the length of his sword, now pointed at his own throat, and said, "It seems that I taught you better than I realized."

"No, *Abatah*," Bilal answered. "What I have learned, I have learned from Salim."

De Ridefort's jaw worked for a moment. Then he said, "Fine.

I am at your mercy; now what do you want?"

"I want you to leave me alone," Bilal answered, "and for that promise, I am willing to spare your life. However — " he added, as de Ridefort began to reply, "I know very well that your word alone is worth little. And so, remember this: I serve the Sultan first, and he knows this. If you ever try to coerce me again, I'll go straight to him and tell him that you are a traitor."

"He would not take your word over mine," de Ridefort scoffed.

"I have fought loyally for him," Bilal answered. "One might even say that I gave him the victory at Amman. What have you given him but empty promises?"

De Ridefort pinned him with a long, icy look and said, "Very well. But if you ever attempt to shame me among my own people, you will not live to tell about it."

Bilal smiled bitterly. "Believe me, de Ridefort, I have no more desire to be known as your son than you have to be known as my father." He lowered the sword. Automatically, de Ridefort reached for it, but Bilal only laughed. "As you say, *Messire*, you taught me well."

With a last, bitter glance at his son, de Ridefort mounted his horse and gave him a vicious kick. When Bilal was certain that he was gone, he slumped down against the wall of stone, shaking and filled with elation. He knew that there would be a price to pay for that night's work, but at the moment, he could not think beyond his victory. For although he had walked the earth for sixteen years, he had not until that moment realized that the reins of his destiny were his for the taking.

28

For two days the sandstorm vented its wrath on the ruined village, and at times Khalidah was convinced that the flimsy hut would finally collapse around them. At last, though, it blew itself out in a violent but short-lived squall of rain. They filled their water skins before the sun dried the puddles, and then set off again under a brilliant sky.

Though the great salt desert was monotonous, it was not actually very big – not, at any rate, compared with the vast deserts of Arabia – and within a couple of days another clutch of mountains rose on the horizon. "Say good-bye to the sand," Sulayman said, and then, pointing to the mountains, "we'll see little but that until we reach Qaf."

They passed from the desert into the province of Sistan, which, according to Sulayman, had once been known as an earthly paradise, a vast garden of a country housing a refined and peaceful civilization. But peaceful civilizations never fare well in a world wedded to war, and over long years of ravage by invading armies Sistan gradually retreated into itself, becoming at last a circumspect no-man's-land between Persia and Khorasan. It was still a fertile place, though, its mountains interspersed with tilled valleys where wheat, melons and sesame grew in abundance.

The farmers of these valley fields belonged to a tribe called the Baluchi, who lived in wicker huts with roofs of cloth and spoke a language even Sulayman could not decipher. They rode curious horses with fine heads on long necks, bodies somewhat heavier than the Arab horses', and long ears that curved toward each other to touch at the tips. Despite the language barrier, the Baluchi understood trade and appeared to have goods to spare for it. Sulayman and Khalidah replenished their supplies, and found ample grazing for the horses when they stopped at night.

After the lands of the Baluchi they crossed dry steppes dotted with crumbling ruins, and once an entire abandoned city, its broken columns thrusting skyward like the ribs of some ancient slain beast. They climbed hills and came down again into a marshy region bisected by the Hirmand river, which flowed from the heart of Khorasan. Its water was pure and freezing cold, and welcome after days of warm water tainted with the taste of the skins.

On what Sulayman said would be their final day in Persia, they stopped at a small city called Zabol. It was a collection of low mud buildings baked to the dull, dun color of the mountains at its back. But it was also green: behind its walls were gardens fed by the same great river. They had not stopped at a town of any size since Domat al-Jandal – a place that now seemed the provenance of dream – and Khalidah felt a strong reluctance to enter the city.

"Is it really necessary to stop here?" she asked.

"Unless you want to freeze in the mountains," Sulayman answered. "There are things we need to buy here, before we can go on."

Sighing, Khalidah nudged Zahirah onward. Once they were inside it wasn't so bad. Many of the town's people spoke Persian, especially in the *suq*, where Sulayman bought men's clothing for them both.

"The hills are rife with bandits," he answered, when Khalidah questioned the need to maintain the disguise. "Better they believe you are a man."

He handed her a porridge-colored woolen hat which he called a *pakol*, tubular in shape and rolled to sit as high or low on the head as the wearer desired. Next he bought long woolen coats woven in somber stripes, and generous woolen shawls, a red one for himself and a blue one for Khalidah. They also bought a new load of provisions, paying for it all with the last of the silver from the horses' bridles.

"And now we are as ready as we can be," he said to Khalidah as they packed their food and new clothes onto the pony. They rode away from the *suq*, and the chaos of the streets dissipated. Now the houses they rode past dreamed within walled gardens full of violet shade and the muted sounds of moneyed life.

"This is not the way to the mountains," Khalidah observed.

"No," Sulayman answered. He hesitated, then said, "We may have reached the last stage of our journey, but it will be by far the most difficult. Tonight we should have a proper meal, and sleep in real beds."

"We have no money for an inn."

"We do not need it. I have a friend here."

"You have a friend everywhere," Khalidah said.

"Are you angry?"

"No; only, why did you not tell me this before?"

"I didn't know whether our road would take us here, and I didn't want to raise your hopes."

It was a strange thing for him to say. Nomad's daughter that she was, Khalidah was indifferent to the charms of a stuffed mattress, and though a hot meal would be welcome, she hardly pined for it. She was about to question him further when he pulled 'Aasifa up outside the largest house on the street, a sprawling two-storey place surrounded by the ubiquitous wall and date palms. Somewhere beyond the wall Khalidah could hear children's laughter, and the subtle harmonics of falling water. Their interlacing tones and rhythms filled her with an unfathomable longing.

"How will you explain me to this friend?" she asked as they dismounted by the gate.

"There will be no need," answered Sulayman. "Sandara knows the truth already – probably more of it that we do."

"What do you mean by that?" Khalidah asked sharply.

"This is not the place to discuss it," Sulayman answered, then rapped on the door. It was opened by a boy of about six, a skinny child in fine clothing that had clearly been clean that morning. He was unremarkable except for a pair of huge, black-fringed eyes the color of the palms' shade. At the sight of Sulayman, his sharp little face broke into a grin of delight, and he launched himself into the man's arms.

"You've come back!" he cried.

"I promised you I would," Sulayman answered, kissing both of his cheeks and then setting him down again. "Daoud ibn Aslam al-Tamuri, may I introduce Khalidah bint 'Abd al-Aziz al-Hassani."

The child said his *salaams*, and then, "I thought you were a boy."

Khalidah smiled. "That is what I wished you to think."

"Is your mother at home?" Sulayman asked.

"I will fetch her," Daoud said. "Come in, and let your horses drink."

He indicated a fountain set at the convergence of four pebbled paths and surrounded with well-tended apricot trees. Two little girls a year or two younger than Daoud leaned over the stone rim of the fountain, dropping pebbles into the water. As Khalidah and Sulayman led the horses toward the fountain, they looked up with smoky green eyes like Daoud's. Their pretty oval faces were so alike that if they had not worn different colored headscarves, Khalidah would not have been able to tell them apart.

"Sulayman!" they cried together, and flew at him as the boy had done. He caught one in each arm, and kissed them both.

"What have you done to charm these children?" Khalidah asked him, as she stripped off the horses' tack.

"It's they who charmed me," Sulayman said, collapsing back onto the rim of the fountain with a little girl on each knee. "These are Daoud's sisters, Madiha and Maliya." To the girls he said, "This is Khalidah."

Khalidah nodded to the twins, and then cupped her hands to drink from the fountain. She was swallowing water as greedily as the horses when a shadow fell over her. She turned to find a woman standing between herself and Sulayman. She was tall and slim and clad head to toe in black, including a crepe veil over her face that admitted no glimpse of her features, except for a faint, sporadic glint that could have been an eye. The woman bent down and took the wriggling girls from Sulayman, then regarded him silently. Or she seemed to: it was impossible to tell, through the veil, where her eyes fell.

In a sweet, retiring voice she said, "I am so glad that you have returned, Sulayman." As she spoke, the veil fluttered like the apricot leaves in the evening breeze. "And you, child," she said, turning to Khalidah. Her voice wavered between wonder and tears. "Can you be Brekhna's daughter?"

Khalidah had a sudden, powerful sense of ingenerate nobility in this veiled woman, not unlike what she had felt when she first met Sulayman. *Am I so in need of leading that I make royalty of strangers?* she asked herself, but a part of her knew better, perhaps already anticipating the truth.

"By all accounts, I am," she answered.

A nod; the veil fluttered over the glint of a shadow-green eye. Sandara set the twins down, and to Khalidah's shock and mortification, she knelt before her in a graceful sweep of black robes. "*Ya hala, Khalidah bint Brekhna bint Tor Gul Khan; assalaamu 'alaikum.* You will always find welcome in the home of your most humble servant, Sandara bint Arzou al-Jinni."

*

Over the lavish dinner she laid out for her guests and her children under the apricot trees, Sandara told Khalidah of her childhood in Qaf, which she had left for the first and final time as part of a small battalion hired by a Persian *amir* to settle a land dispute.

"I did not know it then," she said, her voice like softly falling water, "but I would never return to my childhood home. Like your own mother I married an outsider, and was thereby exiled."

"Where is your husband now?" Khalidah asked.

"Dead," Sandara answered, with a sudden hardening of her tone. It only lasted for a moment, but when she continued with her story, Khalidah could not help hearing its echo. Sandara spoke of the cloth business kept her family in comfort; the gardens she took pride in tending; the children who were her greatest joy. Yet like her voice when she had pronounced her husband deceased, her account of her life grasped at wholeness while it circled a jagged rent as black as her widow's weeds. Khalidah longed to know the cause of it, and did not dare ask.

When they finished eating, Sandara left to put the children to bed. As soon as she was gone, Khalidah demanded, "What is she hiding?"

"That is for her to tell you, not me," Sulayman answered, tuning his *qanun*.

"I do not like prevarication," she said, though truly what she did not like was the reverence with which Sulayman seemed to regard the older woman.

"You will like the truth even less," he said bleakly.

Khalidah sipped her tea, watching the stars come out between the apricot leaves and contemplating this response until Sandara returned, carrying a lantern and a coffee pot. "You are good for them, Sulayman," the woman said as she set the light by Sulayman's knee and knelt to pour the coffee. "They have little contact with men, now; they have little contact with anyone but me. It is a sad life for them. Sometimes I wonder if I should return to Qaf...I think that my father would take the children in, if not me." She paused, then sighed. "I should do it, and yet I cannot bear to be without them." A laugh that sounded very near to a sob. "What a terrible mother I am. A selfish, weak woman..."

Moved past jealousy by the wretchedness of her voice, Khalidah reached out through the darkness for Sandara's hand. The older woman took it and clutched it with desperate strength. "Play something, Sulayman," she said. "Play something before I drown us all with my self-pity."

"I will play," he said, "and I hope Khalidah will sing." Khalidah nodded.

They performed Chauras's lament, and whether it was Sandara's clinging grief, or the sweetness of the garden night, or simply the specter of the journey's end, Khalidah's voice had a soulful sweetness, Sulayman's strings a tenderness that they hadn't before. By the time they finished, nightfall was complete, the garden a sea of shadow challenged only by the oil lamp that had lit Sulayman's path over the strings.

Sandara said, "I sincerely thank you both. I know that you have given something of yourselves to ease my pain; and in return, Khalidah, I will tell you what you wish to know, though I think that it will hurt you." She paused, then continued, "I have shared with you most of my history, but there is one thing that I have not told you. As a girl, as well as being a promising *ghazi*, I was a beauty. So I was told, anyway – I didn't think much of it. Well, I told myself I didn't, but perhaps I did…perhaps flouting my beauty was a greater vanity than accepting it as the gift it was." She shook her head.

"It was my beauty that caught Aslam's eye. I knew that, but I was too young, too naïve to realize that for him, it was also the whole of my worth. He was the only son of a wealthy family. He could have any beautiful thing that caught his eye, and that was the problem. However dutiful, a woman is still a living being with a will of her own, and I was not just a woman, but a Jinni – duty means something different to the Jinn. But though I knew this, and all the other reasons why Jinn should never marry outside our own kind, I was young, and love in youth does not suffer reason.

"We had not been married long before I realized my mistake. Aslam did not like the way that other men looked at me. First he forbade me to go out. Then he insisted that I go veiled even within the house. Later I was forbidden to show myself to visitors, even family, veiled or not. But even that was not enough. He was convinced that someone would take me from him. I watched as jealousy slowly drove him mad, and yet I never thought that it would master him."

She paused, and then slowly she put back her veil, revealing a profile so exquisite that Khalidah caught her breath: skin pale as dawn, long gold-green eye, nose a delicate aquiline and black eyebrow like a bird's wing. But something was wrong: Sulayman, seated on her other side, was looking at her with tortured pity. For a moment Khalidah did not understand. Then Sandara turned to her with the terrible truth. The other half of her face was a monster's, a livid mess of slabby scars, the eyelid melted into the surrounding skin leaving the milky, unseeing eye exposed, the lips peeling back from the teeth in a permanent snarl.

"He got drunk, and poured burning oil on my face as I slept," she said, her voice at last capitulating to bitterness. "You see, he had convinced himself that it was better to obliterate my beauty than to live with the knowledge that he could not possess it entirely." She smiled a rueful, hideous smile, then dropped her veil with a tangible finality. "He succeeded, and yet he failed, for when he was told that I would live he impaled himself on his own sword. And so I am a widow, rich but unmarriageable, and if it were not for the children I would have followed Aslam in his fate long since."

When she spoke next it was to Khalidah, who had not yet begun to recover from her shock. "I have heard every denigration of your mother," she said gently. "I grew up with her as a chastisement, a threat: 'See what will happen if you deny the tribe? Even our princess was not spared exile and humiliation.' But I for one will never condemn her, and whatever the Jinn may tell you, nor should you; for we who give up Qaf pay for it every day of our lives thereafter, each in our own way."

She paused, and then she said slowly, "It is futile to wish that I had not left the Jinn, since I do not think that it was in my power to resist Aslam, and what I took for love. But this – " she gestured to her face " – is my own doing. He began to erase me as soon as I gave myself into his keeping, and for pride – for weak and willful pride – I allowed him to do it. No Jinn woman should ever have submitted to the treatment he gave me, but it seemed

easier to forget that than to admit that I had been wrong; and so
it reached its obvious conclusion.

"Go to Qaf, Khalidah. Meet your grandfather and hear what
he has to say. Learn what it means to be a Jinni, see if there is a
life there for you. But never, never forget who you are." Sandara
stood abruptly and retreated into the shadows, leaving the echo
of her words to dissolve slowly into the sound of falling water.

29

Sandara was distant when Khalidah and Sulayman said good-bye the next morning, and her children crestfallen. But she sent them away loaded with still more food and water and warm clothing. As Khalidah leaned down to embrace her from Zahirah's saddle, Sandara whispered in her ear, "Do not forget me, Khalidah. I will not forget you." She said something to Sulayman that Khalidah couldn't hear, but which caused his eyes to flicker inadvertently toward her. And then they were leaving, and with one last, yearning look at them, Daoud shut the door on that hushed, haunted garden.

They rode in silence out of the city. Only when they reached the arid foothills did either of them dare to break it. From a rocky precipice they looked out across a vista of undulating red hills that marched ever taller toward the horizon, where they could just make out snow-capped peaks.

"This is Khorasan," Sulayman said at last. He looked at Khalidah, who looked back at him with troubled eyes. "And Sandara has made you wonder whether you should have come at all."

She didn't answer, but by the sudden down-cast of those eyes, Sulayman knew that he had guessed correctly. He sighed. "Sandara is a good woman," he said, "and I thought that meeting her might help you understand your mother, also perhaps protect you from some of the things you will hear about her in Qaf. But you must also remember that Sandara views the world through a lens of loss and regret, and that is at best a skewed view. I have met her father, Arzou. He has long since forgiven her, and would welcome her back with open arms, if only she would come."

"And you have not told her so?" Khalidah cried.

Sulayman answered with a rueful laugh. "I told her so when I returned from Qaf, and I told her again this morning, before you awakened. You might even say that I begged her to hear reason, for the sake of her children and her ageing father if not herself. But Aslam's fire burned away more than her beauty. She is lost in a labyrinth of remorse, and without being able to forgive herself, she can allow no one else to forgive her. It is killing her. I only hope that she loves her children enough to save them before she succumbs."

Once again, the silence spun out across the empty hills.

*

As time shifted her perspective on Sandara, Khalidah's apprehension for Qaf faded. Once again she looked eastward with anticipation, though it was more circumspect now. To keep her mind from dwelling on her worries Sulayman filled their evenings with lessons in writing or the *qanun*, and their days relating what he knew of this barely-tamed frontier of Islam. He worked through Khorasan's history until he reached the Ghaznavid Turks, whose King Mahmoud had plucked the country from the Persians like a ripe apricot. But Mahmoud had no sooner secured Khorasan than he was off again eastward on a mission to convert the sub-continent to Islam.

"And it's from his bloody conquest that the Jinn's part of the Himalaya takes its name," Sulayman concluded. "'Hindu Kush' means 'Slaughter of Hindus.' And it's not just the Hindus who have been slaughtered. When Mahmoud died – not fifty years ago – the country dissolved once again into a chaos of battling dynasties, and that is how it has been ever since. Therefore, no matter how deserted it seems, you must be vigilant on this road; for in reality these mountains are full of bandits looking to kill or co-opt you, depending which side you're on."

Khalidah had nothing to say to this, though now she rode with the decided sensation of hostile eyes, if not arrows, trained on her back.

For some days they followed the river Khash, with the snowy peak of Kuh-e-Sangan towering to their left, rendered a searing violet by the lucent air. After that they turned their backs to the mountain and rode down into the valley of the Helmand, a green hurtle of meltwater cold as knifestrike. They followed this river for several days, and all the time the mountains surrounding them grew in stature.

"There," said Sulayman one morning as Khalidah shook off the dew that had frozen over their blankets in the night. He pointed north through the blazing sunrise to the faint plicae of a mountain range, higher still than anything they had yet encountered. "That is the Hindu Kush. Somewhere in those mountains…"

You will discover whether it is me you love, Khalidah thought, *or my connection to the land you long for*. She was immediately ashamed of the thought, yet she could not quite banish it. She gulped her tea, shivering even as it burned her mouth. They had camped in a place where the river was narrow and its valley deep. The sunlight would not reach it until midday, and then only for an hour or two. Khalidah looked sadly at the horses, who were growing thin despite the now-abundant grazing: they could not eat the grass as fast as the cold and exertion ate their flesh.

"Soon it will be better," she whispered to Zahirah, and indeed, for a few days the conditions grew gentler. They turned away from the river somewhere south and west of Kabul and crossed the Shomali Plain, a vast, fertile expanse of vineyards and fruit trees with little baked-mud villages rising from their midst like anthills. When they passed through these settlements, children smiled and women offered them tea and dried apricots and mulberries, the new season's fruit being still green and hard.

The respite didn't last long, though. From the gardens of
Shomali their path rose into the Baba mountains – the first bony
fingers of the Hindu Kush – growing narrow and rutted with the
violent rains and searing sun that continually battered the land.
The road clung to the sides of the mountains, at times covered
with ice, at others overhanging sheer drops of thousands of feet
down to desolate valleys of reddish stone and dust.

Despite the inhospitable nature of the road, there was a steady
stream of other travelers, particularly as they neared the Khyber
Pass, which was the only route from Kabul to the Orient. When
they met travelers moving west, Khalidah would shut her eyes
and pray that Zahirah's feet not betray her as they maneuvered a
passing on a path barely wide enough for one. Sometimes they
came upon little villages clinging to the sides of the mountains
like fungi on the trunks of great trees. Women and children
would squat in front of their mud huts, watching the travelers
with a look of abject longing.

After two grueling days of climbing, they reached the Pass
and crossed into the Bamiyan range. From the giddy air of that
towering gateway they began to descend: Sulayman with a look
of mild expectation, Khalidah trying not faint with the altitude.
Down and down they went, until the muscles of Khalidah's
thighs, so long used to climbing, seized from all the hours of
riding with her weight pushed back. But when she asked to stop,
Sulayman said, "Not yet."

She was angry with him – angrier than she had yet been – for
what she thought was wanton stubbornness. For an hour she
imagined all the imprecations she wanted to hurl at him and then,
abruptly, she understood. They had arrived in a sandstone valley,
still high enough that the air was dilute, but low enough that
the snow-crusted peaks beyond the surrounding foothills looked
every *farsakh* of their dizzying height. The floor of the valley was
green with meadow grass and the cultivated fields of the farms
scattered across it. Beyond the farms, at the base of the foothills,
huddled a small town, and soaring high above the town were
three great arched niches carved into the sandstone cliffs. They

contained stone carvings of human figures. The westernmost one was the largest, the central one was the smallest, but Khalidah was still too far away to make out any more detail than that.

"What is this place?" she asked as they rode toward the town between fields of ripening wheat.

"Bamiyan," he said. "Once it was the most important city in Khorasan, and the hub of the Silk Route. It didn't matter whether you were traveling from Beijing to Rome or Samarqand to Jaipur, you passed through Bamiyan."

"Are the statues idols of *kafir* gods?"

"The statues represent Buddha," Sulayman answered, "a prophet who lived – "

"Yes," Khalidah said testily, "I know about Buddha. But what are his statues doing in a Muslim country?"

"This was not always a Muslim country." They were close enough now to the cliffs to see that they were honeycombed with caves. Indicating them, Sulayman continued, "You see those? They were Buddhist chapels and monasteries. Once, thousands of monks lived there, and they would put up travelers and pilgrims. They're empty now, but you can still see the paintings and statues the monks made while they were there – the monks, and others too. In those caves you'll see Chinese calligraphy and Tibetan mandalas side-by-side with paintings of Ganesha and Zeus and the Prophet Iesu."

They were close enough now to make out the features of the Buddhas in the sunset light, their heavy-lidded eyes and tranquil smiles cast to the valley below. The largest of them stood as high as the cave above the camp at Wadi Tawil, where months ago Khalidah had hidden from what she thought was her destiny.

"Once, I am told, they were colored," Sulayman said. "Painted and gilded and covered in jewels. I suppose time and thieves have taken care of that."

"Let's go up there," Khalidah said. "Let's sleep tonight in the Buddhists' caves."

Sulayman smiled. "That was my plan. They have done for countless travelers in the past, and at any rate, we have no money left to stay in town."

So they rode around what was left of the town of Bamiyan – huddling, it seemed, in the shadow of its own glorious past – and then led the horses up onto the cliffs, over narrow paths and crumbling stone staircases. They found a cave that was deep enough to give shelter from the evening wind, and high enough for the horses to stand. Sulayman lit a fire, and by its flickering light Khalidah examined the walls, covered with frescoes as Sulayman had promised. In one, men with long Oriental eyes and blood-colored robes drifted through a field of flowers. Another showed a golden chariot drawn by moon-white horses, driven by a man with magnificent hair that flowed across an azure sky. She turned from them at last to find Sulayman lying on the floor, looking up at the paintings on the ceiling, eyes half-lidded like the Buddhas'.

"How far now to Qaf?" she asked.

Sulayman was silent for a few long moments. At last he said, "I don't know."

Khalidah came and looked down on him. "What do you mean?"

He sighed and sat up. "Remember when I told you about my first journey to Qaf? I arrived there and left it in oblivion. We could be one *farsakh* away or one hundred. But the village where I awakened under the cannabis bush was only a couple of *farsakhs* from here: the best we can do now is ride that way, and hope."

Khalidah looked out into the blackness beyond the cave's mouth, wondering, suddenly, what it was she hoped for.

30

In the following days Bilal came as close to happiness as he'd ever been. The windstorm raged on with tedious ferocity and he prayed to Allah to preserve it, if it meant that he could stay forever in that dusty wadi with Salim and their chessboard and their pipe of *banj*. But as his mother had been fond of saying, the only certainty in life is change, and with gritty inevitability the storm finally blew itself out. Once again the Sultan's small army set off south.

Two days' steady riding would have brought them to Kerak, but instead Salah ad-Din led his band in a zigzag course along the King's Highway, sending raid after raid across the border into Franj territory. It maddened Salim, who after his success at Amman was itching for battle, and as the days wore on even Bilal began to long for Kerak as an end to the monotony, though he did not entirely share Salim's delight in bloodshed. But Salah ad-Din met his son's pestering with a calm, indulgent smile.

"To take back Al-Quds," he said, "we must engage the Franj; to do that, we must first draw them forth. And, as Amman taught you, the Franj do not like to come forth from a fortress. This will be truer still when their fortress is their Holy City." He paused, his eyes rambling the horizon where sand hazed to sky. "Yet my biggest problem by far is how to occupy my own army in the meantime."

"So you send them on raids to keep them busy?" Salim asked incredulously.

"Precisely."

The Sultan had caught sight of a far-off wisp of dust, no bigger than the plume from a spent lamp, but he knew that it spelled another victory. He turned at last to his son, who stood waiting with tremulous eagerness to oblige him, and was struck all at once by Salim's resemblance to his mother. The only child of a Persian *amir*, she should never have been a harem wife. She was too used to autonomy and also to significance, all spit and fire over a deep and devastating need to please. Though for a brief time he had loved her with a consuming passion, Salah ad-Din wished now that he had never touched her. He ought to have known that a son of hers would break his heart.

"Yet like the best tactics," he said at last, "it serves more than one purpose. Our successes here keep the public in our favor, and bolster the morale of those waiting at Ras al-Mai'. But the primary reason why we do not make straight for Kerak is that I have had word from Al-'Adil."

At the mention of his father's brother, the atabeg of Egypt, Salim perked up. "Does he mean to bring his army to join us?"

The Sultan gave him a smile of circumspect approval. "They are on the road already, and should reach Ayla in a week's time. With his help and Allah's grace, we stand to gain not only a castle, but a province. Now, does that not seem to a fair trade for a few days' patience?"

This delighted Salim beyond further questioning, and the Sultan watched with troubled eyes as he ran off, no doubt to repeat it all to the Bedu boy. He had his doubts about their sudden intimacy – not for its nature, but because he was not yet certain that the boy was trustworthy. Still, this was not the primary source of his present anxiety. Rather, he was thinking of the other reason for his hesitation in moving on Kerak, the most significant and the most shameful: doubt. For Salah ad-Din had challenged Kerak before, and however his chroniclers might choose to apotheosize his efforts, the simple truth was that he had failed.

That campaign had begun in much the same fashion as this one. Arnat had raided one too many *hajj* caravan, and the Sultan, losing patience, had brought his army south to teach the renegade prince a lesson. He arrived to find the castle packed with Franj nobles come to celebrate the marriage of Arnat's stepson, the sixteen-year-old Humphrey IV of Toron, to the eleven-year-old Princess Isabella of Jerusalem. Salah ad-Din laid his siege despite it, but since his only quarrel was with Arnat, he kept his artillery away from the child-bride's chamber. It had the makings of an entirely civilized conquest – Stephanie de Milly, Kerak's chatelaine, even had portions of the wedding feast sent out to his men – but in the end the mighty castle proved too valuable to the tenuous Latin states. The Leper King came with his army to deliver it, and doubting that his own force was strong enough to withstand a direct confrontation, Salah ad-Din retreated north.

It was a decision he would come to regret bitterly, as a second siege a year later also failed, and Arnat grew ever bolder, the forces restraining him weaker. Now the Sultan rode south slowly, to buy time to think. Yet when the castle rose at last like a wart on the wavering horizon, he was no nearer to knowing how to take it.

*

"The Franj have learned much over their hundred years in our land," the Sultan mused to his *umara* in camp that night. "They do not come out from cover without cause, nor, more to the point, unless the circumstances are favorable. Our raids will have given them cause; now we must convince them of favorability. Therefore I will go myself to challenge them, and I will take only my own guard and my son's."

He silenced the ensuing clamor of protest with a raised hand and continued, "The rest of the division will wait until the Franj come forth, and then you will strike as you have struck all down the backbone of Oultrejourdain – quickly and ruthlessly."

And so it was. Salah ad-Din rode forth at first light, flanked by his own guard and Salim's. Bilal rode near the front of the detachment, watching the castle as they drew closer to it with a disconnected vigilance. There were the tower and the wall he knew so well, there the great gate that had once admitted him as an ally. But now the portcullis was drawn, and daylight sharpened the walls' arrow-slits to bared fangs, the crenellated battlements broken teeth. All along the walls the garrison ranged with their wives and their whores, to jeer at this paltry party come to challenge them.

The master of the garrison, a blunt-bodied man with a face like a pale, stubbled pudding, rode forth with a handful of cavalry to meet them. To the Sultan's *salaams*, he replied, through a translator, "What do you want?" in a voice that suggested he would far rather be back in the keep, drinking his absent master's wine.

"Do you really need to ask?" Salah ad-Din answered contemptuously. "Can you not see the smoke of your burning villages? Have your people not yet come to you for refuge?"

"We have seen it, and they have." This time, his voice was coldly serious.

"Well then: I come to offer terms."

The Franji uttered a low chuckle. "And who has asked for terms?"

The Sultan held the knight in his gold-brown gaze until the knight looked away. Then he said in a calm, conversational tone, "News of your master's outrages travel farther than perhaps you realize: as far, in fact, as Cairo. My brother commands the army there. You might have heard of him. He is called Al-'Adil – that is, 'The Just' – and it is not without reason. He is waiting at Ayla to extract justice from Arnat, if he will not give it freely."

"Arnat is not at home," the Franji said.

"Do you think that this is news to me?" Salah ad-Din asked

in a low, merciless voice. The Franji didn't answer. "Believe me, I know all that you know about your present circumstances, and a good deal that you don't. Now, will you hear my terms?"

"There will be no terms!" the officer roared at the Sultan's tranquil face. The stunned translator paused for a moment, and then relayed his message.

"Very well," said Salah ad-Din, holding the officer in his mesmeric gaze such that the man did not notice when he drew his sword. But there was a brief, lucid moment as the Sultan raised his blade, in which the Franj knight realized that there had never been any terms at all.

*

It was easy after that. The whey-faced officer's rolling head goaded a band of cavalry from the castle keep, and the *mamluk* horse archers and auxiliary cavalry fell on them like lightning strike. Deep in their midst Bilal fought with a will, and when he found himself looking too closely at the faces of the men he slew, he looked instead at Salim, whose own face beneath his helmet glowed with the ephemeral joy of proving his worth. In little more than minutes the field was reduced to a mire of bloody mud and broken Franj bodies, soon battered further by the rider-less horses that plunged among them in terrified confusion.

The Sultan's men turned back to the gates then, beating their shields and calling out for further contest, but no one came to meet them. The castle was still and silent, the battlements empty, the garrison and all their retinue retreated into the keep. It wasn't quite the victory Salah ad-Din had longed for, but then, it would serve his purpose well enough. Plunging his sword into its sheath, he divided his detachment and set them in a ring around the castle.

"Contain the garrison," he said to the *umara* and then, gesturing to his son, he wheeled his horse to the west.

"Where are we going?" Salim asked.

"To rouse my brother," he said, "and teach Arnat a lesson he won't forget quickly."

*

For a week Salah ad-Din and the Egyptian army razed the province of Oultrejourdain, their earlier exploits paling in comparison to the earthly hell they now made of Arnat's lands. They burned the fields where the first crops were ripening, slaughtered livestock and anyone who raised so much as a hand against them. To begin with Bilal was ambivalent about the wanton destruction; this, after all, was not the same as killing men in self-defense. But a human heart can absorb only so much brutality before hardening to it. Soon enough he rode to the slaughter as avidly as the rest, heart burning and throat screaming praises of Allah and of the Sultan who worked His will.

Yet at night when he lay against Salim's beating heart, he knew that his battle cries were empty. He did not fight for the Sultan or even for Allah, but for the human boy he loved. As successive victories fired them with a passion beyond anything either of them had imagined on that first moonlit night in Busra, Bilal realized too that he had no people but Salim, nor did he want any. He knew that someday the wars would end, that for all Salim's brave words about living unbeholden, life would in reality demand things of both of them that might make their love impossible. But for the moment at least, he preferred to do as Salim had told him in the narrow, windy wadi: survive the next day, and then consider what lay beyond.

31

They reached the village with Sulayman's cannabis bush and passed it without incident, except for the contemptuous stare of a nanny goat munching the resinous leaves. Soon they were climbing again, this time into hills as inviolate as they were fearsome. Not even a mud village broke the monotony: snow fields and glaciers, meltwater torrents and lakes all had the unyielding, viridescent beauty of a land untouched and untouchable.

Sulayman no longer knew the names of mountains and rivers; Khalidah doubted that they even had names, beyond what Allah had given them at the beginning of time. The grazing grew thin and finally nonexistent; the horses reluctantly reverted to their rations of camels' milk and dates. *At least*, Khalidah thought, *there is no longer any shortage of water*.

Further and further they traveled into those mountains, shivering through their nights and stumbling through their days. Early on they abandoned riding, since the footing was so treacherous and Zahirah's leg-wound was not healing properly, and led the horses on their winding path between glacier and mountain. Though they were running low on supplies again, they dared not approach the shepherds who occasionally crossed their path with their flocks: ferocious looking men in dirty woolen clothing with faces like the granite cliffs above and eyes blood-red where they should have been white. When she saw these eyes, Khalidah thought that they were devils, and Sulayman had a hard time convincing her that it was merely a custom of these men to stain their eyes with madder, to make them look fiercer.

"It's hardly necessary," Khalidah said, not quite believing him but even less inclined to test the theory.

"Come, Khalidah," he soothed. "It can't be long now."

But his reassurance was transparent. They had traveled further east than he had ever been before, yet there was no trace of human habitation of any kind, unless they counted the demon-eyed shepherds and their fat-tailed sheep, which moved across the landscape like filthy caravans on their way, apparently, from nowhere to nowhere. At last Sulayman came to the decision he had been avoiding for days. It was only mid-day, but the sky to the north looked ugly and the wind was picking up, so they set up camp in the lea of a tumid glacier which offered as much protection as anything could. They huddled together over their smoking fire, having covered the horses with the blankets, for if their sweat froze on them it would kill them.

As Khalidah stirred their meager rations into a kind of stew, which would at least be hot if not particularly appetizing, Sulayman said, "It's over."

Khalidah's eyes flew to his face. "What?" she asked, to stall the inevitable.

"We cannot go on," he said in a small, defeated voice. "We have barely enough food to get us back to the last village, assuming that nothing stalls us on the way."

She stirred the stew, saying nothing for several minutes. At last, handing him a spoon, she said, "No."

He looked up at her incredulously. "No? Do you think we can survive on ice and gravel?"

"I think," she said, sipping a spoonful of the noxious concoction, "that I have come too far to give up now."

"Khalidah – "

"Think about it. Last time, you reached Qaf only when you

were at the very end of your endurance. Perhaps it is the same now. Perhaps it is a kind of test, a measure of our worth, and the Jinn will come for us when they think we are ready."

"I would think they'd tested my worth already," he said dryly, "and yours is beyond question."

"Is it?"

"You're a Jinni."

"No – I am the daughter of an exiled Jinni and a foreign sheikh. Nobody likes half-breeds."

"Then why did Tor Gul Khan send me to find you?"

"I imagine because he hoped that the Jinn half of me would prove the stronger. Perhaps this is a way of testing his theory." She paused, then added, "And perhaps he is also testing our faith."

"Our faith in what?" he asked, with hard, bitter eyes.

"Mine in you," she answered calmly. "And yours in him."

"How can he expect us to have faith in him when he has offered nothing to sustain it?" he cried. "How can I have faith in something of which I have not the smallest memento to prove that it ever existed outside of my own mind?"

"Is that not the meaning of faith?" she asked softly. Her golden eyes rested on him without question or presumption, with little more than a raptor's steady certainty. Sulayman decided then that he would rather die in this nameless, frozen valley, than live in a world which would betray such a look. Picking up his spoon, he began to eat.

*

That night a blizzard raged, and they clung together with the horses curved around them, marking a tiny, tenuous circle of life in that vast wilderness of stone and ice. Khalidah was afraid to sleep, because she knew that if she did, she might never wake up again. But at last she could hold out no longer, and the sting of blowing snow gave way to soft warmth and gentle hands stroking her head. She knew then that she must be dead. She opened her eyes to the flutter of a white shawl embroidered with colorful birds and flowers.

"*Ummah*," she said, struggling to sit up, but the hands pressed her back down. She could see nothing of Brekhna's face except the penetrating golden eyes, and as she looked they dissolved into the blowing sand of a desert evening, where an army raged in battle. They were Muslims – that she could tell by the fluttering banners with their Qur'anic inscriptions – and so vast in number that at first she thought they fought each other. Then, gradually, among the flying dust and flashing steel she began to make out white tunics crossed with red – the Templars. But they were bodies only, torn and broken, trampled beneath the hooves of the Muslim army's horses.

Then, after another moment, she realized that this was not quite right either. In the midst of that vast army of Islam one Christian knight still stood, a young man with a face that should never have belonged to a soldier. Tears rolled from his brown eyes into his auburn beard as he raised his sword again and again, hacking at the enemies who surrounded him with doomed determination. Behind him, on horseback, another young man watched: a Muslim, wearing a bloody yellow tunic over a prince's armor, his troubled soul written all over his fine face. He watched as the soldiers taunted the Franj knight, drawing out the inevitable, his own bloody sword lying on the pommel of his saddle and his knuckles white on the hilt. Khalidah found herself praying for the prince to deliver the failing knight, and as if he had heard her, he raised his sword. The Franji never saw it coming. With one clean stroke, the prince split his helmet and his skull, and the Franj knight fell. Then he turned his horse away from the bloody field and kicked her into a gallop, but not before Khalidah saw the tears on his face.

As he rode away, she heard the incongruous, reedy voice of a *na'ay* playing a melody she did not recognize, though it seemed to echo the bitter sorrow in her heart. Gradually the sounds of the battle faded and its image collapsed into darkness, but the *na'ay* remained, calm and steady and sweet, and there were arms around her, and a beating heart beneath her ear. She opened her eyes to find that she was lying against Sulayman's chest, clutching his coat in two white fists. She remembered snow and fractured rock, but she could not find them now, nor the ranging army and setting sun. There were only a flickering fire, a soft cushion beneath her, the moon shining through a high window and perfect, blessed warmth.

"I did not know that you spoke Pashto," Sulayman said, looking down into her face, smiling around the worry.

"I don't," she said.

"And yet you were speaking it a moment ago, in your dream… screaming it, really. What was it you dreamed of?"

"Do not ask her yet," said a man's low voice with an accent she could not place. She realized then that the sound of the *na'ay* had ceased when the man spoke. She turned and saw him sitting on the floor near them: an old man, but still vital, wearing a white robe and a dark turban, with a reed flute resting on his lap. He smiled at her, though it did not quite reach his golden eyes.

"Where are we?"

She had directed the question to Sulayman, but it was the old man who answered: "In my home."

"And you are…?"

"Tor Gul Khan. Your grandfather." He bowed to her, hand over his heart. "*As-salaamu 'alaikum*, Khalidah bint 'Abd al-Aziz al-Hassani. May I be the first to welcome you to Qaf."

PART II

CASTLE OF TIBERIAS
COUNTY OF TRIPOLI, GALILEE
LATE APRIL, 1187

I

Count Raymond III of Tripoli stood on the wall of his wife's castle at Tiberias, watching the dusty glitter of an approaching band of cavalrymen. He suspected that they were an envoy from Jerusalem, come to demand that he pay tribute to Guy as king, and no doubt led by Gerard de Ridefort. It was ironic, really: the favorite lament of Guy's supporters was that Tripoli's stubbornness had caused the split in the kingdom, when in reality it was due to an old quarrel over a woman, which their champion, the allegedly celibate de Ridefort, could not forget. Of course, Tripoli was too honest a man to pretend that the fault was not partly his. If he had it all to do again, he would marry Lucia to de Ridefort without a second thought, for a wife and family and the headache of running an estate would have gone a long way toward defusing de Ridefort's political aspirations. But what was done, was done, and now he had to concentrate on the present situation.

The group of horsemen had drawn close enough now to make out their heraldry, and as Tripoli examined it, his antipathy turned to puzzlement. This was not the court faction after all – the banners were all of the Ayyubid yellow. He knew that Salah ad-Din was still away harrying Oultrejourdain, therefore his visitor would be one of the Sultan's sons. Tripoli frowned. Though he held the Sultan in the highest regard, he had never been able to stomach his heirs. The eldest was an arrogant brat, the second a charmer with a dangerous disrespect for his skill, and the third a prodigy with a sword and no brains to balance it. A visit from any of them was likely to result in a good deal of trouble.

Sighing, Tripoli turned his back on the bright morning and retreated into the castle. He descended to the great hall, sent a serving girl after refreshments and then sat down at the banquet table. The table was made of Lebanese cedar, and had borne the elbows of Saracen kings a hundred years before the Franks began their march to Jerusalem as torchbearers of the True Faith. Tripoli was ruminating on the improbability of any faith incorporating much truth beyond avarice when a page – some plain little relation of his wife's, whose name he could never recall – appeared with the stammering announcement: "Th-the Sultan's s-son for you, please, *Messire*..."

Tripoli looked past the page to his visitor, certain that there had been some mistake. The boy who stood before him was none of the three princes he knew, nor anything like them. While all of them had inherited the Sultana Nua'm's solid, stocky frame, this boy was tall and slender, with a feline grace and quick, intelligent eyes in a face of luminous beauty. He could be no more than sixteen, yet he moved across the echoing hall with the nonchalant assurance of a man certain of his own significance. He stopped at the far end of Tripoli's table, and inclining his silk-turbaned head, he said the *salaams*.

"*Wa 'alaikum as-salaam,*" Tripoli intoned automatically, and only then realized that he had stood and bowed. "Whom do I have the honor of greeting?" he continued in Arabic.

"Maslamah 'Abd al-Rahman Salim ibn Yusuf al-Ayyubi," the young man answered, with another courteous inclination of the head. But he lowered his chin not a fraction more than courtesy demanded.

Sultan's son indeed, Tripoli thought, *and the only one I've yet seen worthy of his father*. But it would not do to let the boy know that he had impressed him. Tripoli sat down again. Leaning back in his chair he said, "What brings you here, Salim ibn Yusuf?"

The faintest of smiles touched the boy's face, and at last Tripoli saw the familial resemblance. "I come on behalf of my brother Al-Afdhal," said Salim, "with a message from our father." He handed him a letter with the Sultan's seal. "He most humbly requests passage across your territory tomorrow, in order to inspect the shores of Lake Galilee and the region of Acre beyond."

There isn't a humble hair on your father's body, nor your own, Tripoli thought. He said, "I understood that your father was still in Oultrejourdain."

"With respect, *Messire*: does your own king not make a habit of directing his army, even when he is not able to do it personally?"

Touché, thought Tripoli. He asked, "How many men will he send?"

"Seven thousand," Salim answered, as if it were the most natural thing in the world for Salah ad-Din to send a quarter of his army on a reconnaissance mission.

Tripoli concealed his shock admirably. "I suppose," he said after a moment, "that this 'reconnaissance party' will be armed."

"As every man goes armed in these troubled times," the prince answered evenly. "But my father holds you in the highest regard, *Sayyid*, and as you know he is a man of honor. He has no intention of breaking your agreement."

Indeed, Tripoli thought. Yet their hasty truce had made no claims for self-defense, and this request was, at best, irregular.

At worst, it looked like a set-up. All at once he was angry: at the
Sultan for forcing his hand; at the boy who stood before him
now with his wide-eyed, outrageous request; but most of all at
himself, for the stubbornness and pride that had brought this
upon him, for he knew already how it would end. By virtue of
their truce he could not deny the Sultan's request, but the local
Christian garrisons would consider the reconnaissance an affront.
They would hurl themselves at the Muslim army with all their
zealots' fervor and they would be destroyed, which in turn would
vindicate all the Latin nobles who'd called Tripoli a traitor. He
would have no choice then but to capitulate to the idiot king, or
break from the Latin states entirely, and that, for all the respect
he bore Salah ad-Din, he could not afford to do.

For a long time Tripoli held the prince's eyes, looking for a
way out and knowing that it was futile. At last he said, "Tell your
brother that the Sultan's request is granted – but only on the
condition that his men are out of my territory by nightfall, and
that they attack neither person nor property subject to me."

In the prince's ensuing smile, Tripoli saw the measure of his
ruin.

*

In fact, disaster was nearer at hand that day than the count realized, for on the previous morning, the court envoy Tripoli had
expected had left Jerusalem for Tiberias. It was the result of a
long, bitter battle of wills. Most of the nobles favored diplomacy
in bringing Tripoli to heel, but de Ridefort and Kerak, who had
hounded Tripoli's county with raids throughout the past winter,
held to the conviction that he was a traitor, to be coerced rather
than courted.

In the end the moderates won out, but the feeling among
the members of the envoy as they rode forth was one of distinct
uncertainty. In large part, this was due to de Ridefort. Though
Guy – entirely hopeless when it came to matters of diplomacy

– had been persuaded to stay at home, and Kerak had stomped off in a huff, de Ridefort would not be dissuaded from joining the mission. Moreover he rode at its head, despite the presence of so many of his equals and betters: Roger des Moulins, Master of the Hospitallers; Joscius, archbishop of Tyre; Reginald, lord of Sidon, and the powerful secular knight Balian d'Ibelin. Rather than object to this arrogant effrontery, not one of the nobles even attempted to catch him up. They knew by hard experience that when angry, de Ridefort was best left alone, and not one of them had ever seen him as angry as he was now.

By the time the king's envoy reached Galilee, the vein Bilal had marked on de Ridefort's forehead on their first meeting throbbed visibly. The party had lost both Balian d'Ibelin and Reginald de Sidon to vague errands of sudden and indisputable necessity, and when the others arrived at the fortress at La Feve, they discovered chores and duties similarly in need of immediate attention. Jakelin de Mailly, however, was at de Ridefort's mercy, and therefore he alone witnessed the Master's reception of Tripoli's letter.

The news was superfluous. From the moment Tripoli informed his troops of the agreement with the Sultan's son, the news had spread like wildfire, and Guy's envoy had already heard a dozen heavily-embroidered versions of events on the road north. Still, de Ridefort's expression as he read the letter could not have been fouler if its news had been a complete surprise, and he ended by balling it in his fist with a string of colorful curses he would have whipped one of his knights for uttering.

"Traitorous cowardly son of a Saracen whore!" he concluded, though Tripoli's mother had in fact come from good French stock. De Mailly waited, certain that the Master wasn't finished, and a moment later de Ridefort rewarded his foresight with the demand: "Where is des Moulins?"

De Mailly knew that the Hospitaller Master had slipped away with a young and particularly beautiful serving girl soon after their arrival at the fortress. However, he also knew that to remind de Ridefort now of his chief gripe with des Moulins would be disastrous. So he answered, "I will find him for you."

"You will indeed," de Ridefort said. "And send someone with wine!"

"*Messire*," said de Mailly, and bowing to his Master, he made his escape.

As he reached the courtyard, the exhaustion of two fraught days caught up with him all at once. He would have given anything then to lie down and sleep, rather than roust des Moulins from his bed of sin. As he tried to remember which door he had seen the Hospitaller Master take, his look was as close to grim as it ever came. Though he didn't know what de Ridefort was planning, he was certain that it would end in a good deal of spilled blood.

Sighing, he began knocking on doors until at last he was rewarded with a gruff, "*Oui!*" followed by a curse and what sounded very like a body falling out of a bed.

"It's de Mailly," he said. "De Ridefort would like to see you."

"And I would like nothing less," des Moulins grumbled. A moment later he added, "Tell him I'm coming…"

There was a pause, then a girl's muffled laughter, followed my des Moulins'. De Mailly sighed. It wasn't that he found any particular fault with des Moulins' lecherous predilections: for one thing, they were far too common within the Orders (no matter what the Rule claimed) to be shocking, and secondly, de Mailly was of the broad-minded opinion that every man is a sinner in one way or another, and to attempt to assign degrees to sin is essentially pointless. He only wished that des Moulins had chosen a manner of transgression that was somewhat less time-consuming.

To his credit, des Moulins was outside and decently dressed within ten minutes, though his face was unnaturally flushed and his exasperation obvious. The Hospitaller Master wore anger to great effect. His gaunt height and bleak, black-and-white tunic made him look stern at the best of times, and threw any degree of irritation into relief.

"And what does His Highness want with me?" he inquired as they walked across the courtyard.

De Mailly shook his head. "I do not know, but I suspect it

involves the Muslim reconnaissance."

"I fear you are correct," des Moulins answered grimly, "and God help us."

The two men retreated into silence until they reached the hall. There they found de Ridefort pacing the room, mumbling to himself. "Careful," des Moulins said dryly as they entered. "One might mistake you for Kerak."

De Ridefort glared at him, but he said, "Let us lay our disagreements aside for the moment and concentrate on the problem at hand."

Sighing, des Moulins sat down at the table, on which someone had placed a jug of wine and a bowl of fruit. He poured some for himself and de Mailly. "As I see it," he said, "there *is* no problem, as of yet."

"Tripoli has insulted us!" cried de Ridefort. "He has agreed to allow this 'mission' to take place on the very day we intended to bring our envoy to Tiberias."

Des Moulins sipped his wine. "As far as I know, Tripoli's abilities do not extend to prophecy. We did not send word that we were coming, and therefore he could not have known that his plans interfered with our own until it was too late – a fact that he has demonstrated by sending this letter, which is more than either chivalry or justice required of him."

"Chivalry and justice! To leave the king's people open to attack –"

"The Saracens have promised *not* to attack," des Moulins reminded him, "and the Sultan, for all his sins, has never shown himself to be anything other than a man of his word."

"No reconnaissance mission requires seven thousand men," de Ridefort said coldly. "Mark my words, des Moulins: this is a plot constructed by the Sultan and Tripoli to draw us into a fight, and if it's a fight they want, it's a fight they shall have!"

Des Moulins gave de Ridefort a shrewd look which incorporated, for the first time, a tinge of anxiety. "What are you suggesting?"

Ignoring the question, de Ridefort asked, "How many knights

are there in this garrison?"

"Not nearly enough," the Hospitaller answered at last, "for what you are thinking."

De Ridefort began pacing again. "Then we will have to find more. De Mailly, go and rouse the Templar garrison at Qaqun. I will gather the secular knights from Nazareth, and des Moulins —"

"Will not aid you in this madness!" des Moulins roared, his patience spent at last. He looked like death incarnate. "You are talking about a hundred knights, two hundred at most, against seven *thousand!* You may have cowed the king, de Ridefort, but you do not command me, and until you do I will not order my men to certain death!"

"Of course you will not," de Ridefort answered with soft cruelty, "because you are a simpering cowardly fornicator, far more concerned with satisfying your damnable lusts than meting God's justice."

De Mailly caught des Moulin's hand before he could throw the punch he had aimed at de Ridefort's face. "Stop it," he said. "Both of you. We will gain nothing by fighting amongst ourselves, certainly not God's favor. Now, *Messire,*" he addressed de Ridefort, "while I see that Tripoli's actions could be interpreted as an affront to us, two facts are clear: first, by virtue of his truce with Salah ad-Din, the count has no choice but to allow this reconnaissance; and second, he has shown his loyalty to us by his letter of warning. For the good of the kingdom, let us not respond to his gesture with an insult."

De Ridefort considered this for a moment, then his face darkened again. "The only insult here is Tripoli's," he said. "Des Moulins may do as he likes, but I order you, de Mailly, to go now and rouse the garrison, or I shall have you tried before your brethren as a traitor to God!"

De Mailly looked at his Master for a long moment, his kindly face cold with fury. The very rarity of the expression made it far more terrible than de Ridefort's foulest rage. "Very well, *Messire,*" he said at last. "But tomorrow when you call the charge, remember that you and you alone have crushed the flower of Outremer."

Des Moulins felt a shiver of premonition, and even de Ridefort looked slightly abashed. "I ask no more of them than I am willing to risk myself," he protested. "I will fight by you tomorrow, and die by you, if God wills it…"

But de Mailly was already shaking his head. "Tomorrow *I* will die in battle as a brave man should," he said, "but you, *Messire,* will flee like a traitor." And as he turned to leave, for the first time in many years, de Ridefort felt the spectral chill of doubt.

2

When Khalidah awakened, she lay for a few moments without opening her eyes, praying that she wasn't dreaming. She couldn't remember the last time she had awakened to anything but freezing wind and hunger, shivering despite her woolens and Sulayman's body beside her. Rather than receding, however, the warmth and stillness became more apparent as her consciousness increased. At last she opened her eyes, and found herself looking into a girl's face, less than an arm's distance away.

Khalidah started up, clutching the blankets around her. The bed on which she lay was really no more than a pile of quilts on the floor – much like her bed in the *maharama* had been. Looking past the girl who knelt beside her, Khalidah saw rows of beds like her own, stretching along the walls of the room. There were small windows at the roof-line, a fire-circle full of glowing embers in the centre, and little else.

"Where are we?" Khalidah asked at last.

The girl smiled and said something unintelligible. Khalidah shook her head, and the girl spoke again, this time in oddly-accented Arabic, "We are in the valley of Qaf." At the same time she gave her a strange look, as if to say that this should have been obvious.

"Whose is this house?" Khalidah continued. "Whose this bed

in which I have slept?" She indicated the thick felted mattress and blankets.

"This is not a house," said the girl, "but one of the girls' dormitories at the hermitage. And the bed is yours. It has been ready and awaiting your arrival these last months, Bibi Khalidah – ever since Tor Gul Khan told us that you would come."

"Bibi?"

"'Lady'. Because you are the khan's grand-daughter."

Khalidah digested this for a moment, then said, "Thank you, ah…"

"Abi Gul," the girl answered.

"Abi Gul," Khalidah repeated. "That is a beautiful name."

The girl bobbed her head, looking slightly abashed. She was about Khalidah's age, perhaps a year or two younger, and tiny, with a bird's paradoxical look of fragile strength, a round face with a pointed chin, and wide green eyes flecked with gold. Her skin was fairer than Khalidah's, her hair black and tightly plaited in four sections, one looped around her head in a coronet and the other three hanging free to her waist. She wore clothing like what Brekhna had worn in Khalidah's dreams: a long, creamy woolen robe and loose trousers caught in at the waist with a deep red sash, the hems and collar covered in bright, intricate embroidery. There was a tiny gold stud in her nose, and delicate patterns inked on her forehead and cheeks – curving, vine-like patterns quite different from the angled henna designs of the west.

"How long have I been here?" Khalidah asked, once she'd taken it all in.

"Two nights and a day."

"And I have slept all that time?" she cried, dismayed.

"You were given a draught," Abi Gul said, "the first night, after you dreamed. Tor Gul Khan thought it was for the best. You were distraught."

Khalidah shuddered, remembering the bloody field, the single Franj knight fighting for his life and the beautiful Muslim boy who had delivered him. "Where is Sulayman?" she asked.

Abi Gul's eyes twinkled; she appeared to be suppressing a smile. "Do not worry – your man is safe."

"*My* man?"

"Do you know," she continued, leaning in confidentially, although they were quite alone, "Zhalai had to drag him out of here last night."

"Zhalai?"

"Our house-mother. You spent the first night in Tor Gul Khan's rooms, then they moved you here. Of course, only women are allowed inside, but Sulayman barged right in, saying that he would not leave you." A bright peal of laughter. "Oh, you should have seen it! He and Zhalai facing off in the middle of the room, and all the girls shrieking and screaming because there was a man in our dormitory." Khalidah marveled that she had slept through it all. "Anyway, Zhalai tossed him out at last and he's sat outside ever since, never sleeping a wink...honestly, I've never seen a man so smitten – wait! You cannot go out like that, you aren't properly dressed!"

Indeed, Khalidah found when she stood that she was wearing nothing but a linen shift. However, she had long since gone beyond modesty where Sulayman was concerned. She flung the door open, and there against a backdrop of towering peaks and lush grass, his face wan and eyes bloodshot with exhaustion, was Sulayman.

"Khalidah!" he cried as she flung herself into his arms, and they embraced as though they had been parted for years, rather than days. He pushed her away after a moment to look at her. "Are you all right? Tor Gul Khan gave you something after that nightmare, he said it would help you sleep, but I did not think he meant an entire day and night through. If I did not trust him so well – "

"Honestly!" cried Abi Gul, who had caught up with them. She stood with her hands on her hips, like an irate nursemaid with recalcitrant children. "Zhalai would have my hide if she knew I'd let you out half-dressed! Please, Bibi Khalidah, come back inside and put on some proper clothing, before somebody sees you!"

Khalidah looked at Sulayman. "Don't worry," he said. "I won't go anywhere."

Abi Gul shook her head. "Smitten," she pronounced emphatically, though her look was rather wistful. Then she drew Khalidah to her feet and guided her firmly back into the dormitory.

*

Half an hour later, Khalidah was dressed in a robe and trousers much like Abi Gul's, a sapphire-blue sash and soft leather sandals to replace her others, which were falling to pieces. Abi Gul combed out her dirty, tangled hair, commenting grimly that there was not time to wash it, then plaited and bound it like her own.

"There," she said when she was finished, and held a small piece of polished metal for Khalidah to look into. Khalidah hardly recognized herself. Her cheeks had hollowed over the course of the journey, lengthening her face, but the change was deeper than that. She couldn't put a finger on it, other than to recognize Brekhna in it. But because Abi Gul was waiting for her verdict, she nodded approval.

Abi Gul smiled. "Let us go, then." She led Khalidah back outside to Sulayman, who was waiting where they had left him.

He blinked in surprise at Khalidah's appearance, and then smiled. "It suits you," he said.

"Tor Gul Khan says that you are free to look around today," Abi Gul told them. "At sundown, the *Psarlay* festival begins."

"*Psarlay*?" Khalidah asked.

"What is the word...'spring'. We have a festival to mark each season," she said, "but *Psarlay* is the most fun. Sulayman can tell you."

Khalidah bridled at the complicity in her tone and shot Sulayman a look.

"My time here last year overlapped *Psarlay*," he explained.

Abi Gul nodded. "Now, I must leave you. If you need anything, ask anyone – they will all be glad to help."

Khalidah wondered if this were indeed true, or if Abi Gul was merely being polite; surely their feelings for Brekhna's daughter would be mixed at the least. But she thanked her, and Abi Gul smiled, dipped her head again and then turned and trotted back toward the dormitory.

"You're tired, Sulayman," Khalidah said when she was gone. "And I'm quite capable of showing myself around."

He smiled, touched her hand. "I want to come with you."

"Very well."

"If you'd rather I didn't..."

"I'm trying to be solicitous! Haven't you learned yet that I don't lie to appease?"

He laughed. "It seems I haven't, though you've certainly given me ample opportunity. What first?"

"I want to see Zahirah."

Sulayman sighed. "Why did I even ask?"

As they walked down toward the river, Khalidah took in her surroundings for the first time. It was just as she had glimpsed in her long-ago dream: snow peaks shot the distance with shimmering brilliance, and in the foreground the valley's circumscribing foothills were green with grass and trees. There were tilled fields on the valley floor, and some of the hills had been terraced for crops. All were hazed with the soft green of new growth and dotted here and there with people working among them. Orchards of fruit and nut trees extended in orderly rows on the far side of the river, which flowed across the valley floor in its wide, golden bed, ripples glinting in the morning sun. On the near side, a small herd of horses grazed amongst goats and fat-tailed sheep.

Zahirah broke from the group as soon as she spotted them, galloping toward her mistress with the occasional skip and bunny-hop, as if she'd already forgotten the vast distance they had traveled to reach this horse's paradise. Khalidah kissed her grass-stained nose and then ran a hand along her flank to her bandaged leg. Somebody had taken a good deal of care over her: her coat shone like a copper coin, and the bandage was clean. There was no heat or swelling in the leg.

"You needn't worry," said Sulayman, patting 'Aasifa and Ghassan's grey pony, which had trotted up behind their friend. "The Jinn love their horses at least as much as you love yours."

"Have they been at this grass since we arrived?" Khalidah asked, ignoring him. "They will get colic...laminitis too, if they keep eating like this."

"Don't worry," Sulayman repeated. "They let the horses graze here for a few hours in the morning and then they move them higher up into the hills, where the grass is not so rich."

Satisfied at last that her horse was being properly cared for, Khalidah began to examine the others. Like her tribe's horses, they were mainly solid-colored, with occasional splashes of white on their faces or legs. Their coats were in good condition, though many of them were marked with battle-scars. They had wide, deep chests and strong legs, prominent withers and lean bodies, with the kind of square, well-muscled backs that made it easy to ride without a saddle. Their heads and necks were heavier than Bedu horses', without the distinctive dished profile, but they had similarly large, liquid eyes with a kindly look. This was borne out as Khalidah walked among them, for they nuzzled and whickered to her, and didn't protest when she felt their legs and picked up their feet. They wore no irons, and the walls of their hooves were thicker even than those of the desert horses. Khalidah found this strange, given the valley's soft, grassy footing.

"They bred them that way," Sulayman explained when she commented on it, "crossing in the best of the local mountain ponies, which have the hardest feet I've ever seen – for as soon as they leave Qaf, they need them."

"There's more than mountain pony in these," Khalidah said, admiring a particularly fine honey-colored mare. She blew gently into the horse's nostril, and the mare pricked her ears forward, snuffling curiously, then sprinted away, showing off a liquid gallop. The others ran after her, wheeling across the valley floor like the wing of a great, mottled bird.

"I told you that many of the tribes of these mountains claim descent from Alexander the Great," Sulayman said. "Well, the Jinn turn their noses up at the idea of a bloodthirsty Macedonian ancestor, but they insist that their horses bear the blood of Alexander's famous stallion, Bucephalus. Of course, they also claim that the breed was founded on a god's mount."

"Perhaps they are right on both counts," Khalidah answered, "for I've never seen horses quite like these."

They continued on a slow circuit of the valley, during which Khalidah gained an impression of the Jinn as happy, industrious farmers and herdsmen; an impression which increasingly troubled her. Leaving a group of women who had showed her their weaving – a fine, light silken cloth which, inexplicably, they informed her was to be used for underwear – Khalidah said, "These people do not strike me as fearsome *ghuzat,* Sulayman."

"I suppose that is because most of the time, they are not," he answered. "But hand any one of them a bow or a spear – " he gestured to the gossiping women " – put her in front of an enemy, and he would be felled within seconds." Khalidah looked doubtfully at the silk-weavers and Sulayman said, "Let me show you something."

He strode off along the valley, away from the temple and hermitage, passing the herds, the fields of turned earth, hillsides tumbling with stone and wooden dwellings. When they passed the last of these he led her up a grassy bank. From the top, Khalidah found herself looking down into a wide natural arena, perhaps a *farsakh* long and wide, where forty or fifty horsemen were practicing cavalry maneuvers. Or so she assumed, for they rode and bore arms; yet their methods were unlike anything she had seen before.

The group was split into five squadrons. They practiced a kind of a charge against a straw army, which began with the squadrons ranged loosely across the field, two before and three behind. At some indiscernible cue, the three rear ranks would spur their horses, which broke from standing into a glorious flying pace, their legs moving laterally in two beats rather than the four beats of a gallop. The smoothness of the gait allowed the riders great precision with their bows, which they raised as they burst through the loose fabric of the front ranks. Once through, they proceeded to fire volleys of arrows at the dummy army. They timed the volleys such that one horseman was firing as his neighbor was nocking the bow, making the barrage continuous. When they were within yards of the straw army, the archers split and veered off to the sides, riding parallel to the enemy front line, still firing continuously. As they reached its edges, they veered again to encircle the enemy from behind, and simultaneously the two front ranks charged, changing bows for swords as they joined ranks with the straw soldiers. They shredded them briefly, then re-formed their lines to do it all over again.

"They are very good," Khalidah ventured at last. "Especially with the bow."

Sulayman nodded. "It is probably their greatest skill. They carry two types of bow, and three types of arrow with them: light ones for long distances, heavy ones to pierce armor and scissor-headed ones for...well..."

Khalidah shuddered, imagining the effect of a scissor-headed projectile on an extended sword-arm, an unarmored leg, an exposed neck. And then something else occurred to her, a discrepancy that had been niggling all the time she watched the maneuvers: the field was silent. A Bedu raid was underscored by war cries and ululation, prayers and consignments to Allah, but aside from the thumping of their horses' hooves and the whistle of their arrows, the Jinn riders made no sound; nor were there any apparent visual signals.

"How are they organizing these charges?" she asked.

"By impeccable training, and discipline, and their trust in and knowledge of each other. Perhaps it is their isolation that accounts for it, or their communal way of living...whatever it is, it is what makes them invincible. They can disperse and then rally in an instant; even separated, they think as one."

"That's all very well when one is fighting straw men," Khalidah answered, "or even a matched field of real ones. But however silent or well-coordinated, these charges would not work if the Jinn were even moderately outnumbered."

"That is true, and they've accounted for it."

"How?"

"If their charges are brilliant, their retreats are spectacular. They use them as an offensive: when they are outnumbered or out-maneuvered, they feign retreat, luring the enemy into a chase. Here, their horses come into their own, for they are tireless. Once the enemy is exhausted and far from help, they turn and encircle him. It comes from the fighting philosophy of the Far East: yield where the opponent is strong, attack where he is weak."

"Salah ad-Din's cavalry has been known to do the same," Khalidah pointed out.

"But Salah ad-Din's cavalry does not possess Jinn horses, nor the advantage of being able to maneuver independent of signals."

Khalidah watched a small figure on a steel-grey stallion fire a spurt of arrows at the straw men, then wheel away with the grace of a bird in flight. She recalled her nightmare, and wondered aloud what a band of Templars would do, faced with fighting men like these.

"Die of shock, most likely," Sulayman answered.

She glared at him, baffled. His eyes were laughing at her.

"Those are no fighting men, Khalidah," he said. "They are mere apprentices. Not one of them is older than sixteen, and every one of them is female."

As if to prove his point, the archer on the grey stallion pulled off her helmet, releasing waist-length black plaits. Abi Gul turned her grinning face up to Khalidah and Sulayman and waved.

3

"What do you mean, you are not going?" Salim cried, trembling with indignation. "It is an insult to your men and to our father!"

From the pile of pillows on which he reclined, Al-Afdhal shrugged and drew on the mouthpiece of his hookah. He offered it to Salim, who waved it away with a look of disgust. "Ah, Salim," he said, letting out a gust of acrid, resinous smoke, "you take yourself far too seriously."

"And so I should be like you, and take nothing seriously at all?"

"You are a child, *Akhah*. You know nothing."

At the prodding of a sudden instinct, Salim looked closely at his brother. True, Al-Afdhal was very stoned, but even so Salim would have expected to see some vestige of irritation at the blatant insult. Yet he saw nothing in his brother's face but a heavy-lidded smugness. All at once, he was worried.

"And what is it that *you* know, Al-Afdhal, which I do not?"

"If I'd meant for you to have the answer to that," his brother said, "then you would not be asking." And he smiled, as if his words had somehow shown great wit.

Salim studied him for a moment longer, then said, "You have been talking to Gerard de Ridefort." Though this was no more than a guess, he spoke it with conviction, and his gamble paid off: his brother's face drained suddenly of color, and he sat up, hookah forgotten.

Gesturing to a servant to close the front of the pavilion, Al-Afdhal drew his brother down until they faced each other, then hissed, "Who has told you? Was it the Bedu boy?"

In fact, Bilal had spoken to Salim quite recently about his fears that de Ridefort would attempt to double-cross the Sultan in his absence. But Salim kept his face blank and said, "What would Bilal know about the Templar Master?" He shook his head. "What I know, *Akhah*, I have taken the trouble to learn for myself. And do not forget that I have been privy to all of our father's negotiations in the south."

Al-Afdhal gave him a narrow-eyed look and said, "That does not mean that you will be privy to mine."

"Very well," Salim answered. "But I cannot in good conscience allow our father's men to ride to Tiberias tomorrow if I suspect that they are riding into a trap." He stood up. "So, if you'll excuse me, I shall go now and call the *umara* – "

"Stop!" cried Al-Afdhal, as Salim had intended. Salim turned and regarded him coldly, though what he felt was cruel delight as he watched defeat and fury fight for purchase on his brother's face. At last Al-Afdhal said, "There is no need to say anything to the *umara*. Quite likely it will all come to nothing, and if it does, it will only be to our benefit."

"What will?" Salim asked.

Al-Afdhal sighed. "All I know is this: an envoy from Jerusalem arrived in Al-Fulah today. Since then, the local Templars have been gathering at Nazareth."

"And de Ridefort was among the members of this envoy," Salim said, watching carefully for his brother's reaction.

"He was," he answered, with an odd, wistful note in his voice.

"Has he sent word to you?"

"No." Al-Afdhal sighed. "I do not even know whether he still has an agreement with our father or not. Do you?"

"If I'd meant for you to have the answer to that," Salim said, smiling coldly, "then you would not be asking."

"Watch your tongue, you little son of a whore. You aren't in the south anymore."

"No, I'm not; and if you'd ever known a real whore's son, you'd know better than to threaten him."

Al-Afdhal frowned at him and took up his pipe again.

"Now, there cannot be more than a hundred knights in the local Franj garrisons," Salim continued. "If they are so foolish as to attack us, they will be crushed. Why then do you fear to join the mission?"

Al-Afdhal smoked in silence; he would not meet Salim's eyes.

"I suppose Al-Zahir and Al-Aziz will be going; and of course, I will be there with my *saqa*." He paused, then added, "It would certainly be a neat way of ensuring that nothing interferes with your succession..."

"You insult me!" Al-Afdhal cried.

"No, *Akhah*," Salim said. "You insult yourself and all of the men who follow you. For if this army cannot withstand an attack by a couple hundred Franj knights, then who but you would care to lead it?"

*

Salim's words did nothing to sway Al-Afdhal's decision, so the command of the detachment was given to the Turkish *amir* Muzaffar ad-Din Gökböri. Salim told him about the Franj muster at Nazareth, but in the end they agreed that it was pointless to tell the men. If the Franj attacked, the Sultan's men were well-equipped to defend themselves. But if they were expecting something of the sort, they might be tempted into picking a fight with Tripoli's subjects, and that must be avoided at all costs.

Even so, by the time they rode beneath the walls of Tiberias, where all the town's people stood watching them in eerie silence, the tension was palpable. The Muslims moved slowly by virtue of their great number, and the fierce heat made the men irritable.

But to their credit, their swords remained sheathed, and at last they reached the lake. After a brief stop to eat and to water their horses, they turned and re-traced their path toward Ras al-Mai'. Gökböri was beginning to believe that the mission would actually come off without incident when, in a sparse wood near a watering-hole the Franj called the Springs of Cresson, a band of knights appeared from nowhere, lances couched and mounts at full gallop.

De Ridefort had managed to gather almost four hundred infantry along with the hundred and forty knights supplied by the garrisons, but even so his army was no more than a fluttering scrap against the vast fabric of the Muslim force. Besides that, the suddenness of the charge left the foot-soldiers stranded and the mounted ones vulnerable to a counter-charge, which Gökböri ordered as soon as the few Franj knights who had not broken themselves against the Muslim defense turned to re-form their line. They didn't get the chance. Within minutes, the Muslim front line had surrounded them.

Back in the ranks, Bilal and Salim hung on to their battle-crazed horses, looking for something to fight. Seemingly from nowhere, a man in a white tunic with blood pouring from a wound in his neck reared up, raised his sword over his head, brought it down and then fell dead at their feet. The blow had landed on Bilal's own sword-arm half way between elbow and wrist. His armor had kept the limb from being severed, but he knew immediately that something was very wrong. At first he felt only numbness, but when Salim pulled off his gauntlet, Bilal nearly fainted with the pain. The lower half of his arm flopped uselessly onto his thigh.

"It's broken," Salim said, tearing a piece of his tunic to make a sling, "probably both bones. You cannot stay here. Go back to camp, my father's physicians will tend to you. Tell Imad ad-Din what has happened, and have him write immediately to my father and tell him of our victory."

Victory? Bilal thought dumbly, for he was in shock, his mind clouded by pain. Looking across the sea of heaving bodies that stretched and writhed to the horizon, though, he saw not a single red-crossed banner, and the meaning of what had just happened finally dawned on him.

"De Ridefort – " he began.

"I know. I will look for him."

"Do not let him escape!"

"You don't need to tell me. Now go."

"One other thing," Bilal managed to say, though he thought he was about to be sick. "There is a knight called de Mailly…the Marshal of the Temple. If you find him alive, spare him."

Salim gave him a puzzled look. "Why?"

Why indeed? Bilal wondered, but he was in no frame of mind for introspection. "Please," he said.

Still puzzled, and inclined now to think that the pain had addled Bilal's mind, Salim nodded. "I promise to spare him if it is in my power," he said, and because Bilal appeared to be considering another request, Salim slapped Anjum's flank with the flat of his sword, sending her streaking towards home. But as he turned back to the battle – if that was a fair term for the uncontested slaughter unfolding before him – he knew he needn't have bothered with the promise. With seventy *mujahiddin* to every Franj knight, there could be none left to spare.

*

Bilal was dozing in the grasp of a draught of poppy juice, dreaming of blood-soaked white tunics and warm brown eyes, when a gust of cold air wakened him. He opened his eyes to a blurred image of Salim standing in the doorway with the tent-flap in his hand, looking vaguely around as if he could not remember where he was. After a moment the prince drew a deep, shuddering breath, let it out, and came inside. He was caked in dust and dried blood and his face looked defeated, years older than it had when they had parted.

Bilal was too stunned to do anything but stare at him as he

dropped his sword and helmet in the corner, then took off his tunic with slow, dreamlike movements and held it up, studying the rents and blood-stains before dropping it, too. It drifted to the ground like a shot bird. After that he tore at his clothing, hurling bits of armor and cloth into an indiscriminate pile until he stood naked and shivering. Then he gathered it all into his arms and threw it out into the night. At last he saw Bilal watching and approached him, the night-lamp revealing stark tear-tracks in the dirt on his face.

"How is your arm?" he asked, so ponderously that Bilal thought the impression must be a result of his own drugged state.

"You were right," he answered, and his own voice sounded perfectly normal to him. "Both bones are broken, but the physician said they were clean breaks, and they should heal quickly. Though the setting of them was no pleasure..."

"I'm sorry," Salim said in the same strange, detached tone.

"It was not your doing."

"I should have seen it coming."

"And so should I. Now don't tell me that's why you have been crying."

"No," Salim answered softly.

"You cannot have lost the battle, so what is the matter?"

Salim looked at him for a long moment, his lips open but not quite forming the words, and all at once Bilal knew what was coming. "I killed him, Bilal. I killed Jakelin de Mailly."

Bilal drew a deep breath and released it. "Then I am sure that you had no choice," he said.

"Oh, but I did," Salim answered miserably, his voice brave and brittle at once. "He was not even fighting me. Ah, Bilal – I do not know the words for it!"

"Begin at the beginning," said Bilal gently, "and you will find them."

Salim nodded. He sat on the bed by Bilal, wrapped his arms around himself and began: "When you left, it was already over. The Franj who hadn't died in the first charge were dying by then, or else they'd surrendered; all except one."

"Him," Bilal said.

Salim nodded. "You did not tell me that he was so beautiful, Bilal. Like those Persian paintings of angels…" Salim's look had retreated with memory, and at last Bilal felt the beginnings of grief. "When I saw him, he was trying to fight three men at once, and he was almost spent. He had to have known that his fellows were dead or captured, but he fought as if he had an army of thousands at his back. I told them to stop – those who were fighting him, and the others who were taunting him. They obeyed me, and he swayed there, leaning on his sword, but he nodded to me like the well-bred Franj do. I asked him his name, and he said that it was Jakelin de Mailly." Salim paused, then repeated, "Jakelin de Mailly. Our language flowed from his tongue like water, Bilal – not like the other Franj, who sound as though they've drunk too much wine. I told him that I was taking him prisoner, and he told me that he would rather keep fighting. I answered that he would certainly die if he did not let me help him, and he thanked me, but declined. He did not fear death, he said. The only thing he feared was breaking his vow to God.

"I thought that he was mad, and I told the men to take him prisoner. But he raised his sword when they came near, and so it began again. That was when I realized that he wasn't mad at all. He was, perhaps, the sanest man I've met in all this mad land, because…" He paused, his jaw working and eyes filling again. "Bilal, he didn't want to do it! He didn't want to fight us, and he didn't want to die, but he believed that God required it of him and so he did it anyway. He trusted his God beyond even his own heart, and how can a man who believes like that be an infidel? How can he deserve anything but our respect?"

Bilal offered no answer; he had none. After a moment Salim shook his head, casting tears that sparked for a moment in the light before expiring. "I could not bear to watch him then. The men were taunting him again, making a game of his death. I saw how they would draw it out, I knew that I would not be able to stop them, and I could not bear it. So I killed him. I cut straight through his helmet when his back was turned to me. I wanted to give him deliverance, but the moment I struck that blow I knew that I had cheated him, for I was not God, nor any better than a heathen to him, and worst of all I had broken my promise to you." At last he capitulated to the tears.

"Come to me, Salim," Bilal said, and he came, curling up beside him and weeping into his lap like a frightened child. Bilal pulled the blanket over him and said, "It will be all right."

"No," Salim answered, his voice full of despair. "Nothing will ever be all right again."

And Bilal could think of no answer to that, because he knew that Salim might very well be right.

4

"All right, Sulayman," Khalidah said as they walked back toward the hermitage late in the afternoon, "you've made your point. But I am lost as to the ultimate purpose of all of this. Qaf is virtually impossible to access, and aside from the horses there doesn't appear to be much here to protect. So why the need for an elite army?"

Sulayman sighed. "That is equivalent to asking why the Jinn exist at all."

"You promised me an explanation when we got here," Khalidah reminded him, "and though this day has been nothing if not interesting, I have no better idea of who these people are or what they want with me than I did when we left Wadi Tawil."

"You will, tonight."

"Stop being cryptic!"

"I'm not being cryptic. One night of a Jinn festival will tell you more about them than I ever could. Besides, my time here was really not long. You should give them the chance to explain themselves to you in their own way."

Before Khalidah could reply, someone called her name. She turned and saw a group of girls approaching, led by a sweaty, beaming Abi Gul. Their white robes were mud-spattered and the patterns on their faces smudged. All of them carried padded leather armor and metal helmets. They had bows slung over their shoulders and short-swords tucked into their sashes. Having witnessed the girls' skill, Khalidah felt shy in their presence; but they looked equally intimidated by her. Only Abi Gul appeared unperturbed.

"You were watching us," she said. "What did you think?"

"I was humbled," Khalidah said. "You put my father's *ghuzat* to shame."

The girls looked at each other, blushed and giggled. There were four of them besides Abi Gul, and she introduced them in a blur of names. Ambrenn was tall and auburn-haired, Hila small, sturdy, with brown hair and dark skin, Afshan rosy and laughing with fugitive black ringlets escaping her plaits, and Shahascina an unparalleled beauty, with hair as astonishingly yellow as a Franji's. Though the shades varied, every one of them had golden eyes.

"And this is Bibi Khalidah," Abi Gul told her friends: unnecessarily, thought Khalidah. No doubt they had watched and discussed her at length while she slept.

"Come with us," said Abi Gul, taking her hand, "it is time to get ready."

"Sulayman?" Khalidah said, suddenly panicked at the thought of surrendering to this group of girls. She had had no female friends among her father's tribe, and after their long months of solitary travel, she couldn't imagine being without Sulayman.

"Go with them now," he said. "I will not be far away." He turned before he noticed the looks the girls exchanged, but Khalidah saw them. She turned her own eyes away, mortified.

"Ah, come now," Abi Gul said when she noticed her charge's embarrassment, pulling her firmly toward the dormitory. "Who would not envy you such words, from such a man?" Another peal of giggles.

"You don't understand – " Khalidah began, but seeing Abi Gul's raised eyebrows, she abandoned the denial. After all, what they assumed was likely very near the truth.

Sighing, she followed them into the dormitory, which was heaving with girls ranging roughly in age from twelve to sixteen. Khalidah had counted twenty-five beds that morning, but there had been twice that number on the practice field.

"Where are the others?" she asked Abi Gul, who was hanging her gear in an alcove by the door.

"This is not the only dormitory," she answered, wiping her sword carefully before she sheathed it and hung it with the others, between two long pegs extending from the wall. Khalidah caught a glimpse of her own sword standing in a corner beside her saddle, bags and travel clothing. All had been cleaned. *By whom?* she wondered. *Was it a chore or an honor?*

"There are four in all," said Abi Gul, "two for the girls, two for the boys. We live with our families until we are twelve, then we move here." Khalidah followed her to one of the beds, where Abi Gul began to undress. "For four years, we live with the other apprentices, and do nothing but train. It's the only time in our lives when we do not help with the crops or the herds or anything else."

She tossed aside a long garment of finely-woven silk – the underwear, apparently, for which the women had been weaving cloth earlier – and then stood stark naked, to Khalidah's mortification, her finger to her lips as if she were trying to recall what to do next. At last she reached for a woolen robe and tied it around her body with her sash.

"When we turn sixteen," Abi Gul concluded, "we are sent on our first battle. If we fight honorably, and if we return, then we are Jinn."

"What are you until then?" Khalidah asked.

Abi Gul shrugged. "Children."

Khalidah considered this. Though her unmarried state had put her somewhat in limbo, she had been a woman in the eyes of her tribe since she started bleeding, aged twelve. When she had left with Sulayman, many of her peers already had two children; if she had been a boy, she would have been a seasoned *ghazi* by now. She tried to imagine what it would be like to live all one's life in a single setting, and to leave it the first time to go to war. She wondered what kind of courage it would take to forsake Qaf for a world one had only glimpsed from an arrow-sight; how common were Sandaras or Brekhnas.

"Look, you are still dressed!" Abi Gul cried. She reached for another robe, which hung on a peg by the neighboring bed: her own, Khalidah realized. "Come, or there won't be time to wash your hair."

Looking around, Khalidah saw that the dormitory was nearly deserted. She stripped quickly, wrapped herself in her robe and joined the exodus. The girls streamed down the hill toward a large wooden building on the banks of the river, with smoke rising from a hole in its roof. Inside was filled with steam and chattering girls. Their robes hung from pegs near the entrance, and they shrieked and giggled as they washed themselves or each other's hair. The water, apparently re-directed from the river, ran in a trough down the length of the building, and then away again out through an opening at the other side. Older women, dressed in shifts, warmed water in massive kettles over a fire at the centre, ladling it into the bowls and pitchers the girls brought them.

Khalidah had never bathed with anyone but Zaynab, and she was mortified at the thought; but Abi Gul seemed to understand this, and led her to a quiet corner where Ambrenn and Hila were sharing a bowl of hot water. "I'll get more," said Abi Gul, and left Khalidah with them.

Hila smiled kindly at her, and Ambrenn nodded. Khalidah could not decide whether the latter was haughty or shy, but thought it best to give her the benefit of the doubt. She smiled, and hesitantly, Ambrenn smiled back. Shy, she decided, and this knowledge gave her courage. She untied her robe and hung it by theirs. When she turned back, Ambrenn was proffering a chunk of soap.

"Wash in the cold," she said in Arabic less fluid and more heavily accented than Abi Gul's, "and rinse in the warm."

Khalidah accepted the soap and took it to the trough of running water. She could not remember the last time a bath had constituted more than a quick plunge in an icy river, and soap was a distant dream. She embraced the luxury wholeheartedly, scrubbing herself from head to toe, and was trying unsuccessfully to rinse her hair in the cold trough when Abi Gul joined her.

"Not like that," she said, and filled a pitcher partly from the bowl of hot water she had brought, mixing it with cold before she tipped it over Khalidah's head. She repeated the process until Khalidah's hair was rinsed, the soapy water running away through the slatted wooden boards of the floor.

By the time she was finished, Khalidah had grown less shy of her nakedness, and she listened with interest to Ambrenn and Hila as she worked a comb through her tangled hair. They were speaking in Pashto, and as she listened, Khalidah felt a strange kind of *déjà vu*: not quite understanding, but like the memory of understanding. One or two words seemed to form the basis of the girls' conversation, and when Abi Gul returned, dripping and goose-pimpled from the cold-water trough, Khalidah asked her what they meant. In response, Abi Gul burst out laughing. She said something to her friends in rapid Pashto, and Hila joined in her laughter as Ambrenn flushed red, and Khalidah wondered what terrible thing she had said.

"I told them that they should watch their mouths around you," Abi Gul told her, "you have a sharp ear for our tongue! *Aghundem* means 'to dress, to put on'. *Meerre* literally means 'warrior', but in this case, it also means 'husband'. My friends are talking about how to dress tonight to best attract a husband."

The other girls objected loudly to this. "She'll think we are feather-headed fools!" Hila cried.

"I have seen evidence that you are anything but," Khalidah answered.

Hila inclined her head, acknowledging the compliment, and continued, "It is true, we were discussing the dresses we will wear tonight. I doubt there is a girl here who is *not* discussing them – our mothers have spent the past month making them for us."

"Then it seems you would be ungrateful daughters not to boast," Khalidah said, thinking with a pang of the red silk dress Zaynab had made for her wedding. She wondered what had happened to it, and then made herself stop, for to wonder that was to open her heart to a stampede of painful speculation.

"As for attracting husbands," Hila continued, "that is only half the story, as Abi Gul knows full well." She flicked water at her friend. "You see, it is during *Psarlay* that betrothals are made official. And although everybody pretends that the official betrothal is the first they have heard of an intended union, in reality everybody has known about it for months...or in Ambrenn's case, for years." She grinned, Abi Gul giggled, and poor Ambrenn blushed still more deeply.

"So, you are to be married?" Khalidah asked her gently, wondering whether congratulations or commiserations were in order.

Ambrenn looked up at her, and by the shining eyes above her flushed cheeks, Khalidah saw that it was the former. "After we both return from our first battle."

"Indeed, poor Ambrenn and Mirzal must eye each other chastely for a while longer," teased Hila.

"How do you know that they are chaste?" Abi Gul asked wickedly.

"Of course they are chaste!" Hila retorted. "Ambrenn is too well-behaved to suggest anything else, and Mirzal too dreamy to think of it until she does." She and Abi Gul collapsed into laughter, and Ambrenn stood up, tied her robe on, and stomped away. The other girls sobered immediately.

"Ah, now we'll have to apologize," sighed Abi Gul. "Honestly, she should know that we tease her out of jealousy."

"Then neither of you is betrothed?" Khalidah ventured, hoping that she wasn't overstepping any boundaries by asking.

Abi Gul shook her head. "We are still 'free', alas...though rumor has it Sarbaz means to speak for Shahascina this *Psarlay*. He has certainly mooned over her long enough, though she plays her cards close...we'll have to wait and see. Come now, let's catch Ambrenn before she works herself into a state." They tied their robes and collected their combs, and made their way back up the hill to the dormitory.

Though still crowded, the scene was more ordered than the one they had left. Khalidah suspected that it was due to the presence of an older woman who was stoking the fire in the center of the room. She was perhaps in her early twenties, tall and thin with gleaming blue-black plaits and skin like new milk. Abi Gul led Khalidah to the woman and introduced her.

"Zhalai, this is Bibi Khalidah; Bibi Khalidah, Zhalai, our *Mor* – that is, mother."

Zhalai smiled, bowed to Khalidah, and seeing her confusion elaborated: "*Mor* being a relative term. I watch over the girls in this dormitory for the years that they live here, taking over where their mothers leave off. I am, therefore, an honorary mother to them all – and honored indeed that you have joined my house, Bibi Khalidah." She bowed again, and this time Khalidah reciprocated. "I trust that Abi Gul is taking good care of you?"

"The best," Khalidah said, smiling. "Thank you."

"Don't thank us," Zhalai said, her look suddenly sober. She drew breath as though she meant to add something, and then appeared to think better of it, but not before the unspoken thought had time to infect Khalidah with a seed of curiosity, and doubt. It was a look she had encountered many times that day amongst her mother's people. It was not comfortable to know that they expected something of her which they were afraid to ask for outright. "You had best get ready," Zhalai said then, and turned back to her fire.

Khalidah wanted to ask Abi Gul what it all meant, but the other girl had launched into a chattering tirade, perhaps to preclude just such a question. "...dress is on your bed," she was saying, when Khalidah tuned back in, "and when you have put it on I will help you with the rest."

Khalidah nodded vaguely, noticing another white woolen robe laid out on her bed, this one more finely-woven and intricately embroidered than the last. As she put it on, she wondered who had made these things for her. They didn't look like hand-me-downs, and they fitted perfectly. But before she could think long about that new mystery, Abi Gul produced a comb and made Khalidah sit so that she could re-plait her hair. This time she wove strings of beads and cowry shells into the plaits, and when she finished she produced a shawl, deep blue and covered with embroidered horses.

"It is beautiful!" Khalidah exclaimed, running a hand over the minute stitches. "Who made it?"

For once, Abi Gul was silent, but by her heightened color and pleased embarrassment, Khalidah knew the answer. Moved, she said, "Thank you, Abi Gul…but please don't be offended if I ask you how you knew?"

"We have always known that you would come, Khalidah bint Brekhna." She took up a pot of kohl and a brush, and indicated to Khalidah to sit so that she could line her eyes. "Does it bother you to hear me say so?"

In fact, it was a bit like the Pashto words: unexpected, yet unsurprising. "How could it," Khalidah answered, "after everything else?"

"Tell me," Abi Gul said, pausing, brush in hand, "how did Sulayman ever convince you to go with him?"

So Khalidah related the story of her short-lived engagement to her cousin, Sulayman's warning, and their subsequent flight. Abi Gul listened with a mixture of laughter and awe, and when Khalidah had finished, her only comment was, "Well, that's your Jinn blood showing." Then she put away her pot of kohl and brought out another pot and a brush so fine, it seemed to be made of only a few hairs.

"What is that?" Khalidah asked dubiously.

"It is ink made from…ah, I cannot remember the word…we call it *tut*."

"Mulberry," Khalidah said abruptly.

Abi Gul nodded, surprised. "Yes, mulberry – but how did you know?"

"I have been thinking about this since Sulayman told me that I spoke Pashto during that dream on my first night here: I think that my mother must have spoken it to me, and perhaps, long ago, I spoke it too. Understood it, at least. Now that I'm here, bits of it are coming back."

Abi Gul nodded. "That makes sense. Perhaps you will be able

to speak it again before too long…well, anyway, this is ink made from *tut*, and we use it to paint the *harquus* on our faces. You have seen them on the women?" Khalidah nodded, and Abi Gul began painting something on her forehead, between her eyebrows. "When we return from our first battle," Abi Gul continued, "we are given permanent *harquus* – the mark of the Jinn. Until then, we paint them on."

"What about the men?" she asked.

"They get them too, but theirs are on their backs."

"Why?"

"Why not?"

Khalidah could think of nothing to say to this. She sat in silence, considering the day's many revelations until Abi Gul finished. She held the scrap of mirror for Khalidah's approval. She had put a delicate, vine-patterned triangle on Khalidah's forehead, and tiny mandalas on both cheeks. To their equal surprise, Khalidah leaned forward and hugged her.

"I am glad to be here," she said.

"And we are glad to have you," Abi Gul answered.

5

The sun had sunk behind the mountains when Khalidah and
Abi Gul emerged from the dormitory, leaving the sky bluish-
green with the first scatter of stars and a waning moon. A bonfire
had been lit on the riverbank, and it was already surrounded by
people. Many of them were dancing, and as the girls drew closer
Khalidah began to make out the sound of instruments – drums,
a high-pitched flute, and some kind of stringed instrument, its
voice louder and more brittle than an *oud's*, and underscored by a
drone. When they reached the fringes of the dancers, the *oud*-like
instrument suddenly picked up a melody, plaintive and strange
and beautiful.

"Where is that coming from?" Khalidah asked. Abi Gul took
one look at her rapturous face and rolled her eyes. Khalidah
didn't understand until she followed her friend's pointing finger.
Seated by the fire was a group of musicians; Sulayman sat at their
centre, holding the strange *oud*. He looked up then, saw her, and
smiled. She smiled back, then turned to say something to Abi
Gul, but she was gone.

Khalidah joined the ring of people watching the musicians.
The instrument Sulayman played had a neck far longer than that
of any *oud* she'd seen. Standing on end, the instrument would
be nearly her height. It had five wire strings, and thirteen frets

marked by colored thread wound around the neck. As far as she could tell, the two sets of outer strings were tuned to the same note, and the middle one tuned a fifth above. Sulayman played all the strings in unison, but worked the frets only on the first two, accounting for the distinctive drone. He played on and on through a series of serpentine variations, and when at last the tune ended he was met by cheers of delight. He smiled, thanked the other musicians, and then handed the *oud* to a woman in the circle of listeners.

"What was that instrument?" she asked Sulayman, when he joined her.

"A kind of *sitar*," he said.

"How did you learn to play it?"

He shrugged. "It's not so different from an *oud*."

"What about the tune?"

"I learned it on my last visit here."

"Will you ever run out of surprises?" she asked dryly.

He smiled. "I hope not, or you will tire of me."

"No," she answered, "it is only then that you will *cease* to tire me."

He laughed and slipped an arm around her waist. She looked around anxiously, but no one seemed to notice or care about this show of appropriation. In fact, as she looked, she saw other couples behaving similarly. "They see things differently here," he said, picking up on both her apprehension and its source. "Do not worry – your honor is quite intact among the Jinn." Khalidah nodded, though she still could not quite believe it. "Come, you must see the dancing."

They moved toward the outskirts of the crowd, where bodies spun and whirled in the darkness. The dancers formed a ring, the men and boys at the center, moving to the music with wild, individual abandon, while the women linked arms across each others' shoulders in small groups and moved together in slow, elegant lines around the periphery.

"What is this all about?" Khalidah asked. "And please don't tell me that someone will tell me later on!"

Sulayman shook his head. "I won't. But you'd do better to ask Abi Gul."

Khalidah turned to find that her friend had re-joined them. "They are asking the gods and goddesses to bless the herds and crops during the growing season," she answered, handing each of them a fresh cup of wine.

"And who are your gods and goddesses?"

Abi Gul paused, then said, "At the end of the night, someone will recite the creation story. It explains most of what you are wondering, and probably a good deal that you haven't thought of yet."

Sighing, Khalidah sipped from her cup and resigned herself to waiting. The night wore on with food and drink, music and dancing. The girls dragged her into some of the dances, and she found them more fun and less difficult than she had expected. After a time the *sitar* player gave up, leaving the drummers to play alone. They seemed to be competing to make their rhythms ever faster and more complicated, while the spectators called and cheered. The dancers gradually retired, settling into a ring by the fire, until only the boys and girls were left, barging each other's lines in a good-natured attempt to make the others step down. When the last of them had collapsed in exhaustion, the drums suddenly went silent. After a moment, a figure emerged from the shadowy throngs and made his way to the center of the circle: Tor Gul Khan.

He wore a robe like the others' but without embroidery, and on his head, in place of the other men's rolled woolen caps, was a multi-colored turban with the glint of golden threads running through its weave. He had a face the color of tea with a splash of milk, eyes as brilliantly golden as an eagle's, an aquiline nose which was prominent, but not overly large. His eyebrows were white, his chin clean-shaven as all the Jinn men's, and his skin ridged and valleyed with age. He regarded them in silence for a moment, and then he cried something in Pashto, his voice rolling across the crowd like an ocean wave.

"What is he saying?" Khalidah asked Abi Gul.

"Hail to Khuday, the creator of all things!" she translated. "Hail to His creation which sustains us, and to the deities who serve Him, who keep us by their grace! Hail to the consecrated Kings of Hewad, from whom our race descends!"

"Hewad?" Khalidah asked.

"Literally, 'homeland'; the place where our people originated."

The crowd was murmuring something in response to Tor Gul Khan's words, and when they finished, he turned in a slow circle, carefully examining the faces of his rapt spectators. They looked back expectantly, even hopefully. At last Tor Gul Khan's eyes came to rest on a young woman with golden hair – Abi Gul's friend, Shahascina. He nodded to her, and she beamed with pride. Amidst the sudden buzz of whispers around her, she stood and approached the leader. Laying one hand on her shoulder, Tor Gul Khan addressed the people again.

"Shahascina is Khuday's voice tonight. Give her all the respect you give Him." With that, he retired into the shadows, and Shahascina knelt at the center of the circle. She looked around at the throngs of people, as had Tor Gul Khan, and with no less composure she began to speak:

"In the beginning, when Khuday formed the earth, He placed the great mountain Luy Ghar at the center of the world, which rose all the way to heaven. The upper regions were screened by clouds, and above the clouds on the mountain peak was the land of Hewad, where the lesser deities made their home. They were divided in two groups, one to oversee the west and one the east of the world of men.

"In time, each group wanted sovereignty over the earth, and so they went to war. They fought, tearing each other to pieces, and when the pieces fell to earth they became evil spirits which wreaked havoc on the world of men. They salted the fields and poisoned the waters, sent pestilence among the herds and plagues among the people.

"The shamans of earth appealed to Khuday for help. When

He saw what was happening, and the cause of it, He was furious. He came down to Hewad and put Himself between the warring deities and chastised them, for they had decimated not only the people of earth but also their own number by their quarrel. Only twelve remained: six women of the east and six men of the west.

"'Your war ends now,' He said to them, 'and to seal the peace you will each take a spouse from your rivals. The first child born of these unions will be sent to earth to live as a man. He will be a great warrior, and he will deliver the people from the monsters you have created.'

"The deities obeyed him, and within a year a child was born to a goddess of the east and a god of the west. When he was delivered of his mother, the infant raised his right hand up as if to strike out, bent his left leg as if to kick, and looked at his parents with his right eye open and his left eye squinted. He said, 'With my right hand I will strike the enemies of men; with my left leg I will kick them. With my wide eye I will see the path of righteousness, and with the narrow I will see through deception. Now take me down the mountain to the valley and give me to the barren woman who lives there.'

"The child's parents did as he bid them. They brought him to the valley, sun-scorched and teeming with evil spirits. The village was nearly deserted, the few remaining people dying. The baby directed them to a little stone hovel in the shadow of the mountain, with a rag for a door and a sheep's skeleton in the yard. A wizened woman sat on the sheep's skull, watching them.

"'This is where you leave me,' said the child. His mother wept and his father protested, but in the end of course they had no choice but to leave him in that terrible place of their own making.

"Well, the evil spirits knew that the child had been sent to drive them from the earth, and they knew also that they must destroy him while he was still an infant and helpless. So they made a giant rat of bronze, gave it life, and sent it to dispatch the child. But when the baby saw the rat, he grabbed a whip and struck it so that it shattered into a hundred harmless mice, which scurried away. Next, the spirits sent a raven made of iron, but the child grabbed a bow, strung it with the old woman's hair, and shot the raven down. Then the spirits sent a mosquito as large as a horse, but the baby took a sword and struck it, and it turned into a cloud of ordinary mosquitoes and flew off into the grass.

"The old woman, who had lost all her family to the deities' plague, was overjoyed when she realized the nature of the child she had been given, but she knew that she could not raise such a child in a dying town. So she bound him to her back and walked until they came to a place where people still lived in comfort. She took a job in the kitchen of a wealthy family, and there her son, whom she called Arman for all the hopes she pinned on him, grew up.

"Being the child of deities, Arman grew quickly, so that within five years he had the stature of a young man. The nobleman's sons were jealous of him, for he was well-built and handsome, and they set him tests of strength and cleverness so that he would fail and they could ridicule him. But he succeeded at their tests, and gradually the townspeople became aware of his feats. 'He is no ordinary man,' they said. 'A warrior of such strength and cleverness must have been sent by the gods!' And they begged him to fight the evil spirits which had plagued them for so long.

"Not knowing what to do, Arman decided to appeal to the deities. He climbed to the clouds that marked the border of Hewad and appealed to them: 'If I am truly of your blood, and have been sent by you to deliver men from the evil spirits which plague them, then show me some sign.' When he had spoken, the wind stilled, the clouds shifted, and he found at his feet a pool of water. When he looked into the pool, he knew that it was as the people of earth had said, for it was not his own face that he saw there, but the fearsome face of a warrior, set with eyes that flashed like stars, above a warrior's broad chest and powerful arms,.

"Looking down from Hewad, Arman's mother recognized her son. Taking pity on him for the bitter battles that lay ahead of him, which had been partly of her making, she took his father's armor and sword and bow and sent them down to him on a coal-black war-horse, with a mane and tail thick as sheaves of wheat and hooves so hard they struck sparks from the stone and eyes that flashed like the fire that lives at the heart of mountains.

"Arman, who had now by the grace of the deities become Mobarak Khan, our Sacred Leader, said a prayer of thanks, then mounted the horse, which he called Ghar Sawghat, since he had been the mountain's gift, and rode down toward the world he had pledged to deliver from evil. As Ghar Sawghat galloped down the mountain, the thundering of his hooves awakened boulders which became mounted warriors who followed Mobarak Khan until they were a hundred strong. When at last they reached earth, the men knew that their Mobarak Khan had come and they, too, followed him, until he led an army ten thousand strong. And so the army of Mobarak Khan met the army of monsters and evil spirits in the shadow of Luy Ghar, and there they fought until the evil spirits were destroyed, the few survivors driven back into the barren places of the earth.

"But the battle raged so long and so fiercely that the gods' mountain trembled, then shook and finally toppled. The people of earth did not notice, for they were too wild with joy that the evil had at last been driven from their lands. But Mobarak Khan silenced them, saying, 'Do you not realize what has happened? Our ladder to the gods is broken forever, but the same cannot be said of the ladder between the evil spirits and the world of men. Evil is not vanquished, only driven back, and when it rises again it will be up to us to defend ourselves against it, for the gods can no longer help us.'

"'But you are the son of the gods,' the people said. 'Will you not defend us?' And Mobarak Khan answered, 'I will fight for you, for I have pledged to do so, but I was born a man and my strength will be no greater than that of the best of you; nor will I outlive my appointed time.' Then the people asked him to be their king. But he said, 'I am a warrior; for a king, look to your princes.' So they asked him what he would do instead, and Mobarak Khan said, 'I will go in search of a place I have seen in dreams. It is far from here. The mountains protect it, the sun smiles upon it, its soil is fertile and its water clean. It reminds me of the land of Hewad, which we have lost. My people shall live there in peace, but they shall be trained as warriors worthy of the gods from whom they are descended; and if ever the evil spirits rise again, you will find them at hand with their weapons, ready to serve you.'"

Shahascina looked up and around at her audience, as if surfacing from a dream. "And so Mobarak Khan left with his band of warriors born of the rocks of Luy Ghar and went in search of the valley of dreams. In good time he found it, and in good time he and his men married and had sons and daughters, who had sons and daughters in turn."

Shahascina's voice had grown soft, reverent, and yet the silence of the listeners was so complete that it reached every one of them as distinctly as a cry. "And this is the story of Mobarak Khan our sacred Father; of Qaf, our home; and of us, the Jinn, the children of the fallen mountain. Forevermore, we uphold our Father's pledge."

"We uphold his pledge," murmured the Jinn, as one. And Khalidah too found herself speaking the foreign words, with tears in her eyes.

6

It was several weeks before the full impact of the massacre at the Springs of Cresson made itself felt and for both sides to realize how fundamentally they had been changed by that short, brutal battle. For Gökböri and those who had fought with him, it meant instant celebrity. Even those of the Muslim forces who had not taken part were inspired by it. As news of the victory spread, a whole new wave of would-be soldiers flocked toward Damascus, fired with dreams of the glory to be found fighting in the Sultan's army.

Yet Salah ad-Din himself received the news with mixed feelings. Though he was glad to be rid of so many of the troublesome Templars, he was distinctly put out that he had not been there to witness the event. He considered his situation – the returning *hajj* caravans slowed to a trickle, the battle season imminent, the Franj of Oultrejourdain beaten and cowering – and decided that it was time to go home. He sent a letter to Al-Afdhal instructing him to find a good mustering point for their ever-expanding army, then he requisitioned half of the Egyptian troops, sent his brother back to Cairo and turned his camel north.

The news that Salah ad-Din had finally departed from Oultrejourdain did little to cheer the reeling Franj. The loss of so many of their best knights at Cresson was a disaster, but perhaps the greater disaster was their ensuing loss of faith. Those dead

knights had charged Gökböri's army with the conviction shared
by most of the Christians of Outremer: that it was God's will
that they drive the Saracens from their kingdom. As such, they
could not believe that He would let them fail. But at Cresson
they *had* failed; there was no possibility of denying it, for of the
five hundred men who followed Gerard de Ridefort into battle
that day, de Ridefort was the only one to have escaped with his
life.

The ensuing whispers of treachery, the suspicion that he had
purposely led the knights to their deaths, might have grown into
a whole lot more had the kingdom not faced more immediate
practical problems. Though the castles of Kerak and Shawbak
had not surrendered to Salah ad-Din, there was little else left
intact in Oultrejourdain. Farms had been abandoned, entire
towns deserted as terrified peasants flocked to Muslim-ruled areas
to escape the Sultan's wrath. This was exactly as Salah ad-Din had
intended, for without peasants to provide food, the castles would
be easy prey to sieges the following winter.

There could only be one response to such unmitigated disaster.
At the end of May, King Guy sent out the *arriere ban*, summoning
every able-bodied free Christian man in his lands between the
ages of fifteen and seventy into his army. For once, he acted on
no advice but his own, for even the likes of Guy de Lusignan
could see that war with Salah ad-Din was now inevitable.

*

Tal 'Ashtara had been Nur ad-Din's favorite campground, due
to its many springs and the resulting meadows, which could
support an army's worth of horses in a good season. Al-Afdhal
saw no reason to look any further for a muster point, so as Salah
ad-Din rode north, his son directed the relocation of the army
to the new site south of Ras al-Mai'. Like some ponderous beast,
the city of tents that had grown up around the desert town began
to disperse, until there was nothing left of it but piles of litter,

trampled circles where the pavilions had stood and the feeling of vast abandonment that clings to ancient ruins, but not to living towns.

Meanwhile, the soft green meadowland of Tal 'Ashtara was rapidly disappearing as the old tents and pavilions were pitched anew and then new tents were pitched around them. It was as if the camp had taken nourishment from its new, fertile setting. Day after day it swelled as new soldiers streamed in with their gear and their animals, until a man standing on a siege tower at its centre would not have been able to see its edge.

Salim and Bilal and pitched their tent by the edge of a trickling spring, in the shade of a sprawling pomegranate bush. Or rather, Bilal pitched the tent while Salim looked listlessly on, going through the barest motions of life as he had every day since Cresson. Over the course of those weeks, Bilal had begun to feel that Salim had somehow departed himself, as lost to the battle as if he'd died there. The prince was sad and circumspect, passing his days in bruised silence, speaking only perfunctorily. At night, though he permitted himself to be held, he lay like an effigy of himself, steadfastly ignoring Bilal's gentle attempts to break through his torpor.

At first, it seemed the move to Tal 'Ashtara had made no difference to Salim. But the sound of running water, the days full of heat and little else, seemed to soothe him, and little by little he began to return. It started with a gradual re-focusing of his eyes on the things around him; then one day, for no apparent reason, he reached for Bilal's hand, his own as tremulous and uncertain as Bilal's had once been. Bilal matched his steps as he'd learned to do long ago when breaking a young horse, careful not to show too much of a reaction one way or another, but to accept each overture as the gift it was.

One stifling afternoon, when they'd been at the new camp for about a week, Salim said abruptly, "What if we are wrong?"

They were sitting with their feet in the spring. Salim did not look at Bilal but at the pomegranate bush, which was dropping scarlet flowers into the water. Bilal did not have to ask what he meant: it was the only thing he'd thought about since Cresson.

"I don't think that it's a question of right and wrong," he answered carefully, poking around inside his splinted bandage with a stick in an attempt to relieve the itching. "It's about belief. We act according to the dictates of Allah, as the Franj do their God. We each fight for our holy city. Unfortunately, it happens to be the same one...ah, merciful Allah!" The stick had broken off inside his bandage. Now he was casting about for another with which to remove it.

Salim lay back on the grass, resting his head on his outstretched arm and considering Bilal. "That is not quite what I meant. Although in a way, it is..." He paused. "As you say, we share the same holy city. Has it never struck you as strange that Islam and Christianity and Judaism too, to be fair hold so many of the same places sacred? We speak different languages," he continued slowly, as if he were working out the thoughts as he spoke them, "we and the Franj, and yet we mean the same things. Cut out our hearts and you could not tell one from the other."

Bilal frowned at his broken arm. He'd succeeded at last in removing the stick from the bandage, but it had left shards of wood behind, which would no doubt give him sores and earn him a lecture the next time the physician changed the splint. Giving up, he brought his eyes to rest on Salim's.

"I loved Jakelin de Mailly," he said. "Truth be told, he was the first man I loved. But there are not many Franj like him."

"No, nor many men at all," Salim answered, but his voice was speculative rather than bitter. "Don't mistake me, Bilal. I do not pine for the Templar Marshal; I do not even blame myself anymore for his death. But he haunts me all the same. It isn't that I've found a love for the Franj, but after him, I cannot hate them. Nor can I simply call the things we've done to them the will of Allah, or just retribution, because..." He lowered his voice against the blasphemy he was about to speak. "Because, what if these warring Gods in whose names we fight are all one, and none of us are infidels at all, but only too human to realize it?"

Bilal studied Salim, and for a moment Salim had the strange

sensation that Bilal's eyes were not a part of him at all, but little windows punched out of the corporeal world onto the silent blue beyond.

At last Bilal said, "I think that you may well be right; but I do not think that it would change anything even if all the world knew it. Because in the end, none of it is about God."

"It's about power," Salim answered bitterly.

"No," Bilal said, "it's about the nature of men. For by our nature, we must master others or be mastered by them."

"Must we?" Salim asked softly, and the sadness in his voice turned Bilal cold. He pulled his feet from the water and crossed them under his legs. They sat in silence for a long time, watching the flowers swirl on the stream like bits of blood-soaked silk. "What will happen to us, Bilal?"

"I thought that you didn't worry about the future."

"That was before I realized how much can change in a moment," Salim answered.

Bilal considered the drifting flowers. "Well then, it seems to me that there are two choices. We can stay and fight for your father…or we can leave all of this and look for a place to live where de Mailly would not have died."

"Do you think that there is such a place?"

Bilal looked at him, thinking that for Salim, he would build it with his own hands; but he knew that this was not the answer that Salim sought. He was silent for a long time, his eyes searching the water, the hazy sky for the right words.

"Bilal?"

In the end, he could only tell the truth. "I do not know."

Salim gave him a strange, resigned smile that he didn't like at all. But before he could protest, Salim had pushed him onto his back and kissed him in a way he had almost forgotten, shattering his anxiety with the sudden sharpness of desire.

Before he lost his will entirely, Bilal caught Salim's chin with his good hand and said, "Promise you won't leave me."

"I could not live without you," Salim answered, and it was so long since Bilal had heard such passionate conviction in his voice that he was willing to ignore the fact that Salim had not really answered at all.

*

On the 27th of May by the Christian calendar, Salah ad-Din at last re-joined his army. Despite the influx of new soldiers, the first thing he did was to send out another round of recruiting letters. The second thing he did was to call upon his sons and formally congratulate them for the victory at Cresson. Only Al-Afdhal took it as his due. Al-Aziz had his eyes fixed on his elder brother with withering jealousy, Al-Zahir looked abashed, if pleased and Salim, whom the Sultan had last seen flooded with the sanguine glow of success, and whom he'd expected to be swelled with the pride of having personally executed the Templar Marshall, was wan and distant. Salah ad-Din wondered momentarily if he'd fallen out with the Bedu boy. Then, deciding that it was probably a good thing if he had, pressed on with the business at hand.

"Indeed, you have acquitted yourselves admirably," he said, "but I do not need to tell you that our work has only begun." He sipped his tea, noting that of the four boys, only Salim had not touched his own. "Cresson was a victory, but no victory is without its consequences and as such, we can consider our truce with Tripoli nullified."

"Has he said so?" asked Al-Zahir, his wide, good-natured face uncomprehending.

Salah ad-Din sighed, wondering how Al-Zahir could possess such a genius for combat, so unmitigated by any other vestige of intelligence. "No, he has not said so," he said patiently, "but the other Franj nobles will blame him for the debacle, as indeed I would do myself in their situation. I believe that Tripoli wants to live in peace with us, but he is a Franji, and I have never met the Franji who would turn his back on his people for the sake of a Saracen."

Al-Zahir appeared to be attempting to follow his reasoning.

Al-Aziz's attention was clearly wandering and Al-Afdhal's had been absent from the start. Only Salim seemed to be taking in what he was saying, but Salah ad-Din was struck by the false note in his interest, a cast to his attention that was too much like antipathy.

Sighing, the Sultan said, "It will not be long before Guy sends another envoy, and this one will not ask for Tripoli's compliance – they will demand it. Tripoli will have no choice but to acquiesce. Once the Latin states have patched up their differences, they will turn on us. Your men have been lazy while I have been away – it is time to make them start working again. We must be prepared."

"How long?" Salim asked abruptly, and though his voice was as distant as his expression, the Sultan could not conceal a slight smile that encompassed both approval and humility, for once again, the son he had nearly written off was the only one to have asked the right question.

"A few weeks," he answered. "A month, perhaps. I am calling Taqi ad-Din back from Antioch and Lu'lu from the south with his ships. I will meet with the *umara* after I have finished speaking with you, to begin our strategy for drawing the Franj into battle." He paused, looking at each of his sons in turn; at last, he saw with approval, he had the attention of all of them. "Before this summer is out, I will raise the crescent over Al-Quds."

7

Psarlay lasted for a week and continued much as it had begun, with music and dancing and offerings to various gods, to enlist their help for the growing season. There was a *wradz de shode*, "milk day", on which everyone went from house to house with offerings of week-old milk, singing and entreating the sheep and goats to eat well and produce plentifully. There was another ceremony in which all of the children of the valley danced holding slender walnut branches, to give thanks to the gods for this staple of their diet. There were blood sacrifices of livestock on altars to various deities, which Khalidah studiously avoided, and informal gatherings at which the elders recounted legends of Mobarak Khan's brave feats, along with those of more recent Jinn heroes. There was almost always music: quick-paced songs that spurred energetic dances and others, long and slow, which were like the camel-songs of Khalidah's tribe, elegies to former battles or lost loves.

Though Khalidah could not quite let go of her reticence regarding a *kafir* festival, she also found it impossible to dismiss the Jinn as mere unbelievers. They conducted themselves with a reverence for all living things, approaching even their sacrifices with honest regret and entreaties to the dying creatures for forgiveness. There was none of the fretful longing for an afterlife that seemed to characterize the religions of the west. Rather, the

Jinn saw Qaf as their heaven, since their gods had equipped it with all that they could need or want: fertile land, clean water, ready means to clothe and shelter themselves.

On the last day of the festival, the girls from the hermitage rose at dawn and went down to the meadows where the horses grazed. There, they filled baskets with wildflowers and long grass and then brought them up to the temple. It was the first time Khalidah had been inside, or, for that matter, seen the carved wooden double-doors standing open at all. She followed Abi Gul into a vast, echoing space lit by more rows of high, narrow windows, their shutters propped open to the spring breeze. The floor was covered with beautiful carpets: plush, knotted rugs like the Persians', rather than her tribe's flat-woven ones. There was no pulpit, but many little altars covered with wood carvings, banked with hundreds of tiny, flickering lamps.

The girls moved toward one of the larger altars. As they drew close, Khalidah saw that its carvings were of horses – thousands of individual figurines, spilling from the top of the altar onto the lamp-laden steps and the floor around it. Each was uniquely detailed, carved and painted apparently with great care. Some of them looked new, others very old.

"When a war-horse dies, we carve his effigy and place it here," Abi Gul told Khalidah. "We honor them as we honor our dead warriors, because without them, we would not be warriors at all."

She sat down with the other girls, took up a handful of grass and flowers and began to plait them into a wreath. After watching her for a moment, Khalidah began her own clumsy attempt. While they worked, the girls sang, and Khalidah recognized enough of the words to know that they were singing praises to their horses.

After a while, Abi Gul said to her, "You have an extraordinary voice."

Khalidah had not realized that she had been humming along. Mortified, she nodded.

"I have heard that Brekhna did, too," she continued. "You must sing something for us – one of your own tribe's songs."

"I don't think – " Khalidah began, but she was immediately drowned out by protests and urgings.

Sighing, she considered her options, and in the end she chose her own arrangement of Shánfara's "Ode in L". Her voice echoed strangely in the vast hall, taking on an ethereal quality. The girls kept working while she sang, never really focusing on her and after a while Khalidah relaxed. When the song ended the girls thanked her, and Khalidah was surprised and pleased to detect neither the discomfort nor the reverence with which she usually met when she performed. Rather, another girl began another song a few moments later. And so they worked on, until all of their grasses and flowers were woven. Then they laid them at the foot of the altar, saying something in Pashto as they did it.

Abi Gul repeated it in Arabic for Khalidah: "May your spirits guide your sons and daughters to glory."

Once they had laid their wreaths, the girls left the temple. "Will it bother anyone if I stay here for a little while?" Khalidah asked Abi Gul, when they had added theirs to the pile.

"Only Sulayman," she grinned.

When Abi Gul left, Khalidah knelt before the horse-altar, searching for the one she could not hope to find and yet which must be here, for surely, if Brekhna was dead to the tribe, then her horse was too. All at once a wizened, white-robed arm reached over her shoulder and plucked a bright chestnut from the ranks. The horse had been carved mid-trot, head and tail high and proud. She turned and found herself looking up at Tor Gul Khan.

"Husay," he said, handing her the carving. "It means – "

"Falcon," she interrupted. "I…I remember him." For all at once, she did. She had ridden this horse, or rather, ridden in a sling on her mother's back as her mother had ridden him, the wind whistling past her ears, drawing her delighted screams like a banner behind them.

Tor Gul Khan gave her a pensive smile. "No doubt, if you remember your mother at all. She loved that horse more than life. Besides, I'd be willing to bet your pretty mare bears some of

his blood."

That was a thought stranger even than the memory. Tor Gul Khan knelt beside her, looking at the altar where the wooden horses seemed to leap and gallop in the flickering light. At last he said, "You have borne up well."

Khalidah shook her head. "There has been nothing to bear. Everyone has been very kind to me."

"As I would expect them to be. But I referred to your journey, not to the days you have spent in Qaf." Khalidah wondered how he knew the details of that journey. "Tell me," he said after a moment, with a glimmer of humor, "what do you think of our Abi Gul?"

Khalidah smiled. "She is kind. And she talks like the west wind."

Tor Gul Khan nodded, smiled back. "And yet, if you will believe it, her precision with an arrow is preternatural."

"I know. I saw her practicing."

"She will be one of our best warriors, one day," Tor Gul Khan said ruminatively, "if she does not fall prey to her beliefs."

Khalidah felt a chill of premonition, as she had on the long-ago eve of her wedding, just before her mother had appeared to her. "What do you mean?"

Tor Gul Khan scrutinized her as the wind scoured the stone tower above them, swelled by the distant calls of animals, the far-off cry of a raptor, the beat of a drum and the droning voice of the *setar*.

"Your mother was my heir," he said. "But that was only incidental to the fact that she was Mobarak Khan's heir. When Brekhna turned her back on the Jinn, not only the succession, but the natural order of Qaf and its people were displaced."

"And you think that I am meant to restore it?"

"The truth, Khalidah," he said with weary sincerity, "is that I have no idea." His eyes were recalcitrant, though unblinking, crowded with questions rather than answers. Before she could respond, he spoke again: "Do you know what a *betaan* is?"

Khalidah shook her head.

"He, or she, is a prophet. Not a prophet like Iesu the Christ or your Muhammad, upon whom a religion is founded, but something rather more mundane, more functional and yet indispensable – a kind of oracle and priest in one. A *betaan* speaks to spirits, who in turn speak to the deities, and so he is in that sense the voice of the gods."

Tor Gul Khan paused, perhaps guessing that she would need a moment to digest this. Then he continued: "Alipsha is our current *betaan*. He lives in the high pastures, where we graze our flocks in summer, to keep his mind pure. I go to him when I am in need of advice; more rarely, he comes to me with messages or warnings. For instance: on the eve of my marriage to your grandmother, he told me that I would have no son, that after me Mobarak Khan's line would pass to a woman. Naturally, when Brekhna was born, I assumed that she would be this woman. But you see, I had not listened carefully to Alipsha, as he pointed out when I went to him with my fury and accusations after Brekhna left us. A woman would succeed me, that was all that the spirits had told him, and all that he had told me. Neither they nor he had said anything about her being my daughter, or even of my blood at all."

Tor Gul Khan stopped abruptly, as though the words he needed to continue were too painful to speak.

"Then you called me here to find out if I am the one to succeed you," Khalidah said.

Her grandfather drew a deep breath, but rather than answer her question, he said, "You have heard the story of our origin and of Mobarak Khan's pledge, and you will understand from that, from your days here in Qaf and from what Sulayman has no doubt told you about us, that we devote ourselves to fighting evil and injustice whenever and wherever it shows itself. For we believe these things to be the progeny of the evil spirits which Mobarak Khan drove back at the beginning of time. But there is an addendum to the story."

Another pause, coupled, Khalidah thought, with some kind of internal bracing. Then he said: "In Mobarak Khan's time, there was a shepherd among the Jinn named Pamir. He was a strange man. Some called him simple, but he was known for having visions that often came true. Today, he would most likely have become a *betaan*. At the time, the Jinn did not recognize any prophet but Mobarak Khan.

"Pamir was in the high pastures with his flocks when Mobarak Khan died, and yet three days after Mobarak Khan's death, on the morning when he was to be laid to rest, Pamir appeared at the gravesite. He showed no surprise to find the leader dead and lying in his coffin, but he *was* surprised at the grief of his people. 'Why do you carry on so?' he asked them. 'Mobarak Khan has not truly died, only left us for a time, like a shepherd gone to the summer pastures.'

"The people dismissed his words as a sign of his madness, but he was not finished. He told them that he had been visited in a dream by the spirit of Mobarak Khan, who had told him that the Jinn would prosper for many generations, winning the battles they were called to fight, making a good life in their valley when they were not. But one day, he said, the evil spirits he had once scattered would band together again and form an army of great strength. They would come from the west – from over the sea – with swords raised to slaughter. The army of evil would roll across the lands of the east, the cities would drown in blood, the people who survived would be slaves. But when that day came, Mobarak Khan would once again take human form, to lead the armies of men against the evil spirits."

Khalidah found herself clutching the model of Brekhna's horse so tightly that it hurt. She waited, barely breathing, for Tor Gul Khan to continue.

"Prophecy is seldom so specific as one would like," he said at last. "Mobarak Khan's spirit had told Pamir, for instance, that he would be reborn to a tribe of local nobility but relative obscurity; that he would not be born a leader of men, but would have to prove himself as such. He would be a child of a new religion and a model of its virtues, while still fulfilling those of the old. But Pamir could not tell his people when this rebirth would come to pass, nor where, nor even whether Mobarak Khan would reincarnate as a man or a woman."

Khalidah drew a deep breath and then let it out. "Please do not tell me that you think I am this Mobarak Khan reincarnate," she said.

Tor Gul Khan turned finally to look at his grand-daughter. To her consternation, he smiled. "No, Khalidah, I do not." She felt an unexpected stab of disappointment at this. "I'm afraid that the implications of this story – and your part in it – are a good deal more complicated than that. Religion, as you of all people must be aware, is inherently divisive. Take Iesu: your people, the Jews and the Christians all believe that he once walked the earth and delivered an important message. But depending on one's viewpoint, he is an outdated prophet, a madman, a heretic, or a god. To me, it seems madness to spill blood over the discrepancy, for at the core of it all, was he not a man who preached the sanctity of love and kindness? Yet to the people fighting for control of Al-Quds, it is the difference not only between life and death, but also salvation and damnation.

"And then there is Islam itself. You all agree on Muhammad as its figurehead. Yet from the moment of his death you have been divided over a matter of succession, and once again, blood pools in the divergence." He sighed again. "Well, our own religion is no different. Though it must seem primitive to you, hardly comparable to the ones you have known since your infancy, if you scratch the surface, you will find that it is at least as contentious as Christianity or Islam. From the moment Pamir spoke his vision, the Jinn have been divided on whether the shepherd was an oracle, or a madman spurred by grief at the death of a beloved leader. Some of us, therefore – like Abi Gul and her family – believe that Mobarak Khan was a messiah, who will one day take human form again and lead us. Others believe that he was a man – helped by the gods, perhaps even bearing godly blood, but flesh and blood like you or me, subject to the finality of death.

"If Pamir's prophecy had been the end of it, the rift might have healed. The factions might have softened with the softening of grief over Mobarak Khan's death. But unfortunately, that was not the end of it. You see, Khalidah, we do not burn nor bury our dead, but place them in wooden coffins in hillside cemeteries, open to the elements. We believe that this is the quickest way for the body to return to its source. But it also means that graves are occasionally attacked by animals or robbers. On the day after Mobarak Khan's burial, a group of women, led by his wife, went to lay bread on the grave – a custom of ours, food for the gods – and when they arrived, they found the coffin empty. The lid had been prized off, and no sign remained that anyone had ever lain there."

"Like Iesu," Khalidah murmured.

Tor Gul Khan gave her a sharp look. "There were plenty of mundane explanations, but of course, to those desperate to believe that he had not truly left us, it was a sign that Mobarak Khan's body had been taken by the gods, to be returned at that time of need Pamir had spoken of. From then on, we have been divided by our beliefs. The division has, at times, been contentious, but we have managed to live with each other and our differences. That is why the Khan is so important: his job is, first and foremost, to keep the peace.

"Of course, to do this he must remain neutral in the eyes of the tribe, no matter what his personal beliefs, and by luck or by wisdom this has always been possible."

"Until now?" Khalidah asked warily.

"Until now," he agreed. "For now the Franj have come – from the west, across the sea, with swords raised, drowning cities in blood and vanquishing the native tribes – and the Kurdish prince is raising an army against them."

"Your people think that the Franj are the evil spirits," Khalidah said slowly, "and Salah ad-Din the messiah." She looked closely at Tor Gul Khan. "But you do not."

"In every generation," he answered after a moment, apparently choosing his words with great care, "there are an evil and an opponent who accepts its challenge. Sometimes it is on a small

scale and resolves in little battles whose villains and heroes are
quickly forgotten. But sometimes he infects others with his zeal,
capturing a broader imagination, as when Musa led his people
out of slavery in Egypt or Iesu took on the might of Rome. As a
man committed to fighting evil, I can honor these men's ideals
and the sacrifices that others make to them. But as a leader I must
protect the future of my people, and just now my people are as
vulnerable as they have ever been. They know that I am growing
old, with no heir in line to replace me; and they know why."

The coin dropped at last. "Brekhna believed it," Khalidah said
wonderingly. "My mother left here to fight the Franj, because she
believed the myth."

Tor Gul Khan stiffened, and Khalidah knew that she had hit
on a painful truth. Yet when he answered, his voice wasn't angry,
only weary and terribly sad. "She met him, you see – Salah ad-
Din. It was long ago, before he was Sultan or anything much
more than his uncle Shirkuh's lackey. They fought together
against some petty tribe or another, and unlikely as it might seem
they took to each other. He infected her with his ideas about
ousting the Franj – and with the fear of what might happen if he
couldn't. He asked her to bring the Jinn back to help him when
it was time. She came back to Qaf full of fire and asked me to let
her lead the believers west."

"And you said no," Khalidah guessed.

Tor Gul Khan's look was one of abject despair. "How could I
do otherwise? You are young, Khalidah, like Brekhna was when
she first saw the Franj. I know that they must seem to you the
epitome of evil and indeed, they have wreaked havoc the like of
which the lands of Islam have never known. But an army of evil
spirits that threaten the sanctity of a continent?" He shook his
head. "I have fought evil in many forms, and I tell you, though the
Franj are brutal, they are no more brutal than any other power-
hungry men. More than that, they do not have the strength – nor
the inclination, I imagine – to expand to the east."

"But they could," Khalidah answered. "If they believed their
God demanded it of them, they would march from Al-Quds to

Qaf as mercilessly as they marched from their homeland to Al-
Quds one hundred years ago."

"That was Brekhna's argument," he said, "and it is the argument
I fear will be the end of us."

"Why?"

"Because, although some of the Jinn revile Brekhna for
abandoning us, many more revere her."

"For what?" Her tone was bitter. "Running away and marrying
an outsider? Then abandoning him and her only child?"

"They do not see it as you or I do," he said gently. Khalidah
saw in his eyes the desire to comfort her and to be comforted. She
wished she knew how to accept it. "All legends are the same, at
their heart: they are built on a few twigs of fact and a good deal
of wish and hope. My people – those of them who believe that
Mobarak Khan was a supernatural being – think that Brekhna
was called by him, and followed that call."

"So, I will tell them that it is not true. That she married an
ordinary man and lived an ordinary life."

"It will not matter, any more than the disappearance of
Mobarak Khan's body mattered to those who wanted to
believe him immortal. If anything, it will add credence to their
speculation, and determination to follow in her footsteps."

"Which is all well and good, except that nobody knows where
she is…unless you do?"

Tor Gul Khan gave Khalidah a strange, intense look.

"You do?"

He shook his head. "I have a guess, but it is based on nothing
more than a father's intuition; and at any rate, it does not help us
in our immediate problem."

"But – "

"Khalidah," he said sharply, startling her into silence. Then,
more gently: "Please – if I am right, then your mother is beyond
reach, and certainly beyond helping us. We have too many
present problems to go seeking more."

Khalidah desperately wanted to press him on this, but his
momentary flash of anger told her that it would be futile. Sighing,

she said, "All right, then; where do I come into it?"

"You," he sighed, "are the answer to the prayers of those faithful to Pamir's prophecy. As Brekhna's daughter, you are the obvious choice to lead them to their messiah, Salah ad-Din, and their lives' purpose, eradicating the Franj. But I fear that if they go, it will be the end of the Jinn, for our skills will not save them in the kind of war Salah ad-Din will fight."

"Then why, in the name of Allah, did you send Sulayman to bring me here?"

Tor Gul Khan did not answer, only looked at her, his eyes no longer those of a proud leader, but of a helpless, pleading old man. Khalidah saw the answer in them and was torn between pity and rage.

"You hoped that I would tell them that Salah ad-Din is not what they think he is," she said. "You want to use me to keep them here."

"I would never use you," he said vehemently, "nor ask you to lie. If you truly believe that the Jinn's place is with Salah ad-Din, then I will not stop you telling them so."

"I do not dictate the actions of others."

He gave her a level look. "Tell me: what is your view of the Sultan and his *jihad*?"

"I believe in Salah ad-Din and what he fights for."

"And do you intend to fight for him yourself?"

"If it is Allah's will. After all, he is not in the habit of taking women into his army. But even if I do, it does not translate into a suggestion that your people follow me."

"A leader inspires others' actions by his – or her – own."

"I am not the Jinn's leader!"

"That is not your choice, but theirs," Tor Gul Khan answered with infuriating calm. "Therefore, before you act, be certain that you have chosen the right course."

"How?" Khalidah snapped.

"Live with us for a few weeks; understand the people whom you would lead. Decide for yourself whether *jihad* is the answer they seek."

Khalidah considered this. She was little inclined to do anything for Tor Gul Khan, but she could not forget Abi Gul's open-armed friendship, nor the kindness shown her by all of the Jinn over the past week. That, at least, had been sincere. She sighed. "Three weeks. No longer."

8

Over the next few days, Khalidah had a good deal of time to consider her discussion with her grandfather and to wonder whether her promise had been folly, for as he had predicted, *Psarlay* was hardly finished before the questions began. It was the unquenchable Abi Gul who sent out the first tentative feelers, asking Khalidah, as they groomed their horses, whether or not she had ever met Salah ad-Din.

"I would be lucky if Salah ad-Din allowed me to serve in his kitchen," Khalidah answered warily.

This surprised Abi Gul. "I can see that he might not recognize your Jinn ancestry, but you are still the daughter of an Arab king."

"Hardly," said Khalidah, picking stones ruminatively from Zahirah's hooves. "I'm the daughter of the sheikh of a Bedu tribe. The Bedu may be useful to the settled nobility when it comes to war with a common enemy, but they have little time for us otherwise and certainly no respect. To them we are the *harafish* – the rabble – little better than your hill bandits." She sat back on her heels, looking at the river. "Though perhaps that is not entirely fair to the Sultan. I have heard that he takes a rather more generous view of us than others of his kind."

"And will your people fight for him against the invaders?"

Khalidah sighed. "I don't know. My father wanted to, but his brother, who controls the other branch of our tribe, was against it. My leaving might have made it impossible for my father to follow his own wishes."

Abi Gul seemed to know better than to press her on this, but the possibilities opened up in Khalidah's mind's eye anyway, each more grim than the last: 'Abd al-Aziz drawn once again into war with his brother, sacrificed to Numair's greed, victim of a treacherous knife in the back; the tribe scattered or subjugated, Bilal a martyr and Zaynab a slave.

"I hope that he has gone to Salah ad-Din," she said at last, ruefully. "I pray for it every day."

Abi Gul worked silently for a time, then she said, "Do you believe that your creator – that is, your Allah – has sent Salah ad-Din to drive out the invaders?"

"I know that the Sultan believes it," she said carefully, "and that his belief infects others, so that perhaps in the end it comes to the same thing: by believing in him, they will believe in themselves enough to ensure his success."

Abi Gul had forgotten her work and her horse wandered away. "We have a story," she said, inevitably, "a prophecy, which tells us that Mobarak Khan will be reincarnated at a time of great need. To many of us, he is like your Muhammad – or perhaps, more accurately, the Christian Iesu, who died to rise again." She seemed about to add to this, and then to think better of it; but her wide eyes were full of questions.

"Abi Gul," Khalidah said, "I know that many of your people think that the Franj are the army of evil that was scattered by Mobarak Khan so long ago, and that Salah ad-Din is his reincarnation, come to fight them. Perhaps they are, and he is…but 'perhaps' is the best I can do. I do not know whether the Sultan can be what you would have him be. I do not even know whether he can defeat the Franj. For all I know, he has already tried and failed."

"He has not," Abi Gul answered with surprising conviction. "Our *betaan* has seen him, and though the time is drawing near, the Sultan has not yet made his move."

Khalidah took a moment to digest this, making a mental note to find a way to speak with this *betaan*. "Very well," she said, "but consider what it would be like if the Jinn really went to fight for him. His army is huge, his tactics entirely different from yours. You would be made to surrender the skills that make you such perfect warriors."

"Would we?" the other girl asked softly, but still with the conviction of someone who has pondered something long and hard and already countered all of her own doubts. "Or would we teach his army something that would make the difference for them in this coming war?"

Khalidah sighed. "I suppose anything is possible. But there is something else: we are a long way from Damascus. If you decided to go to Salah ad-Din, how would you find him, and find him in time? And then, if you did find him, how you would convince him of your worth and your loyalty, given that he is a devout Muslim and you are a tribe of foreign *kuffar*?"

Abi Gul smiled. "Do you truly need to ask?"

Khalidah didn't like the implication of the words. "What are you suggesting?"

"It's why you have come to us, Khalidah," she said, like an echo of Tor Gul Khan. "You are the link between Salah ad-Din's people and the Jinn." Khalidah only realized that she was shaking her head when Abi Gul contradicted, "Yes, Khalidah, it is true. Call it the will of the gods or Allah; one way or another, there is a reason why you have been sent on this particular journey, at this particular time."

Khalidah wondered how many more times she would have to hear this before she believed it.

"You are the heir of two proud races, and right now the future of both hangs in the balance. What is your purpose if not to be the link between them and thereby the foundation for that future?"

Khalidah saw that it would be useless to argue against Abi Gul's passionate certainty. Instead, she asked, "How many of you believe that I am this…link?"

Abi Gul didn't answer, but her look told Khalidah everything. She dropped her face into her hands. "You are mistaken," she muttered, "oh, how you are mistaken. I am nothing but a silly girl who ran away because she didn't want to marry her cousin..."

She felt Abi Gul's hand on her shoulder. "If you truly believed that," the girl said softly, "you would not be here now." She was silent for a moment, giving Khalidah time to compose herself; then she said, "Come. If you are going to lead us, then you must learn to fight like one of us."

"I did not say that I would lead you," Khalidah answered querulously.

But Abi Gul only smiled.

*

They taught her how to shoot with bow and arrow, and ways with the sword that she had never imagined. They bound her hands and put her on one of their own horses and sent her through grueling dressage drills until she could sit the two-beat battle gait with perfect balance, then they returned her bow and taught her to shoot while she rode. Though she began by hating it, after a couple of days Khalidah developed a great enthusiasm for that smooth, quick pace and asked why they didn't ride that way all the time.

"It is too taxing on the horse," said Zhalai, who oversaw the training of her dormitory. "Many of them must be taught to pace, but even those which come to it naturally are worn down by it quickly. If you ride a horse too hard at the pace, he will go shoulder-lame. Then he cannot be ridden in battle, for the lameness can re-emerge at any time, without warning."

Khalidah nodded, humbled by the realization of how much she had to learn.

Though she hardly saw Sulayman, Khalidah didn't have time to miss him. The days were taken up by training and at night she wanted nothing more than to fall into bed and sleep.

Sometimes this was possible, but on other nights the girls, who seemed to possess boundless reserves of energy, would climb up into the foothills and dance on a hilltop late into the night, singing praises the stars and the moon and their own youth and happiness. And they were happy: that was what struck Khalidah most profoundly about the Jinn. They seemed secure in their love for their beautiful valley, the simple purpose of their lives, the righteousness of their beliefs. Khalidah quickly came to envy them this; but she feared for them too. Though she knew that they faced it habitually, she couldn't quite believe that they could withstand the outside world, its neuroses and duplicities and its dereliction of faith. Their reverence for life was so different from her world of vengeance and honor, their *kuffar's* faith somehow far more civilized than the warring gods of Christianity and Islam.

As the days passed, Khalidah came grudgingly to agree with her grandfather that to join Salah ad-Din's *jihad* would be brutally hard on the Jinn. Yet she also saw how deeply the faith in Pamir's prophecy ran amongst those who had embraced it, and nearly all of the younger generation had. As the days turned into weeks, their expectant faith in her began to fill her with a bleak despair, until at last she couldn't stand it and went looking for Sulayman.

He was too old for the boys' dormitory. Though he joined their training during the day, he had been living with Warda and Batoor – Shahascina's parents – who had kept him during his first stay in Qaf. Khalidah had met them, but had never been to their house, and she approached it now with some reluctance. It was a big house, situated at the end of one of the terraces, with clear views to the practice grounds from its rooftop terrace. The wooden door was covered in intricate carvings of scenes from Mobarak Khan's life. An ibex skull hung from the lintel, its fantastic horns reaching outward like a two-pronged claw.

The door stood half-open to the sweet evening breeze, which splayed the drift of wood-smoke from the smoke-hole in the roof, enveloping Khalidah for a moment in a smell as heady as incense. Before she could knock, a child appeared in the gap. She was about six years old, with a fairy's face and hair the color of ripe wheat. Like many of the children of Qaf, she carried a pet Mynah bird on her shoulder, which studied Khalidah with eyes as inquisitive as its mistress's. After a moment the child grinned, showing two missing front teeth, and started hollering for her mother. Warda appeared a moment later, wiping her hands on her apron. She too smiled when she saw Khalidah and immediately invited her inside, scolding the child, who was called Mahzala, for neglecting to do so.

"Please, sit," she said to Khalidah, indicating one of the low wooden chairs pulled up around the central hearth. "Sulayman is outside with Batoor – I will fetch him for you. Mahzala, fetch tea for Bibi Khalidah."

As Warda went out to find Sulayman and Mahzala busied herself with the tea, Khalidah looked around. The room was as Sulayman had described it long ago in the desert: there were the closed doors leading off of the central living area, and above them the gallery with the high windows, dark now, though they showed a spatter of stars. There was no sign of the other two girls who still lived at home, nor of the grandparents who also shared the house. The room was silent but for the crackle of the fire and the sigh of the wind through the smoke-hole and the open doorway.

Khalidah had almost settled into the easy peace of the dwelling when Mahzala returned with her tea and promptly announced, "Ghairat says that you know Mobarak Khan."

She nearly choked on her mouthful of tea. "Who is Ghairat?"

"He is my friend," the child answered, feeding her Mynah crumbs from a plate of bread spread with sheep's butter, which she'd put down by the teapot.

Khalidah sighed. "Well, tell Ghairat that he is mistaken."

Mahzala looked up at her with wide-eyed appeal. "But he says that you have come to show us the way to Him. If not you, then who?"

"Mahzala!" Warda said sharply from the doorway, precluding

an answer. "I am sorry, Bibi Khalidah," she said, but there was a hint of curiosity beneath her mortification. Khalidah was very glad to see Sulayman stooping through the doorway behind Warda. "We will leave you alone to talk," Warda said.

"It is not necessary," Khalidah answered politely, but was intensely grateful when Warda ignored her words, taking her daughter firmly by the hand and leading her upstairs. Sulayman watched them go, then sat down in another of the chairs by the fire and poured a cup of tea.

"I take it from your expression that you are not keen on your role as intermediary to a messiah," he said with a dry smile. Khalidah put down her tea and dropped her head into her hands. After a moment she felt Sulayman's hand on her hair, stroking and soothing. "Ah, Khalidah – you knew that they would expect something of you."

She laughed wryly. "I did not think that I would be expected to introduce them to a god."

He chuckled. "Has it been that bad?"

She was comforted to find real sympathy on his face along with the humor. "Oh, yes. They are polite about it, but their expectations are quite precise, and also intractable. Do the boys talk about it too?"

"They talk about almost nothing else."

"What am I going to do, Sulayman?"

He sighed. "What can you do, but follow the path that Allah has laid out for you?"

"I would like to believe that that is what I am doing; and yet, could Allah really have intended that I lead a tribe of *kuffar* to their false deity?"

"Are you questioning His will?"

Khalidah didn't answer. She didn't know whether he was teasing or serious, nor how to account for her own doubt.

"Khalidah, you know I have always believed that there was a purpose in your coming here, even when I didn't know what it was. Whatever the circumstances, under whatever pretenses, if that purpose is to lead the Jinn to the Sultan...well then, that is what you must do."

She looked at him. His eyes were gentle, but troubled, too. "I am afraid for them, Sulayman," she said at last. "I fear that if I agree to take them west, it will be to their destruction."

"I know," he said, "but however great your fear, don't forget that only Allah knows. You must leave it in His hands: that is, make your own decisions and allow the Jinn to make theirs. If you truly believe that your destiny is to stay here and do Tor Gul Khan's bidding, then do it. But if you believe that it is to fight for Salah ad-Din, then you cannot turn aside from that calling, and you must be prepared to lead these people if their choice is to follow you."

"Who am I, to lead them?" she asked bitterly.

"Who else, Khalidah?"

Once again, she found herself at a loss for words; for once again, however little she liked it, the answer was obvious.

9

Once again, Raymond of Tripoli stood on the battlements of the castle at Tiberias watching an approaching envoy, but this time he had no doubt about its identity or intentions. He was only surprised that it had taken them so long: more than a month had passed since the debacle at Cresson. Then again, he thought wryly, with so many of their best knights lost on that day, it was no wonder that it had taken time for the court faction to gather enough fighting men to confront him.

The envoy drew closer – close enough at last to discern that Guy of Lusignan was absent from their number. Tripoli could not stem the disgust that rose in him then. Baldwin IV, consumed by leprosy, had led his army until he had to be tied to the saddle to stay in it. When that had failed he had nevertheless continued to direct his affairs with clear-headed wisdom until he drew his final breath. But then, Tripoli hardly needed further proof that Guy was unfit to rule.

Though Guy was absent, most of the key nobles were there, along with various priests and monks and knights of the holy orders. At the centre, the banner of the Patriarch of Jerusalem whipped out like a challenge. Yet even the presence of the Patriarch was not as surprising as that of the man who rode at the head of the column: Gerard de Ridefort. Tripoli's astonishment came not from the fact that de Ridefort had sworn when he left his household never to set foot in it again – de Ridefort wasn't the kind of man to miss the subjugation of an old enemy – but because he could not believe that the other nobles had forgiven de Ridefort's betrayal at Cresson. Shaking his head, the count watched as his guards opened the gate and de Ridefort rode through, stirring the dust that was all that remained of the Saracen detachment, a look of haughty triumph on his face. Tripoli watched a moment longer, then he turned from the window to meet the inevitable.

*

When de Ridefort and his entourage entered the great hall, they found the count seated at the head of his banquet table, wearing an expression of guarded serenity. De Ridefort looked him over carefully for signs of repentance, or at least a knot-hole in the audacity that had brought him to his present position. But at forty-five – an age which in those harsh, warring lands was an achievement in itself – the count was still lithe-bodied, his stature erect. His beard was still more black than grey, his dark eyes keen with intelligence, and the swarthy skin that many mistook for an Arab's was lined more with wisdom than with age.

Stifling his reflexive fury, de Ridefort approached the table. Tripoli gestured for the nobles to be seated. He paused, surveying them. Once, de Ridefort would have assumed that the count was waiting for one of them to break the silence. He knew from experience, however, that Tripoli was waiting until their discomfort peaked before breaking it himself.

"It is kind of you to come so far out of your way on my account," he said at last. "To what do I owe the honor of your illustrious presence in my home?"

"You know very well why we are here," de Ridefort answered tersely, before any of the others could. Tripoli's head snapped upwards, accompanied by a click of his tongue: an Arab gesture of negation that infuriated de Ridefort as much as his faint accent. "Well then," de Ridefort continued, "I shall spell it out. Your refusal to recognize your rightful king, as well as your traitorous alliance with the Saracen leader, has cost me half of my knights. I am here now to exact payment."

Tripoli leaned his elbow on the table and rested his head languidly on two extended fingers, looking as though de Ridefort had asked his opinion of the weekend's weather, rather than charged him with treason. "It was not I who called the charge," he said.

"You put the infidels there to taunt us!" de Ridefort roared.

"I did no such thing," Tripoli answered with icy composure. "I was honoring my agreement with Salah ad-Din and he honored his with me. No man would ask another not to defend himself, but no blood would have been shed on that day if you had not attacked."

This time it was the Patriarch, Heraclius, who answered. "This is no time for casting blame," he said, what had once been a powerful voice dulled now by his richly embroidered robes and layers of fat. "We are here to ask you, Tripoli, whether or not your agreement with the Saracen king still stands."

"I am not a man to break my word," Tripoli answered carefully.

"Not break your word!" de Ridefort began. "You are a traitor and – "

"Silence!" roared Heraclius. He turned from de Ridefort to Tripoli. "Where is your loyalty, Count? Do you honestly mean to tell us that you have given it to an infidel?"

Tripoli smiled bitterly. "Not one year past," he said, "every man here swore his *loyalty* to a dying king. We all gave our word that his sister would not succeed him, unless it was by decree of the Pope in Rome. I do not recall the Pope being consulted before Sibylla was crowned."

"You know as well as anyone that Princess Sibylla was the rightful heir to Jerusalem," said William Borrel, who was serving as custodian of the Hospitallers until they elected a new Master, des Moulins having lost his life at Cresson with the rest. "*Not* her dying child. Naming him his heir was an act of spite on the part of the Leper King."

"Sibylla," Tripoli mused, drawing the name out, rolling it on his tongue. "More of a man than her husband, when it comes right down to it…and yet it's in his name that you come here, not hers."

"Things are as they are, Tripoli," snapped de Ridefort. "If you do not pay homage to Guy now, you brand yourself a traitor."

"And then?"

"Then?" De Ridefort was florid with rage, the vein in his forehead pulsing to its beat. "Can you really mean to defy us again? You pride yourself on being like the Saracens, and you must surely have converted to Islam or you could not tolerate what happened at Cresson! To allow the infidels to cross your territory, to slaughter Christian knights and take them prisoner without ever raising a hand to stop it, you must be a traitor to God Himself!"

Heraclius frowned at de Ridefort's words, but he did not ask him to retract them. Instead, he said to Tripoli, "In answer to your question: by continuing to defy your rightful king, you defy God. If you do not repent immediately, I will have you excommunicated and your marriage annulled, for I could not ask a good Christian woman to remain married to a heathen."

Tripoli stared at the Patriarch, stunned; but the gauntlet had been thrown. Tripoli might despise Guy and all the rotten politics that had set him on the throne, but he loved his wife and her children beyond anything. Heraclius was wiser than the count had ever realized: he had found Tripoli's price, when Tripoli himself had not known it.

And so he said, the words like sand in his mouth, "My lords, I beg your pardon for any part that I had to play in the tragedy of Cresson and I am prepared to make reparation to the kingdom as you see fit."

De Ridefort opened his mouth for a sharp retort, but Balian d'Ibelin, whom Tripoli respected for his level-headed intelligence despite his staunch loyalty to the king, put a restraining hand on his arm. "For that we thank you, Count," he said graciously, "and the only reparation we require is that you pay homage to Guy as your rightful king."

Shaking off d'Ibelin's hand, de Ridefort added, "And you'd best pray that he's still in a mood to receive it!"

D'Ibelin, Heraclius and several of the barons were looking daggers at the Grand Master, but Tripoli only smiled. "Still in a mood to receive it?" he repeated. "He would fall to his knees and grovel for it if you'd let him; or more likely, send his wife to do it for him. That is precisely why you are here, and he is not." He shook his head. "Do not mistake me – I still believe that you are fools to put your faith in Guy de Lusignan, but for some reason God has set him on the throne of His kingdom, and for God I will call him king."

He stifled the barons' sighs of relief with a look like a sharpened blade. "However, I must say this: though I may have been the instrument of our defeat at Cresson, I was not its instigator. I will fight Salah ad-Din if God requires it, but I will not follow you on another fools' mission."

Hastily, before de Ridefort could think of a response, d'Ibelin said, "Very well then. Come with us now to Acre, where your king is waiting, and let us all welcome you back."

De Ridefort and his erstwhile mentor stared at one another for a moment of frigid surmise. Then Tripoli nodded, and with a swirl of colored cloth, the lords of Outremer stood and departed.

*

Early in June, Guy's army began to muster at the oasis town of Saffuriyya. It was a good position, with plenty of water and grazing land and proximity to Salah ad-Din's own growing army. But despite the success of the *arriere ban* and the addition of Tripoli's troops, Salah ad-Din's army still outnumbered the Christians' by a good margin. While the barons mooned and debated about how to remedy the situation, de Ridefort did something that his supporters considered long overdue, and the rest suspected was calculated to further dispel the suspicion of treason that had hovered around him since he fled the battle at Cresson. He countermanded a large sum of money belonging to King Henry II of England, which the king had given to the Templars and Hospitallers several years earlier to atone for the murder of Thomas Becket. The money was to have been kept by them until the king made his way to the Holy Land on the pilgrimage that would serve as the second part of his penance. De Ridefort spent the lot of it on mercenaries, dressing them perfunctorily in England's colors.

"Will he not notice that the money is missing?" Guy asked de Ridefort fretfully, when he announced what he had done.

"Only if he comes looking for it," de Ridefort answered dryly, "which, given his response to the Patriarch in '84, looks unlikely."

De Ridefort referred to the failed attempt several years earlier by Heraclius, des Moulins and his own predecessor, Arnold de Toroga, to convince the monarchs of Europe to take the cross and join them in the Holy Land. All of them, including Henry of England, had declined the offer. Guy nodded, although he had only a hazy understanding of de Ridefort's reference and still less of what he himself had just agreed to. As usual, he was happy enough to let someone else shoulder the burden.

Meanwhile, Salah ad-Din watched his own army's preparations for war with considerably keener interest. He knew that he had a good majority on the Franj, though it would take a full review to know exactly how large it was. New *muttawiyah* were arriving all the time, the Tiberias detachment had returned a couple of weeks earlier, and the previous day Taqi ad-Din had re-joined the army after quickly drawing up a truce with Antioch. This last addition brought the Sultan particular pleasure, for Taqi ad-Din was the epitome of the Muslim warrior – fine-mannered, fearless and handsome – and his men, in their discipline and effectiveness, were the type by which all fighting columns should be judged.

But his enthusiasm was not untinged by anxiety. The change in his son Salim disturbed him, for in their time in the south he had come to rely on the boy more than he had realized, and now this support was gone. Furthermore, he was aware that Numair al-Hassani had not returned with the detachment from Tiberias. With the intuition born of years of leadership in a war-torn land, he suspected a connection between the two, but with so many more pressing problems demanding his attention he made little headway in discerning just what it was.

And then one night in the middle of June, when a dry wind from the desert shifted the sluggish air of the oasis, he heard a voice outside of his tent speaking with the guard. It was only on hearing it that he realized how long he had expected it. A moment later the Bedu boy ducked into the pavilion, said his *salaams* and bowed to the Sultan. His eyes looked bluer than ever, despite the dim light, but it was only when he knelt that Salah ad-Din realized that they were brightened by tears.

"Please, Your Highness," Bilal faltered, looking up at the Sultan, "there is something that I must tell you, only I am afraid..." He faltered. His eyes were transparent as water and deep with sorrow.

Looking at him, Salah ad-Din, who had never felt much of an attraction to boys, understood his son's obsession completely. "You have long since proven your loyalty to me," the Sultan said gently. "Speak your heart without fear."

And, drawing a deep breath, Bilal began.

10

When Khalidah and Sulayman had been in Qaf three weeks, the Jinn received a request for assistance. It came from a Turcoman clan near Mashhad-e-Reza, in the south-west corner of Khorasan, an area still controlled by Persia. They were a small, nomadic clan, an offshoot of the great Mary Teke tribe, who had long lived at peace with the local *amir*. But recently the *amir* had died, and the son who succeeded him had proven very different from the father. He began taxing the Teke on the use of their traditional lands and when the nomads could not pay, he began executing them publicly. The man, Rakan, whom the Teke had sent to Qaf to plead for help, was thin and ragged, with a haunted look in his eyes. Tor Gul Khan took him into his rooms to discuss the situation. Within an hour he had dismissed him to eat and rest and called a gathering of elders.

Khalidah watched them converging in the temple as the girls walked back from the practice grounds for their mid-day meal. "What will happen?" she asked Abi Gul.

"Oh, they will grant the man's request," Abi Gul answered with a dismissive wave of her hand. "Tor Gul Khan will send him home with twenty or thirty warriors tomorrow morning."

"And will you go with them?"

She laughed ruefully. "I am two months short of sixteen. But Afshan and Shahascina will likely be sent." She nodded to the other girls, who looked both hopeful and uncertain.

Khalidah considered them, as well as the note of regret in Abi Gul's voice. "Do you worry about it?" she asked. "Is this first battle something to look forward to, or to fear?"

"It is how we become what we are," Shahascina answered. "Fear has no place in it."

"Nor hope, I suppose," added Afshan, cocking her curly head.

"And yet," Abi Gul said to Khalidah, slowing her step so that Shahascina and Afshan drew ahead and out of earshot, "it is not quite so simple. We may ride from Qaf toward the same goal, but each of us returns to a separate destiny. Afshan and Shahascina both wish to distinguish themselves, to earn their places as adult members of the tribe, and no doubt they will. But when they return as women, Shahascina will marry Sarbaz, move into her own house and, if her mother's fertility is any indicator, she'll be a mother herself within a year. Her first fight could well be her last. Afshan, on the other hand, will most likely join the ranks of the regular warriors."

"And that's it? A Jinn woman either bears children or fights?"

"A Jinni is never forced to fight, nor to marry. Afshan will be a warrior because it is what she believes she has been called to do. She can change her mind at any time. One day she might marry, or become a dormitory mother, or even choose to devote her life to the gods as a temple celibate…though frankly, I doubt the latter."

Khalidah agreed. She had seen these celibates, men and women in unembroidered white who moved silently around the temple tending the altars, or knelt for hours in meditation. She couldn't imagine the laughing Afshan as one of them; but then again, it was equally difficult to imagine her lopping off a man's head.

"And you will lose two friends," she said.

Abi Gul shrugged. "For a while, I suppose. Until I fight my own first battle and join the ranks, or…" She glanced at Khalidah and then away.

Khalidah sighed. "If you are not sixteen, you will not be

allowed to go to Salah ad-Din even if Tor Gul Khan gives his blessing to the others."

"Were you 'allowed' to forsake your marriage and come here?"

"That was different."

Abi Gul gave Khalidah a pointed look: not quite accusatory, but certainly not conciliatory. "Did you not choose to follow the dictates of your heart, rather than those of your people? How is that different from this?" She flung her hands outward in a gesture of exasperation. "Difficult as it may be for you to accept, Bibi Khalidah, I believe that Salah ad-Din is our messiah. I believe it as fundamentally as you believe that Allah is the only God and Muhammad His prophet. My fate is to become a warrior, and though I sympathize with Rakan and the others like him who come seeking our assistance, their fights are only drops in the pool of history. Salah ad-Din's is a flood tide. If I am to spend my life in battle, I would rather join the flood."

They had reached the dormitory. Khalidah gave her friend a long, searching look and found only determination in her gold-and-green eyes.

"I will not let you protect me," Abi Gul said, "so please, do not try."

"Very well," Khalidah answered, "but I will promise no more until you have done something for me."

"Name it."

"I need to speak to Alipsha, your *betaan*."

Abi Gul grinned. "I thought you would never ask!"

*

The afternoon was warm, the sky strewn with cottony clouds. It was the first time Khalidah had ridden Zahirah since her bandage had come off, but the mare's fitness seemed to have improved rather than deteriorated, and there was no sign of lameness. Abi Gul eyed Zahirah from the back of her own blue-grey stallion, who was called Tufan, which, like 'Aasifa, meant "storm".

"She's a fine horse," she said. "She'd bear Tufan a lovely foal."

"Don't even think about it!" Khalidah scolded. "She can't very well make the journey west if she's in foal – never mind ride into battle."

"Perhaps someday, when the battles are behind us…" Abi Gul said wistfully.

"*Insha'Allah*," Khalidah agreed.

They rode over soft grass and in and out of sparse forest until, after a couple of hours, they reached the high pastures, where the air was thin and the sun brilliant between the drifting clouds. Some of the shepherds had already brought their herds up for the summer grazing, moving into *aylaqs*, stone bothies built by the trickling springs that fed the river in the valley below. Near the bothies were stone pens into which the sheep were driven at night, to keep them safe from predators. As they approached one of the bothies, Abi Gul called out in Pashto and a boy emerged, squinted at the riders for a moment and then ran forward, laughing. Abi Gul jumped down from her horse and embraced him, then turned to Khalidah.

"Bibi Khalidah, may I introduce my brother, Arsalan."

Arsalan bobbed his head to Khalidah and she did the same in return. The boy was a few years older than Abi Gul; he looked just like her, except for the plaits and the mulberry *harquus*. Abi Gul spoke to him in rapid Pashto and he answered likewise. Khalidah caught the words for horses and snow and, repeatedly, *betaan*.

At last Abi Gul turned back to her and said, "Forgive us, Bibi Khalidah. Arsalan's Arabic was never very good, and since he opted for a shepherd's life, he has forgotten most of what he knew. Anyway, he says that Alipsha is at home and he will take us to him. We will have to leave the horses here, though, and walk. The melting snow has made the paths too treacherous."

Arsalan helped them removed the horses' tack, then shut them in the sheep's pen. "Ready?" he said in Arabic. Without waiting for them to answer, he turned and set off up the mountain.

He moved like an ibex. Abi Gul and Khalidah followed rather

less quickly. Khalidah still wasn't used to exertion at such a high altitude and they had to stop frequently for her to catch her breath. Even Abi Gul seemed happy enough for the pauses. Soon enough, Khalidah saw why Arsalan had made them leave the horses behind. The grass gradually gave way to stony soil underlaid by mud left by the melting snow. At times, Khalidah could hardly find footing; the horses would have been useless.

At last they reached a stony ridge, where in icy wind whistled from the snow peaks which now looked, if not close, then not quite so distant. Khalidah wrapped her shawl around her head and shoulders and linked arms with Abi Gul as they picked their way along a path by a dizzying drop. Finally they crossed the mountain's backbone and found themselves in a little hollow, just big enough for the stone bothy that huddled in the embrace of the ridge. It was sheltered from the wind, giving respite to sparse grass and a few wildflowers. A tethered nanny-goat munched on a patch of brilliant blue poppies, and a vein of smoke rose from the hole in the *aylaq's* roof.

Arsalan approached first, peering into the darkness past the open door. He spoke to someone within, his voice muffled by the wind that screamed across the ridge above them. After a moment he re-emerged with a man whom, it seemed to Khalidah, life had gnawed to the bone, leaving nothing but sinew and spirit. His threadbare white robe hung off of him like laundry drying on a frame, hands emerging like sticks of the gnarled *irta* shrubs that the Bedu used as fuel. His dark skin hung equally loose, battered by the elements, and his prominent, hooked nose seemed to engulf his hollow-cheeked face. But his eyes, a brilliant Jinn gold, blazed with a young man's fire. He grinned toothlessly at Khalidah, taking her hands in his own and kissing both of her cheeks in between muttered blessings and exclamations in Pashto.

When at last he let her go, he beckoned to them all to come into the *aylaq*. Inside, it was almost as spare as the outside. The packed-earth floor was covered with rugs so old they were beginning to disintegrate. The fire-pit was no more than a

depression in the centre of the floor, the fuel dried goat dung
and there was no smoke-hole. Three flat rocks sat at the edges
of the fire-pit with a cauldron balanced on them, the simmering
liquid within giving off a pungent, not-quite-unpleasant herbal
smell. Alipsha gestured to them to sit down, so they sat directly
on the rugs; there was no other furnishing in the *aylaq*, unless
one counted the enormous ibex skull in one corner. Khalidah
wondered if the old man slept directly on the floor, wrapped in
his moth-eaten carpets, and she was poised to pity him until she
recalled that a *darwish* often embraced equally harsh deprivations
in his quest for unity with Allah.

When they were seated, Alipsha disappeared outside and
then returned with a wooden bucket. He set it before Khalidah
and handed her a ladle. It was full of milk. Certain that she was
consuming the man's weekly sustenance, but well aware that
refusing it would be an insult, she dipped the ladle and took
a small sip before passing it along to Arsalan. Alipsha settled
himself across the fire from Khalidah and studied her for a time
before at last addressing her.

"Welcome, Bibi Khalidah," he said slowly, in Pashto. "I have
been – ."

Khalidah looked at Abi Gul and repeated the end of the
sentence, which she had not understood: "*Matale…?*"

"*Mateledal* – to wait for," Abi Gul explained. "Alipsha has been
waiting for you to come to him."

"Why?" Khalidah asked the old man.

He gave her a long answer, which she quickly gave up trying
to translate. She waited until he had finished and then looked
at Abi Gul, who said: "He has been dreaming of you for the
past three weeks – that is, since you arrived in Qaf. And before
that…" She paused uncomfortably.

"Please, just tell me, Abi Gul."

"He says that he has been speaking with your mother."

Though she knew that Alipsha could not mean it literally,
the words sent a shiver down Khalidah's spine. In Qaf, she was
constantly occupied with the demands of the Jinn's daily life,

but up here in this strange, solitary cell, she was suddenly and painfully aware that her mother was still alive somewhere, perhaps in a place not unlike this.

As if she guessed Khalidah's thoughts, Abi Gul quickly continued, "She appears to him in dreams, he says; she asks him to guide you. But he also says that he needs to know how you would be guided. That is, he wants you to ask him."

"But how can I?"

"Speak," said Alipsha, "and you will find that we understand each other."

The smoke in the hut had thickened, and Khalidah found that she could not recall what language the man had just spoken, only that she had understood him. "How…" she began.

"Because I am the *betaan*," he answered, as if this explained everything. "Now, Khalidah, tell me why you are here."

She looked at his kindly, wizened face through the steam rising from the pot. It seemed to shift and blur into a different face – that of a young man, though with similar features. It was like looking at two images, each with one eye, and it sent her head spinning. She found that it was easier to close her eyes.

"My father," she said, "and Bilal and Zaynab…what has happened to them?"

"Open your eyes," he said, and she obeyed.

The steam from the pot had thickened, hazing the shapes of the room to indistinct blotches; but within them, something was moving. Gradually, it resolved into a band of galloping horses backed by black-clad riders. The one at the front was her father. The image faded, merged into one of Zaynab stirring a pot in a kitchen – her own kitchen, the one beside the *maharama* where she and Khalidah had lived together, and she did not bear the look of a slave. Then it shifted again, and Khalidah was looking at two boys – one with long, curling black hair, the other with a bandaged arm and a head shorn like a Bedu's – sitting on a riverbank by a flowering pomegranate bush in their loincloths, their legs in the water.

As she watched, the long-haired one lay back with his head

on his outstretched arm, turning his fine-boned face toward her. She knew him at once as the Ayyub warrior who had killed the Templar in her nightmare that first night in Qaf. But this had barely begun to sink in before the other boy turned and leaned over him and Khalidah found herself watching Bilal kiss the beautiful boy with a lover's passion. As their limbs tangled, the image dissolved into steam.

She shut her eyes again, her heart racing. "What is he doing?" she asked, knowing even as the words formed how idiotic they sounded.

The *betaan* chuckled. "Did your nursemaid teach you nothing?"

"All right, I know what they are doing; but Bilal, I never..."

She stopped, not knowing how to put her thoughts into words, or even what her thoughts were. Despite what the Qur'an and the *hadith* had to say about it, and the fact that the staunchly traditional Bedu frowned on the concept, she was well enough educated to know that this kind of love was tolerated – even encouraged, within certain parameters – in other parts of the Islamic world. Moreover, what Bilal had done was no more outrageous than her months traveling alone with an unrelated man.

"Very well then: where was my father leading those men?"

"I do not know."

"Do you know who is looking after Zaynab and the rest of the tribe?"

"No, I am sorry."

"What about the boy, the one Bilal was...well...I have seen him before. Do you know who he is?"

"That, I can answer. The boy is the son of the Sultan, Salah ad-Din."

Khalidah's head spun. She had assumed that he belonged to the Sultan's retinue, by the yellow he had worn in that first terrible vision of him, but Bilal the lover of an Ayyub prince? She could not imagine how it had come to pass, and her reaction was to panic, for if the simple boy whom she had thought she had known inside out could change so radically, what might have happened to the rest of her people and her land in her absence?

But Alipsha had sensed her anxiety. When he spoke, his voice was soothing as fingers stroking her hair. "The world never ceases changing, Khalidah, but the ones you love are alive and apparently well...is that not enough?"

Khalidah couldn't argue with this.

"Now," said Alipsha, "if I have put you at ease, then tell me why you are here."

"In Qaf? I suppose because I believed that my mother was calling me here. But now I am not certain, for she is not here herself, and I don't sense her at all. Not even that part of her which called to me."

"The spirit is transient," Alipsha answered, "as is time. Brekhna is here, and not here; but she is not the answer."

"Perhaps not," Khalidah said, "yet Brekhna is the reason why the Jinn believe that I will lead them to their destiny."

"Are you certain of that?"

"If you know something different, I would prefer that you tell me plainly. I have had enough riddles and prophecies to last a lifetime."

There was a pause, a momentary hollowing between them, like a sigh. Then: "Khalidah, a *betaan* does not see in a linear way. For me, cause and effect do not form a chain, but an infinite web, each filament an individual life, and each life a part of the whole. Some threads spin out long and strong, some weaken and break. Some cross others, some gather them; others hardly touch any at all. I am not omniscient – far from it – but at times I am granted glimpses of the web. For whatever reason, your section of the fabric appears to me more often than most. I cannot tell you much, but I can tell you this: while your thread touches Brekhna's only in places, those of the Jinn, it gathers and binds."

"And what does that tell me?" she cried, exasperated. "It could mean that I am to stay here and take Tor Gul Khan's place, or as easily that I am to lead the Jinn to Salah ad-Din."

"Would it help if I told you that your thread is equally bound to those of your father's tribe?" Khalidah was surprised by how much this affected her, moved her even; but there was no time to question, for Alipsha was speaking again. "It also crosses that of Salah ad-Din. In fact, there is a great convergence of lives upon you, from all sides of this land and beyond. Your tugs on the fabric will be felt for a long time."

"Then I *am* destined to lead the Jinn to fight the Franj."

He sighed. "Khalidah...our religion is perhaps most different from yours in that we believe that *nothing* is written, nothing predetermined. I see likelihoods, no more. In other words, despite what I have told you, you can still choose your own fate."

"Then really," Khalidah said bitterly, "you have told me nothing."

"Haven't I?" the *betaan* asked. "Or do you simply mean that I have not told you what to do?" He sighed. "I know that it is difficult. It is always difficult for the ones like you. You could not be blamed for losing faith, as your mother did."

"What?" Khalidah asked, suddenly, stingingly alert. "What do you mean, like my mother did?"

But Alipsha ignored her question, saying, "If you want advice, I will tell you what I would tell any man or woman who asked: choose your path and then follow it to the end. But it is you, Khalidah, who must choose."

11

Salah ad-Din had expected a confession from Bilal al-Hassani and had guessed that it would incriminate his cousin Numair, but for all his years and experience reading the hearts of men, the Sultan had never imagined that the Bedu boy's could hold such tortuous secrets. It was the eyes, he decided. Like clear water, blue eyes had always seemed to him incapable of dissimulation – which was ludicrous, he realized, given the predominant coloring of the Franj.

As he listened to Bilal's strange story – de Ridefort's old transgression, an Ayyubid princess hiding within a Bedu tribe, a bastard child and layers upon layers of deception – he considered his options. And when the boy at last lapsed into tremulous silence, he asked him the last question Bilal expected:

"Tell me, do you love your father?"

Bilal gave him a terrible, twisted smile, followed by a bitter laugh. "I would gladly see his head on a pike."

The Sultan raised his eyebrows and said, with a shimmer of smile, "Strong words from a boy who could be coerced to treason by a mere threat."

"I have changed since then," Bilal said defiantly.

"My son, too, has changed." Now there was a flinty note, a hint of accusation, in his voice. "Tell me, how long has he known what you have told me?"

Bilal considered the wall tapestry across from him, then said, "It is not the reason for the change in him."

"That is not what I asked," the Sultan replied, irritated that the boy had seen so easily through his words to his intent.

"But is it not what you meant?" Bilal gave Salah ad-Din a direct look. The Sultan met it, but said nothing. "He has known since Oultrejourdain – I told him when we were trapped in the wadi by that sandstorm. I have severed ties with de Ridefort since then," he added quickly.

Salah ad-Din nodded, and though he kept his silence, his look told Bilal to continue.

"Your Highness," he said, sighing, "your son is sick at heart. I am not the cause, but sometimes I wish that I were, because then perhaps I could do something about it..." He shook his head, thought for a moment and then continued, "It was Cresson that changed him."

"That does not make sense," the Sultan insisted. "I have watched Salim in countless battles. He is no soft-hearted fool."

"No, he is not," Bilal replied. "But Cresson was different. Up until then, we had always fought men who would kill us given half a chance."

"And at Cresson you fought Templars," the Sultan said, his voice waspish, almost peevish. "Do you think that they would have spared you?"

"No," Bilal answered wearily, "of course not. But there was a desperation to their actions on that day, as if they knew that they should not be there. And then, when Salim was forced to kill the Templar Marshal..." He shook his head. "Did you know Jakelin de Mailly?" He did not wait for the Sultan to answer before continuing, "He should not have died at Cresson. He should never have been there at all. I think when Salim killed him he saw that, and so he saw the darkness inside himself for the first time, and he has been wandering within it ever since."

"Correct me if I am mistaken," Salah ad-Din said slowly, "but are you saying that the change in my son is due to the death of a single Franj knight?"

"Well...that is one way to look at it."

The Sultan was clearly angry, and Bilal thought that the anger was for Salim's weakness. He could never have anticipated the truth.

"Would it help him to know that it was Gerard de Ridefort who was responsible for de Mailly's death – in fact, for all of them?"

"He already knows that de Ridefort called the charge," Bilal answered, puzzled.

"Don't be a fool, boy!" Salah ad-Din said sharply. "I mean that he sabotaged his own men. The last time I met with him, I told him that I no longer wished to deal with him. I have never trusted him, and for some time he has been failing our – well, our agreements." He looked closely at Bilal. "He promised to prove his loyalty, in order to keep our negotiations open. I told him that I did not believe he had it in him to turn against the Order that has raised him so high; that in the end, he would forsake any promise to me. Apparently," he concluded dryly, "I underestimated him. Or at any rate, his greed."

Bilal blinked at him for a moment, digesting all of this. Then he said, "Forgive my impertinence, Sire, but I think you had best not tell Salim this."

The Sultan raised his eyebrows in surprise. "Why not? Will it not cause him to stop blaming himself?"

"Oh, yes," Bilal said. "Instead, he will blame you."

The Sultan's face flushed with anger. For a moment Bilal thought that the Sultan would strike him. But then his expression changed again, looking first puzzled, then defeated. "I fear you are right, al-Hassani; and you are a wiser man than I."

Bilal smiled sadly. "Hardly, Sire. Only, I do know Salim very well."

The Sultan sighed. "At any rate, we have strayed from the matter at hand. Therefore: I admit that much of what you have told me has come as a surprise. Where Gerard de Ridefort is concerned, however, you have only confirmed what I have known all along: he is a man whose only true cause is his own ambition. I know that for every promise he made me, he made two elsewhere. I see that you are wondering why, then, I have dealt with him at all? Well, even a treacherous egoist has his uses…"

He fell to musing, apparently forgetting about Bilal. A moment later, however, he locked eyes with the boy. "As for you, when I said that you had nothing to fear from speaking the truth to me, I meant it. But whatever hand is at work in all of this, it has placed you at the center of a powerful man's quarrel with the world. Any step you take will lead you deeper into danger." The Sultan's eyes softened, as Bilal had seen them soften a handful of times for Salim. A knot of sadness tightened in his chest.

"Listen to me, Bilal al-Hassani, for I speak to you now not as a king to his subject, but as a father to his son: you must be careful, as you have never been careful before. You were always a liability to Gerard de Ridefort, and now you have spurned and humiliated him as well. He will waste no time in trying to be rid of you, and given what I have told you about Cresson, you can see that doing so will not trouble his conscience in the slightest. As for your 'cousin' Numair, I cannot guess what he is plotting now, but it strikes me that he will take no more kindly to your deserting his cause than de Ridefort."

"I am not afraid of them," Bilal answered.

The Sultan smiled. "I am glad to hear it. But if you have no thought for your own safety, then at least consider Salim's."

Bilal froze, then babbled: "Oh, Your Highness, I had never thought – if being with me puts him in danger, then I will – "

"Do nothing, least of all what you were about to suggest!" the Sultan interrupted sharply. Then he sighed, pulling at his beard. "I can think of no one likelier to help him right now than you. He may not be my heir, and I know that I have given him little cause to think that I value him, but I do, more than he knows. So please, be careful for his sake."

Seeing that the Sultan had turned back to his papers, Bilal stood and started to leave. But as he reached for the tent flap, Salah ad-Din said, "Oh, and one more thing: you need not fear for your mother. In fact, that to me is the true travesty in all

of this. Her husband was a brutal man – yes, *was*. He was cut
to pieces by a money-lender whom he'd cheated a few months
after your mother left him. So you see, Numair lied to you,
too: whoever told him her story, it was not Zaynab's husband.
But even if he had lived, you must rest assured, I would never
have allowed any man to cast a stone at Zaynab bint Ibrahim
al-Ayyubi, nor will I willingly allow any man to harm her son.
Bilal ibn Zaynab al-Ayyubi…it has a certain ring, doesn't it?"

Once again, the Sultan smiled. Bilal nodded, then stumbled
out into the night, dazed and euphoric despite everything. For
in all the months that he wrestled with the acquisition of a hated
father, he had never considered that Numair had also unwittingly
bequeathed him a family.

*

The Franj castle at Saffuriyya was hardly worthy of the designation. Numair, who had grown up with the mighty fortresses of
Kerak and Shawbak as his models, thought that the small cube of
rock looked like nothing so much as the product of some third-
rate god's constipation, squeezed out and left to desiccate on the
top of an indifferent hill. But if the castle wasn't up to much,
the lands around it more than compensated for its shortcom-
ings, and so Numair had been happy enough to wait there in
the weeks between his desertion from the Tiberias detachment
and de Ridefort's return. He had lain low, camping in a clutch of
trees, hunting at dawn and dusk when he was unlikely to be seen,
listening from the shadows of village tea-shops and taverns as
news rolled in of the massacre at Cresson, Tripoli's capitulation,
the Franj call to arms and finally of the army that had begun to
gather in the town.

When he learned, via this same web of gossip, that de Ridefort
was in residence, he made his way to the castle. Now he sat
by a window in what passed for a great hall, sipping a glass of
sweet local wine, as the fertile hills of Galilee tumbled toward

the horizon like a kneeling woman's skirts, and a breeze full of verdure wafted the hill. He would have liked nothing better than to relax into the bucolic torpor of the setting, but de Ridefort was in no such mood.

"What do you mean, you are not going back?" he stormed when Numair made his announcement, slamming his cup onto the table so that the wine splashed out and over his hand, further stoking his rage.

"Just that," Numair answered with languid arrogance. "I've had enough of army life, and at any rate I've learned nothing in my time in the Sultan's camp that can help you. Besides, your son seems far better placed to provide you with information than I."

Numair had intended for this remark to placate the Master, but instead de Ridefort's anger deepened. "Do not mention that brat to me!" he rumbled.

With the first fluttering of anxiety, Numair asked, "Why? What has he done?"

"He has insulted me," de Ridefort answered, "and if you had paid the slightest attention, you would have realized that he has deserted us long since in favor of the little Ayyub sodomite. He is of no use to us any longer – if he ever was at all."

De Ridefort's sky-blue glare had settled on Numair with a cast of accusation. Liking this even less than his words, Numair said, "How do you know this?"

"Because he told me."

"He *told* you?" Numair repeated. "And you let him live?"

De Ridefort paused before answering, convincing Numair that there was more to the story than the Master was allowing. "I was not in a position to do otherwise," he muttered. "But it is worse than that. The Sultan has dismissed me from his service. I hardly need to tell you what that means – for both of us."

"You think that Salah ad-Din holds Bilal in high enough regard to take his advice on such a matter?" he scoffed.

"Do you have a better explanation for his sudden change of heart?"

"What does it matter, the reason?"

"It matters a great deal, to me," de Ridefort said coldly. "I do not like to be double-crossed."

Numair bristled at the accusation in his tone. "You cannot blame me for this."

"Can't I? You are the one who brought the boy into it."

"So?"

"So, you are the one who is going to take him out again."

"You do not command me," Numair said, slamming his own cup down, his anger finally piqued.

"Oh, but I do," cried de Ridefort, his eyes alight with malice. "You are a Saracen in a Franj castle. One word from me, and your head rolls."

"And if Bilal has turned the Sultan against you, do you really think he's left my reputation intact? I won't get anywhere near him."

The Templar stood and leaned over Numair, gripping the arms of his chair, pinning him to it. "Oh, you will. Somehow, you will find a way, for if you don't, your head will decorate my lance." He smiled as Numair glared at him. "And just in case you take it in mind to disappear, remember that there is a good deal of Franj territory between here and your home, and I have every means of keeping tabs on you."

"You are despicable," Numair hissed.

"And that is why we make such a good team," de Ridefort answered coolly. "So, am I to understand that you'll take care of my little problem? You will of course be well paid for your services."

Numair only glowered at him, but they both knew the answer.

*

Agreeing to it was one thing; carrying it out was another. Depending on how the Sultan had taken the news of his treachery, there might be scouts looking for him even now. Numair

knew that he couldn't go near the Muslim camp; his only chance
was to draw Bilal out of it. But Bilal was not the gullible boy he
had been on the morning after Khalidah's elopement. For several
days, Numair lay in his tent in a dry, wind-ridden wadi to the
south of Tal 'Ashtara, smoking *banj* and ruminating glumly on
the impossibility of his mission. And then, with the inexplicable
luck that sometimes graces the truly nefarious, the solution fell
into his lap.

It was the sixth morning since he'd left Saffuriyya and three
hours shy of noon it was already sweltering. Numair was seated
on the lip of the wadi in the perforated shade of a tamarisk tree,
cleaning his weapons and hoping for a breeze, when he noticed a
cloud of dust moving along the horizon. It came from the north,
and as it drew nearer he recognized the form of a running horse.
A few more moments and he could make out its coloring: dark
bay. Even as he was telling himself that it couldn't be, he caught
a flash of yellow – the rider's flying robe – and the three white
spots on the horse's flank.

Flinging his gear back into the wadi, but retaining his crossbow and sword, Numair hid himself such as he could behind the
attenuated tree. He knew that this chance was likely to be his
only one, so he loaded the crossbow carefully and then waited,
measuring the distance with the patient acuity that had made
him into a formidable hunter. He spared a moment of regret for
Anjum – he had bred and broken her himself – then he fired.

Even before the arrow hit its target, he knew that he had
judged the shot perfectly. The horse tumbled, hurling her rider
into the sand, and before the stunned Bilal even realized what
had happened, Numair was upon him. He drew his sword and
shoved it against Bilal's throat, where it turned on the iron links
of a mail coif.

"Charmed the prince out of his armor, have you?" Numair
snarled, and went to nudge the mail aside.

But Bilal caught the point of the sword in one gauntleted hand
and with a strength Numair was clearly not expecting, he forced
it back from his throat, and still further back, until he rolled free

and leapt to his feet, drawing his own sword and hoping that his arm would hold. It had only just healed and was still tender enough that he wrapped it for riding in wet strips of leather, which hardened and stiffened as they dried, protecting it from further damage. He doubted, however, that the bandage would withstand the force of a sword fight, and worse still, Numair had noticed it.

"What was it?" he asked, nodding to the bandage. "A lovers' quarrel?"

"Why are you here, Numair?" Bilal asked coldly, as they circled.

"To kill you, obviously."

"What is obvious? You couldn't have known that I would be here, now."

Numair smiled, shook his head. "I consider that Allah's blessing upon my intention. Now – "

He lunged and Bilal dodged the blow, stumbling. Numair slashed while Bilal was recovering, and this time their blades clashed in a shower of sparks, which fizzled away into the searing sand. Bilal managed to recover, but Numair had seen the flash of pain on his face as the wrapped arm took the force of the blow.

"If you kneel to me now like a good boy," Numair said, studying his sweating opponent down the length of his blade, "I promise to make it quick."

"I would suffer the worst of deaths before I would kneel to you!"

"Very well, then…"

Numair attacked again. Though Bilal fought with everything in him, he knew that he was beaten. They were an hour's ride from camp – an hour's ride from anywhere – and he would not have been a match for Numair even if his arm had been sound. His fight rapidly deteriorated into a series of desperate parries as Numair forced him back to the edge of the wadi and then, with a vicious swipe, knocked his legs out from under him, so that he knelt after all.

The fall from the hapless Anjum, the heat and the pain had

all done their work on Bilal. He could not make himself stand; in fact, it was all he could do to keep from toppling into the valley behind him. The blood rushed in his ears with a sound like a flooded wadi, and his vision was clouded with the spots and sparks of fleeing consciousness...and something else. Something that should not be there, but was: a dark wedge on the horizon that resolved improbably into a band of running horses, all backed by black-robed riders except for one at the front, who rode in a flicker of yellow and a stream of dark hair. For a moment he thought that they were angels come to escort him to paradise; but the subsequent thud of the black-feathered arrow was too visceral to be divine, as was the rictus of thwarted vengeance on Numair's face as he stumbled, clawing at the arrow lodged in his back, and pitched over the lip of the wadi.

Bilal clung to the tamarisk's trunk and looked down, forcing his eyes to repeat the truth of the inert body on the valley floor many times before he believed it. It was only when a hand touched his shoulder that he remembered his liberators. He looked up into Salim's face, still etched with the horror of what had almost happened. But when the prince had helped him to stand, he nearly collapsed again, for Salim's entourage had ridden forward and their leader had pulled aside his *kufiyya*.

"*As-salaamu 'alaikum*, Bilal ibn Zaynab," said 'Abd al-Aziz, his narrow, lined face breaking into a smile. "It's a pretty chase you've led us on these last months...and it seems we found you just in time."

12

As Abi Gul had predicted, Tor Gul Khan sent Rakan home the following day with twenty Jinn warriors at his back. Shahascina, Afshan and Sarbaz were among them, their mothers weeping and laughing by turns as they saw them off. All the village watched as they rode off into the foothills to the south and then disappeared seamlessly into the rolling green.

Watching them, Khalidah felt an eerie shiver, knowing that she was soon to follow. She had been certain of this since she had returned from her visit to the *betaan*. Aside from the visions of her friends and family, Alipsha had told her nothing that she had not already known, nor had he pointed her in any particular direction; and yet, when she returned to the valley it was with an odd feeling of clearance, as if the *betaan* had scoured and ordered her mind, leaving her free to see clearly. Even before she and Abi Gul reached the foothills, she had known what she was going to do. She had told both Abi Gul and Sulayman as soon as they reached the valley and both had given their approval. The only hurdle left now was the inevitable confrontation with Tor Gul Khan.

After Rakan's band departed, Khalidah walked up to the temple. She carried the sword she had found in Domat al-Jandal, wrapped in her shawl, since it was not permitted to bring naked weapons into the temple. She had hoped to find her grandfather there, but there were only a handful of celibates, most of them meditating. Approaching one who was not, Khalidah asked her where she might find her grandfather. The woman indicated the door that led into the hermitage, and Khalidah followed her pointing finger.

She had not been to Tor Gul Khan's living quarters since her first night in Qaf, and she realized now that she had no idea how to find them. She walked down a long, whitewashed corridor lined with open doorways. These were the cells of the celibates. Each revealed a neat little room with a narrow bed, a simple woolen carpet and a small altar set with carved deities and flickering lamps. At the end of the corridor was a narrow wooden stairway. She followed it up into another corridor, this one with a row of doors on one side that led onto the gallery at the front of the temple and three on the other, one of which stood open. A faint drift of incense came from within.

Khalidah approached it slowly and looked inside. The room was bigger than the cells below, but almost as spare. Tor Gul Khan sat on a plainly-woven rug in front of a burning censer, meditating. Khalidah hovered inside the doorway, uncertain what to do until, abruptly, her grandfather looked up at her, his golden eyes keen as knives.

"Come in," he said, "and sit."

Khalidah knelt on the rug facing him, still clutching the wrapped sword. Her grandfather glanced at it, but when he spoke, it was to say, "You have decided to go to your Sultan." There was regret in his voice, but not anger. Khalidah nodded. "And you will take the believers with you."

Khalidah sighed. "I have kept my promise to you. I have not knowingly spoken any word to your people to encourage or discourage them from their beliefs. You wanted me to live with them, to come to some kind of decision, but the most I can say is what everyone keeps saying to me: they must choose their own path. When I leave I will not encourage them to follow, but nor will I stop them if they wish to come."

He studied her, saying nothing, the minutes stretching

uncomfortably. At last he said, "Very well, Khalidah. But as you are not here to ask my permission to take my people west, why *are* you here?"

She unwrapped the sword and handed it to him. He looked at it for a long moment, his expression unreadable, though he passed his thumb thoughtfully over the golden jewel in the hilt.

"Was it my mother's?" she asked in a voice she had intended to be firm and clear, but which came out rather more tremulously.

He looked at the sword for a moment longer and then handed it back, sighing. "And her mother's, and her mother's mother's and so on back through time. The jewel is ancient, a yellow diamond from these hills. The inscription is not so old – it was made by an Arab sultan who owed a large debt to your great-great grandmother. I am glad that Brekhna left it to you."

"She didn't," Khalidah said flatly. "I found it in a junk shop in a desert town at the edge of Jazirah."

"I see," he answered evenly, though the shock was evident on his face.

Abruptly, Khalidah flooded with rage. "Tell me what happened to her."

"You know that already."

"Yes," she snapped, "I've been told her story by a hundred different people in a hundred different ways, ever since I was old enough to understand. And yet, none of them ever really told me anything…not until I spoke to your *betaan*."

"And what did he tell you?" he asked, his body very still and his voice nearly a whisper.

"He told me that she lost faith. What did he mean?"

Now, along with the shock, Tor Gul Khan's face showed fear. He shook his head, the movement barely perceptible.

"I don't believe that you don't know!" Khalidah insisted. "There is something you are not telling me. You say that she left the Jinn to fight the Franj with Salah ad-Din, and yet she did not join him, but married my father instead. She abandoned this sword which, if I have understood anything about the Jinn, was like throwing away the purpose of her existence. And then she abandoned her husband and her only child." She ran her finger over the inscription on the sword. "'Life of My Soul', this says...it's what she called me, too. What does it take to make a woman turn from the life of her soul?"

Tor Gul Khan held her eyes for a moment longer, then passed his hand over his face. When he looked at her again, he had become the broken old man of their first conversation, who had pleaded with her to keep his people in Qaf.

Tremulously, he said, "It takes betrayal, Khalidah. Sometimes just one, but in the case of a strong woman like Brekhna it takes many. They chipped away at her soul, little by little, until at last it shattered. That is why she left you, and her Jinn calling. It is why she is not here now and never will return."

Khalidah watched him, willing him to continue, not to lose himself in the remorse and bewilderment now clouding his face. At last he said, "She was such a brilliant girl – talented at everything, it seemed. She was no great beauty, but she had that sparkle that draws the eye despite it. She had many suitors, but there had only ever been one boy for her – Sher Dil. He had a brilliance too, but it came from his kindness. He was sweet-natured, too sweet to make a warrior, really; but still he had the talent for it, and because he knew that it was Brekhna's calling, he pursued it.

"At *Psarlay*, when they turned sixteen, they were betrothed. But though they had finished their training, there was no battle in sight, no chance for them to initiate themselves as adults; no way for them to marry. As the months went by, they pleaded with me to marry them anyway, and I refused. How could I make an exception for my daughter and deny all the others in her situation?"

He shook his head. "But Brekhna wore me down. She made me promise that they would both be sent on the next mission, whatever it was, and like a fool, I agreed. The next call came from a northern village of Tajiks fighting an insurgence of Mongols. The Mongols are difficult opponents, because their methods of fighting are not unlike our own. Their strength, like ours, is in their mounted archers. We had always suffered heavy losses when we fought them, and I did not like to risk Brekhna on such a mission. But what could I do? I had promised. And so Brekhna and Sher Dil rode out on that mission…" His look was distant, bitter.

"And he was killed," Khalidah said softly.

"In the first charge," Tor Gul Khan agreed. "The Mongols use scissor-headed arrows as well, and his arm was severed near the shoulder. He was dead by the time Brekhna reached him." He sighed. "Another girl would have grieved until, with time, her heart softened again. But not Brekhna. It was as if she bled her heart out with Sher Dil on that northern steppe. Afterward she was good for nothing but war. She turned her back on everything that had once delighted her – her music, her horses, the weaving and the planting and the little bits of life here that she had loved – and volunteered for every mission going. A few more fights and she had surpassed every warrior in this valley in skill and brutality. It was as if in every enemy she faced, she saw the Mongol archer who had killed her beloved. She made it her purpose to exact vengeance.

"And then, while they were out on a mission in Persia, she and her warriors caught the eye of a Kurdish *amir*. He asked them to go west with him, for he knew of a man who could use their help, fighting a group of invaders he called the Franj."

"And that was when she met Salah ad-Din?"

Tor Gul Khan nodded. "Salah ad-Din, and the Franj, and her battered mind and heart saw in them, in their struggle, the bones of our old myth. She and her people stayed for many months with him, fighting the invaders. When at last they returned I found Brekhna changed again. I had not thought that anything could be so painful as watching her thwarted love for Sher Dil become such bitter hatred, but now I knew that I was wrong. Now it had changed into religious faith, the kind of burning passion that takes the soul as a flame takes kindling and reduces it to ash as quickly. She wanted to lead the others back to Salah ad-Din."

"And you said no."

"Can you blame me, Khalidah?" he asked, and she saw that a bit of the fire had come back into his eyes. "She was a madwoman by then, without regard for anything but her conviction."

"The same has been said of each of Allah's prophets, in his time."

"Believe me mistaken, if you will," he answered wearily. "There is no changing the past. I told her that I was still the Khan and I would not give her mission my blessing. I suppose in her way she did still respect me, for she didn't take anyone with her, just slipped away one night with her sword and her horse and nothing else. She went back to Salah ad-Din, and for several years she fought for him. I don't know what happened, whether it was a sudden epiphany, or a gradual disillusionment; I know only that at some point, the fire burned out. She lost her faith, or perhaps simply the strength to pursue it. An Arab chief with whom she had ridden on several raids had asked her repeatedly to marry him. At last she accepted, and so she became the wife of 'Abd al-Aziz al-Hassani."

"How do you know all of this?" Khalidah asked, despite a dark premonition of the answer.

Tor Gul Khan paused for a long moment before he answered, "Because she told me."

Khalidah shut her eyes, as if in doing so she could shut her heart against the terrible truth she was about to hear.

"I suppose that she had hoped to salvage herself by marrying," he continued, as if it were a great effort, "in living a simple life as a wife and a mother. But Brekhna was Jinn, and a Jinni never stops being a Jinni, not even after life has burnt her to a cinder." He paused, giving Khalidah a look of terrible sympathy. "War couldn't save her, nor marriage, nor motherhood. By the time she realized that there was a single ember left burning in her, and that was the desire to return to Qaf. That was why she left you, Khalidah: to come here, to ask to be taken back. But she did not intend to abandon you – that, you must understand. She would have brought you with her."

"Would have?" Khalidah repeated.

"Yes," he said softly, bitterly. "It is my fault, Khalidah, that you grew up without a mother. I could not forget my own anger and forgive her. I denied her request to come back. I told her that she would never be welcome here again, nor any half-blooded child."

Khalidah felt the words like a slap; it was only by tremendous effort that she didn't leap up and run from the place then and there. But she knew that there was still more to come, that she must hear it, and so she kept still, kept listening.

"She accepted it with what I thought was meekness. I could not see that I had snuffed that last ember in her heart. With that betrayal, I had killed my only daughter. Oh, she still lives – Alipsha has told me that. She is somewhere far from here, far from anywhere, I suppose. But what her life is like now...well, I wish I did not need to imagine.

"As for me, I realized my mistake the moment she left. Since then I have known remorse the like of which you cannot imagine. I spent a few years looking for her, until Alipsha convinced me that she did not want to be found. Then I began looking for you, and that is why you are here, Khalidah: not because I want an heir, nor to keep the Jinn intact, but because it was what Brekhna wanted, and it is the only thing left for me to offer her by way of an apology."

"So I am here to soothe your conscience?"

He flinched, but held her eyes. "I suppose I deserve that. But if you can find it in yourself, please believe that I wanted you to come here because I wanted you to have a choice. You cannot tell me that you would rather have stayed with your tribe and married your cousin."

Khalidah sighed. Tor Gul Khan's eyes were pleading again, and Khalidah found her heart softening despite herself.

"What can I do, Khalidah, to begin to atone for what I have taken from you?"

She studied him for a long time, imagining the many ways that she could answer this question. But in the end, she cast them all aside in favor of the only one that mattered. "You can let the believers follow me," she said, "and fight for Salah ad-Din, with your blessing."

He closed his eyes and inclined his head and again, despite herself, Khalidah was humbled by the effort this must have cost him. "Along with my blessing, take this knowledge with you, Khalidah: in my eyes you are Jinn, you are my blood, and nothing will ever change that. If you choose the life of your father's people, I wish you well in it. But if you ever find yourself longing for Qaf, then come back to us. I don't care how long you have been away. You and whomever you choose to bring with you will always find a home here."

When Khalidah nodded, she found her hands spattered with tears.

13

"Well?" Abi Gul asked eagerly. "What did he say?"

She and Sulayman had waited for Khalidah while she spoke to Tor Gul Khan, sitting on a wide, flat rock on the riverbank near where the horses grazed. Khalidah sat down with them, winding one of her plaits around her hand as she tried to make sense of all that had passed between herself and her grandfather. Perversely, now that he had given her his blessing, she was suddenly less certain that the path she had chosen was the right one.

"He said that we are free to go," she answered at last, "and that we will go with his blessing."

Abi Gul leapt to her feet, clapping her hands like a child, her face aglow with excitement. "May I tell the others?" she asked.

Khalidah could not help smiling at her friend's delight; she only wished that she felt the same. "Of course you can – and hurry. We must leave as soon as possible, if we are to catch the Sultan's army in time."

Abi Gul waved away Khalidah's words like flies. "Don't worry about that – we have ways of traveling fast, when we need to." And with that cryptic assurance, she was off up the hill to the dormitory to spread the news.

Sulayman had been watching Khalidah carefully throughout this exchange, and once Abi Gul was gone he said, "There was more. A lot more, judging by the look on your face."

Khalidah looked at him. He was almost unrecognizable as the minstrel who had accompanied 'Abd al-Hadi to her father's camp so many months ago, well-fed, bearded, cloaked in the studied obsequiousness of the intelligent servant. Now he was clean-shaven like the Jinn men, his hair shorn close under his *pakol*, and his features had taken on the quality of the Jinn's, something that marked them as creatures of these remote mountains, as if they had been shaped by rock and thin air. Only his eyes remained the same: black and laughing, clever and kind. He smiled encouragement, and Khalidah burst into tears.

Sulayman took her into his arms and held her while she cried, neither asking nor offering anything in response. After a time, the sound of the river and the shelter of his arms soothed her, and she began to tell him all that Tor Gul Khan had told her. Putting it into her own words did nothing, however, to settle her heart on all the torment her grandfather's confession had unearthed.

"I preferred not knowing," she concluded.

"Khalidah, I do not mean this in any way to sound condescending...but are you sure of that?"

Khalidah stifled her initial annoyance and asked him what he meant.

"It is like Ghassan telling me about my own mother. I was angry at him at the time, I felt like it was another burden to carry when I was already overloaded. But now, it has settled. It isn't that I don't think of it, or that it doesn't trouble me, only that time has made me see it as necessary. Now I believe that one day, it might lead to answers, and to some kind of peace."

"Right now, I cannot imagine peace."

"Perhaps not; but maybe that isn't the point. At any rate, it doesn't change the reasons for your deciding to return to Salah ad-Din, so don't let it throw you. Perhaps, once you have met that challenge, the rest will fall into place."

"I hope so."

"Hold on to your purpose, Khalidah – if not for your own sake, then for the people who will follow you."

"What if no one does?" she asked. "What if all of this comes to nothing?"

His face quirked into the expression Khalidah had once thought of as his thief's smile. He indicated the hill behind her. Khalidah didn't know whether to be dismayed or delighted at the stream of people heading toward the rock where she sat, Abi Gul dancing at their head.

*

Khalidah's biggest worry was time, but the Jinn repeatedly reassured her on this point. Every Jinni of fighting age and ability was always ready to leave the valley at a moment's notice, and in terms of reaching Salah ad-Din before he engaged the Franj, the Jinn knew shortcuts through all of the mountains between the Hindu Kush and the Zagros. Once past the latter, they were back into territory that Sulayman knew well. They had every advantage to ensure that they traveled quickly; the rest, they said, was in the hands of the gods.

Khalidah looked out at the people gathered around her. She estimated their number at five hundred: about half of the population of the valley. The volunteers ranged from the not-yet-initiated to their grandparents, but every one of them looked back at her with eager anticipation.

With a deep breath and a prayer to Allah that she would not fail them, Khalidah said, "Tor Gul Khan has given his blessing to this mission. Any who choose to join Salah ad-Din are free to do so, and you will be free to return here afterward."

"And if we are not yet of age?" Abi Gul asked.

Khalidah stumbled; she had not thought to ask her grandfather this. But before she could think of an answer, she heard Tor Gul Khan say, "You may go, Abi Gul." He stood at the back of the crowd, sending a ripple of whispers and exclamations through it as everyone turned and saw him. "That is, if your parents allow it. That goes for the rest of you who are not yet of age."

"And will you join us?" somebody asked.

"I am too old," Tor Gul Khan answered diplomatically. "But I will see you off tomorrow, and I will be here to greet you when you return."

"What will we – " another voice ventured, but Tor Gul Khan held up his hand, silencing her.

"This mission belongs to Bibi Khalidah," he said, meeting Khalidah's eyes with his own, which swarmed with emotion. "I consider her my heir. Whether or not she returns here to take up the position is up to her; but for the duration of this mission, please, treat her as you would me."

He gave Khalidah a slight nod and she returned it. Willing her voice steady, she said, "We will ride out tomorrow at dawn. Go now and make your preparations."

The people began to disperse, but one wizened old man made his way toward the rock where Khalidah sat. He glanced at Sulayman, who gave him a strange, intense look, and then knelt before Khalidah. "Bibi Khalidah, my name is Arzou, and I must ask a favor of you."

Trying to remember why the name sounded familiar, she said, "Please, rise – I am no queen. Tell me what it is you want."

Arzou looked at her for a moment with rheumy eyes and then he said, "Sulayman has told me that you have met my daughter, Sandara."

It all came rushing back to Khalidah then: the horror and the tragedy of Sandara's story, so like in its way to her own mother's. "I have had that honor," she said softly.

Arzou nodded sadly. "I know what she thinks of me and why she thinks it. But Sulayman has told me of her circumstances, and I cannot allow her to live out her life in seclusion, believing that her people have cast her out. She should be here, her children should be raised as Jinn. I am far too old to ride to Al-Quds, let alone to fight if I reached it, but you will pass through Zabol on your way west, and if I might accompany you so far, perhaps you can convince Sandara to return with me to Qaf."

"Of course you can come with us," Khalidah said, "but I do not think that you will need any help in convincing Sandara to come back."

Arzou took Khalidah's hands in his and kissed them.

*

That evening, Khalidah's dormitory was as chaotic as it had been on the first night of *Psarlay*, but this time the turmoil consisted of armor and weapons, saddle-bags and bedrolls, rather than finery and face-paint. Abi Gul brought Khalidah her things from the cupboard where they had lain with the girls' armor and weapons since she had arrived in Qaf. Along with her own saddle and blanket and sword, there were two new bows – one for long range and one for close – and a quiver containing a clutch of the three types of arrow the Jinn used in combat. She had leather armor toughened with fish glue which she had been using in the drills, a metal-and-leather helmet, a suit of plain white clothing cut more closely than the ones they wore every day, and a set of the long silk underwear she had been so abashed to watch Abi Gul remove on her first day in Qaf. Since then, Khalidah had learned its purpose: the silk was so tough that arrows shot from a long distance would not penetrate it even if they penetrated the skin beneath, and so the arrow could be drawn from the flesh intact by pulling on the fabric around it.

She packed what she could into her saddle-bags and made a neat bundle of the rest, then sat on her bed watching the other girls. Only a quarter of them were going, but most of the others joined in the preparations with as much enthusiasm as if they were. A small minority was missing, and Khalidah guessed that this was because they came from families who did not believe in Pamir's prophecy. Though she had heard no one speak out against her, nor against those who were joining her, she felt the absence of the non-believers like a short, sharp dagger in her side, poisoned with doubt.

"You cannot please everyone," came Abi Gul's voice at her shoulder, startling her from her reverie.

"How do you know what I was thinking?"

"Your face is like a clear river – it isn't difficult to see the stones at the bottom."

"That does not encourage me," Khalidah said.

Abi Gul smiled, stuffing her miraculous underwear into a saddle-bag. "I can't imagine anything that would encourage you at the moment. But it will do you no good to sit here brooding. Go find Sulayman; that always seems to help. Take a walk – after all, you might not see Qaf again for a long time."

It was slight, but Khalidah caught the waver in Abi Gul's voice as she spoke the final words.

*

Evening had settled over the valley like a finely-woven veil: the last sunlight burnished, the shadows cypress-colored, the sky a green-tinged wash from an ancient artist's brush. By the river the horses grazed as the last of the workers came in from the orchards and the fields. Blue veins of smoke rose from the terraced houses on the hillside. Khalidah walked along the river bank, looking into water that was opaque now with the falling night. She thought of her first night here – the first she remembered – and its contrast with the present one. There would be no singing and dancing tonight. There was only the hush of anticipation, of speculation and hope and doubt, gathering strength with the falling dark.

Khalidah could already feel the hollow chill of the coming night and she knew that she would never sleep. She also knew then that she could not go back to the dormitory, to the incessant questions and the eager chatter of the girls who had no idea what they were riding into. As the last light faded from the mountains' eastern faces, Sulayman fell into step beside her. They walked for a long time in silence, all the way to the hill above the empty practice field. There the wind was brisker. It blew Khalidah's shawl back against her shoulders and lifted her hair, which was loose for the first time since their journey had begun. It was tradition, Abi Gul had told her, for girls to loosen their plaits the night before setting out on their first mission. There had been some complicated reasoning behind it, most of which Khalidah had forgotten, except that it had something to do with virginity; though she wondered now whether she had that wrong, since she couldn't quite see the connection.

"Are you still wondering whether you've done the right thing?" Sulayman asked.

"No – it's too late for that. But I couldn't face them anymore."

"Stay here with me, then."

"What?" she asked. When she turned to look at him, she saw sadness and longing in his face that confused her further. "What is the matter, Sulayman?" And then it hit her. "You don't want to come, do you? You want to stay here. I should have realized, of course you would, it's all you wanted – "

But he was smiling, half-amused, half-sad. "No, Khalidah, don't think that! Yes, I love this place, but I believe that my first duty is to Salah ad-Din…it is only that I have missed you."

She shook her head, bemused. "Missed me? But I have been here all the time!"

"Yes – and I have hardly seen you in all these weeks. I know that it's jealousy, Khalidah, and I'm not proud of it. But I have begun to wonder whether you have changed your mind…whether the things we promised on our journey here have changed for you, now that you have seen this place and the kind of life you could have here."

She felt a rush of remorse, realizing how it must have seemed to him. And what he said was true, to an extent – she had been absorbed and distracted by all that had happened, all that she had learned and become and stood still to become. Yet he had allowed her to do it, however much it must have hurt him; he had never let his feelings cloud his advice to her. Khalidah realized now that she relied on him, and loved him, more than ever. She reached out to clutch him to her and he reached back. And then he was not just clutching her but kissing her, and she couldn't quite believe that it was her own hands reaching for the knot in his sash, as he pulled her down into a hollow in the lee side of the hill. Somewhere in the midst of it, he caught her hands.

"Are you sure, Khalidah? I thought that you feared – "

But she had already counted the days and knew that it was as safe as it could be, and as for the rest she answered, "I have learned a lot since I said that, Sulayman; and now the only thing I fear is that I will go to my grave never having known this."

He looked at her for a moment, to be certain that she meant it, that this was not something she would regret.

"I will never regret it," she answered, and then smiled.

14

'Abd al-Aziz's men made quick work of Numair's campsite, extracting everything of value and then torching the rest. Bilal and Salim stood together, watching the tent burn.

"Are you all right?" Salim asked.

"More or less," Bilal answered, flexing the fingers of his right hand. They were losing feeling as the arm began to swell against the binding.

"Here, let me..." said Salim. Drawing his dagger, he cut carefully through the leather strips until they fell away, revealing the livid, swollen skin beneath. He stared at it for a moment, then, looking up at Bilal, he said, "I'm sorry."

"It doesn't hurt much," Bilal answered.

"No – I mean, for the rest."

"The rest of what?" Bilal asked incredulously. "You saved my life."

"Yes, and if I had not been such a self-pitying wretch, I would never have left camp without telling you, and you would not have followed me – "

"And if the last straw had not been loaded, the camel's back would have held," Bilal interrupted dryly. "What's done is done, and we're both alive to tell about it. Besides, we're finally rid of *him*."

They both looked over at Numair's crumpled body, the ostrich-feather arrow still protruding from his back. For all that they made free with his belongings, none of the Bedu men seemed inclined to touch him.

"And you?" asked Bilal. "How are you, after – "

Salim smiled. For the first time since Cresson, it had all the arch brilliance Bilal had first fallen in love with. "Killing him?" he finished. "Surprisingly well, actually. In fact, one might say it was just what I needed to snap me out of the dream I've been in these last weeks."

Bilal wasn't quite certain that he believed this, but he wasn't about to argue with it, either. Salim walked over to the body, prodded it speculatively with his toe. "Do you want his head? You can bring it back to camp as a gift for my father."

Snapped out of the dream, indeed, Bilal thought. He found the matter-of-fact brutality in Salim's eyes at least as disturbing as his earlier torpor. "Leave him for the vultures," he said.

Salim looked at the body with obvious regret, but he resheathed his sword. Bilal took Numair's horse, a rangy bay whose name he didn't know. He regretted leaving Anjum to be eaten by scavengers, but there was little choice. Casting a silent prayer over her, he turned Numair's horse and followed the others toward camp.

Despite 'Abd al-Aziz's protests, Salim led him straight to his father's tent. While the retainers kicked dust outside with the Sultan's guard, the two leaders eyed each other with cautious respect. After formally thanking the sheikh for his part in Bilal's rescue, Salah ad-Din sent two of his *mamalik* to find a campsite for his men, then clapped his hands for tea.

"So then, will you remain here with us, or repair to the south now that you have found your wayward…ah…"

"I have always considered Bilal a son," 'Abd al-Aziz said quietly, "whether or not he realized it; now more than ever."

Though he was nominally answering the Sultan, 'Abd al-Aziz looked at Bilal as he spoke the words. The boy nodded mutely, wondering if it would forever be his lot to choke back tears like a girl whenever someone offered him a kind word.

'Abd al-Aziz gave him a brief smile and then turned back
to Salah ad-Din. "As for remaining with you, it would be our
honor. I would have come sooner, but certain affairs" – here his
face darkened momentarily, and Bilal knew that he spoke of his
brother – "have kept me with the tribe. At any rate, I trust that
the men I sent to you have proven useful?"

Though it seemed unlikely that he would remember a small
band of Bedu cavalry among tens of thousands, Bilal didn't doubt
Salah ad-Din's sincerity when he answered, "They have proven
serious-minded and stalwart. I thank you for their services."

The two leaders made small talk while they finished their
tea, and then the Sultan said, "I imagine that you and Bilal have
matters of your own to discuss. Therefore, allow me to detain
you no longer."

'Abd al-Aziz was astute enough to realize that he had been
dismissed. Bowing, he retreated. Salim stayed behind in the
pavilion at his father's request; Bilal and the sheikh followed the
mamluk guard who was waiting outside to show them to the
campsite. They walked for a time in silence, before Bilal found
the words with which to break it.

"Do not think that I am not grateful...but I cannot help
wondering, why did you come for me?"

'Abd al-Aziz paused for a moment, then answered, "What I
said to the Sultan was true, Bilal – you have always been like a
son to me. When I learned that you had left with Numair, I knew
that something was not right. I came after you as soon as my
brother let up on his raiding long enough to allow it."

"Has it been bad, then?"

'Abd al-Aziz sighed. "No worse than usual, though he's been
more persistent. It's spite, I suppose. 'Abd al-Hadi has always
been adept at shouldering me with the blame for his problems,
and his son's defection was no different, if particularly nettlesome
to him."

Bilal paused, working up the courage to ask the question that
had been prodding him since they met. "How is my mother?"

There was a hitch before the sheikh answered: slight, but not so slight that Bilal didn't notice it.

"What is it?" he demanded. "What has happened to her?"

"Nothing," 'Abd al-Aziz insisted, perhaps too vehemently. "She is well."

Bilal looked at him closely. 'Abd al-Aziz met his eyes only for a moment before looking away. "There is something else. Tell me, please."

"I assure you she is well, Bilal," 'Abd al-Aziz said. "Only wretched with worry for you. If you do not believe me, you can see for yourself soon enough, for I have sent messengers to tell her that I have found you here. She will no doubt be joining us as soon as she can find a horse to carry her."

Bilal was still convinced that there was something 'Abd al-Aziz was keeping from him, but for the moment he forced his mind back to the present and asked, "How did you know where to look for me?"

Apparently relieved to have left the topic of Zaynab, 'Abd al-Aziz chuckled and said, "There aren't many blue-eyed *ghuzat* in Oultrejourdain, still fewer fighting for Salah ad-Din...you are a bit of a legend in the south by now." Bilal smiled wanly. "We followed the rumors and we met Salim al-Ayyubi this morning, by Allah's grace. The rest, you know."

There followed another long pause that would have been silence, if it had not been so full of the sounds of calling men and clattering weapons, restless horses and flapping tents. Bilal was keenly aware of all that 'Abd al-Aziz had refrained from asking him, but he could not subdue his own curiosity.

Choosing his words carefully, he said, "Please, *Sayyid*, do not misunderstand me, for you have all of my gratitude, and at any rate I would not choose any life now over the one I have found here...but I cannot help wondering, if you really thought of me as a son, why then – "

"Did I not marry my daughter to you?" 'Abd al-Aziz laughed ruefully and shook his head. "I wanted nothing so much as that."

Bilal stopped, stunned.

"I could see that you loved each other," the sheikh continued, "with the kind of love that may not flash and spark, but which will endure the tests of marriage. I thought that you would temper her and she would inspire you, and that together you would be a pillar of strength to the tribe."

"What happened?"

'Abd al-Aziz sighed. "How much does the answer matter to you?"

"I am tired of secrets," Bilal answered. "They bring nothing but grief."

"I agree with you. For that reason I will tell you, though I break an old promise to do so, and I fear I will sow great bitterness in you. So: I did not marry you to my daughter for the simple reason that your mother begged me not to."

A part of Bilal felt that he ought to be surprised by this, but he wasn't. "Because she feared de Ridefort's threat about turning her over to her husband," he said. "She did not want anything to draw attention to us."

'Abd al-Aziz nodded.

"How long have you known about him?"

Once again, the sheikh sighed. "Almost as long as I've known you. Not long before Brekhna left the tribe, she told me your mother's story and made me promise to protect her, and also to keep her secret as if it were my own. I do not regret the first part, but many times I have regretted the latter. If you had known who you were, who your father was and what your mother feared, so many things might have been different..."

Bilal reflected on this as they walked. Things would indeed have been different, but he could not see that they would have been better. At last the *mamluk* pointed out the campsite that had been chosen for the Hassani. By the door to the pavilion that had been raised for him, 'Abd al-Aziz turned to Bilal.

"Thank you for listening to me, Bilal. Now I must rest, and you have your arm tended. There will be time enough for talk in the days to come. But there is one more thing I would have you know: I have taken a longer view of my daughter's disappearance over these last months. If she should ever return to me, I will hold no grudge over her."

"That is good of you, *Sayyid*," said Bilal, not quite certain why the sheikh was telling him this.

"Bilal, do you…that is to say, if she were to return, and were agreeable to it, would you still wish to marry her?"

Looking into 'Abd al-Aziz's earnest, solicitous face, Bilal could only wonder how he had ever thought that he was in love with Khalidah, or that marrying her would make him happy. He did not have 'Abd al-Aziz's faith in Khalidah's return, and he did not want to hurt the old man; but still, after the sheikh's honesty, Bilal could not bring himself to lie.

"Much has changed for me over the last months, *Sayyid*," he said. "I still hold Khalidah in the highest respect; but you'll understand that I see myself to have a different destiny, now."

To his surprise, 'Abd al-Aziz looked relieved, rather than offended. He smiled at Bilal and bowed, saying, "*Ma'as salaama*, Bilal. May Allah bless you in that destiny, whatever it may be." Bilal watched as 'Abd al-Aziz turned and went into his tent, ruminating on the fickleness of time, and the human heart.

*

Numair was in hell. He knew it because no mortal realm could encompass such pain. It began as a white-hot point in his upper back, radiating down his spine and into his limbs in skewers of searing agony. But when at last he opened his eyes, he found himself looking not at a fiery world of dancing devils, but at the same empty, sandy wadi he had called home for the last week. He did not know whether to be relieved or disappointed. At any rate, he had little strength left for either.

It took him the rest of that day to drag himself to the stream. He ascertained in the process that his right leg was broken and his left arm injured, though still workable. The vision in his left eye was hazed red, and he knew that he had at least one concussion to the head, but all of these ills paled in comparison to the rod in his back, which dragged and screamed against the surrounding muscles every time he moved. He lost count of the number of times he passed out. By the time he made it to the water he couldn't raise his hands to drink, so he tipped himself into the stream and lay there, letting the water run into his mouth.

He fell asleep. By some miracle, he did not drown, but he woke shivering violently. The sky was dark. He dragged himself back out of the water and looked for the tent he was certain had been there in the morning, a few paces from the stream. Now there was nothing but a pile of ashes. Digging into them, he found a few glowing embers, to which he fed the remains of the tent-poles and some dry grasses until a flame flickered to life.

He lay by the tiny fire until his shudders had died to periodic tremors. Then he reached behind him with his uninjured arm, gripped the arrow-shaft and pulled. It seemed to him that he was tearing the soul from his body, but at last it came away. He was so dizzy with pain, it took him several moments to realize what he held in his hand. It was indeed an arrow-shaft, with flights of black ostrich-feather, but where the point should have been there was only chewed wood. The wedge of iron was still lodged in his flesh.

Numair was no physician, but looking at that arrow, he knew without a doubt the course his own death would take. It was enough to make him wish that Bilal had let the prince make a souvenir of his head after all.

15

Khalidah awakened with the first watery streaks of light in the east. The mountains were still ghost-shapes drawn by the absence of stars, the birds still slept. There was no sound but the faint whisper of wind through the grasses. She laid on her back watching the light push its gentle, intractable fingers into the dark, wrapped in Sulayman's arms and their discarded robes and the perfect peace of fulfilled longing, wondering why she had ever wanted anything more.

"Because longing does not end with fulfillment," Sulayman whispered, his lips touching her neck, when she said as much to him. "No human being ever stops wanting for long."

She could feel his hardness against her leg. "So I see," she said, grinning, and turned to him, tracing the line of his back with the tips of her fingers. The light had grown enough that she could see him shut his eyes, see him shiver as well as feel it. Her own body leapt to his desire; but he caught her hands as they reached for him and kissed them.

"No, *habibti*," he said gently. "There is not time."

Khalidah sighed. "Since I met you, it seems, we have been riding a horse which is racing time. Will it ever end? Will we ever be able to lie like this for days and think of no one or nothing else?"

The rising light caught his smile and seared it into Khalidah's heart. It was not the old thief's smile, but one of unutterable tenderness; she knew that whatever happened, he would never smile that way at anyone else, and it would be with her until the day she died.

"*Insha'Allah*," he said. "And I have never wished more for Allah's will to match my own."

*

The girls were only just beginning to stir when she returned to the dormitory. She hoped that they would think she was returning from a trip to the out-house, but none of them seemed to notice her at all, so engrossed were they in their own preparations. When she reached her untouched bed, however, she found Abi Gul sitting on it, regarding her with sharp eyes and a knowing smile.

"I wonder where you have spent the night, Khalidah, for it certainly was not here." The accusation in her tone was teasing, but the question was serious enough.

"Did you watch for me all night?" Khalidah asked, dropping her grass-stained clothing and pulling on a clean set.

"As a matter of fact, I did," Abi Gul answered ruefully. "I could not sleep a wink!" Then, abruptly, "You were with Sulayman."

"I was," Khalidah answered, tying her sash.

"Please, you must tell me what it was like – after all, I may never have the chance to find out for myself."

Checking her saddle-bags, Khalidah answered, "Find out what?"

Abi Gul sighed. "If you would keep it a secret, Khalidah, you'd best comb the grass out of your hair."

Khalidah reached up to feel her hair. It was tangled and, indeed, full of dry grass. In horror, she reached for a comb and began tugging it through the knots. Abi Gul watched her for a while in half-amused silence, then said, "Well?"

"I would tell you if I could, Abi Gul," Khalidah said, meeting her friend's eyes at last, "but I do not have the words."

Abi Gul sighed. "It doesn't matter. It shines from your face like the evening star from the night sky." She sighed again. "How I long for someone to love me like that!"

"Oh, Abi Gul, somebody will! How could they not?"

Abi Gul's face was troubled, but she smiled around it. "It's time to go, Bibi Khalidah. Are you ready?"

By the most merciful Allah, Khalidah thought, I hope so.

*

Though the village came out to see them off, there was none of the cheering and weeping that had accompanied the departure of Rakan's mission. The eerie silence that Khalidah had sensed as she walked by the river the previous evening seemed, if anything, to have intensified. The riders strapped on their saddle-bags and checked the loads on the pack horses and then they were riding toward the hills beyond which Rakan's group had disappeared.

Khalidah rode near the front, behind the guides, with Abi Gul on her left and Sulayman on her right, riding a tall palomino stallion called Sre Zer. 'Aasifa had come into season during their first week in Qaf, and despite the careful separation of fertile mares from the stallions, she and Sre Zer had been found grazing together one morning outside of the pens. Though it was too early to tell whether she was in foal, the stallion's owner had assured Sulayman that Sre Zer's seed never failed to sprout. He insisted that Sulayman leave 'Aasifa with him and take the stallion in her place.

As they passed the orchards and the houses and finally the practice grounds, Khalidah realized that she had no idea how they would get out of the valley, for she had no memory of being taken in. Abi Gul laughed when she asked her about it.

"Is this the first time you've thought of it?"

"You've kept me too busy to think of anything else," Khalidah answered.

"Poppy juice," Abi Gul said.

"What?"

"Do you not know the effects of poppy juice?"

Khalidah and Sulayman looked at each other and burst out laughing. Abi Gul frowned, unaware of anything humorous in what she had said.

"I'm sorry," said Khalidah, "it's only that none of this would have happened at all if it had not been for the merits of poppy juice. Sulayman used it to drug my tribe the night before my wedding. That was how we managed to escape."

Abi Gul looked at Sulayman with raised eyebrows. "Well, we can claim nothing so dramatic. But when the scouts tell us that someone is approaching Qaf, we make them drink poppy juice before bringing them to the valley. We do not wish the way to be known."

"I do not remember anyone asking me to drink poppy juice on that night," Khalidah said, frowning.

Abi Gul shook her head. "There was no need. They dripped it into your mouths while you slept, and you awakened in Qaf."

Khalidah wondered how much of her strange dream of the battle and the dying Templar could be attributed to the narcotic; but then, she had seen the same boy, the Sultan's son, again at the *betaan's aylaq*. There was too much to decipher, and all of it of little importance compared with their present journey.

They rode on in silence for a long time, winding amongst the foothills on paths Khalidah would never have found on her own, and for the first time she began to believe that they might actually make it back to Syria as quickly as the Jinn had promised. After several hours the foothills turned into mountains, topped by the snow-peaks that had looked so distant from Qaf. They rode along a rocky valley that narrowed rapidly, until Khalidah could have reached out and touched both of its sides at once. Great walls of rock reared up on either side, seeming to lean toward each other until at last they did come together, and the little army was riding through the darkness of a cave. There was a dim light coming from somewhere up ahead, and the sound of rushing water. This grew louder and the light stronger as they rode along, until at last Khalidah saw the opening to the rocky passage, curtained by a thundering waterfall.

The horses ahead of her were turning sharply right at the cave mouth. She gave Zahirah her head, letting her follow Tufan. The grey stallion disappeared around the corner and then Zahirah was around as well, picking her way down a narrow, stony incline. At first it was slippery with water and weed, but soon they left the waterfall behind them and reached another valley, this one much wider than the last. It was bordered by dun-colored hills with great rocky mountains behind them, the floor dirt and smooth as a racetrack. With a shock, Khalidah realized that she recognized the place.

"We were here!" she said to Sulayman. "There is a stream up ahead. We camped by it, but that must have been four…five days before we reached Qaf?"

"A week," he answered.

"How is that possible?"

He shook his head. "They are the Jinn. This is what they do." He considered this, then added, "Besides, by the time we camped here, we might have been riding in circles for days."

It was possible, Khalidah conceded to herself; but still, she doubted it.

They picked up the pace through the valley, cantering when the footing was good. Zahirah kept up easily with her larger counterparts; in fact, she seemed eager to best them, for which Khalidah secretly swelled with pride. They rode through that day until the last light had gone, then they made camp on a patch of sparse grass by a little green pond.

The Jinn were as efficient in making camp as they were in picking their way through these treacherous mountains. Within minutes, it seemed, the horses were stripped, rubbed down and given their rations of grain; minutes after that the cookfires were lit and pots of water hung over them to boil. Khalidah shared a fire with Sulayman, Abi Gul and Hila. Ambrenn and her betrothed had stayed behind, at the request of their parents, who were non-believers. They were joined by a few older warriors, cousins of Abi Gul and Hila who regaled them with tales of other missions while they drank their tea and ate their dried mulberries and boiled salted mutton; but nobody had the energy to stay up late, particularly knowing that they would rise again at first light for another day of relentless travel.

The cousins retreated, and after stoking the fire, Abi Gul and Hila lay down by it, wrapped in their blankets, studiously ignoring Sulayman and Khalidah. Khalidah was half mortified, half relieved that she didn't have to make excuses as she and Sulayman picked up their blankets and moved away from the camp.

16

When they rose the following morning, Khalidah found the dust around the patch of grass on which they'd slept riddled with prints. Looking more closely in the dim dawn light, she found one that was whole: the perfect imprint of a canine paw, nearly as large as her own spread hand.

"Wolves," said Sulayman, leaning down beside her. "Several of them, by the look of it."

Khalidah shuddered. "Why did they not attack us?"

"I suppose they weren't hungry…or they don't like Arab meat."

Khalidah gave him a black look.

"Alipsha would say that it's an omen," said Abi Gul, coming up behind them. "Death has noticed you, but let you pass. Still, I'd stay by the fires tonight, if I were you." She regarded them both seriously, and then grinned. "Don't worry – nobody will pay any attention to you. Well, they won't let you know that they are, anyway."

Khalidah flushed to the roots of her hair, and even Sulayman looked slightly abashed.

*

A couple of days later they reached Zabol. While the army camped
in the foothills outside of the city, Khalidah and Sulayman
accompanied Arzou to his daughter's house. It seemed to have
stood still in time since the morning they had left it: the same
leaves ruffled above the garden wall, the same smell of verdure
came from within. But there was also something different. After
a moment Khalidah's musician's ear hit upon it: the sound of
falling water was absent. Sulayman rapped on the gate, and after
a long time Daoud opened it. This time his serious air of the man
of the house did not dissolve into glee. He simply stood in the
doorway, staring at them.

Thinking that it might be the presence of the strange man that
deterred him, Khalidah said, "Daoud, you need not be afraid.
This man is your grandfather, Arzou al-Jinni. He has come to see
your mother."

"He cannot see my mother," the boy answered wearily.
"Nobody can. I am sorry, I cannot let you in." He began to push
the gate closed, but Sulayman put out a hand and held it.

"What has happened, Daoud?"

The child looked at him for a moment and then burst into
tears. Sulayman bent down and took the weeping child in his
arms, at the same time giving Khalidah a look over his head.
She nodded and slipped with Arzou through the gate and into
the garden. Once inside, she saw that the illusion of timelessness
had been just that – an illusion. The garden was dying. As she
had suspected the fountain was dry, and with it the irrigation
channels that had fed the plants. The leaves of the apricot trees
were yellow and withered, the immature fruit fallen and rotting
on the ground. Even the palms were turning brown, and the
smaller, more delicate plants had long since shriveled.

"It was not like this, before," Khalidah said to Arzou. "Sandara
loved this garden…it was a green oasis when I saw it last.
Something has happened."

He nodded, looking around with sad circumspection as they
approached the front of the house. There they found the twins,
Madiha and Maliya, sitting on the door-step, picking through a

bowl of beans. They appeared to be discarding more than they kept. When they looked up and saw Khalidah, they ran to her and burst into tears.

"Where is your mother?" Khalidah asked them gently.

One of them pointed to the shadows of the doorway, as the other one said, "No! She said to let no one see her!"

"Why not?" asked Khalidah.

"Because of the sickness. She said that anyone who sees her might catch it too. We are not allowed to go to her. No one is."

Khalidah and Arzou exchanged a look. "And what kind of sickness is it?" she asked the child.

"A spotted one."

Arzou stood up, ready to push his way into the house, but Khalidah stopped him. "If it is as you fear," she said, "you'd best let me go."

"Why? You are young, I am an old man – "

"And I am immune to the red pox," Khalidah finished. "It is too long a story just now – you must trust me. Please, Arzou, stay here and meet your grandchildren, and do not under any circumstances allow Sulayman to come after me."

She left him puzzling over her words as she stepped into the house. She wandered through shadowy corridors hung with fine weavings and glass lanterns and other signs of the family's wealth, calling Sandara's name and hearing no answer. She had begun to imagine the worst – stumbling onto a room with a bloated, pockmarked corpse – when at last she heard a weak reply to her call:

"I am here – but come no closer."

Khalidah followed the sound of the woman's voice up a set of stairs and into a small room at the back of the house, lit by a single, narrow window. There at last she found Sandara's black-shrouded form stretched on a narrow bed in the corner of the room, a cup and a pitcher on the floor beside her. Her back was to the door.

"You should not have come here," she said. "Now you, too, are doomed."

"How so?" Khalidah asked.

Sandara sat up and put back her veil, turning the burned side of her face toward the wall. The other side, where the skin had been whole and smooth, was now covered in angry red pustules. Khalidah approached Sandara, coming right up to her face. The older woman drew back instinctively.

"I cannot catch it," Khalidah said. "I have been inoculated." She touched one of the pustules on Sandara's face, and the woman shuddered. "Did that hurt?"

"No…no. I was only surprised."

"Do any of them hurt?"

"Not much," Sandara answered, reluctantly allowing Khalidah's fingers to traverse her face. "Some of them itch."

Khalidah nodded and continued to examine Sandara as she explained, "My tribe met a traveling healer once, a man from Hindustan. There was an epidemic of the red pox in our area at the time, and Balachandra – that was the healer's name – told my father that he knew a method of making people immune to it. He carried with him a powder made of the dried scabs of a past victim of the disease. If a little bit of this powder were blown up the nose of a healthy person, he would catch the disease, but in a mild form, and when he recovered he would be immune, as are all who recover from it."

"Do not tell me your father allowed this charlatan to practice his witchcraft upon you!"

Khalidah smiled, lifting Sandara's sleeves to examine her arms. There were no lesions there – they seemed to be confined to her face and chest. "He did indeed," she answered, "but only after testing it first on several prisoners. As Balachandra promised, the men sickened, but mildly, and when they recovered they could not be re-infected, though they were housed for days with a man with running sores. Afterwards, my father had himself inoculated, and me, and Zaynab and Bilal…" She trailed off, realizing that these names would mean nothing to Sandara, nor still her present fears. "Tell me, how long have you had these lesions?"

"Since a few days after you and Sulayman left."

"And did they appear first on your face, or elsewhere?"

"They have been always where you see them now."

"You need not fear, then," said Khalidah. "With the red pox, the lesions come out first on the arms. If you had it, by now you would be covered and so ill that you would not be sitting speaking to me like this. The children would almost certainly be ill too."

"If it is not the pox, then what is it?"

"I am no healer, I cannot say. Has there been anything else? Any other symptoms of illness?"

Sandara lowered her veil, sighing. "I find that the sadness hangs on me more than it used to. There are days when I cannot make myself get out of bed. No matter how much I sleep, my weariness remains. And of course, since the lesions came, I have been so afraid for the children, I have not let them near me, but they can barely cope on their own..."

"Perhaps," Khalidah said, "what you suffer from is not a sickness of the body at all, but of the soul, and it is merely the signs of it that show on your body."

Sandara laughed bitterly. "And so my acrimony has come out in pustules, to eat away what's left of me? Even if it is true, how does the knowledge help me? There is no cure for bitterness."

"Perhaps there is," Khalidah said.

"What do you mean?"

"Come with me," she said, offering her hand to the woman. Reluctantly, Sandara took it and followed her into the corridor, then down the stairs. They found Sulayman and Arzou by the dry fountain playing with the children, who finally had smiles on their faces. Both Arzou and Sandara froze when they saw each other; and then, slowly, Sandara let go of Khalidah's hand, and Arzou stood. They moved toward each other, slowly at first, and then faster, until they fell into each other's arms, both of them weeping.

*

Sandara wanted them to stay that night, but Sulayman and Khalidah declined, saying that the army must move on.

"Very well then," said Sandara, looking at Arzou, "I had hoped to have more time with you, but if this is the way it is to be, then so be it. *Abatah*, I entrust my children to you and to my mother. Take them back to Qaf with you and raise them as Jinn…as they should always have been raised."

The twins were too young to catch the ominous undertone of her words, but Daoud heard it and instinctively clung to his mother as she turned to Khalidah. "Bibi Khalidah, I most humbly offer you my services on your mission. If you will allow it, I will join your army and go to fight for Mobarak Khan in the west."

"No, Sandara, you cannot!" her father cried. "Please, return to Qaf with me. You have suffered too much already, your children need you, and your mother longs for you so."

"My mother longs for the daughter she remembers," Sandara said gently, clasping his hands, "but I am not that girl and I never will be again. Better to give her three beautiful children to care for than one broken woman. I might not have the red pox, *Abatah*, but I am sick at heart – sick to my soul – and the only way to end the suffering is to complete what I began so long ago. I will fight my battle and return to Qaf as a Jinn, or else…well, the sickness will be ended, one way or another."

The children were distressed now, the little girls beginning to cry. Sandara bent down and took all three of them in her arms. "Do not weep, children; you are going to live in paradise. You will have other children to play with, and two grandparents to care for you, and with Allah's mercy we will be reunited there someday. Now go and pack whatever you wish to bring with you – but not too much for a horse to carry."

After a moment they went, still looking dubiously behind them, as if she would disappear. She watched them until they were gone, then she said, "There is little left here that I would keep; but there are some valuables that should go with the children. Can you wait two hours for me?"

Khalidah said that they could, and told her where to find the camp. Then she and Sulayman left Arzou and his daughter to their private farewells.

*

After that they traveled fast – faster than Khalidah had ever imagined possible. They cut their way across the lands Khalidah and Sulayman had crossed so tortuously, sometimes along the same routes, but more often by different ones, shortcuts and secret paths that even Sulayman had never dreamed were there. The Jinn never consulted maps. The routes were chosen by the oldest members of the army, who had apparently memorized them.

When they came to Jazirah they turned north, so that they bypassed the marshes entirely. They followed the course of the great river Al-Furat for several days before turning west again into the rocky Syrian desert. Now they began to send out scouts, who brought back enticing snips of news. Count Tripoli had abandoned the Sultan and turned back to the Franj after some kind of catastrophic battle; King Guy was mustering his army near the coast; the Sultan was moving his own army south, toward the border with the Franj kingdom. It seemed he might be planning to cross the Jordan. The Jinn could not grasp the significance of this, but to Khalidah it was awe-inspiring: Salah ad-Din could hardly choose a more brazen declaration of war.

"The battle you spoke of," said Khalidah to the scout, "the one which made Tripoli turn back to Guy – do you know any more about it?"

The boy shook his head. "Only that it took place about six weeks ago, and that an order of Franj knights was nearly destroyed in it."

"Which order?" Khalidah asked.

"'The Order', that was all the man told me – as if I should know by that what he meant."

Khalidah thought of her nightmare, of the beautiful prince who had cloven the head of the Templar and wished that she were a boy, so that she might go out herself and search for a straight story. But they were firmly back in the land of Islam now, and whether or not it was dangerous for the women to go out on their own, it was pointless: nobody would have told them anything. So Khalidah had to content herself with the news the men brought back.

The army traveled at night now, both for secrecy and to avoid the terrible heat of the desert daytime. The Jinn never complained, but Khalidah could tell that it was hard on them: few would have experienced such heat before. Finally, a week past midsummer, a scout came galloping back to camp one early morning with the news that he had seen the Sultan's army camped on the Golan Heights.

"And it was vast," he gasped, both from exertion and shock, "more vast than any army you can imagine. Their campfires flickered on the Heights like candles on an altar, and I could not see their beginning nor their end."

Many of the Jinn wanted to break the camp they had just made and go to the Sultan then and there; eventually, Khalidah managed to dissuade them.

"It would be suicide," she said. "We would be shot down unapologetically if we were to approach them now, for they are about to make their move, and they will not let anything endanger it. No – we will camp here today, and tonight..."

She trailed off, because in fact, she had no idea what she would do tonight. Khalidah slept fitfully that day, tossing and turning by Sulayman in the heat. She had forgotten its fierceness, how it sucked the sweat from her skin almost before it was finished forming, leaving it dry and gritted with salt. At last she crawled out from beneath their white tent and walked to the edge of the camp, past the hobbled horses faded with dust and heat, until she stood at the edge of the empty desert, looking for her next step on the scorched and windblown horizon. For a moment it felt as though she had never left – as though the past months had been a dream, and if she were to turn she would see not the white tents of the Jinn but the black ones of her father's tribe, ringed around the oasis.

A slender hand slipped into hers. "What do you see?" asked Abi Gul.

Khalidah squeezed her hand. "Nothing," she answered. "We have come so far, and I still don't know how to bring us to our destination."

Abi Gul considered this for a time, her green-gold eyes slitted against the light and the scouring wind. Then she said, "Perhaps you should listen, instead of look."

"What?"

Abi Gul looked at her, her fairy's face serious for once. "As your mother called you to Qaf, there must be somebody who calls you back. Your father, perhaps? Your nurse?"

"Bilal," Khalidah said softly.

Abi Gul nodded, as if this was obvious; as if it could mean anything to her. "And do you know where to find him?"

Khalidah thought of the beautiful Ayyub prince and said, "I think I do."

Abi Gul smiled. "And so, you see, you *do* know, after all."

17

At the end of June, Salah ad-Din knew that his time had come. Battle season was upon them and his army would never be larger or readier to fight. On the twenty-fourth, he called a review at Tal Tasil. While he and his entourage stood on the hill, the army paraded before them. Salah ad-Din counted twelve-thousand professional cavalry plus another thirty-three thousand mixed soldiers, everything from untrained *muttawiyah* to the deadly fire-troops with their balls of naphtha, elite Turkish horse-archers to the Bedu *ghuzat*.

"Forty-five-thousand souls, gathered to fight for Allah," he said to his umara in his pavilion afterward. "The opportunity now before us may well never arise again. In my view, the Muslim army must confront all the infidels in an organized battle. We must throw ourselves resolutely into the jihad before our troops grow weary of waiting and disperse."

Nobody disagreed, so the Sultan continued, "By our best estimate, we outnumber the enemy three to two – beatable odds for a well-trained, cohesive army, but Cresson culled the best Franj knights, the barons are still barely on speaking terms and Guy is as chronically indecisive as ever. They cannot beat us in a field battle, and so that is how we must fight them. It is time to bait the trap, and pray that they take it."

"What trap?" asked Al-Afdhal.

"What bait?" added Al-Zahir.

"Our own arid hills," Salah ad-Din answered, "and their stubborn chivalry."

And however they pressed him, he would say no more that night.

*

If Salah ad-Din remained circumspect on the nature of his ultimate plan, he made his primary aim clear enough. He needed to broadcast his intent to fight in a way that the Franj could not possibly ignore and so, on the twenty-sixth of June, as the Latin nobles bickered at Acre, Salah ad-Din turned his army west. Before the march began he regarded the vast, churning force spreading behind him, and raising his sword he called, "Victory over God's enemy!" His cry resounded through the ranks as his scribes dutifully scribbled, preserving words which would echo undiminished down the next eight hundred years.

They spent the first day climbing and camped that night on the Golan Heights. The next day, they put the plain of Hauran at their backs and picked their way along the western edge of the Heights, where the hills become rocky cliffs that drop abruptly down to the Sea of Galilee. Mid-way through that day they crossed the border into Latin territory south-west of the town of Fiq, but few remarked on it. By that point all who had not been told had guessed that the Sultan's aim was not the fickle borderline between their land and the Franj kingdom, but that far more potent barrier, the Jordan River. Though one might dispute ownership of the dust the mighty Muslim army stirred after Fiq, the river where John had baptized Jesus was a point of no return: the moment the Sultan crossed it, the two kingdoms would be at war.

Late in the afternoon the army reached the river Yarmuk. They followed it for an hour in their descent from the Heights before Salah ad-Din turned them north once again, toward the confluence of the Jordan and the Sea of Galilee. That night he pitched his tent at Al-Qahwani, a morose little sore of a village on the lip of the great river, whose mud-brick buildings looked more than ready to re-join the marshy ground on which they were built. It was damp and fly-infested and equidistant from the recently-wronged Tiberias and the great Hospitaller fortress of Belvoir, but perched as it was within spitting distance of the Jordan, it could not have marked the Sultan's intentions more clearly.

Just as Salah ad-Din had intended, Guy's scouts on the other side of the river took one look at the massing Muslim army and turned their horses north toward Acre, pushing them to the limits of their endurance to bring this news to the king. And again as the Sultan had hoped, the insecure Guy immediately moved his knights and nobles to Saffuriyya, halving the distance between the two armies. At that point, Salah ad-Din allowed himself a cautious sigh of relief, to have the enemy at last in his sights. Secure in his position for the moment, he called his own war council together to discuss his next step, which seemed to Salim to be a step backward.

"More raids?" he said to Bilal as they left his father's tent. "I thought that we were finished with all of that."

Bilal shook his head. "It's the same as Amman – the same I suppose as all of our battles with the Franj since they first took Al-Quds. We may outnumber them, but it does us no good if they remain behind their fortress walls. And Saffuriyya makes a good fortress: plenty of water, open supply routes…they would be fools to leave it for a pitched battle."

"Fools indeed," Salim answered dryly, hacking at a withered yucca with his sword. "But I do not think that they are such fools as to come to the call of a few raids."

"You might be surprised," Bilal said quietly. "There are plenty among them who are hungry for our blood."

They had come to the edge of the water. The light of the campfires shattered and sank into its flow. A few bright points burned like stars somewhere off in the Franj distance. Stabbing his sword into the spongy ground and crouching down beside it, Salim asked, "Why did you tell my father about de Ridefort?"

Bilal sighed. "I had to, Salim. He and Numair could have been planning anything." He paused. "Are you angry?"

"Not that you told him. That you didn't tell me before you did it – yes, a little." He glanced at Bilal, his eyes bright and sharp. "I know that I have not been myself of late, but I am not so weak that I would have shrunk from duty."

Bilal knelt beside him. "That isn't why I didn't tell you."

"Why, then?"

Bilal traced his name in the mud and then, beside it, Salim's. "Because I was afraid."

Salim gave him another keen look. "Don't say that you were afraid for me."

He looked up from his writing. "Well, why not? I love you, Salim. I could not bear a life without you. And since that makes you a target for those who wish to harm me – "

"All right," Salim said wearily. "Well, what did my father have to say?"

"He told me to be careful."

"Of what?"

Bilal shook his head. "For."

"For me?"

"Of course."

"And for yourself."

"He did not say that."

Salim smiled. "It would be like you not to hear it."

"It doesn't signify, anyway," Bilal said, smoothing their names from the mud and drawing an abstract pattern in their place. "A careful soldier is worse than useless."

"We will be like the Thebans, then," Salim said after a moment's thought.

"The what?"

"Thebes was an ancient Greek city-state, and a great military power. They remained autonomous long after their neighbors had fallen to Macedon. The secret of their success was a small band of warriors at the heart of the army: three hundred men, one hundred and fifty pairs of lovers. They were talented soldiers, but it was their love that made them great. There is a quote from Plutarch, I can't remember it exactly...it was something along the lines of men bound by familial ties being unwilling to endanger themselves for each other, but those bound by romantic love being invincible. They'll fight fearlessly, he said, because they cannot bear to be seen as cowards by their lovers. The Sacred Band...that was what they were called. The Sacred Band of Thebes."

"And what happened to them?" Bilal asked, though he suspected that he did not really want to hear it.

Salim shrugged, but the gesture fell just short of nonchalance. "They were beaten at last by Philip II of Macedon and his son Alexander, at the Battle of Chaeronea. It's said that every last one of them fought to the death. I suppose it is no wonder then that Thebes lost its independence that day."

"Hardly an inspiring story," Bilal said with apprehension, because inspiration was exactly what he saw on Salim's face.

"You don't think so?" Salim asked. "That night in Oultrejourdain, when de Ridefort came to challenge you, what made you stand up to him?"

Bilal couldn't speak, not even to ask how Salim knew about that confrontation; but his averted eyes were answer enough.

"Well, if you can fight for me, Bilal al-Hassani, then I can fight for you, too," Salim said. He paused, then added in one breath, "I'm sorry for the way I've been since Cresson."

"I know," Bilal said quietly.

"It was as if I froze on that day; but when I saw you fighting Numair, something in me caught fire, and I came back to myself. It was like...it was – "

"I know," he repeated. "You don't have to tell me."

"There are a heartful of things that I have to tell you," Salim contradicted, "but they can wait."

"What are you doing?" Bilal asked, as Salim began to undress. The prince answered by dropping his clothing by his planted

sword and stepping into the dark water. He reached one hand
back for Bilal.

"I cannot swim," Bilal said.

"I will not let go of you," he answered.

They didn't bother with their tent that night, or either of the
following two that the army camped at Al-Qahwani. When dusk
fell, they swam until they were exhausted and then lay down in
the sedge grass of the riverbank, wrapped in each other's limbs
and the blanket they had shared since the first night in Busra.
Swimming came to Bilal easily, more like memory than learning.
It was an affinity that surprised him, given his childhood on the
sands.

"It shouldn't," Salim said when Bilal told him this. "You are
like a river."

"How?"

"Your face betrays little and overlays much. You love silently...
and yet it's the silence of the hidden water, the layers beneath the
surface that carve valleys out of mountains."

Salim's shoulder curved against the night sky like one of the
gentle hills. "Do you know how I adore you?"

"Heart of my heart," Salim whispered, and pulled him close.

*

On the first morning in Al-Qahwani, Salim had re-assembled
his *saqa*. Each day after that they were ready at dawn, awaiting
the Sultan's orders. The orders never varied. On the maps he had
shown his *umara* on the first night by the Jordan, Salah ad-Din
had marked out an area the shape of a spearhead, its points at
Nazareth, Tiberias and Mount Tabor.

"Raze it," he had said.

Salim quickly realized that he had been mistaken in calling
the raids a step back. These were nothing like their forays in
Oultrejourdain which, though effective, had at times bordered
on chaotic. Now the raiding parties struck with quick, brutal

precision, torching fields and villages and executing anyone who
dared resist them. They took neither prisoners nor plunder. They
did their work and then retreated back across the river before the
Franj army had time to locate them, let alone send troops against
them.

These lightning raids were what the Muslim army was best at,
and Salah ad-Din intended to use them to sow as much confusion
as possible before he struck. But they also had another purpose.
The Sultan needed to be absolutely certain that the main body
of the Franj army was in Saffuriyya before he proceeded with his
plans, and the raiders were able to confirm this for him.

So, on the evening of the twenty-ninth of June by the Christian
calendar, Salah ad-Din called his *umara* together once more and
said: "Strike your tents and ready your men. Tomorrow we cross
the river."

*

They crossed at the Bridge of Sennabra, and it took them the better part of a day. By the time the last stragglers had put the water
behind them, Salah ad-Din had pitched his tent at Kafr Sabt, five
miles west of Tiberias and blocking the main road from there to
Saffuriyya. From this position, he would be able to intercept any
Franj advance.

Meanwhile, he ordered a detachment to blockade Tiberias
("The bait," he said curtly to anyone who asked why), and sent
scouts to Saffuriyya to gauge the Franj reaction to his day's work.
Salim begged to be one of them and at last, against his better
judgment, the Sultan agreed.

"I suppose you will bring Bilal al-Hassani with you," he said.

"I would not go without him."

The Sultan gave his son a hard look and then sighed. "Salim…
do not mistake what I am about to say, for I too have grown
to love that boy, and while as Allah's servant I cannot entirely
condone the nature of your…ah…"

Salim could not help smiling; it was the first time he had ever seen his father at a loss for words. Still, he did not like to see the Sultan embarrassed when he intended kindness, so he said, "I understand, *Abatah*. You need say no more."

Again, Salah ad-Din sighed. "I am afraid that I must, though I would rather not. I know that you love him, Salim, and I would not part you for the world – but the world itself is not so forgiving. You are a king's son and he, though he may not yet realize it, is a desert chief's heir. You will both be leaders of men one day, and leaders must sacrifice whatever is required for the welfare of their people. First and foremost, your people will require that you produce heirs." He paused, looking closely at his son. "Do you understand me?"

Salim was looking at him, his expression that of an antelope that glances up from its watering-hole into the inevitable eye of the hunter. No fear, just regret and a terrible kind of acceptance. Salah ad-Din knew then that he had told his son nothing that Salim had not already known for a long time, and though he was no champion of the kind of love the boy seemed to favor, he felt for him then as keenly as if he had forbidden him some worthy maiden.

The Sultan tried to smile then, and failed miserably. But to his surprise, the boy reached forward and embraced him. With a pang, he realized that he had not touched Salim with affection since he had been weaned. And before he had quite realized the sweetness of it, Salim had pushed him away again, though he still held his shoulders.

"Thank you, *Abatah*," he said.

"For speaking the words you least want to hear?" Salah ad-Din asked with a bitterness he had not intended.

"For your honesty. And for not forbidding me the time I have left with him."

The Sultan passed a hand over his face, suddenly exhausted. "You're welcome, then, and let us speak no more about it until the time comes for...but I assume too much in speaking of the future, when we do not yet know whether it will stretch beyond tomorrow. Go now and bring me news of the Franj. And Salim, I don't suppose I need to remind you that de Ridefort will be looking for his son?"

Salim shook his head. "I will watch his back."

"Indeed," said the Sultan dryly. "And make sure that he watches yours."

And so, as the sun dipped beneath the green hills of Galilee, Salim and Bilal rode out with a handful of other scouts toward the Franj camp at Saffuriyya. The group split up near Tur'an and rode off in a wide semi-circle surrounding the south side of the encampment. Bilal and Salim hobbled their horses in a thick copse of trees some distance from the camp and walked the rest of the way. By the time they spotted the first of the tents, night had fallen. They were small, tattered tents, pitched in a rough circle around a fire. A group of soldiers sat in front of them, passing a jar of wine and kicking the dust. They were rough-looking men, as dark as Arabs with long, tangled hair and beards and filthy clothing. Clearly, it was not their first wine-jar of the evening, for they spoke and laughed with noisy abandon.

"Foot-soldiers," Salim said with marked distaste.

"From where?" Bilal said, frowning. "That is not the Franj tongue they are speaking."

Salim looked at him in surprise. "I did not know that you spoke the Franj tongue."

Bilal shrugged. "Only a little. But what does it matter? I've already said that this is not Franj, though it's odd, some of the words are familiar…"

"That is because it is the *Langue d'Oc* – the tongue of the south of the Franj country," Salim said, looking speculatively at the soldiers. "And since I do not speak it either, they are no good to us. Come, let us move on."

They made their way slowly around the perimeter of the camp, retreating when they caught sight of sentries, then creeping cautiously back in their wake. The northern end, where the ground was flat, was the most populated; to the south it tailed away until at last it petered out in a thread of tiny fires on the

slopes of the Hill of Nazareth. Bilal was relieved to see no sign of
the Templars, though at one point they spotted the black-and-
white banners of the Hospital, not far from a large pavilion of
deep red silk, which Salim told him belonged to the king.

Beyond the central position of the king's tent, there seemed no
order to the camp's sprawling constellation. Even at the perimeter,
they passed everything from the ragged shelters of the untrained
infantry to the silk pavilions of wealthy secular knights. They lost
count of the languages spoken: northern French and the Langue
d'Oc and a handful of strange, stuttering tongues Salim said
belonged to the people of far-off northern countries covered in ice
and snow; dialects of Italian with cadences frustratingly similar
to those of Arabic, but words as foreign as the northerners'; and
a smattering of Arabic itself, spoken by the *turcopoles* – Muslim
mercenaries – and the universally despised *pullani*, the offspring
of Franj-Arab unions. It was at a *pullani* camp that they finally
stumbled on a conversation worth listening to.

"...should go over to the other side while we still can," a dark,
raw-boned man was saying to his fellows. "I heard it from a
squire who was with them at Acre – the barons are at each other's
throats. Mark me, they won't be happy until they've torn this
country apart and fed it to the Muslim pigs for supper."

"The same Muslim pigs you want to defect to?" asked a small,
wiry man to his right, taking a swig from a flask of something
and passing it to the bigger man.

"Better a pig than a slave," he answered morosely. "They say
the Sultan has a hundred thousand men at Caffarset."

"There aren't a hundred thousand men in all his lands
together!" scoffed another.

"You're an idiot," said the first man. "The Sultan rules a
hundred times that many." He shook his head. "De Ridefort's
working on the king already – it will be just like Cresson. How
many men are we? Twenty thousand perhaps, and only twelve
hundred of us knights. The Sultan has at least as many again.
God wills it, my arse – that mad Templar and his friend Kerak,
they'll call the charge, then stand and applaud while the pigs

swallow us whole. Just like Cresson, I tell you."

"Are you sure of those numbers?" the wiry man asked, suddenly humble.

"Sure as I can be," his friend answered. "I told you, I spoke to a squire from Acre."

Salim and Bilal crept back into the darkness. If the morose half-breed was to be believed, they now had an exact count of King Guy's army: precious information indeed. They walked back to their horses, each lost in his thoughts, and rode back toward camp in silence. Once there Salim went off to tell his father what they had learned, and Bilal walked slowly back to their tent. He was so preoccupied with his own thoughts that he did not notice that it was brightly lit until his hand was on the flap, and he had lifted it before he thought to wonder why. Therefore, it took him a good few moments to register the apparition sitting on the rug at the centre, dark head bent over a book of poetry from which Bilal had been practicing his reading that afternoon.

The apparition looked up, and Bilal had a sensation similar to what he had felt listening to the speech of the southern Franj: that what he was witnessing ought to make sense to him, and yet somehow did not. For he knew this heart-shaped face intimately, the fine sweep of the eyebrows, the golden eyes beneath; yet time had translated it into something irrevocably foreign. The change went beyond the heavy kohl lining her eyes, the dark patterns on her cheeks and forehead, the warrior's muscle and grace beneath her white robes and the sword tucked into her sash. But when she stood, offering a hesitant smile, she was, once again, his childhood friend.

"Khalidah?" he said, stepping inside at last and dropping the tent-flap.

"Bilal," she answered, her voice belying the emotion that her new face hid. Hesitantly, she reached out her arms to him, and hesitantly he embraced her. But at the contact all the missing months evaporated, all the bitterness and guilt, until they were left at last holding only each other.

18

Bilal wanted to take Khalidah to her father immediately, and interpreted her reluctance as fear. "He will not be angry," he insisted. "He blames himself, Khalidah, not you."

"He should not," she answered grimly. "I deserve his anger. But that is not why I do not want to see him now. I have a duty to fulfill before I do anything else: a duty to my mother's people, the Jinn."

Bilal blinked at her, and then smiled. "The way you said it, I almost believed you! Now tell me, where have you really been...after the emerald mountains at the end of the world, of course!"

Sighing, Khalidah proceeded to fill him in on all that had happened to her since they had last seen one another, and the mission of the army she had brought with her. As she spoke, Bilal's look of disbelief turned to amazement, then to intentness. Though he stopped her now and then to ask for clarification of one point or another, he took it all in with what she considered remarkable composure.

"So the legends are real," he said softly, when she had finished.

"Real, and not real," she answered. "Like most legends, I suppose. But the question is, what will Salah ad-Din make of it? Will he accept us?"

"I don't see why not," Bilal answered. "He has accepted plenty without half so good a reason to be here. Besides, did you not say that he knew your mother?"

"That was a long time ago, and I don't know the circumstances of their parting. Besides, if he is as pious as people say, I am afraid he won't take kindly to the idea of a bunch of *kuffar* worshipping him as a pagan god…especially if they call themselves after the tricksters of Islam."

Bilal gave her a smile she did not recognize: a man's smile, its humor cut liberally with irony and regret. "Salah ad-Din deals in realities, not rumors," he said, "and though he is indeed pious – perhaps the most pious man that I have known – he is not parochial. You would be surprised at the things he is willing to accept."

"A Bedu bastard as his son's lover, for example," said a low voice behind them.

Khalidah turned and saw Salim standing in the doorway. She knew him at once, though he had changed since her vision in Alipsha's hut. He was thinner, his black eyes guarded and rather sardonic. She knew that he had intended to shock her with his words, but she didn't flinch at them, nor at the kiss he gave Bilal when he saw that she hadn't – a lover's lingering kiss.

"What is wrong with you?" Bilal demanded, pushing him away in irritation.

"He fears that I will turn you from him," Khalidah answered, before Salim could. Then, to the prince: "But I could not, even if I came with such an intention. Though if you are so blind to the strength of his love for you, perhaps it would be better if I had." She fixed him with a pointed look, her golden eyes leonine, almost feral in their thick kohl rims.

Salim scrutinized her for a moment and then smiled. "Forgive me," he said, "you are right: I have long been jealous of you. But you are also wrong, if you do not realize what a wide stake you yourself claim in Bilal's heart. Still, by that very token, you deserve my respect and friendship, and so let us begin again." He bowed low to her, hand over his heart and said, "Welcome, Khalidah bint 'Abd al-Aziz al-Hassani; Maslamah 'Abd al-Rahman Salim ibn Yusuf al-Ayyubi, at your service." He smiled, his eyes glinting now with humor.

Khalidah smiled back, and bowing as well, she said, "As I am at yours, Your Highness."

"Very well, Your Grace; and from now on, let us dispense with all forms of ridiculous etiquette. Do you smoke?" He produced a pipe of *banj* from a deep pocket of his robe.

Khalidah blanched; then she met Bilal's eye, and they both burst into laughter. Salim looked confused, until Bilal said, "Khalidah and I had a somewhat abrupt introduction to *banj*…and it appears her time in the east has done nothing to change her first impression."

Salim shrugged, lit the pipe in the nearest lamp, drew on it, then said, "Wine, then? I hear they drink it like water in Khorasan."

"Tea," Khalidah said firmly.

Salim nodded, stuck his head out of the tent flap, sent a servant after refreshments and then sat down by Bilal. "One thing I don't understand," Bilal said to him. "How did you know who she was?"

"I know of only two women with whom you could sit and speak so familiarly," Salim answered. "Khalidah al-Hassani and your mother Zaynab. Since she's rather young to be the latter, guessing her identity really wasn't much of a challenge. What you should be asking is how *she* knew *me*." Salim arched an eyebrow at her.

"I have seen you," Khalidah told the prince. "Twice, in fact: most recently in a vision, where you sat with Bilal by a stream and a flowering pomegranate bush."

"Tal 'Ashtara," Salim murmured.

"That was when I learned your name – one of the Jinn's *betaans*, or shamans, told me who you are."

Rather than inquire how the *betaan* had known, as she had expected, Salim said, "And the first time?"

"That was in a dream," Khalidah said slowly. "A nightmare,

really, on the night we came to Qaf. There was a battle in which
you killed a Templar. I know now that it must have been the
battle of Cresson."

Salim's face clouded. "The blackest day of my life…and the
blackest act."

"It looked to me like mercy," she said.

Salim said nothing, looking at his hands in his lap, as Bilal's
troubled blue eyes rested on him. It made Khalidah wonder more
than ever what that dream had meant, but this clearly wasn't the
time to ask. After a moment the prince composed himself and
smiled at her.

"Well, Khalidah bint 'Abd al-Aziz, I gather from what I heard
before I so rudely interrupted your conversation with Bilal that
you are here to make some request of my father. If I can help you
in any way, please, allow me."

So Khalidah explained again about the Jinn, about her
relationship to them and their beliefs about Salah ad-Din, which
had led them to the Sultan's army. As she spoke, Salim's face took
on a look of keen thoughtfulness, so like Bilal's when he had first
listened to the story that it was eerie. *Do lovers always come to
resemble one another?* she wondered, and then wondered on the
heels of it whether this might be true of herself and Sulayman.

"It is true," Salim said at last, "that my father will not like to
be petitioned as a pagan god. But on the other hand, he is quick
to befriend any enemy of the Franj, and if your Jinn are as skilled
as you say, then he will be more than glad of their assistance."
He paused, gave her another keen-edged look. "I take it that you
yourself have not forsaken Allah, despite taking on the guise of
a *kafir*?"

"I will never forsake Allah," Khalidah said firmly, "but this is
not a guise. Aside from their religion, I live and fight as one of
them."

Salim nodded. "Come here tomorrow morning, then. Bring
with you a few of your best warriors, but tell them to keep their
mouths shut about this messiah myth. Can they do that?"

"Of course they can."

"Very well, then. Bring them, and let me do the talking. I promise you, Khalidah bint 'Abd al-Aziz, if it is in my power, your Jinn will belong to this army by midday."

"Thank you, *Sayyid*," she said, and bowed low to him; this time he did not object to the formality, only looked thoughtfully at her.

"Will you stay with us tonight?" Bilal asked.

Khalidah shook her head. "I must get back to the others. They will be waiting for word."

"Tomorrow, then," he said, taking her hand and squeezing it.

"Tomorrow," she answered, squeezing back. Then she slipped from the tent and into the night.

*

The first of July by the Christian calendar dawned as hot and bright as all the previous days of that week. There was no wind, and so none of the haze of dust it would stir up. The only movement on the vast, searing plain was that of the Jinn's approaching horses, wading through the shallows of a heat-shimmer sea, the dry grass of the plains poking up through the mirage like reeds. The riders themselves, clad in unadorned battle white, all but disappeared into the bleached sky behind them. There were six of them in all: Khalidah and Sulayman, Abi Gul, Sandara, Shahascina's father Batoor and his young nephew Janduli. All of them had been sworn to silence on the matter of Mobarak Khan; none had seemed to need to be told.

They dismounted at the edge of camp and led their horses to Bilal and Salim's tent, drawing the stares of the people they passed, for their strange clothing and fine horses made them stand out. They found Bilal outside waiting for them. He told them that Salim was already at his father's pavilion and that they were to follow him there.

"The Sultan is not in good spirits this morning," he said to Khalidah in a low voice, as he helped them hobble their horses.

"Because of the Jinn?"

"Because of the Franj. He is ready to meet them, but they are proving intractable."

"Should we come some other time?" Khalidah asked.

"There is no other time. If it is going to happen, it's going to happen now."

"What can we do, then, to win him over?"

Bilal shrugged. "Just tell him the truth. *Insha'Allah,* it will be enough." He paused, with a look that Khalidah knew well. It meant that he was deliberating whether or not to tell her something else.

"Just say it, Bilal," she sighed.

He started, then smiled ruefully. "Very well. Your father knows that you are here."

"Who told him?" she hissed.

"I do not know. I certainly didn't; but news has a way of traveling in this camp."

Grimly, Khalidah resigned herself to a difficult morning. She and the others followed Bilal through the warren of tents, until they reached the Sultan's. The front panel was rolled up, with a clutch of *mamalik* standing guard at a respectful distance. Inside, Salah ad-Din sat beside Salim. Khalidah made herself walk forward, fixing her eyes on him. He looked back at her, his eyes showing neither emotion nor curiosity. He was smaller than she had expected, but his aura was nonetheless that of a large and powerful man. He wore a mail coat under his yellow silk robe, and a helmet wrapped in a gleaming white turban.

The *mamalik* parted to let them pass. Once inside the pavilion, the Jinn bowed to the Sultan and then seated themselves facing him, as he indicated. Bilal sat down by Salim, looking worried; the prince gave her a small, apologetic smile, which told her better than the Sultan's stony countenance what she was up against.

Salah ad-Din looked them all over for a moment, then he said, "Welcome, representatives of the Jinn." His voice was cool, polite but expressionless. "I understand that you have a petition for me. Who is your representative?"

"I am, Your Highness," said Khalidah, putting her shawl back from her face.

The Sultan gave a start, though it was nearly imperceptible, and then his eyes narrowed. "And you are?" he asked.

"I am Khalidah, daughter of 'Abd al-Aziz al-Hassani, and granddaughter of the Khan of Qaf, Tor Gul."

The Sultan frowned. "So you are the girl who ran off on the eve of her wedding and re-ignited the feud her marriage was to have ended. What business have you here?"

"The same business as you," Khalidah answered, her voice plangent with sudden fury at the realization that the Sultan intended to judge her.

"To fight the infidel with Allah's sword? You are a woman – an outcast, I might add – and your Jinn are pagans."

"Yes," Khalidah answered coldly, "and from what *I* understand, you were once more than happy to accept the assistance of a woman and a Jinni both, Brekhna bint Tor Gul. My mother."

The Sultan looked at her for a long moment, then said, "Before the morning is out, I must find a way to lure Guy out of his lair at Saffuriyya and also find some way to shore Lubiyah against the Franj. The only reason you have this audience is because my son, his friend and your father, all of whom I trust implicitly, have spoken on your behalf." Khalidah was so surprised to hear her father's name included in this, that she did not heed the menace that had crept into the Sultan's tone. "So tell me now and tell me quickly, why I should listen to the petition of a whore and a tribe of infidels?"

Khalidah was as stunned as if she had been struck, and then the anger flooded in. She saw Bilal and Salim exchange a look of despair, but it was Abi Gul who leapt to her feet, flinging her headscarf aside, and faced the Sultan with eyes blazing. The *mamalik* were on her at once, ringing her with spears, but she ignored them.

"How *dare* you!" she cried. "Do you not realize that this woman is princess of my people, descended from a royal line that stretches back to the beginning of time?"

The Sultan had raised his eyebrows and gave her a condescending smile. "And who, exactly, are your people? Who for that matter are you?"

"My people are a race at least as old and as worthy as yours," she spat back, "and I am no more or less than one of them!"

"Which tells me only that your people must be exceptionally weak in both body and morals, to make warriors of little girls."

Khalidah had time to realize what Abi Gul was going to do, but not to stop her. With a nearly-invisible motion, she ducked the *mamalik'* spears and turned, casting a look as she did so to the other Jinn. In an instant the situation was reversed. The Sultan's guard found themselves ringed by Jinn with daggers in one hand and swords in the other. Khalidah thrust herself into their midst, crying for them to lower their weapons. Miraculously, they listened. She gestured for the Jinn to sit down again, and once they had done so, Salah ad-Din ordered his reluctant *mamalik* to lower their spears. Khalidah had resigned herself to defeat; but when she raised her eyes to the Sultan's again, she saw that his look was speculative rather than angry, and a tiny hope flickered into life.

"Tell me, Khalidah bint 'Abd al-Aziz," he said, "are all of your Jinn so quick and so cunning as these?"

"They are," she said, trying to keep her voice from trembling.

"And why, if they have no quarrel with them, do they wish to fight the Franj?"

Taking a deep breath, she answered, "Because they believe that their gods are calling them to it. Your Highness, though these people do not answer to Allah, and though you have made it clear why you believe my opinion to be of dubious value, I swear to you that you would not make a mistake in accepting them into your army. The Jinn are loyal and wise, they are the best warriors you will ever see, and they believe that their duty is to fight the Franj – to fight for you. Will you honestly turn them away?"

Once again, he studied her. At last he said, "How many do you lead?"

"Five hundred, Your Highness."

"Send one hundred of the best to me immediately. They will come with me to Saffuriyya. After that, I will decide. Oh, and I would prefer it if the women among you did not appear as such. I will not have my men distracted by brazen pagan girls." He glared at Abi Gul as he said this. She looked ready to argue, but to Khalidah it seemed a small concession if it won them their goal.

"It will be as you wish," she said, before Abi Gul could change his mind.

The Sultan gave her a curt nod. "And now, you are dismissed – you too," he said to Bilal and Salim. "Divide these Jinn among the *umara*. You," he said, turning abruptly to Sulayman, "stay here."

Sulayman met Khalidah's eyes. His were curious, hers worried, but the Sultan had spoken; they had no choice but to do as they had been bidden.

19

Sulayman returned to the Jinn camp south of Kafr Sabt as the chosen hundred were putting the finishing touches on their preparations. The younger ones were giddy with excitement, hardly able to believe their luck at being taken to the Franj camp by the Sultan himself on their first mission. The older ones were subdued, well aware that they had not been chosen so much as tolerated, and that they must conduct themselves perfectly, or risk being sent home in disgrace. They pestered Khalidah with questions about how to speak, how to behave, how to impress, until she thought she would go out of her mind. She felt she had never been as relieved as she was when Salim and Bilal finally came to take them to their *umara*. Sulayman was with them.

"Take the others now," he said to Salim and Bilal. "We will catch you up once I am ready."

"You don't mean to join this mission to Saffuriyya?" Bilal asked Khalidah.

"I certainly do," she answered sharply. "The Jinn are my responsibility; I will not send them into this alone."

"It will be dangerous, Khalidah. If the Sultan has his way, it will turn into a full-scale battle…" But he trailed off, seeing the defiance in her eyes. "Hurry, then," he finished, and wheeled his horse to lead the Jinn to the muster point.

Khalidah turned to Sulayman and said, "What did the Sultan want?"

Sulayman turned from the retreating Jinn to look at her, frowning. "I still don't quite know. He remembered me from the time I was taken to his camp and played for him. But he did not talk about that. He asked me questions about my childhood and my days with the troupe."

"What did you tell him?" Khalidah asked, tightening the straps on her armor.

"The truth," said Sulayman, donning his own.

"And?"

"And nothing." He shoved his helmet onto his head and gave her a troubled look. "He listened to all of it, then he sent me away again."

"How very strange. Do you think that he knows something about your family?"

"Perhaps. Or perhaps he thinks he does. I don't see how it signifies."

If Khalidah's journey had taught her anything, it was that almost everything signifies sooner or later; but because she knew that this would not help Sulayman now, she said nothing. Checking her armor one final time, she mounted Zahirah and rode after her people.

*

They were split into ten groups, each given to different *umara*. Khalidah purposely separated herself from Sulayman, knowing that they would distract each other if they rode together, but she brought Abi Gul and Sandara with her. The older woman and the younger one bolstered her, each in her own way. They rode in the Sultan's own battalion, because Khalidah wanted to see and judge his reaction to the Jinn first-hand. Before they departed, Salah ad-Din rode down his ranks, inspecting them. He stopped before Khalidah, giving her a long look. Zahirah skipped and danced with days of pent-up energy.

"That's a fine horse," the Sultan said at last.

"Thank you."

"You sit her well." Khalidah waited. After a pause, he continued, "I will not spare you because you are a woman."

"I would not ride with you if you would," she answered.

He narrowed his eyes at her for a moment, then wheeled his horse and cantered back to the head of his line.

It should have been a short ride to Saffuriyya, but their progress was slow because of their numbers and their need for secrecy. A few *farsakhs* into the trip the battalions split up, and then they moved faster, though no less carefully. Abi Gul was quiet, her wide eyes taking in the details of the terrain they passed, and it seemed to Khalidah that she could almost hear her friend's brain whirring as she sorted and stored the information.

Action, however, had made the usually silent Sandara loquacious. She rattled on to Khalidah about former missions and battles of which her father had told her, her tone almost as giddy as Abi Gul's generally was. Then, at the end of one story, she turned abruptly to Khalidah and said, "You have impressed him."

"Whom?" asked Khalidah, who had been only half-listening, preoccupied as she was with the other Jinn in her group.

"The Sultan."

Khalidah smiled. "Have you forgotten that he called me a whore?"

"He was testing you. Obviously, you passed."

"If anyone passed," said Khalidah, "it was Abi Gul."

"It was you who put yourself in danger to avert bloodshed. Believe me. He is impressed."

"Then we must live up to it. Until then, he is humoring us, no more."

Sandara kept silent, but Khalidah caught the edge of a smile through the fluttering black veil.

By mid-morning, the castle at Saffuriyya was visible: a little dirty cube on a stark swell of hill. "It does not look like much," Abi Gul observed, the first words she had spoken since they departed.

"It *isn't* much," Khalidah answered. "A token only, to show that they hold this place. Many of the Franj castles are like that. The army will be camped on the plain, near the water."

And indeed, it was not long before they could make out the smear of smoke and dust on the sheet-metal sky that marked a place of close-packed habitation, and a little later, the first of the tents among the low hills. Salah ad-Din stopped them then, to water the horses and decide on the best plan of action. His battalion had converged with the one led by his nephew Taqi ad-Din, in which Sulayman was riding. Sulayman sought out Khalidah as the Muslim leaders met to discuss their plans.

"How has it been?" he asked Khalidah, but it was Abi Gul who answered.

"Boring," she said. "There hasn't been sign of a single Franji all this way."

Sulayman nodded. "They're certainly playing it close. We saw one of their scouting parties in the distance, but they turned and ran back to camp when they spotted us."

"What about Taqi ad-Din?" Khalidah asked. "What is he like?"

Sulayman shrugged, taking a sip from his skin of water. "Just as you'd expect of a favored *amir*: assured, arrogant. Certainly competent. His men respect him. It's hard to tell more, without seeing him fight."

Khalidah nodded. "The others – how are they?"

"Bored, as Abi Gul says," he answered. "Not quite certain how they are to prove themselves, with nothing to fight. But they're quiet. They follow their orders like lambs."

"That's good," said Khalidah and she had no time to say more, for the *umara* were calling them back into line.

The Sultan and his nephew had decided to continue on toward the Franj camp and try again to lure them forth. Though a wise leader would stay put in Saffuriyya, Guy was just volatile enough that he might be goaded forth by the sight of the Sultan so near his lines. So they continued on toward the pall in the sky, more slowly now than ever, wary of ambush. But for all Abi Gul's vigilance, it was the half-blind Sandara who called the warning.

"Look," she said softly to Khalidah, indicating with a thrust of her chin a slight movement in an olive grove to their right. Khalidah looked and caught a flicker of white, so miniscule and gone so quickly that it could have been a bird – but she knew instinctively that it was not. She had insisted that the Jinn who rode with the Sultan remain in her sight, and now she was glad of her own caution. It took only a moment to alert them and then they were off, dividing into two groups to gallop down either side of the column and surround Salah ad-Din. He looked at them in anger that turned momentarily to surprise as an arrow whizzed by his right ear, and then to grim determination as he realized what was happening.

As he turned to call his orders, a small band of knights charged from the trees. Judging by the arrows that still flew among the Muslims, they had left a clutch of archers hidden there. The knights were already engaged with the Sultan's guard, which had thickened around him as soon as they realized what was happening. A quick look told Khalidah that the Franj swordsmen were lay knights, their fighting skills as rusty as their weapons, and that the Sultan's men would subdue them easily. But she was worried about the archers: their aim seemed too good. Pulling an arrow from the armor of a man at her side, she examined it. The shaft was smooth, the flights made of neatly-cut pheasant feather, the tip well-forged iron.

Casting it aside, she gathered the Jinn in her sights, caught the eyes of the nearest and saw that they had come to the same conclusion as she. Immediately they left what they were doing and gathered again into two groups of five, which then dispersed to either side of the wood. She caught a glimpse of the Sultan, who glared at her from his ring of *mamalik*, no doubt believing that they were deserting, or worse. Then she turned back to the trees and put him from her mind. There was no time to explain to him now, no time to lose.

Once among the trees they spread out further, though they always kept within sight of at least one of their fellows. The intermittent arrows she dodged told Khalidah that the Franj archers had seen them enter the grove and guessed what they were about, but they also gave her a means of locating them. She unslung her short-range bow and fitted an arrow, riding now with her legs only, her reins knotted in front of her. Zahirah had taken to this training like a bird to flight, and she seemed to guess Khalidah's next command almost before it had formed. They moved silently, keeping to the thickest trees and undergrowth when they could. At last she located the archer who had shot at her, though by now he had turned back to the main battle and the aid of his failing knights. He was only lightly armed, and dressed to blend in with the trees. Khalidah raised her bow and Zahirah, sensing the motion and its meaning, froze. The arrow hit the man cleanly in the neck. He crumpled without a cry.

Khalidah had begun to ride toward him, when she felt an arrow thud into her own armor at her back and then another, with a harder blow and a sting that told her it had pierced through to the flesh. She whirled and saw the archer just as he let another arrow fly. Swerving before the arrow hit, Zahirah side-stepping with sure-footed precision, she nocked another arrow – this time a scissor-headed one – and fired it at the man's drawing arm as he aimed at her again. It sliced straight through his shoddy leather armor, cutting deep into his forearm. He crumpled to his knees, holding the wounded arm to his chest, and Khalidah kicked Zahirah forward, grasping her bow with her left hand and her sword with her right. The archer looked up, but he hardly had time to cry out before his head rolled.

Blood sprayed across Khalidah as the body toppled. It was only then that she saw the man's long, black beard, the color of his skin and the shape of the helmet over his glazed eyes. He had been a Muslim – a Turk most likely, given his skill with the bow. A mercenary. Riding back to the one she had felled with the arrow, she confirmed that he too was a native. Somehow, the thought of Muslims doing Franj work sickened Khalidah more than the violent deaths she had just inflicted.

After that, it was over quickly. Khalidah re-joined Sandara, who reported that the archers she'd killed had also been *turcopoles* and that their skill had deserted them at close range. They formed a line with the other Jinn and combed the olive grove, but it was as Khalidah already suspected: all of the Muslim mercenaries were dead. They re-joined the Sultan's band in time to see the *mamalik* cut down the last of the fleeing knights.

Khalidah rode straight up to the Sultan, who indicated to his guard to part ranks for her. "The archers are dead, your highness," she told him.

"All of them?" he asked, raising his eyebrows.

"All of them."

He gestured to his guard, half of whom plunged off into the trees, apparently to verify this information. In a few minutes they were back to confirm what Khalidah had said. Salah ad-Din allowed her the hint of a smile.

"Very well, Khalidah bint 'Abd al-Aziz," he said, "your Jinn may join my army. But," he added sharply, the smile flattening, "do not ever let me see you break ranks without permission again. If nothing else, my guard might very well have cut you down before you had the chance to prove that you were acting in my defense, not attacking."

Khalidah nodded, subdued.

"I am aware that your people have done us a great service on this field today; but nevertheless, this is my army, not yours."

Once again, Khalidah nodded. The Sultan held her eyes a moment longer, before the glimmer of smile returned. "And now, we've spent enough time idling here."

"You don't think that Guy will send out others against us?" asked Khalidah.

"I know that he will not. He would have done already, if he meant to. No – it is time to go to Lubiyah."

"Is that not an abandoned village?"

"Very good," said the Sultan. "It is also the best place to put a battalion to block the road between Saffuriyya and Tiberius."

Khalidah knew that she had ventured into impertinence, but because the Sultan had answered her other questions, she chanced one more. "And why, if your wish is to draw him forth, would you want to do that?"

This time, the Sultan allowed her a full smile. In the shock of its warm luminosity, she nearly forgot her question. But his answer jolted her back to reality like the hard ground after a horse's back: "Because tomorrow, we lay siege to Tiberius."

20

They returned to Kafr Sabt with the last of the daylight. In all of their days on the road from Qaf, Khalidah had never been so tired. She was told that the Jinn had moved into the main camp while her hundred had been gone, and she turned to follow those who had come to meet them, longing for her bed. However, Khalidah had taken only a few steps before Bilal touched her arm and told her that she and Sulayman were wanted in the Sultan's tent.

"What for?" she all but wailed.

Bilal gave her his strange new smile. "To plan for tomorrow," he said. "It is the price of the Sultan's respect."

Khalidah was tired enough to wish then that she had never sought it, but she called to Sulayman and they followed Bilal back through the warren of tents toward the Sultan's pavilion. It glowed like a paper lantern in the falling dark. Inside was crowded with *umara* and scribes and servants bringing coffee and food for those who had been out all day.

Khalidah had wound a turban of white linen around her head and stuffed her plaits inside it. As she entered the pavilion, she pulled a tail of the fabric across her face to better disguise her sex, but she need hardly have bothered. The *umara*, engaged in their chattering and squabbling, gave her little more than a cursory glance. In the course of the day, apparently, the Jinn had been accepted and forgotten as just another band of *muttawiyah*.

Khalidah sat with Sulayman far back against the cloth wall, while Bilal pushed his way through the crowd toward Salim, who was sitting with the Sultan's other sons near his father. Soon afterward, Salah ad-Din called for attention. He looked as exhausted as Khalidah felt, but still his voice was strong and clear as he began to speak, as warm in its assurance as his smile. Its quality was such that it almost made his mad plan seem reasonable, but Khalidah caught herself before she slipped into its lull, snapping to attention once again, not wanting to miss anything; for this, she knew, was the beginning of the end.

"As many of you know," Salah ad-Din said, "I rode out today to the outskirts of the Franj camp at Saffuriyya, in hopes of luring their army onto the field. In this, aside from a minor skirmish, we failed, and therefore I am left with no choice but to employ the alternative plan I had hoped to avoid. Tomorrow, I am sending a detachment to Tiberias. At the moment the town is lightly guarded, its lord and the main body of its garrison having been deployed to Saffuriyya, and I have it from good sources that the castle itself is left in the hands of the Lady Eschiva. My intention is to take the town and the castle and thereby goad the Franj army into coming to its rescue."

"Begging You Highness's pardon," an elderly *amir* spoke up immediately, "but Guy would be a fool to give up the security of Saffuriyya for the sake of one little town."

"And do you doubt that Guy is just such a fool?" the Sultan answered dryly, followed by a runnel of laughter. "Besides," he continued, "there are those in the Franj camp who will push Guy toward this decision." He glanced, perhaps involuntarily, at Bilal as he said this.

"And if it works?" said another *amir*, an Egyptian with a long, pale, lugubrious face. "Our detachment will be trapped between a hostile town and the approaching Christian army."

"That is true," agreed Salah ad-Din, giving the man a cold, calm look, "and it is why I will stay with the heavy cavalry here at Kafr Sabt, until we see how our invitation has been received. Gökböri will lead the Tiberias detachment and Taqi ad-Din will

lead another to the plain beneath the hill known as the Horns
of Hattin, to blockade the second route the Franj might take to
relieve Tiberias, if they do not choose to engage us here. I have
made up my lists already; those of you whose names I call will
have your men ready tomorrow at first light to ride to Tiberias."

Khalidah's mind wandered as he began to read out a long list
of names and so she almost missed "al-Jinni", squeezed in as it
was among the others. It registered only when Sulayman touched
her hand. He smiled at her. She felt little but overwhelming
weariness. On the way back to their tent, she kept trying to make
herself understand that she would ride into battle tomorrow – not
reconnaissance, not a skirmish, but the siege of a town – but she
could feel nothing beyond her longing for sleep. Yet even now
she wasn't free to give into it, for as they approached their new
camp, they found it full of light and noise and commotion: a
party, she might have said, if the sounds had not all been wrong.
Abi Gul appeared at her side and then Bilal, looking as confused
as Khalidah felt. Abi Gul was tugging her hand, pulling her away
from her dusty little tent and toward another, bigger one, its
front flap rolled up and its light spilling out along with a *na'ay's*
reedy melody.

The girl was chattering to her excitedly in Pashto, but the odd
numbness in Khalidah's mind would not allow the words to
penetrate. She looked toward Sulayman for help. Sulayman,
however, was looking at the lit tent, his face sober and
strange. Khalidah followed the line of his gaze and saw a
small robed figure come forth, silhouetted against the light,
another one standing hesitant in its wake. It only made sense
when Sulayman at last spoke the words that should have been
obvious all along:

"It's your father, Khalidah."

'Abd al-Aziz approached his daughter. His face looked more
deeply lined than she remembered, its bones stood out more
starkly, but the wrinkles were lax with relief. It was only
as he reached out for her that Khalidah realized he was
smiling. He embraced her – clutched her, in fact, as if not

quite believing that she was real – speaking her name over and over again. When at last he released her, she saw that the hesitant figure had come up behind them and was hugging Bilal with equal ardor. Zaynab. And then Zaynab was reaching for her, hugging her, praising and scolding at once and weeping through it all.

"But what are you doing here?" Khalidah asked, when she could get a word in. "This camp is no place for you."

"No place for me!" Zaynab cried. "Will you listen to her – as if it were a place for a girl child, either!" She shook her head and said, "No doubt you're right, Khalidah. But I don't have much choice, do I? If it's his place" – she indicated 'Abd al-Aziz with a jut of her chin – "then it's mine."

Khalidah looked from her father to Zaynab in confusion, and then at Bilal, who seemed equally baffled. But Sulayman, when she glanced at him, had begun to smile; and then she saw that Zaynab and her father had joined hands. Before she could make sense of this, her father was speaking again.

"Children, you must congratulate us, and then kiss each other as siblings. Zaynab and I are now man and wife."

*

Zaynab, it seemed, had known for some time what Bilal had only just learned: that her first husband was dead and she was free to re-marry. She spoke of protection, 'Abd al-Aziz of politics, but for all their logical reasons Khalidah could see that there was a real affection between them. Still, it was strange: stranger even than Bilal and Salim. Khalidah could not stop thinking of her father and Zaynab as the opposite poles of her childhood, converging, it seemed, only to battle over points of her upbringing. She had rarely seen them converse without arguing, let alone agree. But perhaps, she ruminated as she watched them, she herself had been the impediment to their discovering their true hearts. Without her to divide them – and to remind them of her absent mother

– it was not really so odd that Zaynab and 'Abd al-Aziz would find that they were essentially married already.

All at once, the burden of guilt Khalidah had carried since the night she left her tribe lifted from her. It slipped up and away with the campfire smoke toward the crystalline stars. She felt liquid, giddy, as she did after over-exertion; as though her limbs, if she had been inclined at that moment to stand, could not have supported her. But she had no desire just then to stand. Instead, as she watched Bilal and 'Abd al-Aziz boast and exaggerate their adventures to one another (Sulayman and Abi Gul had tactfully made their excuses after 'Abd al-Aziz's announcement) she slipped her arms around Zaynab's shoulders and embraced her.

"What is this for, child?" Zaynab asked, surprised to find tears slipping down Khalidah's cheeks and into the cloth of her dress.

"Because I'm sorry to have left you like I did," she said.

Zaynab uttered a low chuckle. "I was ready to throttle you at the time, but don't think I don't know why you did it," she said. Then, lower still, "And I'd have done the same, in your place. Tell me, did you find her?"

Khalidah was silent for a moment, still clutching Zaynab, though her tears had stopped. "I suppose I did, in a way; though not to see or speak to."

"What are they like?" Zaynab asked. "The Jinn?"

"They are like us…and nothing like us. Like the legends and unlike them too." She paused, then said, "I am afraid for them, Zaynab. I'm afraid for myself."

"Of course you are," she soothed. "All of us are. But you're living your truth, Khalidah. That is what matters. Oh, don't start again! Why are you crying?"

"Because I'm so glad," Khalidah answered, "to finally be able to call you *Ummah*."

*

Khalidah slept that night beside Zaynab in the *maharama*

that had been set up for her in the sheikh's tent, knowing that it might be the last time. They stayed up long into the night, each filling the other in on all that she had missed. It seemed to Khalidah that she had hardly shut her eyes before the trumpets and drums were waking her again and the muezzin calling to the faithful. She rinsed her sleep-fuzzed eyes with water, then her arms and feet. Finally she ran her wet hands across her head. But the actions were jerky, like a second language not spoken in many years. It had been so long since she had said her prayers she wondered whether she would even remember the words. As she knelt by Zaynab, though, bowing to the still-black southern sky, she found the words of the *Salatu-l-Fajr* tumbling from her lips, as a once-familiar tune would come back to her fingers on the *oud* if she did not think about it too hard.

By the time they returned to camp the Jinn had risen and pulled together a breakfast of sorts. Khalidah's stomach turned at the thought of food, but she drank the glass of tea Abi Gul handed to her, grateful for its heat in her cold hands and knotted stomach. Then they went and readied their horses. By the time the red sun had prized the sky from the horizon, they were riding toward Tiberias.

The weather was clear, the wind dry, and before long the day had grown hotter even than the previous one. Khalidah felt the sweat running down her back inside her layers of clothing and armor and wished for nothing so much as to tear all of it off. Yet she knew that the Jinn leather was still preferable to the nobles' mail and metal. She had caught sight of Bilal as they rode out, fine and shining in armor and brocade fit for a prince, but she had not envied him. She wondered how he was faring now.

Despite the heat, they made good time. By mid-morning the lake had shimmered into view, and with it the bleached stone walls of Tripoli's castle. To Khalidah, the high walls and bright banners (though slack now in the windless heat) were impressive; but to those who had lived for months as the castle's guard, and the others who had ridden beneath its walls on the fateful reconnaissance two months earlier, it seemed an eerie, desolate place by comparison. It had the air of having been abandoned, and in a way it had been, for with the garrison gone to Saffuriyya its numbers had dwindled, and Eschiva had brought most of the remaining citizens inside the fortifications as soon as Salah ad-Din had crossed the river.

The detachment ranged around the walls, the siege engines and towers rumbled into place, and still there was no sign of life. Khalidah had begun to wonder whether the people of Tiberias would surrender without a fight when a volley of arrows, pitifully thin, whizzed out from the walls. The Muslim army tumbled into action: *umara* began calling orders and the sky darkened briefly as the archers send a cloud of arrows in response. There were cries from beyond the walls to tell them that some of the arrows at least had found their marks, and then the catapults were firing, the air filling with the shriek and dust of shattering masonry.

Far back in the fidgeting ranks of the light cavalry, Khalidah wondered how long it would continue. The Muslim detachment was easily strong enough to obliterate the vulnerable castle by mid-day, and yet in accordance with the Sultan's orders, they were not operating at full force. "Spare the town as best you can, while still taking it," he had said, for he had no interest in the little Galilean port other than as a means of drawing out Guy's army, and no wish to harm the family of his old friend Tripoli.

The Muslims flung their stones until the few men of Eschiva's guard retreated to the keep, and then they fired the town. No knights rode forth to challenge them. There was no point, and both sides knew it. Khalidah's Jinn, like most of the detachment, never drew their weapons that day. They surrounded the silent town, watching the catapults taking half-hearted pot-shots at the castle's towers as the town burned. Khalidah herself saw the messenger pigeons released from the roof. They fluttered for a moment as the windless banners ought to have, finding their bearings before turning south and west with their inevitable message. There was nothing for Salah ad-Din's men to do then but return to camp and wait to see how it would be answered.

21

City lost. Confined to the citadel. Quite well. E.

Tripoli sighed and rubbed his forehead. It felt as if someone was trying to drill through his skull. The headache had begun when they heard of Gökböri's march toward Tiberias that morning and it had not shifted since. Still, he could not help smiling grimly to himself as he handed the note back to Guy. It summed up the character of his wife perfectly, as well as the seed of his love for her. In all his crazed land, he had never met a woman so unflappable, so stoic in the face of danger. That she would approach a siege with the same pragmatic nonchalance as she would a pile of dirty linens was worth more to him than her beauty and money combined.

Tripoli could not imagine a woman less in need of saving than the Countess Eschiva, and indeed her note had said nothing about needing to be saved. Nevertheless, Tripoli knew that this was exactly what the barons would propose. It was only a question of who would speak first, and only surprising in that it turned out to be Guy rather than de Ridefort or Kerak.

He did, however, look to the latter for approval as he made his statement: "We must of course go to her aid."

"Unquestionably," agreed Kerak, delighted as ever at the possibility of spilling Arab blood, particularly after so many days of inactivity.

"We might even leave today," de Ridefort mused. "There is light enough left for a few hours' travel – "

"Why bother," asked Tripoli dryly, "when we could simply hand the Sultan our kingdom on a silver platter?"

"Do you intend then to leave your wife to the mercy of the Saracens?" asked de Ridefort, with studied horror.

As he considered the possible answers to this, Tripoli revised his opinion of his headache: it was not, after all, something external trying to drill into his skull, but the pent-up words of reason trying to escape. He had held them back all day, knowing that they would fall on deaf ears or worse, fuel Kerak's and de Ridefort's latent accusations of treachery. Now at last he spoke them, not because he expected to be heeded or even heard, but because the pain left him no choice.

"I tell you just what my wife would if she were here: to march on Tiberias is folly at best, but to do it tonight is suicide." He held up his hand to stay de Ridefort's protest and was bolstered to see, from the corner of his eye, that the brothers d'Ibelin were nodding and most of the other barons were at least listening. "Can you not see that this is a trap? Here we are well-watered, our supply line is secure, our position strong. Between here and Tiberias there is nothing but heat and barren plains, with only two springs to break them – that is, if this heat has not caused them to run dry. If we leave tonight, I tell you, by morning we will be sitting ducks for the Sultan's army."

"Why should we not march out and meet him like men," roared Kerak, "rather than cringing here like mice?"

Guy looked nervously at Tripoli, but the count kept his composure, his anger showing only in the sudden heat in his black eyes. "Because we are outnumbered," Tripoli said, "and very nearly outmaneuvered. We are unlikely to beat Salah ad-Din's army in a field battle, still less so if we are hungry and thirsty and surrounded on a desert plain. But if we can maintain our patience for a few days more, we can fell the Sultan by his own sword."

Kerak opened his mouth to retort, but Balian d'Ibelin said

sharply, "Stay! I would hear what the Count would say; then you will have your turn."

Before Kerak could think better of it, Tripoli plunged on. "The strength of the Sultan's army is also its greatest weakness. He is in enemy territory now. Soon he will run out of supplies. When he does, he will be forced to attack us here or to retreat. If he attacks us in this secure position we might well best him. And if he retreats, well, the battle is won with no bloodshed."

"Spoken like the traitor you are," de Ridefort said, his voice supple, sibilant with hatred.

"I would beware how I bandied that word, *Messire*," Tripoli returned, with only the barest hint of sarcasm as he spoke the title. "The same has been said of you not long since. What better way to revive the suspicion than to urge this army onto a fool's mission?"

"You accuse me?" bellowed de Ridefort, the vein standing out on his forehead, his fury buffeting Tripoli's calm like the sea raging impotent around an ancient stone. "You, who would leave your own wife and children to the mercy of the infidels? You are not only a traitor, Count, but a coward!"

Rather than rise to the taunt, Tripoli merely shook his head, his face stoic, almost beatific in its acceptance. "Tiberias belongs to *me*," he said softly, "and it is *my* wife who is besieged. Not one of you here can imagine how I love that woman or our home. But I would allow the citadel to be taken and my wife to be captured if I could be sure that Salah ad-Din's offensive would stop there; for in God's name, I have seen many a Muslim army in the past, but none as numerous or as powerful as the one Salah ad-Din commands today. I tell you, if we march from here it will be to our deaths, and the destruction of God's kingdom."

De Ridefort was shaking his head, Kerak sneering, but Guy, for once, seemed to have come to a decision.

"I believe that Tripoli may be right," he said, looking to the nobles for affirmation, "and at any rate, things always look clearer in the morning." He laughed feebly, hoping perhaps for encouragement which was not forthcoming. "Let us put off any big decision until then. You are dismissed."

Not quite certain they believed it, the nobles drifted away, though de Ridefort remained behind, his angry eyes boring into his hapless king.

*

Tripoli had known when he left the king's tent that nothing had really been settled. In fact, if he was honest with himself he knew even as he was leaving that it was a mistake to do so, that he left the king open to influence by the bloodthirsty Kerak and the far more dangerous de Ridefort. He had long suspected that de Ridefort was playing both sides, and since Cresson he had been certain of it. But he had no way of proving it, not even any clear idea of how the treachery manifested, and more than anything he was exhausted, worn down by the constant debate and indecision and the brutal pain in his head. So he left Guy to the mercy of de Ridefort and Kerak – a decision he would spend the rest of his days regretting.

It seemed he had barely closed his eyes when Eschiva's eldest son, Hugh, was shaking him awake again. He read the whole story on the boy's face before he had even opened his mouth, but allowed his stepson to fill him in anyway on their walk back to the red tent.

"They say that de Ridefort has been hounding him since we left," Hugh said, "and Kerak with him."

"As they were before," Tripoli answered. "What, then, has changed his mind?"

The question was rhetorical in that Tripoli knew that little but persistence was required to change Guy's mind, and still less of that. So he was surprised to hear the boy answer, "King Henry's money."

"What?" he demanded.

Hugh sighed. "Guy held firm until de Ridefort reminded him that they had spent the penance money that Henry of England had given into the keeping of the Templars, without consulting Henry. They spent it on mercenaries," the boy added helpfully, though Tripoli knew this already.

"Idiot," Tripoli grumbled. He said no more, but strode out with renewed vigor, leaving his stepson to wonder whether the Count referred to Guy or de Ridefort. In fact, Tripoli had been referring to himself, and the anger with which he entered the tent was also directed at himself, though none of the others could have known this. Even de Ridefort recoiled from the palpable force of Tripoli's wrath.

"What is this about?" Tripoli demanded. "How can you change your orders in the middle of the night?"

"It has taken exactly this long to undo your handiwork," retorted de Ridefort, "and to remind the king of his duty."

Guy smiled wanly at Tripoli, who pointedly ignored him. "And what is reasonable about breaking camp now?" he demanded. "Could this not wait until daylight?"

"You yourself reminded us about the heat we will encounter tomorrow," said de Ridefort. "Is this not, then, the best time to march?"

Tripoli shook his head, glaring at his erstwhile protégé. "One might think you had an appointment to keep," he said, so low that the others could not hear it.

But de Ridefort heard and smiled. At full volume he answered, "Only with God, Count...for we Templars are appointed by God to protect this kingdom and we would sell our mantles rather than let a Christian city go so easily."

Tripoli was shaking his head. "You will live to rue this day."

"We've heard your song, Tripoli," Kerak snapped. "You try to frighten us with talk of the strength of the Muslim forces simply because you like them and prefer their friendship. Otherwise you would not proffer such words. If you tell me that they are numerous, I answer: the fire is not daunted by the quantity of the wood to burn!"

There were nods, murmurs of agreement from the sleepy barons jostling for space in the red tent. Tripoli might have

ignored them all and argued further if he had thought that Guy
might still be swayed by reason. But one look at the king's face
told Tripoli that he had been captured by Kerak's crude images
of glory. He glowed with his imagined victory in a battle that
Tripoli knew was as lost as their holy city, perhaps their whole
kingdom.

"Very well," he said, too weary now for bitterness, "as I am
one of you, I will do as you wish. I will fight at your side, but you
will see what will happen." And he went to rouse his men, leaving
a strange, vacant silence in his wake.

*

If Guy had decided to ignore Tripoli's advice, he had at least remembered some of his warnings, and he knew that he could not
march his army straight across that desert plain. Despite Salah
ad-Din's shrewd positioning of his forces, there were still several
routes open between Saffuriyya and Tiberias, and Guy realized
that his choices were limited to those with water. Therefore they
must either go by Tur'an with its small spring, or Lubiyah and
Hattin, which possessed a larger one, as well as access to the lake
at Al-Majdal. In the end, Guy chose to march south toward Kafr
Kana, then north-east, where they would re-join the main road
to Tiberias near Tur'an.

Tripoli, wedded now to this doomed mission, insisted on
leading the advance guard. Guy rode at the center, flanked by the
bishops of Lydda and Acre who carried the reliquary containing
the shard of the true cross, which had been brought from Jerusalem
for the purpose. Though the Templars rode in the rearguard, its
command was given to Balian d'Ibelin rather than their Master.
That de Ridefort didn't argue this was suspicious at best, but
Tripoli didn't have the energy to wonder anymore what his old
rival was up to. Nor, in the end, did it particularly matter.

Guy's midnight glow of inspiration had quickly dampened as
the tired soldiers formed ranks. They knew by the stars' crisp

clarity the precise nature of the hell that awaited them when the
sun rose. Their grim mood turned black when the horses refused
to drink, though their water was tasted and pronounced sweet.
It was an idiosyncrasy that might well prove lethal both for the
animals and their riders, for every knight of that unforgiving
country knew that without his horse, he was dead. As if that
were not enough, just as they were about to move out there
was a commotion toward the front of the ranks. Tripoli, who
had positioned himself near the center of the vanguard, pushed
through the knights and surrounding infantry to see what was
causing it. What he found sent a chill down his spine, a cold
portent of disaster so far out of keeping with its cause that he
knew it must be heeded.

An unveiled Saracen woman in a tattered dress was struggling
against the restraining arms of two infantrymen. She had a look
of the devil in her eyes, and as soon as she spotted Tripoli she
began screaming at him: "By Allah and his Prophet Muhammad,
I curse you! By all the prophets before him and all the angels in
heaven, I curse you! Lead your men forth this day and you are
damned, every last one of you, to the fire of hell – "

"Enough," he said to her quietly in Arabic.

She spat in his face.

"You'll burn for that, you infidel whore!" snarled one of her
captors, at which she turned to him, smiled, and then sank her
teeth into his arm.

"You'll burn!" the man screamed. Some of his fellows had
already broken ranks to stoke one of the dying campfires to a
roaring blaze.

"There is no time for this!" Tripoli cried, furious. "Leave her,
she is of no account!"

"The devil is in her," one of the men replied. "Witches must
burn."

"Stop this, I tell you – "

But they had already lashed the woman's hands and feet and
were dragging her toward the fire. Tripoli could only watch with
appalled resignation as they lifted the woman like a sack of barley

and hurled her into the flames. Her clothes and hair caught at once and burned away, but she did not scream or cry out. In fact, her skin seemed impervious to the fire. The flames ran off of her like rain as she struggled into a sitting position. When she met Tripoli's eye again she was smiling.

"You see, you have no power over us," she cried. "We are like the deep-rooted tree which grows back after each cutting. You who survive this day will find that you have lost everything. Your blood will water this land and we will drink it, we will – "

At that moment one of the infantrymen, his face twisted by rage and fear, lifted his battle-axe and split her head in two. The woman's body toppled into the flames, but one eye still stared up at Tripoli as he turned his horse and barked at the foot-soldiers to re-join ranks, or face his sword. Yet all his fury could not erase that mocking, taunting eye from his mind. He did not know it, but it would hound him, waking and sleeping, until the day he died.

22

The Muslim scouts rode into Kafr Sabt just after dawn with the news that the Franj army was moving. At first Salah ad-Din could hardly believe that his plan had worked so well, and found himself wondering whether there could be a trap somewhere within the Franj's apparent gullibility. But when his son Al-Afdhal voiced this same suspicion, it polarized the Sultan's opinion.

"*Alhamdulillah*," he said to the gathered *umara*. "We must thank God for this gift, for that is what it is. Break your camps this morning and take your men to the plain between the Horns of Hattin and the lake. Make certain that there is no gap by which the Franj might reach the water. We will fight them there tomorrow."

"Why not just march out and fight them today?" asked Al-Afdhal, querulously.

His father gave him a cold look and said, "Why not, Salim?"

Startled, Salim surfaced from his reverie. "Because tomorrow is Friday?"

"Indeed," his father answered dryly, still looking at his eldest, who was crimson now with shame and fury. "It is always my preference, when possible, to fight Allah's battles on His most sacred day. But that is not all. Al-Afdhal?"

Al-Afdhal merely glowered, so his father continued, "The Franj, by their decision to relieve Tiberias, have declared a war

of attrition upon themselves – for who among you remembers a
week of such brutal heat, or can name a road so poorly watered
as the one the Franj have chosen?" He waved his hand, as if these
matters were trifles rather than the lynchpin of his plan. "Still, we
cannot leave our victory entirely to nature, or even to the Franj
king's stupidity. We must do everything we can to intensify the
invaders' misery on their march, everything to make sure that by
the time they see my army between themselves and the lake, they
will beg to be taken prisoner. I want the horse-archers mounted
within the hour. They are to harass the Franj ranks from both
sides and slow the march as much as possible."

Khalidah, squeezed in amongst the *umara*, felt a shiver run
down her spine. Beneath the folds of their robes, Sulayman took
her hand and held it tightly. In its taut muscles, she could feel
her own fear and excitement. The Sultan looked out at them all
for a moment, his golden-brown eyes stern, without the hint of a
smile, but benevolent all the same.

"*Bismillah ar-Rahman, ar-Raheem*," he said. "In the name of
Allah, Most Gracious, Most Merciful, go now and tell your men
that the time has come. By tomorrow, Al-Quds will once again
be ours."

*

The Jinn rode out with the Turkish horse-archers, half of them
led by Khalidah, half by Sulayman, one group in each of the
two main battalions. Batoor led them in a prayer to their gods
and Mobarak Khan, and then they were riding out, a silent
white presence against the metallic heat of the day. Even before
Khalidah saw the Franj army she had begun in a corner of her
heart to pity them. The country over which they had chosen to
march was rocky and harsh, not quite desert but a far cry from
the green hills that made up so much of the Galilee. It was less
than three *farsakhs* from Saffuriyya to Tiberias – less than a day's
march for a fit army – but without water or fodder for the horses

it would be a march across hell.

At last, with the sun a finger's-width above the horizon and buzzing in the sky like an angry hornet, Khalidah had her first sight of the enemy. Her detachment crested a wooded hill between Lubiyah and Shajarah and found themselves looking down through the trees onto the Franj vanguard. Even so early in the morning, the heat was having its effect. The Latin division, which should have appeared as a tight formation of knights boxed by infantry, was instead stretched and frayed like a threadbare runner along the plain that ran between the hills to the north and south.

Across the valley to the east Khalidah could see the stacked cubes of the village of Tur'an emerging from the wooded hillside and she knew that they must be heading there, for it possessed the only spring in the area. Khalidah's band of Jinn had been put under the command of a wiry little Turkish *amir* called Burakghazi, who was obsessed with the arrow and therefore enamored of the Jinn. Now he called his detachment together, and dividing them quickly into smaller groups, each with an equal number of Jinn, he said:

"The time has come to commit ourselves to our Sultan and Allah. Strike quickly, strike hard. Aim for the horses – without their mounts, they are easy prey. But remember, Count Tripoli leads the vanguard and the Sultan has commanded that we spare him at any cost. *Allahu Akbar!*"

He kicked his horse and hurtled off down the hill, toward the hapless knights on their scorching plain. "*Allahu Akbar,*" Khalidah whispered, and unslung her bow.

*

Raymond of Tripoli looked up at the group of shrieking *ghuzat* hurtling toward him. He could muster no more than a weary sigh in response. He was stewing within his armor, his headache pounded as if to burst his helmet, and he could barely see for the

glare and the rivulets of sweat running into his eyes. He watched
with dreamlike detachment as the arrows whizzed past, barely
flinching as two of them lodged in his armor. On all four sides
the infantry were crumbling against the onslaught, barely managing in their exhaustion to raise their shields before they were
shot down. The Count rested one gauntleted hand on his sword
but made no move to draw it; there was no point. By their skill
alone he could tell that these archers were Turks, and as such they
had no interest in close combat. They would fire off their arsenal
and then turn tail and run, disappearing back into the trees from
which they had come. And indeed, almost before he had finished
thinking it, it had happened. The whiz and thud of the arrows
fell silent, leaving only the sounds of his own men, crying out in
confusion or pain.

Now Tripoli roused himself to action. He pushed through the
ranks to survey the damage, which turned out to be considerable.
The infantry had been sluggish in their response, numbed by
weariness and thirst and perhaps already by the realization that
their mission was doomed, and they had paid for it. All around
him men lay wounded and dying, the lucky ones pierced cleanly
through their throats or hearts, many more gut-shot or broken-
limbed and screaming in agony.

But there was something else, as well – a false note in the
wounded men's collective cry which Tripoli felt before he made
sense of it. The next moment he was staring it in the face: a severed
arm, over which his horse stumbled. The man to whom it had
belonged was already dead, but Tripoli dismounted anyway and
examined the wound. It was a clean cut, and if he had not known
that it was impossible he would have said that it had been made
by a sword. He scoured the ground until at last he discovered
the culprit – an arrow with a forked head, not unlike his wife's
sewing shears.

Before his men could see it and panic, he cried, "Back in
line! Onward!" But the command was half-hearted, and half-
heartedly obeyed. From the woods to which her division had

retreated, Khalidah watched as the Franj leaders tried to pull
the scattered troops back together with the last frayed threads
of order remaining to them. As the battered knights stumbled
forward, her pity was genuine.

*

The rest of the Christian army was faring little better. Even before
the Muslim onslaught they had been far too spread out for safety,
their formations sabotaged by the heat and their own thirst and
exhaustion. Now, as they neared Kafr Sabt and the Muslim front,
more and more *ghuzat* were sent to harass them. Their horses
succumbed to heat and arrows and knights were forced to walk
in their armor. Some collapsed; others simply cast the armor
aside, preferring to expose themselves to Muslim artillery rather
than slowly cook to death.

By ten o'clock in the morning, the king's center division had
reached Tur'an. Those of his men who had not dropped away
had, for the past several hours, marched with the sole purpose of
reaching this town, with its promise of springs and fodder and
respite from the terrible heat. The left flank broke ranks as soon
as the water was spotted, paying no heed to the commanders
who called them back.

"What are they doing?" cried Guy from the center of his
formation, where he rode behind the reliquary of the True Cross,
surrounded by packhorses carrying water-skins. "They cannot
stop here!"

"They have seen water, Your Highness," one of his knights
answered. "They have marched a long way without drink."

But Guy had grown increasingly panicked over the course of
the morning, as the Muslim onslaught became more fierce and
his own army stumbled and straggled. Now that panic took hold
of what little reason he possessed.

"They cannot stop here!" he repeated, his voice rising. "We are too close to the Sultan. We must press onward!"

"Your Highness," the knight began gently, but Guy interrupted.

"I order you onward! Send someone to bring the left flank back into line, and do not allow the others to break ranks!"

"Your Highness," the knight answered and spurred his horse forward to do the king's bidding.

To be so near the antidote to their suffering and yet be denied it did more to degrade the Franj army's morale than any number of Muslim arrows could have done. By the time they crossed Salah ad-Din's front, they were barely moving. Even for the few who were lucky enough to have access to water skins the heat was maddening, intensified by the blowing dust and the steady pounding of drums from the Muslim camp, which seemed to rise up from the parched ground like a heartbeat from Hell. At noon, Tripoli and the vanguard reached the village of Miskinah. As they paused there, a messenger reached them with the news that the rearguard had been forced to halt. Leaving the division temporarily in the command of his stepson Hugh, Tripoli turned and retraced his steps until at last he reached the center division. He picked out Guy's standard at the center and forced his way toward it until he rode beside the king.

Without ceremony he said, "We cannot possibly continue on this road, for if we do, we will meet the main body of the Muslim army, and my men can barely stand, let alone fight. We must find them water and a place to rest, or we are finished."

Guy's eyes were dull and faraway. There was neither emotion nor curiosity in his voice when he asked, "Well, what, then?"

"Not far from here a track leaves the main road to the left. If we follow it we will come to Hattin village. It is only a few leagues, and there are springs there. More than that, it is close to the lake. We could reach it the next day, and with the water on our side we just might salvage this disaster."

Kerak, riding at the king's other side, had been listening to Tripoli's proposal with a darkening countenance. Now, at this insult, he burst forth: "The only disaster would be for Your

Highness to listen to this – "

But to both Kerak's and Tripoli's surprise, Guy interrupted, "Silence! It was *your* advice that landed us here." He glowered at Kerak with uncharacteristic vitriol. "I ought to have listened to Tripoli when he told us to remain at Sephorie. As I did not, I can at least heed him now. Give the command: we ride now for Hattin."

Though it was unclear to whom this order was directed, Tripoli wasted no time in which Guy might once again vacillate. "Your Grace," he said, and with a curt nod he turned his horse and rode as fast as it would take him back to the vanguard with their new orders.

*

"Have they gone mad?" Al-Afdhal asked his father.

They sat on their horses atop a hill above the camp, watching as the Christian army in the valley dissolved into chaos. Salah ad-Din watched for several moments without comment, eyes slitted against the brightness. The *umara* around him stood equally silent, awaiting his judgment (and perhaps the chastisement of his arrogant son.)

At last the Sultan spoke. "They have realized that they cannot reach Tiberias," he said, "and now they are trying to change direction. They are making for Hattin."

"How do you know?" Al-Afdhal persisted.

The *umara* expected a sharp retort, but the Sultan maintained his odd serenity when he answered, "Because they are dying now of thirst, and Hattin has the only springs within their reach." He turned abruptly to face his *umara*. "Taqi ad-Din!"

The Sultan's nephew had engaged the Christian vanguard already that day, skirmishing with the stragglers amongst Tripoli's men. He had ridden back into camp only a half hour earlier, to report to the Sultan and take new orders. He was dusty and sweat-stained, his yellow robe rent and blood-spattered over his mail, but the look in his eyes was as fresh and eager as it had been at dawn.

"Your Highness," he answered, urging his horse forward.

Salah ad-Din sighed, wishing once again that this man could have been his heir. "Your division is still blocking the main road to Tiberias, by Lubiyah?"

"It is."

"Take them now and block the road to Hattin instead."

"It will not work," Al-Afdhal muttered. "The Franj are much closer to Hattin than we are."

"The Franj are closer," his father said shortly, "but we are faster."

"Your Highness," Taqi ad-Din repeated. Bowing to the Sultan, he turned his horse and rode toward Lubiyah, flanked by his guard.

"Will you leave the main road to Tiberias unguarded, then?" Salim asked his father quietly.

Salah ad-Din shook his head. "We must move my center division to cover it. We will make camp tonight at Lubiyah." He spurred his horse, and as they rode down the hill the Sultan recounted their position, though it seemed to his listeners that he spoke more to himself than to any of them. "Taqi ad-Din and the right wing at Hattin; Gökböri and the left wing in the hills near Shajarah. If all goes well, Gökböri will attack the Franj rear-guard and Guy will be forced to order a halt."

"But if the Franj make camp at Hattin," Salim persisted, "will it not be the same as Saffuriyya? Worse, since they have learned their lesson – we will never draw them forth."

"We will not need to."

"How can you be sure?"

The Sultan gave his son a smile of beatific wisdom. "Because by then, we will have them surrounded."

23

The Franj rear guard had been under constant attack by Gökböri's division for eight hours when the order came. The halt boded no relief for the men, for without water or shade it only prolonged their misery. While the troops hung and wavered on the shimmering road, swatting at the intermittent Muslim arrows as if they were flies, Balian d'Ibelin and Joscelin d'Edessa called a hasty meeting with Gerard de Ridefort.

"We cannot go on like this, my lords," de Ridefort said, before either of his commanding officers could take control. "We must strike back, or be cut down little by little."

D'Ibelin had never liked de Ridefort, and since Cresson he had not trusted him either. Now the Templar Master's face was eager, florid, little reflecting the gravity of the situation. If he had not known better d'Ibelin might have attributed this to religious fervor, but as it was he smelled treachery.

"Your haste has condemned us to this march, de Ridefort," he said. "Let us not now allow it to finish us."

Immediately, de Ridefort was fuming. "If I had allowed the king to listen to that traitor Tripoli, the Lady of Tiberias would be a Muslim whore by now!"

"And who is to say that she is not?" d'Ibelin asked. "We have certainly not succeeded in delivering her."

"Which is why we must act now, and act decisively!"

"With what, *Messire*?" d'Ibelin roared, his fractured patience finally shattering. "Look around you! The foot-soldiers are finished. Let the Saracens say the word and they will convert for a cup of water. As for the knights, they are little better off, and I will not order mine to charge an enemy so superior to them in their present condition. I might as well order a foundering ship to steer for rocks!"

"Well, d'Ibelin," de Ridefort answered coldly, "not all of these knights are yours to command. Mine answer to God, and God demands that His soldiers do more than make themselves willing pincushions for infidel arrows."

"Do you call yourself God, now?" d'Ibelin hissed.

"Enough," d'Edessa broke in at last. "We have enemies enough amongst the Saracens without making more of each other. I agree, d'Ibelin, that a charge is unlikely to win us much ground. On the other hand, it will certainly be more effective than sitting here and succumbing to the heat. If de Ridefort wishes for his Templars to engage the Saracens, we may as well let them. If nothing else, it will give us a few moments' relief from their arrows."

D'Ibelin's head swam with heat and exhaustion. D'Edessa's words had deflated him as a needle would a pig's-bladder balloon. He could not even muster words to answer, just waved his hand in acknowledgement of his defeat, and watched de Ridefort gallop away with a deepening sense of doom.

*

To Gökböri it was Cresson all over again, the only difference being that this time he was prepared. Even so, he could hardly believe his eyes when he saw the little wedge of white-robed knights galloping toward his lines, lances couched and ready to shatter on the infantry's shields – which, a moment later, they did. He caught the flash of drawn swords, and then the scene succumbed to its own raised dust.

Like Cresson, it was over before it began. The Templars had

spent themselves in the initial charge. By the time they joined ranks they were swaying in their saddles, hardly able to draw their swords, let alone use them. It was like picking fruit, thought Sulayman, who was fighting in the front lines: a comparison which he could not subsequently banish from his mind, though as the dust turned to crimson mud and his horse's hooves sucked and squelched in a mire of tattered flesh and spilled entrails, he longed to do so. There was no second charge. Those Templars who survived the first retreated as quickly as their tired horses could carry them, leaving their fallen brethren to the vultures and the captured or wounded to the mercy of the Muslim swords.

Meanwhile, to the east, the king's division had at last caught up with the vanguard near the village of Miskinah. They were still nearly two *farsakhs* from Tiberias when the news of the Templar's charge reached them. When he heard it, Tripoli cursed himself bitterly for accepting the command of the vanguard and thereby separating himself from the Templar Master. He ought to have stayed by him, where he might have had a chance of curbing his impulsiveness.

"Lord God, the war is over," he said bitterly. "We are betrayed to death and the land is lost."

"Betrayed?" asked Guy, his voice thin now and showing cracks.

Tripoli had forgotten the king in his self-recrimination. Now he looked over at him. Seeing the whiteness of Guy's face, the tremor of his hand on the reins, he knew that he must act quickly and decisively if they were to retrieve anything of this disaster.

"Betrayed," he answered coldly, "by those whose hot blood burns away reason. If you would salvage anything of your kingdom, Your Grace, then you will order a halt immediately."

"Another halt? But that cannot possibly help us. Perhaps we ought to turn back to *Sephorie*..."

Tripoli gave a derisive snort. "It's a bit late now, Your Highness, to think of Saffuriyya. Even if the Sultan's men would allow the retreat, our own would never make it so far. Order them to set up camp for the night by Miskinah. We will wait there for the rearguard to catch up, and we will try for Hattin spring in the morning."

"This is travesty!" cried Kerak, who had ridden up to listen when he saw Tripoli speaking with the king. Heat and sun had already ruddied his face, now fury deepened it nearly to the color of his hair. "We must attack the Saracen pigs' main position now while we are near it – it is our only chance of victory!"

"Victory?" said Tripoli softly. "Is it possible that you are still so deluded as to imagine we might escape from this with our lives, let alone as conquerors?"

"You speak blasphemy, Tripoli, to suggest that God would see us vanquished by infidels."

Tripoli looked not at Kerak, but at the king. Guy's hands were shaking harder now and his face, if possible, had gone whiter. He looked as if he would gladly hand over his crown to the first taker, if only to escape the crushing responsibility for this mess. But Tripoli had no pity left for him. With a voice like the strike of a blacksmith's hammer he said, "You have succumbed time and again to bloodthirsty fools, *Messire*. You might as well fall on your own sword as listen to this one now."

Kerak reached for his sword, but at the rasp of metal, Guy spoke: "Stand down, Kerak."

It was so unexpected that for a moment, Kerak's vitriol dissolved. But only for a moment. "Your Highness, would you have this lover of infidels dictate – "

"Silence," said Guy, and if he did not sound entirely certain of himself, his hand had at least stopped shaking. "Your advice has proven worthless. Let us see if Count Tripoli's serves us better. We will halt now and make camp as he has suggested, and let us all pray that tomorrow the Lord sees fit to deliver us."

*

By the time the time the rear guard caught up with the rest of the Franj army, they were surrounded. Taqi ad-Din was stationed with his division on the plateau between the village of Nimrin and Horns of Hattin; Salah ad-Din and the center held the hills around Lubiyah; and Gökböri had closed in behind the rearguard, stoppering the valley up which they had just marched. That night the two armies were camped so close that their pickets, had they been so inclined, could have conversed with each other.

The Franj at least were not so inclined. They were thirsty to the point of madness or despair, depending upon each man's particular inclination. The situation was made worse by the raging drums from the enemy camp, their prayers and songs broadcast by the surrounding hills, and most of all by the knowledge that the infidels making the racket were replete with water. For as soon as his troops were installed in their new position, Salah ad-Din had organized a camel caravan to bring water from the lake in goat-skins, which were then emptied into temporary reservoirs dug by the *muttawiyah*. Now the Muslims drank to their hearts' content.

Further groups of volunteers collected brushwood and dry thistles, lining it up in piles along the windward side of the Franj camp and setting it alight. More brushwood was ranged along the road they were expected to take the following day, and left to be lit at dawn. As the smoke and heat from the fires began to do its work, the Sultan had water pots placed at the edges of camp where the Franj could see them. He ordered them filled and then emptied in view of the miserable Christian soldiers. Many of the Franj infantry gave in then, throwing away their weapons and pledging their souls to Allah for the privilege of a handful of muddy water salvaged from the dust.

"What will be done with them?" Bilal asked Salim as they watched the muddy converts being led away.

Salim shrugged. "They'll be put to work with the *muttawiyah*."

"Even the knights?"

"Have you seen a knight surrender yet?"

"No," Bilal answered, "but I imagine they will. They have little choice now."

"They won't surrender without some attempt at a fight."

"Surely even the Franj are not so arrogant as to imagine that they have any chance at victory now."

Salim thought about this for a moment, then said, "I cannot claim to know what they hope for, but I do know that they won't lay their faith aside so easily. They believe that God wills this war, so even now they must believe that God will provide them with a victory."

"Those infantrymen don't seem to believe it."

Salim waved a dismissive hand at the trickle of ragged converts. "Those men are poor and ignorant, and most of them are probably half-breeds anyway." As soon as the words were out of his mouth Salim realized what he had said, and turned stricken eyes on Bilal.

But Bilal only smiled. "Don't say it, Salim."

"Truly, Bilal – "

"Don't. It doesn't matter. Very little matters now."

Salim's eyebrows drew together. "What does *that* mean?"

"It means that by tomorrow, all of this will be over one way or another and, *Insha'Allah*, you and I on our way to someplace better."

Thinking of his father's words, Salim gave Bilal a troubled smile. "You have discovered that land, then, that we spoke of long ago?"

"Perhaps I have," he answered.

"And where is it?" Salim asked, without trace of a smile now, his eyes once again fixed on the sad and miserable converts shrouded in the smoke of his father's fires.

Bilal paused, thinking of the conversation he had had with Khalidah the previous night about her hidden valley far to the east, and the spark of longing it had awakened in him. He knew that Salim would be skeptical at best, and he didn't have it in him after their long day to hear his idea rejected. Bilal knew that the next day would be hard however Salah ad-Din managed to soften the Franj, and he needed hope tonight and harmony, not despair and bitterness.

So he said, "As you once said to me, let us see whether we survive tomorrow's battle, then worry about the future."

Salim seemed about to say something, but in the end he only nodded, then rested his chin on Bilal's shoulder as they watched darkness fall. In the shadow of the Horns of Hattin Khalidah sat between Abi Gul and Sandara, watching their campfire burn and thinking of Sulayman far off down the valley with Gökböri's division, just as Sulayman thought of her. And on the muddy shores of the Jordan a strange, filthy figure with a splinted leg and a devil's eyes pulled himself from the water. He was half-mad now, burning with the slow poison of iron sunk in flesh. Yet as long as he could place one foot in front of the other, he could put himself to the single purpose left to him; and so he turned west toward the sound of beating drums, and revenge.

24

Near dawn on July 4th by the Christian calendar, King Guy, who had sat through that night in his red tent with his head in his hands, called his commanders to him. He looked around at them as if searching for somewhere to lay blame, his eyes coming to rest at last on de Ridefort.

"You," he said, and if his voice hadn't trembled it might have held accusation. "You have brought us here; now it is up to you to get us out."

"Out, Sire?" de Ridefort repeated incredulously. "We came here to fight the Saracens, and it is God's will that we are now so placed that there is no way out but by our swords."

"God's will?" the king whispered, shaking his head. He looked around for Tripoli, and found him back in the shadows by the doorway. "Count? What do you say?"

Tripoli raised his head and looked at the king. After a moment he smiled, and it was like the grimace on the face of a dead man. "What is there to say? If we stay here we will die of thirst by nightfall. To reach Hattin spring we must march straight through enemy lines. Either way we are dead men. It is up to you to choose our doom."

"Very well," Guy trembled. "Yes, I fear that you are right. We must fight our way out. Aimery!" he called to his brother, the Constable of Jerusalem. "Organize the squadrons!"

And so it was that Count Tripoli was given the first division, and rode once again at the front of the army. He took with him his four stepsons, Hugh, William, Ralph and Otto, and Raymond, son of the prince of Antioch. Balian d'Ibelin and Joscelin d'Edessa once again commanded the rear guard, and the king rode at the center with the other nobles, his bishops and the relic of the True Cross. As dawn streaked the sky with light the color of blood, they turned toward Hattin village and their last hope.

*

"Sire, they are moving!"

Salah ad-Din, who had lain all night in his armor, came immediately to the *mamluk*'s call. From his position at the top of the camp he had a clear view down into the valley, where the Franj army had indeed re-formed and resumed its shuffling march north-east. After a time his sons joined him, but it was several more moments before any of them ventured to break the silence.

"Are we not going to stop them?" demanded Al-Afdhal.

Salah ad-Din looked at his eldest. The boy's face was taut with anticipation and anxiety. It stifled the caustic reply that was forming on his tongue. "We will wait," he said at last. "I need to know whether they intend to try for Hattin village or to launch an attack on us, before I decide our next move."

"Then we will do nothing?" Al-Afdhal asked incredulously.

Taking pity on him, Salah ad-Din answered, "Send word to the *muttawiyah* to light the fires along the road. Tell them to light them in sequence, as the army moves, so that they do not burn out too soon to do their work."

Inclining his head to his father, Al-Afdhal ran off. When he was gone, the Sultan surveyed his remaining sons with a distracted look. At last his eyes settled on Bilal, who stood behind Salim like a pale shadow.

"Al-Hassani," he said.

"Sire?" Bilal answered, stepping forward.

"Do you know the whereabouts of the minstrel Sulayman?"

Bilal raised his eyebrows in surprise, then quickly recovered himself, saying, "I believe that he led a contingent of Jinn under Gökböri."

Salah ad-Din gave him a curt nod. "Go then and find him. He is likely camped at Miskinah. Bring him to me." Catching Bilal's glance at Salim, he added, "No, you must do this alone. I need Salim here."

"Of course, Your Highness," Bilal answered, and cursing Sulayman all over again he went to saddle his horse.

The horse was a fine black mare which Salim had given him to replace Anjum. She was fast and sure-footed and even in the dim dawn light it did not take him long to reach Miskinah. But a search of the camp there turned up not a single Jinni. Bilal rode on past the town to the north, where yesterday's brush-fires still smoldered. Beyond them was a smaller camp, and on its fringes, a cluster of white tents. Bilal found Sulayman untying the guy-ropes of one of them.

"The Sultan wants you," he said.

Sulayman looked up at him as the tent collapsed. He was dressed in his armor already, his sword slung through his sash. "Why would he want me?" he asked.

"The Sultan is not in the habit of confiding in his servants," Bilal answered irritably.

"You are hardly a servant," Sulayman said. Before Bilal could retort, he added, "Don't worry, I am coming." He called something to a small, slight Jinni in a language that Bilal didn't recognize. The boy – or girl, Bilal couldn't tell – ran off to do whatever Sulayman had ordered. Then he went and spoke for a moment with an older man, who nodded and put his hand on Sulayman's shoulder for a moment before the younger man turned away.

"Let's go," said Sulayman, shoving his helmet onto his head and picking up his bow and quiver. He had barely finished speaking the words when the little Jinni was back, this time leading his horse. Sulayman swung up into the saddle and followed Bilal south again.

By the time they returned to Salah ad-Din's camp, it was full daylight and everything had changed. The tents had been struck, the horses saddled, and those men who had not slept in their armor were busy donning it now. The Sultan was no longer at his lookout point, so Bilal turned toward his pavilion. When he reached it, however, he found a large crowd gathered outside.

"What is happening?" he asked a cavalryman at the fringes of the crowd.

"Christian deserters," the man said. "They've asked to speak to the Sultan."

"There was a steady stream of deserters yesterday," Bilal said. "They were not given an audience with Salah ad-Din."

The man gave him a sharp look. "They were not knights."

"Knights?" Bilal repeated, but he did not wait for the man to confirm it before he pushed his way through the crowd, finally winning a view of the Sultan's pavilion. The flap was rolled up, and Salah ad-Din sat within in full armor, surrounded by his sons and his chroniclers. In front of him knelt nine beleaguered-looking men, each with his hands bound behind him and an armed *mamluk* at his side.

"...one more time," the Sultan was saying.

One of the Franj, a young man with bloodshot eyes and a red-gold beard, answered in French; one of the Sultan's men translated for him. "They are marching for Hattin – for the spring – but even if your own army were not in the way it is unlikely that they would reach it. Yesterday's march has finished them, Sire. If you attack them now...well, they are as good as beaten."

The Sultan studied the knight for several moments, and then gave a nearly-imperceptible nod. The *mamalik* hauled the bound men to their feet and began to lead them away. The strawberry-haired knight cried: "Wait! It is good information I have given you!"

"And you need not fear that it will go unrewarded," the Sultan answered calmly. "The guards will not harm you. You will be given something to drink and to eat. But you will understand that in these circumstances I cannot allow you to walk free. Not, at least, until our victory is certain. Until then you will be my guests." The Sultan offered him a recalcitrant smile, and the knight allowed himself to be led after his comrades. But Bilal was certain that he saw the glint of tears on the man's face as he turned away.

After the knights had gone, the crowd around the pavilion dispersed rapidly. Bilal came forward, with Sulayman a step behind. After a momentary reverie the Sultan's eyes focused on Sulayman. Sulayman met them unselfconsciously, and after a moment Salah ad-Din rewarded him with a faint smile.

Turning to his sons, he said, "In a few moments we will begin our attack. Go and ready yourselves and your men. I must speak for a moment with this man, and then I will join you."

When they were alone, Salah ad-Din gestured for Sulayman to come closer, then to sit down by him in the shade of the pavilion. Sulayman was grateful for this: the sun was already strong, and he was sweating inside his armor. He knew that the heat of the coming day would be brutal, but for the moment he tried to focus on the present.

"Thank you for coming," said Salah ad-Din.

"You are welcome, Your Highness."

"You are wondering why you are here."

Sulayman said nothing.

"You are here," Salah ad-Din continued after a moment's thought, "because it is your right."

Sulayman frowned. "Forgive me, Sire, but I do not understand."

Salah ad-Din sighed. "Do you remember Cairo, Sulayman?"

"I was only a child, perhaps my perception is skewed – but yes, I remember it as a heaving, filthy, vibrant and beautiful place."

The Sultan smiled. "I could not have put it better. Few people know this, but I loved it there. Partly because it was all of the things you say, but also because it was there that I first felt freedom. In Damascus I had answered to my uncle Nur ad-Din, and for the first part of my time in Egypt it was the same, though by then it was Shirkuh, his lieutenant, to whom I answered. After a few years there it became clear that we would defeat the Fatimids, and I knew that I would be appointed *wazir*. I would be something in my own right." He shook his head, then looked at Sulayman. "Did you ever see the Jewish quarter?"

It took Sulayman a moment to absorb this abrupt change of tack, and when he did, he felt suddenly cold. He could not make himself speak, so he shook his head, his eyes fixed on Salah ad-Din. The Sultan met them squarely.

"It was my favorite part of the city," he continued. "The caliphate was by that time an old man rotting on his feet, infecting everything with a terrible lethargy. But the Jewish quarter was different. Alive. I used to walk through it in the mornings, when the bookshops and apothecaries were opening and the streets smelled of baking bread...well, you do not care about that. You want to know how I met Haya."

Sulayman sat very still, afraid that if he moved or even breathed the Sultan might change his mind and retreat into silence.

"She was far from home. Her family was Persian, from Shiraz, but her sister had married an Egyptian physician the previous year, and had just borne him twins. Haya had been sent to Cairo to help her...and no doubt to find a husband of her own."

"And instead," Sulayman heard himself saying bitterly, "she found you."

Salah ad-Din looked at him calmly. "We found each other, Sulayman. I have never forced any woman against her will, and though Haya was young, she was not a child. She knew exactly what she did. She chose me, as I chose her."

"And then you abandoned her, pregnant, to fend for herself."

The Sultan raised his eyebrows, smiled humorlessly. "Is that what you have been told? I'm sorry, Sulayman, but the truth is that *she* abandoned *me*. I could not marry her – our religions forbade that – but I had made it clear that I would take care of her. I had already chosen a house for her when she disappeared. For a long time I didn't know why she had left. By the time I

traced her back to Cairo she was dead, but I did learn that she
had had a child. A son called Sulayman. And that is the nearest
I can come to an explanation: that somehow, she had convinced
herself that I would drop her once I knew that she was with
child, and so she left, probably to go back to her family."

"That is correct," Sulayman answered. "But they would not
have her. She was on her way back to you when I was born in a
ma'dan village. But I do not know when, or why, she returned to
Cairo."

Salah ad-Din sighed. "Well, I looked for you, but you too had
disappeared. I had long since given up any hope of finding you
when you stumbled into my camp in the mountains that night,
the very image of your mother."

"Why didn't you tell me this then?" Sulayman asked.

Salah ad-Din shook his head. "It took time for me to believe
it. But also, I suppose, because you were a grown man with your
own life. I did not think you needed to know."

"Then why are you telling me now?"

"Because Allah seems to keep setting our paths to cross, and I
cannot keep ignoring it. Because we might die here today, and it
does not seem right that I should take this knowledge with me to
my grave. And because if I cannot recognize you as a legitimate
son, I can at least honor the blood we share. I would like you to
fight with me today."

Sulayman looked at his father for a long moment. He felt
detached, almost as if he were dreaming, but the blowing smoke
and dust, the sweat running down his back and neck, the crying
of buzzards overhead were too mundane for that. He sighed.

"I thank you for telling me this, Sire," he said, "though it is a
shock indeed. And you honor me by your request, but I believe
I must decline. I have promised to lead the Jinn through this
battle, and I do not break promises. But perhaps, when this is
finished," here at last his voice trembled, "we may speak to each
other again?"

The Sultan studied him for a moment, and then smiled his
rueful smile. "*Insha'Allah*, we shall have that chance. Here, take

this." He handed him a silken robe of Ayyub yellow. "Good luck, Sulayman."

Sulayman accepted the garment. "Good luck, Sire," he said, and bowing low, he retreated.

25

While he prized innovation, Salah ad-Din was not a man to discount tradition. Therefore, after he had dismissed Sulayman, his first action was to send messages to Taqi ad-Din and Gökböri by carrier pigeon instructing them to anchor their divisions on nearby hills, as had been done by Muslim cavalry armies for hundreds of years. Taqi ad-Din and his right wing would position themselves between the foot of the Horns of Hattin and Nimrin village, to cut off the route to the springs at Hattin village. Gökböri would station his own division between Lubiyah and Jabal Tur'an, making it impossible for the Franj to retreat west to the springs at Tur'an. The Sultan's centre division would complete the triangle around the Franj, spreading out between the foot of the Horns and Lubiyah, thereby blocking the main road to Tiberias.

"Do not underestimate the motivating power of despair," Salah ad-Din added at the end of his orders to both generals. "The Franj will try to break out toward water – quite likely the lake – and they must be stopped at any cost. Hold firm. Leave Tripoli and the Templar Master alive if it is in your power. *Allahu Akbar!*"

When the pigeons had disappeared into the searing sky, Salah ad-Din took the helmet proffered by the *mamluk* on his left and mounted the horse held by the one on his right. He looked out over the glittering expanse of his army, its banners fluttering proudly in the hot wind, then down at the Franj army, crawling along the valley in its ragged square formations like some great, ailing insect. The disparity did not deceive him. He knew exactly what kind of day lay before him. He knew that he could not be defeated.

"*Allahu Akbar*," he repeated softly, and the spurred his horse forward.

*

Salah ad-Din's center and Gökböri's left flank were the first to attack. The Franj rear-guard had a momentarily perfect view of the endless ranks charging down upon them before the raised dust and the smoke of the *muttawiyah's* bonfires obscured it. The Muslim army slammed into them with the force of a sandstorm in the empty desert. Only the Templars held firm, doggedly defending as the *tawashiyah* systematically hacked their way through the infantry and Turkish arrows felled their horses. For a moment in the midst of the chaos, de Ridefort wondered if he had made a terrible mistake. But he balked at the brink of that chasm, and forcing the doubt aside, he called for his knights to regroup.

"Counter-charge!" he screamed against the shriek and whine of metal, the thuds of arrows and the screams of fallen men and horses. "Regroup and counter-charge!"

The smoke and the dust and the forest of flailing weapons were too thick to accurately assess the Muslim position or even the extent of either side's losses, but de Ridefort had been fighting in this land long enough to have developed an instinct for it. He sensed a lessening in the onslaught and once again screamed his orders into it. This time they were heeded. The knights who still had mounts formed a line behind what remained of the infantry.

"God wills it!" cried de Ridefort, spurring his horse. Though few repeated his cry, the surrounding thunder of hooves told him that they were with him. They slammed into Gökböri's lines, crushing foot-soldiers and toppling lighter Muslim cavalry. The dust and smoke swayed this way and that, like a curtain in a crazed breeze. For every Muslim soldier that de Ridefort cut down, three more seemed to spring into being. They came like a river, rank upon rank of them, a blackness on the hills; and then suddenly they were gone. A tattered remnant of some Muslim battalion was all that stood between de Ridefort and freedom.

"*Messire,* we are through!" cried one of his knights. "Call another charge, and their line is broken!"

Broken, thought de Ridefort. His head was ringing with the din of battle, with the heat and thirst and exhaustion which had at last caught up even with him. He could not make his mind work. The internal compass that infallibly led him down whatever path would be to his greatest benefit had failed.

"*Messire!*" cried the knight, a voice bleeding despair.

But it was already too late. The gap had closed again, filled in by strange apparitions in white with marks on their faces and bows in their hands. *Retreat* – the word crawled across de Ridefort's sluggish mind. By the time it penetrated, his horse had been shot from under him. At last he came back to himself. To his right he saw the knight who had tried to rouse him to call the charge, fighting one of the white riders. Perfunctorily, he shoved the boy from his saddle and onto the infidel's sword and then, hurling himself onto his horse, de Ridefort turned and raced back into the valley.

*

From the slopes of the Horns of Hattin Khalidah looked down into the valley where the two armies fought, darkening the bright sands. There were the wooded hills, there the vastness of water; there even the standards waving in the morning breeze, though the colors had lost their dream clarity to the reality of smoke and dust. Still, she could see the Templars bloodied white and the

Hospitallers' black, the colorful banners of the warrior houses of Franj and Muslim, the brilliant yellow of the Ayyubids and *mamalik*, the green and white of the Fatimids, black again for the Seljuqs. There was a charge and a counter charge, and Khalidah knew that had she been nearer the ground would have shaken with their force. But she did not cry "Now!" She did not cry anything. She sat on Zahirah's back, still as a statue, with Sandara on one side and Abi Gul on the other, watching the storm of flesh and steel, awaiting orders.

"So much for prophecy," she said, not realizing that she'd spoken aloud until Abi Gul answered, "What do you mean?"

Khalidah only shook her head. She knew that somewhere down in the dusty valley everyone she had ever loved – everyone but the few Jinn who waited with her now – was fighting for his life. She knew that in a moment she would be fighting for hers. She was wondering why she had ever thought that she should come here, that she could be anything more than fodder to these two battling gods.

"Nearly time," Sandara said calmly.

"What?" asked Abi Gul.

"Look – the vanguard is lining up to charge."

Sandara was right. The closest Franj square was spreading out, the horsemen lining up behind the infantry. Khalidah's heart came into her throat.

"Do not fear, Khalidah," Sandara said gently. "The Jinn have taught you well. Remember, take down as many as you can with your bow; don't draw your sword until they are upon you."

Sandara settled her helmet more firmly on her head and readied her bow. With numb fingers, Khalidah fumbled to do the same. And then the Franj vanguard was charging, heading straight for Hattin village, straight for Khalidah and her Jinn. Sandara had been right: the Jinn had taught her well. Once she was moving she forgot her fear, firing her arrows with speed and precision equal to Sandara's, if not to Abi Gul's. The Muslim force was larger, but as Salah ad-Din had pointed out to his generals, the Franj had the motivation of despair. Once the two divisions had joined ranks the Franj fought with all of its strength.

Khalidah had long since changed her bow for her sword. Blows rained down on her seemingly from all sides, but her armor held. She rained blows in return, but in the raging of tight-packed men and horses, the deafening clash of metal and the cries of men and animals, she had little concept of their effectiveness. She did not even know which side was prevailing, though at some point she felt the tide-like push against her slacken and then reverse, so that slowly, slowly, she was pushing forward. And then the man whom she was fighting turned and galloped away, and she looked up to see that all down the line the Franj were retreating. She didn't know whether to be elated or disappointed.

Their *amir* was calling them to re-form ranks, and Khalidah turned Zahirah back up the hill with the others. The diverging armies left a detritus of bodies in their wake, as the retreating tide leaves weed on the strand. There were white-robed figures among them, but both Sandara and Abi Gul had survived the charge. There was blood seeping through Sandara's right sleeve, however, and Abi Gul looked pale and drawn beneath her helmet.

"All right?" Khalidah asked them as they resumed their position on the hill.

Abi Gul nodded mutely, but Sandara shook her head. "This is not going to work."

"What isn't?" Khalidah asked.

"If the Franj charge again, they will break through. You must speak to the general."

"Taqi ad-Din? And tell him what?"

"Have you forgotten already, Khalidah?" Sandara said, exasperated. "Yield where the opponent is strong, attack where he is weak. We will gain far more right now by yielding."

"You mean that we should let them through?"

Sandara nodded.

"But – "

"But nothing, Khalidah. The Franj charge, we open our ranks, they ride through the gap and we close them again. They will find themselves on their way down a steep, narrow cleft in the rock of this hill. They would be unable to charge back up it again even if they had the will. And with water in their sights, they will hardly have the will."

Khalidah considered this. It made sense, but the idea of her approaching Taqi ad-Din with the idea was preposterous, and she said as much to Sandara. "After all," she added, "what reason does he have to listen to me?"

"He has as much reason as he has to listen to any of us."

"It was your idea," Khalidah said.

"It is a Jinn idea. It belongs to us all, but you are our leader. Now go, Khalidah, or you will lose your chance. They are lining up again already."

Khalidah glanced down at the Franj and saw that this was true. Taking a deep breath, she turned toward the waving Ayyubid banner that marked the general's position and kicked Zahirah into a gallop. In seconds, it seemed, she was there.

"I must speak with the general," she said to the *mamluk* guard.

He looked at her as he might a scorpion he intended to crush.

"Please," she said. "I have a message from the Sultan."

She didn't like to lie, but she knew that there was no time. The *mamluk* looked at her for a moment, and then barked something over his shoulder. A moment later Taqi ad-Din rode up. He was streaked with sweat and blood, his eyes irritable on either side of his helmet's filigreed nasal.

"What is it, Jinni?" he demanded.

Show no weakness, Khalidah thought, then said, "I can tell you how to defeat Tripoli's division, *Sayyid.*"

"Indeed?" said the man, his look and tone now mocking. "And perhaps you can magic this entire Franj army back to their pox-ridden country…or better yet, to hell!"

"That I cannot do," Khalidah answered, forcing herself to remain calm, "and there is no magic involved. We must simply yield to them. Form our line, allow them to charge, and then open a gap as they engage. By the time they manage to stop their horses they will be far down the ravine, and I do not think that they would choose to charge us again from such a disadvantaged position."

"You suggest allowing the entire Franj vanguard to go free?" Despite the incredulous words, his tone held a flicker of interest.

"Free?" She shook her head. "Perhaps for a few hours. But without the vanguard the king will be an easy target, and when the king surrenders there will be no freedom for any Franji in this country."

For a moment, Taqi ad-Din wavered; and then his face hardened. "Back to your battalion, Jinni, and leave the strategizing to the generals!"

With a sinking heart, Khalidah rode back to her position and took up her place between Sandara and Abi Gul. Neither of them needed to ask her how the interview had gone. Once again they readied their bows, and once again the Franj charged. Before Khalidah had really registered any of it, she was caught again in the thicket of swords and spears, hacking and stabbing with her mother's sword before she could be hacked and stabbed herself. But something was different this time. The onslaught was not as fierce, and instead of the tidal reach and retreat of the first charge, the force of the action seemed to be spiraling away to her left.

When she killed the man she had engaged she found herself momentarily clear, and looked in the direction that the Franj seemed to be heading. A gap had opened in the Muslim ranks where an entire section of the line had swung aside, and the Franj were pouring through it, disappearing like water into parched sand. A moment later the last Franj horse had been swallowed, and the Muslim ranks had closed again. And when Khalidah turned again to face the infantry, she found nothing but their retreating backs.

26

Though Tripoli and his knights were now expunged from the battle, his initial charge had weakened the Muslim triangle where Taqi ad-Din's division met Salah ad-Din's. Tripoli's abandoned infantry could see Lake Tiberias to the right of the Horns, and they began to move east toward the thinned patch in the Muslim ranks, hoping to reach water. It was a delusional hope, but for the Franj it had devastating effects. Seeing their brethren deserting, the infantry of the remaining center and rear-guard finally cracked and began to follow them. Before long there were no infantry left to defend the knights. The Muslims concentrated their arrows on the Franj horses then, until most of the Franj knights were fighting on foot.

"We must form some kind of barrier against their cavalry," said Guy to anyone who might be listening, in a tone that suggested he would like that anyone's approval. Nobody answered him. All of his men were either fighting or sunk too deep in their despair to soothe the qualms of their king.

"The tents," Guy said to himself after a moment, and then cried, "the tents! We must pitch the tents between ourselves and the enemy, for surely that will slow them."

Ignoring the withering looks of his commanders, Guy proclaimed the order. His men turned grudgingly from the battle to obey it, but they only managed to pitch the king's tent and two others at the foot of the Horns before the rain of arrows grew too fierce for them to continue. Guy huddled inside his red tent, trying not to hear the screams of the failing cavalry that still fought around him, trying not to breathe the smoke that rolled over him thicker than ever, trying to make his mind work. He wanted nothing more than for someone else to take responsibility. He cursed the nobles who had pushed him toward the throne to thwart Tripoli, cursed Sibylla who had put the crown on his head. It never occurred to him to curse himself.

After a time a squire came in, a skinny boy dripping sweat and blood onto the fine carpet. "Sire, I am to tell you that all of the infantry is now on the northern Horn. We have sent your orders for them to come down, but they refuse. The bishops have threatened damnation if they will not come down to defend the Cross, but still they will not listen."

"Oh?" said Guy faintly. "And what do they give as their reason?"

The squire made a helpless gesture. "They say that they are dying of thirst."

Guy smiled bitterly. "And will death spare them on the northern Horn? No, never mind. I will come."

When the king emerged he found the remaining cavalry fighting solely to keep the encroaching Muslim forces away from his tent. The rest fought on foot, though more for their lives, it appeared, than any cohesive goal. Looking east, Guy could see the Horns of Hattin: the larger southern one flat-topped and still pristine, the nearer northern one crawling black with his own infantry. He was reminded of a rose he had once seen in his mother's garden back home, so infested with blackfly that its color was no longer discernible.

He turned to the squire. "What is your name, boy?"

"Ernoul," the young man replied.

"Ernoul," the king repeated. "I know that name."

"Perhaps, Sire. We have met before. I am squire to Balian d'Ibelin."

Guy raised his eyebrows. A knight, for some reason missing

his helmet, stumbled past them with an arrow protruding from his forehead and died. "Then why are you here, and not with him?"

"There was no one else to bring you the news, Sire."

Guy nodded as if all of this information was perfunctory. "And what would you do, Ernoul?"

"Do, Sire?"

"Yes. If you were in my shoes, what would you do right now?"

Ernoul looked around at the chaos, the dwindling Franj forces and the surrounding ring of the Saracen army, bristling with weaponry and bitter intent. "Well, Sire," he sighed, "it seems there is little that *can* be done, except perhaps to follow the infantry onto the Horns and hope that there, they will do their duty."

"Very well, *ecuyer*," Guy said. "Let it be known."

"Sire?"

"Go and tell the rearguard that we are moving onto the Horns."

Still gaping at him, Ernoul went.

*

Khalidah was glad of the sudden respite in the fighting, though she could not immediately see what had caused it. It was Abi Gul who first realized the truth.

"Look!" she cried, shaking her plaits back over her shoulders. "They have pitched the king's tent on the Horns!"

Khalidah watched for a moment as the red fabric billowed on the hilltop and then stretched taut. "They are taking the army after the infantry," she said. "But we will surround them and, *Insha'Allah*, that will be the end."

For a few minutes they watched as what was left of the Franj army took up position on the flat-topped southern Horn. Then their commanding *amir* rode up with the order they were all expecting:

"Surround the Horns! Move out!"

They turned their horses to follow the rest of their division toward the hill. It was slow going. The Franj center seemed to be heavily burdened and the Muslims wasted no time in capitalizing on this, engaging them wherever they could, which slowed everything further. The Jinn detachment was toward the back of the division and therefore free of the fighting for the time being. As they rode, Sandara, who had been silently studying the Franj for some time, suddenly broke her silence.

"What is the significance of the golden cross?"

Khalidah looked in the direction of Sandara's gaze. A short distance away a golden cross bobbed on a long pole at the center of a cluster Franj, surrounded by waving banners. Though it had been there throughout the battle, Khalidah had not really registered it until that moment.

"That is the reliquary containing the fragment of the True Cross – the cross on which Iesu the Christ was killed. Or so the Franj believe."

Sandara nodded. Though she wore her black veil even with her helmet, Khalidah could tell by the tilt of her head and the very stillness of her hidden gaze that she was plotting something. "And so, that golden cross is precious to them?"

"More precious than anything," Khalidah said slowly, for she saw now where Sandara was heading, and she did not like it. "It is the representation of their God. They always carry it into battle. I suppose it motivates them."

"So, if they were to lose it," Sandara concluded, "then they would lose their will to fight?"

"Sandara," Khalidah said, "you cannot."

"Why not?" the older woman asked.

"Because you are unlikely to succeed, and very likely to be killed. Think of your children."

"I *am* thinking of them, Bibi Khalidah," she said. She pulled her veil away and jettisoned it to the churning hooves. For a moment the dust-laden air gave the illusion that her face was whole, her smile a perfect curve of certainty. "I am going to the

front now. I need to be near the Franj the next time we charge.
Good luck, daughters. Remember me."

And before Khalidah or Abi Gul could say anything, Sandara
had plunged off into the roil of men and horses in the direction
of the Franj cross.

*

Within the hour the Franj were surrounded on the Horns. The
north and east slopes were too steep for horses, but the Muslim
right and center divisions fought their way up from the south and
the west. Early in the afternoon the Muslim foot soldiers, who
had been marching as one toward the northern Horn, finally
arrived and engaged their Franj counterparts. There was little
contest: those Franj who did not immediately surrender were
easy targets for Muslim swords, or else they were thrown down
the steep hill to their deaths.

Salah ad-Din was cautiously pleased. His sons were fighting
well. Salim had apparently recovered from his ennui and was
cutting down Franj like a demon, while Sulayman had proven a
strong, steady swordsman. More than that, his men – men and
women, the Sultan corrected himself, for he must not forget that
the heathen Jinn were both – followed his lead with obvious
respect. There were definite possibilities for the boy, the Sultan
thought; but this was not the time to consider them, and of
course, he had not yet survived the battle.

Studying his situation once again, Salah ad-Din made two
immediate decisions. The day would not be won until the king
was taken, and the king could not be taken without an action
more decisive than their current slow trundle up the slopes of
the horned hill. He evaluated the two paths to the top as possible
routes for a charge. The southern one, guarded by his own
division, was the steeper. It might tire the horses unduly before
they engaged, which could give the Franj just enough of an
advantage to repel the charge. Though longer, the western slope

had a gentler incline. The west was also Taqi ad-Din's position, and this decided the matter for the Sultan. If he could not make the final charge himself, he could think of no one better to entrust it to than his nephew. If the fact that Khalidah al-Hassani rode in that division was also present in his mind he did not acknowledge it even to himself.

Upon receiving his orders, Taqi ad-Din wasted no time in organizing the charge. The Jinn – minus Sandara – rode at the back. They would not take the brunt of the attack, but still Khalidah's heart was in her throat as they lined up and the call sounded. Then the horses were moving forward, gaining momentum as they climbed the slope toward the flat saddle between the horns where the Franj knights had gathered to repel them. There were not many of them, but there were enough to form a solid line, and far too many of them wore the Templar white for Khalidah's liking. She didn't have much time for anxiety, though. Within moments they had joined ranks and then they were fighting, even the Jinn at the back of the charge. Khalidah had not yet engaged the Templars, and she soon saw that their reputation was justified. It was all she could do to fend off their swords; she doubted that she had made a dent in any of them. But gradually she became aware of the tide she had felt that morning during Tripoli's doomed charges, and it was moving slowly but inexorably against the Franj.

During a lull in the fighting she looked up. Ahead of her the Franj banners fluttered red and gold and purple, and behind them the king's tent trembled in the wind of the heights like a coward's heart. In between them was a bright spark, which resolved as she watched into the golden reliquary of the True Cross. For a second it hovered above the banners. Then it swayed drunkenly to the side, swung wildly for a moment, and sank beneath the churning waves of the battle.

"Did you see – " Abi Gul began.

"I saw," Khalidah interrupted. And more importantly, the Franj had seen. Many of them had thrown down their weapons to run back to the place where the cross had fallen. But they would not find it – Khalidah knew that with as much conviction as she knew that she would never see Sandara again.

*

Later on, thinking back on the battle, Khalidah would realize that they had won it the moment that cross fell. At the time, however, things weren't so clear. After its loss and the initial confusion, those Franj knights still in possession of horses regrouped between the Horns and made two counter-charges that fell on the join between the Muslim right and center divisions. They knew that their only chance now to salvage the day was to take Salah ad-Din himself, and in fact, one of their charges came so close to the Sultan that the men around him disbanded their offensive in order to surround and protect him. But Salah ad-Din sent them angrily back to their work, crying, "Away with the Devil's lie!"

Not long afterwards the Muslim cavalry charged again up the Western slope. This time they succeeded in driving the enemy off of the saddle between the Horns. Watching from the valley with his father, Al-Afdhal cried out, "We have conquered them!"

Salah ad-Din turned him and growled, "Be quiet! We shall not have beaten them until the red tent falls, and as you can see, it is still standing."

Up on the hill, the assessment was much the same. "Onto the southern Horn!" the *umara* were crying to their men. "Take the tent – take the king!"

The Muslims battered their way onto the flat-topped hill where the final few mounted Franj knights attacked them with the wild abandon of the beaten. The hot wind blasted the exposed hilltop, the sun beat down, and Khalidah felt as though she'd slipped into a nightmare. The hill was so crowded that movement was nearly impossible, and she could think of little beyond the brutal heat and her own exhaustion. She kept catching glimpses of familiar faces as one does in dreams, ghost-like and gone in an instant, but disturbing and somehow indelible despite it. There was Bilal, fighting on foot with blood running down his face and by him Salim, his yellow robes torn away and his long hair slick with sweat or perhaps blood. There was Abi Gul, still clinging to Tufan and hacking doggedly away at a black-robed Hospitaller twice her size. She saw Jinn fighting and Jinn dead beneath Zahirah's hooves, neither penetrating far into her consciousness. She even saw Sulayman once, but this, she was sure, had been a hallucination, for over his white Jinn trousers he seemed to be wearing a tunic of Ayyubid yellow.

For a time she succumbed to the eddies of the battle, allowing them to shunt her one way and another. And then something else swam into her field of vision; something red. It took her another moment to realize that it was the king's tent, and she was almost upon it. The next moment someone was attacking her again, but she had regained her clarity of purpose. Looking down, she saw that her attacker was an unhorsed knight. She hacked down on his sword arm when he raised it and wheeled Zahirah as he dropped away howling. She knocked away the subsequent arms raised to stop her and then it was there before her, mundane and solid: a thick hemp rope tied hastily to a wooden peg hammered into the dry earth. A shadow fell on her. She looked up. It was Sulayman, and this time there was no mistaking the yellow tunic. For a moment this distracted her from her purpose. Then he smiled.

"Well, are you going to do it or should I?"

She blinked at him, then raised her mother's sword. The yellow jewel caught the light for a moment, flashing like a Jinni's eye as she brought it down, severing the rope. For a moment as the king's tent drifted to the ground there was perfect silence. And then, the deafening roar of victory.

27

If Guy ended that day as Salah ad-Din's prisoner, he was in good company. Along with the king and countless of his knights and barons, the Muslims had taken Gerard de Ridefort and Prince Reynald of Kerak. Despite the capture of the man he had sworn to kill, the Sultan left the field in rather more circumspect a mood than his soldiers. He repaired to his tent amidst their rejoicing and ordered that the high-ranking Christian prisoners be brought to him. He also requested the presence of his scribes, his sons, Bilal al-Hassani and the minstrel Sulayman.

When Salah ad-Din and his attendants were settled, the erstwhile Latin nobles were brought before him, each with his own *mamluk* guard. Guy, de Ridefort and Kerak were among the first to be presented. Salah ad-Din looked them over and then, his eyes settling on the king, he said, "Come, Your Grace, and sit by me."

The Sultan's words were translated for the king, who spoke no Arabic. He looked as though he did not quite believe them, or anything that he was seeing. In fact he looked, Sulayman thought, much as 'Aasifa had looked on the night he stole her and fled from the Hassani camp. Trembling with fear or exhaustion or perhaps with both, Guy obeyed the Sultan and knelt beside him on the fine carpet.

"And you," Salah ad-Din said to Kerak. "Sit beside him."

Kerak gave the Sultan a long stare after the interpreter had spoken and then, so slowly that the movement itself was an affront, he sat down beside his king. Salah ad-Din subjected him to a long scrutiny, during which Kerak met his gaze with one of unflinching venom.

"How many times," the Sultan said at last, his voice calm but steely, "have you sworn an oath and then violated it? How many times have you signed agreements that you have never respected?"

Kerak answered, and the interpreter spoke hesitantly: "Kings have always acted thus. I did nothing more."

Salah ad-Din said nothing to this, but turned to the Franj king beside him. Guy's water skins had long since run out, and if he was not quite as beleaguered as his soldiers he was at last coming close. He swayed drunkenly, his head hanging like a beaten mule's.

"You are thirsty, Your Grace?" Salah ad-Din said gently. "And afraid, I see. You have nothing to fear from me." With a glance at Kerak as short and sharp as a poisoned dart, Salah ad-Din gave a quiet order to one of the servants. The man slipped away and returned a moment later with a cup of shaved ice. The Sultan took it from him and handed it to the king, but the king would not accept it.

"Ah," said Salah ad-Din, "you fear treachery...and so might any king, though I have told you already you need not fear me."

He took a sip from the cup himself, then handed it back to Guy. This time the Franj king received it with good grace. He drank his fill and then, recalling himself, he handed the cup to Kerak, who finished it off. To the Franj, Salah ad-Din appeared to take all of this in with calm circumspection. Those who knew him better, however, recognized the sudden coldness in his eye.

When Kerak had set down the empty cup the Sultan turned to Guy, "You did not ask my permission before giving him water. I am therefore not obliged to grant him mercy." For it was Arab tradition that a prisoner who had been offered refreshment must then be spared – a nuance of the culture of which Guy had been ignorant.

As the interpreter was attempting to explain this to him, Salah ad-Din lifted his right hand and Salim placed the hilt of his own sword into it. With a smile that had nothing of its usual warmth and welcome the Sultan stood, raised the sword, and brought it down between Kerak's neck and shoulder-blade. Several of the Franj knights cried out. Guy shut his eyes and moaned, shaking now like a man with quartan fever. Kerak fell forward, his eyes bulging and his hands fluttering around the wound in his neck. The Sultan's sword had severed an artery, and dark blood poured forth, soaking the carpet. But the job was not finished, and so Salah ad-Din raised the sword again. With an almighty strength he brought it down again on his old enemy, and this time Kerak's head rolled free, fetching up at the feet of the Franj king.

Salah ad-Din handed the bloody sword back to Salim and turned once again to the miserable Guy. "This man was killed only because of his maleficence and his perfidy. But you have nothing to fear. Kings are not generally in the habit of killing kings." Salah ad-Din bent then and dipped his fingers into the blood that had drenched the carpet. He sprinkled it on his head as tradition demanded, in recognition of the fact that he had taken vengeance on the dead man.

"Take his head to Damascus," he ordered the *mamalik* when he had finished, "and drag it through the streets, so that all might see that vengeance has been taken upon this vile man. Take the prisoners to the city as well and confine them as befits their station. I will tolerate no mistreatment of any of them."

And then, leaving his interpreter to attempt to explain, he strode from the tent to supervise the return of the troops.

*

Khalidah and Abi Gul intended to find Sandara's body and give her a Jinn burial, but even before dusk made the job impossible they had given up. The magnitude of the slaughter was beyond

anything that Khalidah had ever imagined. Where the valley and
the horned hill had earlier been a forest of swords and spears
without apparent beginning or end, now it was a carpet of
mutilated bodies. A horse could not move without stepping on
squelching human remains, and there was little to distinguish
one bloody, muddy tunic from the next. Besides, the *muttawiyah*
had already begun digging graves for the Muslim dead, and it was
entirely possible that Sandara would be under the earth before
they ever got near her.

"It does not seem right," Khalidah said to Abi Gul as they
turned at last from the terrible field and headed back toward the
Sultan's camp. "The Jinn would not wish to be buried beneath
the earth."

"No doubt there are many here who will not be laid to rest
according to their customs," Abi Gul answered. "It is one of the
many casualties of war. At any rate, Khalidah, do you imagine
that we usually carry our dead back from our missions?" She
shook her head and smiled sadly. "It is part of being Jinn, the
knowledge that our bodies may well come to rest far from home.
But wherever our bodies lie, our souls are free. Once the two
are separate, nothing can keep us from re-joining our gods in
Hewad."

Khalidah considered this. It made sense, and there was a degree
of generosity to the philosophy that she envied. Nevertheless, she
did not like the thought of being buried by anyone who would
not understand and implement her own traditions. Sighing,
she turned to her friend. Abi Gul looked more exhausted than
Khalidah had ever seen her. Her eyes were wide in shadowed
hollows, there were countless gashes in her armor and skin, and
she was favoring her left arm; but still she rode upright and
proud.

"How are you?" Khalidah asked.

Abi Gul smiled. "Alive, praise Khuday! You?"

Khalidah's own smile was grim. Her right shoulder had been
wrenched sometime in the final charge, and now she could not
lift her sword arm. There were lacerations on her arms and legs

and she'd had cause to put her silk underwear to the test when a Franj arrow had lodged in her upper left arm. It had worked precisely as described, but she suspected that the wound would take some painful cleaning before the night was through. But as Abi Gul said, she was alive, and none of her wounds seemed likely to kill her.

That she was surprised by this made her wonder if she had expected to die on this day. At any rate, finding herself alive after this battle she had thought about so long left her oddly detached, and dazed. Khalidah had known that any clash between the Sultan's army and the Franj's would be cataclysmic and yet somehow, the result was still shocking. It was difficult to witness such rampant destruction and not wonder why she had been spared to ride over the bodies of the countless thousands who had died. And when she considered the trinkets for which all of these men had given their lives – a gold-leaf cross that might contain a relic, a red pavilion, even the city which was not in the end the holiest or even the second holiest in Islam – she had to wonder whether it had been worth it.

She told herself that she needed to sleep, that morning would clear her head. But when she and Abi Gul finally located the Jinn camp, they found that the Sultan had given out apricot spirits in honor of the victory. Those who were not drunk already were well on their way. Khalidah used the portion that was handed to her to clean Zahirah's wounds, and then, when the horse had been fed and watered, she retreated to her tent. She was stripping off her armor when the flap opened and Sulayman's flushed face peered in.

"You cannot mean to go to bed!" he cried.

"That is just what I mean to do," Khalidah said shortly. She wasn't sure whether her irritation was a result of her exhaustion, her grim search through the bodies of the fallen or the fact that Sulayman still wore the yellow tunic, tattered and bloodied as it was. But it was on the last that she seized. "Have you tired already of the Jinn?" she demanded. "Is it more glamorous to be the Sultan's man – ah!" Rancor turned to a yelp of pain as she tried to pull her tunic over her head and her wounded shoulder screamed protest.

Sulayman's brewing anger turned to concern. "Careful, Khalidah. Let me help you." He tried to ease the tunic over her arm and shoulder, but in the end he had to cut it off. "Let me find a physician," he said, gently touching the swollen joint. "This doesn't look good."

"No," she answered. "There are others who need them more tonight." She lay down in her silk under-clothes, pulling the blanket up to her chin. Though the tent was close with the residual heat of the day, she was shivering. Sulayman came and sat beside her.

"I have not tired of the Jinn," he said in a tone Khalidah could not quite read. "It is only that I learned something today which changes everything."

"What?" Khalidah asked, not really wanting to hear the answer.

Sulayman paused, then said, "Salah ad-Din informed me this morning that he is my father."

Khalidah had thought that she was beyond shock, but these words were like the thud of an arrow into armor. Slowly she sat up, looking warily at Sulayman. He looked back with equal bewilderment.

"How could he possibly be your father?" she demanded.

"He and my mother were in Cairo at the same time in their youth, it seems – "

"No, no," said Khalidah crossly, "that is not what I meant to ask. How is it that he could know this?"

"How did you know that a sword in a junk-shop in a desert town was your mother's?" he asked, exasperated. "Blood calls to blood, Khalidah."

She was silent for several long moments. "Very well; but I do not see that it changes very much. He cannot recognize you, so you cannot inherit, and even if you could there would be all those other princes to challenge you."

"It is true that he cannot recognize me publicly," he said. "But he loved Haya, and because of that he wants to do something for me."

"Like what?" Khalidah asked, her gut heavy with foreboding.

"He has offered me land – not much, just a little town near Edessa and the surrounding farmland – but it is enough to give me a name and the rank of *amir* in his army."

Abruptly, Khalidah began to cry. "So that's it? All that time pining for Qaf and you'll give it up for a backwater town, an indifferent title and a chance to kill yourself in Salah ad-Din's name?"

"Have we not all come here today for that chance?"

"I have not," Khalidah said bitterly. "Nor have the Jinn." She turned her back to him and lay down again.

"Khalidah," he said, the hurt and confusion in his voice so strong that she almost gave in and pitied him. But then he continued, "This way, I can give you the life you deserve."

She laughed. "If I had wanted that life, Sulayman, I would have married my cousin, not followed you to Qaf."

"Khalidah, please try to understand…"

"If this is your decision then I will never understand! The Jinn too have offered you a name and a country, one far worthier than this. But if you are so fickle that the Sultan's finery can blind you to it, then you are not the man I thought you were."

No matter how he coaxed and pleaded, Khalidah would say nothing more to him. At last he lay down beside her, listening to her sob all through that long night of their victory.

*

The next day Salah ad-Din began his re-conquest in earnest. The first thing he did was issue a declaration that the Countess Eschiva and those of her people who were still holed up in the citadel at Tiberias were permitted to leave the castle and to go unmolested wherever they wished. Count Tripoli had not joined his wife at Tiberias after his disastrous charge the previous day, but had gone on north to the city of Tyre. Therefore, Tiberias passed to Salah ad-Din peacefully, Eschiva personally handing him the keys.

This bloodless conquest would set the scene for his many further ones in the days to come, but before the Sultan could continue his redistribution of the Holy Land he had another pressing problem to solve. Amongst the many prisoners taken the previous day were over two hundred Templars and Hospitallers. Muslim chivalry forbade killing prisoners of war, but Salah ad-Din knew very well that these knights were the Franj's only means of challenging his newly-won authority. As such he could not allow them to go free. And so he issued another, darker decree, saying, "I shall purify the land of these two impure races," and ordered them all beheaded.

He had wondered whether some of his more devout followers might raise objections, but before the morning was out his little white pavilion was swamped with men begging to be allowed to play the role of executioner. The Sultan found himself dispensing with the task as a privilege to those he wished particularly to thank or impress, and as such, one of the first invitations to the mass beheading was issued to Sulayman.

"You are not thinking of accepting?" Khalidah said when he told her.

"Why shouldn't I?"

"Because it is barbaric! Because it flies in the face of Muhammad's teachings!"

They bristled at each other for a long moment, but Sulayman was the first to drop his eyes. Khalidah went back to cleaning her armour. "I hope that the Sultan is impressed by your zeal," she said, and though she had intended sarcasm her tone was flat.

"Khalidah, please try to understand…"

"How?" she cried. "How can I possibly understand?" She shook her head. "A woman does not change her mind lightly! There is no allowance for it. I made my choice the night I left my father's camp with you, and I knew that I could never revoke it."

"But he has forgiven you, Khalidah," he pleaded, "and at any rate, what would it matter to anyone once you are my wife?"

She laughed mirthlessly. "Do you really think that I could be a nobleman's wife, having been a Jinni?" She shook her head. "Consider my parents, Sulayman, and tell me that you think it could work."

The silence between them cauterized. Sulayman picked up his sword and turned toward the Sultan's tent.

*

"What has happened?" Abi Gul asked Khalidah later as they washed clothing in front of her tent.

Khalidah considered denying that anything was wrong, but Abi Gul was too good a friend. "Sulayman has left me," she said.

"What?" Abi Gul cried. "Do not tell me that he has found another woman – I won't believe it!"

Khalidah smiled grimly. "Not a woman," she said. "A man. The Sultan – his father." She filled Abi Gul in on what Sulayman had told her, and when she was finished Abi Gul sat thinking for a long time.

"It does not make sense," she said at last. "Sulayman is not fickle. Are you certain you aren't mistaken about his intentions?"

Khalidah shook her head. "He has been perfectly clear. To give him his due, I do not think it is fickleness. Until you have longed for a mother or a father it is difficult to understand the hold they can have over you."

"And yet you are the woman he loves," Abi Gul said gently. "You are his future, not this ageing Sultan."

"I am afraid," Khalidah answered, her voice wavering dangerously toward tears, "that he does not see it that way."

"And you could not stay here, for him?"

Khalidah smiled sadly, shook her head.

"Ah, Khalidah," Abi Gul said, and she might have said more if something had not caught her attention then. "Look – what a strange man! Do you think that he is a stray Franji?"

Khalidah looked up distractedly, but a moment later her frayed attention had focused on the man Abi Gul pointed out. He rode a skinny, mangy cart-horse, swaying in the saddle as though he were drunk, and he seemed to be accompanied by a swarm of flying insects, though with the distance it was hard to be certain.

"No, he is not a Franji," Khalidah said, dropping her washing as she stood up.

"How do you know?" asked Abi Gul.

"Because he is my cousin, to whom I was once betrothed."

"But what is he doing here?"

Khalidah did not answer, for she had seen something else: a little knot of figures walking toward camp from the direction of the execution field between herself and Numair. Without waiting to see whether Abi Gul followed, she grabbed her sword from the tent and ran. Long before she reached them Khalidah had confirmed that the figures she saw were Sulayman, Bilal and Salim. The way that Sulayman laughed and sauntered with the two boys told Khalidah more clearly than any words they had exchanged that he was lost to her in the glamour of this new world. But Numair had swung down from his horse by now, and so she pushed the pain aside to concentrate on the immediate threat.

"Khalidah," Sulayman said when he caught sight of her, "what is – "

"Numair!" she cried, not stopping. "Behind you!"

Sulayman and Bilal turned, but Salim laughed. "That is impossible! I killed him. You must be – "

But he would never finish that sentence or any other, for the next moment he was sinking to his knees, a look of shock on his face and the shaft of a spear protruding from his chest. For a moment the world seemed to stop; then it resumed again in chaos. Salim collapsed and Bilal fell on him, wailing and tugging at the spear that had gone clean through his chest. Abi Gul was down beside Bilal, Sulayman drawing his sword. But Khalidah was a step ahead of him, running again toward the fly-ridden wraith with the swollen, grinning face, the tattered clothing stained with old blood and filth. By the time Sulayman caught up with her Khalidah had already felled him, finding the strength even in her injured arm to knock his knees from under him and plunge her mother's sword into his throat.

28

Bilal did not cry. He could not. He would have believed that he had turned to stone in that moment when Salim fell if it had not been for the deep, rending ache within him. Unable to think of anything to do but to keep moving, he alone carried Salim's body back to camp, laid him in their tent and brought water to wash him. He alone performed the *ghusul*, lifting Salim into the bath and washing him three times, then drying him and wrapping him in a white linen *kafan*. Throughout the process he didn't speak, except to lash out at anyone who tried to help him, sending away everyone from the servants to the Sultan himself.

Khalidah's was the only presence he seemed willing to tolerate. She sat just outside the tent as he worked, for she was forbidden to enter while a man was being prepared for burial. But when Salim's brothers came to carry him to the place where he would be buried later that day, Khalidah at last entered the tent to find Bilal curled into a ball, sobbing tearlessly on the bed that was now his alone. She lay down beside him and put her hand on his head, expecting him to pull away. Instead he moved toward her, clutching the skirts of her black *thoub* as an infant clutches for comfort at whatever is nearest to hand. When a servant came to tell them that the *Salat al-Janazah*, the funeral prayers, were about to begin, they were lying like that still.

*

The grave had been dug on the hill above the camp. It was one of many, and it seemed to Khalidah as they threaded their way amongst them that the earth had opened a thousand mouths to weep for all the vast hordes of dead. Yet still she felt that it was not enough to account for the suffering of those left behind. Looking from Bilal's ravaged face to the still-smoking valley, she wondered if there were enough tears in all the ages of man to account for what had been sacrificed to the Sultan's great victory.

The *imam*, standing beside Salim's shrouded body, was already facing Mecca; the lines of mourners were already forming behind him. Khalidah saw Sulayman standing near the front by the Sultan, the late sun blazing on his yellow tunic. He looked back at her and she met his eyes, then took her place between Bilal and her father. Though women were forbidden to accompany a body to the grave, nobody questioned her right to be there.

The *imam* raised his hands to his ears, and in a low voice he began, "*Allahu Akbar.*" Khalidah repeated the words and then, with the other mourners, she folded her right hands over her left on her stomach. As the *imam* continued the prayers Khalidah's mind drifted with the sun-stained smoke, so that she only half-heard the words. "O Allah! Forgive our living and our dead, those who are present and those who are absent, our young and our old, our males and our females. O Allah! To he among us to whom you grant life, help him to live in Islam, and to he whom you cause to die, help him to die in faith…"

Khalidah wondered how many *imams* were reciting these same words that evening in the surrounding hills. She wondered what the Christians who had escaped were doing with their dead. When the prayers ended, Salim's brothers lowered his body into the grave. Though the Sultan had beckoned to Bilal to join them, he remained in his place by Khalidah's side, still clutching the fabric of her dress. Salah ad-Din looked puzzled, but Khalidah understood: this was a finality that Bilal could not bear. And so the Sultan himself stood in the grave and laid his son down on his right side, his head propped on a stone and his face turned toward Mecca.

"In the name of Allah and with Allah," Khalidah whispered along with the others as the earth claimed the body, "and according to the *sunnah* of the messenger of Allah upon whom be the blessings and peace of Allah…"

Al-Afdhal heaved a shovelful of earth into the grave. It fell with dull irrevocability. Bilal turned and ran.

*

Khalidah sat with her friend through the three days of his official mourning. Bilal received the inevitable visitors as tradition demanded, but their condolences seemed to fall on him like dust into a dry well. He neither smiled nor thanked them, and none of them stayed long. When the mourning period was over and he was left alone once again, Bilal at last broke his silence.

"He had no child," he said in the voice of an old man.

"What?" asked Khalidah.

"The Prophet – peace and blessings be upon him – says that at death, everything in the earthly life is left behind except for charity given during the dead one's lifetime, knowledge which will benefit others and a child who prays for him. Salim was not given to charity, and I do not know that he much influenced the world's knowledge, and as far as I know he had no child."

Khalidah thought for a long moment before she answered. "He had little time to give materially, nor to come up with worthy philosophies, nor yet to procreate…and yet he loved, Bilal. From the little I knew of him, I could see how deeply he loved. And is love not a greater gift than money or knowledge? Is it not a kind of progeny? For though he is gone, the love you shared with him is not, nor will it ever be as long as you are alive to feel it."

"Perhaps you are right, Khalidah," Bilal said wearily.

"But it is poor consolation?"

"It is no consolation at all."

Khalidah sighed, looking at the stone boy who had been her dearest friend. "I would do anything to ease your pain, Bilal."

He gave her a brittle smile. "I know that. But there is nothing you can do, unless you can give me a world where he would not have died."

Again there was a long silence. At the end of it she said, "Do you know, Bilal, I think perhaps I can."

*

Sulayman was waiting for her in their tent when she returned, splendid in his yellow silken tunic, and Khalidah's deathly weariness flared immediately to anger. "Why are you here, Sulayman?" she asked coldly. "You will not make me change my mind."

"What if I told you that I am not the only one?" he asked. "Half of the Jinn want to stay here and help the Sultan with the rest of his conquest."

"Conquest?" she asked dully, wiping the smudged kohl from her eyes with a wet cloth. "I thought that they came here to find Mobarak Khan."

"They did," he answered, growing angry at last, "and they have, and that is why they want to stay. *His* mission is not finished, so neither is theirs."

"And the others? What do they think?" she demanded.

"Like you," he said bitterly, "they believe that their duty to the Sultan finished at Hattin."

"My duty was never to the Sultan, Sulayman," Khalidah said softly, "but to Allah, and to the Jinn, and perhaps to myself." He opened his mouth to retort, but she pressed her fingers to his lips. Silenced, his eyes filled with despair. "It is no use, Sulayman. You will not sway me, nor I you. We have traveled a long way together, but our road parts here."

"That is all you can say?" he demanded when she released him. "You will give up our future, just like that?"

"I could ask the same of you. Please, Sulayman, leave me now. I cannot bear any more."

"Khalidah – "

"Leave me, Sulayman!" she cried, her eyes filling at last. "If that is what you mean to do, then do it, and let me have what peace I can find!"

He looked at her for a long moment, but in the end, of course, she was right: there could be nothing else to say.

*

At dawn the next day Khalidah rode out of Salah ad-Din's camp with a third of the Jinn behind her, and Bilal and Abi Gul on either side. Her father and Zaynab were there to see them off. Zaynab muttered blessings through her tears, but 'Abd al-Aziz seemed to be taking their departure with remarkable equanimity.

"I am sorry, *Abatah*," Khalidah said to him as they faced each other for the last time.

"For what?" he asked.

She smiled. "For not being a boy; for not having pure Bedu blood; for proving everyone right about my mother..."

"Ah, *habibti*, any blame is mine. And at any rate, I would not change anything about you."

"Truly?" she asked.

He shook his head. "You are everything a father could hope for in his child."

"Headstrong, impulsive and intractable?" she smiled.

"Resolute, courageous and loyal. And I believe that despite everything, you are still devout." Khalidah bowed her head. After a moment he said, "You are so like her, it breaks my heart."

"Better, then that I am going," she said with a shaking voice, but she smiled and kissed both of his cheeks. "Good luck, *Abatah*. By Allah's grace, we will meet again. And if not I wish you joy in your new marriage, and many sons who are nothing like me!" She kissed her hand to him, and then turned Zahirah toward the rising sun.

EPILOGUE

If Khalidah had hoped to leave her past in Salah ad-Din's camp, she did not succeed. One way or another, news of his conquests managed to reach them until they were deep into Persia. Khalidah and Bilal and the returning Jinn heard how Salah ad-Din took Saffuriyya after Tiberias had surrendered, and then all the towns and castles along his slow road south until at last he reclaimed Jerusalem. They heard that Gerard de Ridefort had alone been kept alive of the captured holy knights, to be used as a barter-piece in the surrender of the more recalcitrant Templar castles. They even heard that the Pope in Rome, after learning of the Franj's terrible defeat at Hattin, had died of grief, and how his successor immediately called for a new holy war. After that the chain of whispers fell silent.

Though neither Khalidah nor Bilal spoke of their grief, they found comfort in one another's presence. They rode side-by-side during the day and at night they slept with their backs together as they had in their earliest childhood, their breathing assuming a common rhythm. One night, camping in the foothills of Khorasan, Bilal finally broke his heart's silence.

"I would not mind as much," he said, "if he had died in battle. The way it was, it seems such an abject waste."

"I thought the same of Sulayman at first," Khalidah answered.

"And now?"

"Now I am not so certain that we didn't both lose our loves to the battle."

"Sometimes I don't think that I can survive it," he said after a moment.

"Sometimes I don't think so either."

But when Bilal reached out through the darkness to squeeze her hand, Khalidah knew that both of them would.

*

When they reached Qaf, Bilal asked to be given a flock to tend in the high pastures. For a time Khalidah took up residence in the temple with the celibates, but she soon grew bored, the peace she had hoped to encounter there continually eluding her. So she went back to training with the cavalry, and the first time a request came for help she asked to be included in the mission. Tor Gul Khan hesitated only a moment before he agreed, and so Khalidah began her life as a Jinn warrior; but still she was no closer to finding peace.

One evening, nearly a year after she first came to Qaf, she was walking among the horses when she came upon 'Aasifa, lying prostrate and breathing hard. Khalidah knew at once that she was in labor, and a moment later that she was in trouble. A single tiny hoof extended beneath her blood-matter tail, flexed upward toward it: a hind leg, a breech birth, as dangerous in horses as it was in humans. Kneeling by the mare's side, Khalidah lifted away layers of thick membrane and bloody tail, and found as she had feared that the foal's other leg was still inside the mother.

Rolling up her sleeve, she pushed her hand inside the horse's birth canal past the protruding leg until she felt the other, bent and wedged at the top. She waited until the current contraction relaxed, then slowly she straightened the leg and guided it down beside the first. Khalidah waited to see whether the next contractions would push the foal further out, but it didn't move.

Sighing, she unwrapped her sash and used it to grip the slick little legs. With the mare's next contraction she pulled downward toward her hooves in hopes of rotating the foal's pelvis to a better position. After three contractions with well-timed pulls the foal began to come, first the long matchstick legs, then the rump, and finally, in a rush of blood and amniotic fluid, the head and forelegs. Khalidah pulled the remnants of the sac from the foal's face and body. He was a colt, a palomino beauty like his father, with four white socks, a white star on his forehead and a snip on his nose. He wasn't moving.

Wearily, Khalidah picked up her ruined sash and began vigorously rubbing the colt's nose and sides, pressing to expel the fluid from his lungs. "Breathe!" she yelled at him. "*Breathe!*" She hardly believed it when at last he obeyed, drawing a shuddering gasp and coughing up another lungful of fluid. He lay there, exhausted as his mother, but breathing with increasing regularity. Khalidah looked at the umbilicus still joining him to his mother, but without a knife and cords to tie it off this was beyond her.

Looking up then she saw a small, middle-aged man standing watching her. His mane was Emal, and he was the owner of Sre Zer, the foal's father, which for all she knew Sulayman was still riding in his battles for Salah ad-Din. Wordlessly, Emal pulled his dagger from his belt and handed it to Khalidah. Tearing strips from her sash, she bound the cord and cut it.

"That was well done," he said, kneeling to inspect the mare and foal.

Khalidah shrugged. "My father bred horses. Any child of our tribe could have done the same."

"Still, you have saved two fine horses. I would have been sorry to lose them." He looked at the little colt which was already struggling to raise himself, and then back at Khalidah. "What will you name him?"

"Is it not left to a horse's master to name him?" Khalidah asked.

"You saved his life; he is yours."

"But you have lost his father."

"And gained a broodmare," he said gently, "whereas I think that life has not treated you so fairly."

Khalidah looked around at the hills and houses and trees, but saw nothing to suggest a name worthy of what would no doubt be a beautiful stallion. Then, high above their heads, she caught sight of two birds drifting on the valley's warm updrafts. They were hawks, or possibly some type of eagle.

"Shahin," she said, turning back to the little man and his horses.

He nodded. "A fine name," he said. "Leave him to me now, but come back in a few hours and see him standing."

Khalidah nodded, still overwhelmed. "If you change your mind – "

"A Jinni does not go back on his word," he said sharply.

She looked at him for a moment, then touched her forehead and her heart, and bowed deeply, a Jinn gesture of the highest respect. "Thank you, *Sayyid*. You have honored me."

He shook his head, and smiled. "Do you not yet realize, Bibi Khalidah, that it is you who have honored us?"

*

Shahin grew into as fine a stallion as Khalidah had imagined, and he took to his training quickly and easily. With time his coat darkened almost to chestnut, though his mane and tail remained silvery white. The crossing of the Jinn and al-Hassani horse-lines had proved so successful in him that 'Aasifa and Zahirah were soon in great demand as broodmares, and Khalidah took to riding Shahin on her missions.

She was not the best of the Jinn warriors, but she fought doggedly and dealt fairly with the enemy, and in the end even the skeptics accepted her as one of them. When she wasn't fighting she spent time with her grandfather, who instructed her in the history and customs of the Jinn. Little by little she felt her Jinn self eclipsing the Bedu, until even their religion ceased to seem strange. She did not think that she could ever be entirely a *kafir*, but at the same time she knew that she was no longer entirely a Muslim. When she voiced her concerns about this to her grandfather, he only shrugged.

"All things change, Khalidah. Even beliefs."

"But how can I be Khanum to the Jinn if I am still partly Muslim?"

"As I told you long ago, our continued peaceful existence has always relied upon the Khan taking an even view of our clashing beliefs. I do not see that this is much different, as long as you respect and uphold our religion, and I know that you will do that."

Khalidah couldn't argue with this, and when at the end of her first six years in Qaf Tor Gul Khan contracted the pneumonia that would kill him, she no longer balked at the thought of taking his place.

"I have two regrets," he said to her during one of their last conversations.

"If there are only two then you may count yourself luckier than most," she answered, smoothing the wispy hair back from his forehead.

He sighed. "They are plenty, for they are the two things dearest to me."

Khalidah considered this, then said, "It is sad about you and Brekhna; but as my father's people would say, it was written. You cannot regret what is inevitable."

"Perhaps not," he said, "and yet I regret never having the chance to tell her that I am sorry."

"I think that she knows, *Dadaji*," she answered. "But if ever I should meet her, I will tell her for you."

He squeezed her hand. "You are a good grand-daughter, Khalidah-*jan*. Too good."

"Don't tell me that you regret me?" she asked, smiling a little.

"I will never regret having known you," he answered, "but I regret very much what I have taken from you by calling you here."

"What?" she asked. "A life of drudgery in a nomad camp? A husband I did not choose, and children I would raise only to leave me?"

"I know that you left him to come back here," he said softly. "Sulayman."

Khalidah had to swallow hard to loosen the knot that still formed in her throat when she thought of him. "That, too, was written," she said at last. "And remember that it was *I* who left *him* – I chose to come back here."

"And still, you are very young to be so resigned to solitude."

"Don't worry about me, *Dadaji*," she said. "I will be all right."

*

They buried Tor Gul Khan two weeks before *Psarlay*, and Khalidah wondered how she would be able to get through that most important of Jinn ceremonies on her own. A few days before the festival, as she was sitting in her rooms in the hermitage reading, there was a soft knock on the door. It was Bilal. He was hardly recognizable as the heartbroken boy who had ridden beside her out of Salah ad-Din's camp. He had taken to herding, showing no interest in the life of a warrior, and he was good at it. His sheep always threw live lambs, and he had a talent for seeking out the best grass so that his ewes gave the richest milk in the valley.

Early on he had befriended Abi Gul's brother Arsalan, and at first Khalidah had thought that they might become more than friends. But Bilal had only laughed when she suggested it, saying, "Arsalan is a good man, but as hairy as a sheep! Besides, he likes girls. He is my friend: no more, no less."

"Well, Bilal," Khalidah said as he stood before her now, "what brings you down from the mountain?"

He knelt on the carpet across from her. He wore the traditional clothing of the Jinn, plus a long dagger in his sash and a heavy woolen waistcoat against the predators and the cold of the mountains. The waistcoat, Khalidah noticed, was covered with intricate embroidery, brilliant blue poppies on a deep red ground. The poppies were the color of Bilal's eyes, brighter than ever in his sun-darkened face.

"That is a lovely piece of embroidery," she commented, "and I think I could put a name to the artist, for no woman of this valley plies a needle like Abi Gul."

To her surprise, Bilal blushed deeply. "Yes, Abi Gul is the artist. And it is because of her that I have come here today."

"Oh?" Khalidah asked, with the sudden feeling that the ground beneath her was sliding away.

Bilal nodded once toward the floor and then looked up at her. He was smiling. Beaming, she might have said, if she could have thought clearly. "Khalidah, I am here to ask you to marry us – Abi Gul and me. I would like to announce our betrothal at *Psarlay*."

Khalidah hesitated, and Bilal's face fell. The next moment she recovered herself, forcing a smile. "Of course you may marry; you are both adults and free to choose. Forgive me if I seem startled, it is only that I thought…I assumed that your inclinations…"

She stopped, uncertain how to continue without offending him. But Bilal only smiled again. "I do not claim to be much of an expert on love, Khalidah," he said, "but it seems to me that it is about the soul within, rather than the body containing it. Salim and Abi Gul could not be more different on the surface, and yet their spirits are as like as any two people I have known."

Khalidah looked at him for a long moment, trying to swallow her jealousy. She knew that it was ridiculous. She had never been in love with Bilal, and would not have wished to marry him even if their parents' marriage had not made it impossible. Besides, Bilal had suffered at least as much as she, and he deserved to be happy now. Yet his joy threw a spotlight onto her own loneliness, the shallow grave of her sorrow, and it was very hard to look past it to her duty.

"Let me be the first to congratulate you, then," she said at last, leaning forward to embrace him. "Nothing could make me happier than joining my two dearest friends in marriage."

He held her tightly for a moment, then he stood. "Thank you, Khalidah."

"You're welcome, Bilal," she answered. "Send Abi Gul to me, so that I may congratulate her, too." And she managed to hold her smile until he had shut the door.

*

Khalidah shook when she had to address the people on the first night of *Psarlay*, but as soon as she began speaking the words rushed back to her and her confidence with them. After that it was almost as if she had always done it. She saw the ceremony through, and a few days later she married Abi Gul and Bilal, and life returned to normal.

And then at the end of May the news reached Qaf that Salah ad-Din had died the previous March, not on the battlefield but in his bed in Damascus, of a short illness. The Jinn took the news silently – those who had believed in him as Mobarak Khan incarnate for grief, the rest for relief and, perhaps, for vindication. Nobody spoke of the warriors who had stayed behind in Palestine to fight for him. Nobody dared to wonder whether any of them would return.

The first of them arrived at the beginning of June. There were not many, but they continued to come in a steady trickle throughout that summer. They were worn out if not defeated by the hard fighting they had seen over the last years, first to take back the Latin territories and then to secure them against the new waves of Franj sent from Europe to re-capture Jerusalem. All of them spoke well of the Sultan, but they had little good to say about his sons. It was because of them, and the chaos into which the once-mighty Sultanate had dissolved as they fought each other for sovereignty, that the Jinn remaining in the west had at last turned for home.

Khalidah steeled herself after the first few arrivals. She knew that she had nothing to hope for, yet when she saw the joy of the reunited families she hoped all the same. So she remained apart from them, resolving not to ask them what she was aching to ask, not knowing whether she could bear the answer. When the pain of it because unbearable she did what she had done since childhood: she rode. She galloped Shahin up the valley and into the hills, the wind and the motion dulling her mind and heart for a little while.

She was riding like this one August evening as the shadows deepened toward night when she saw a solitary figure stumbling up the valley. He was on foot, leaning heavily on a walking stick, and she thought at first that he was a supplicant looking for military aid, though she could not see how he could have come to the valley on his own. Kicking Shahin into a gallop, she rode down toward the figure. As she approached he stopped, and then, seeing him, she froze too.

Slowly she slid down from the saddle and stood clutching Shahin's mane. She could not speak; she could only stare at him, wondering if grief had at last driven her mad. For it was Sulayman standing before her: older, thinner, scarred by his countless battles and with something very near despair in his eyes. But there was hope there too as he looked at her. After a moment, he offered a tremulous smile.

"Is it you, Khalidah?" he asked, his voice unsteady.

"It is me," she said.

He looked at her for a long moment, taking in the plain white robes and fine striped headscarf of her rank, the thick kohl around her eyes and the blue-black *harquus* on her face. "You are Khanum now," he said half-wonderingly.

She nodded.

"Then it is you whom I must ask for sanctuary."

Again, she nodded. Slowly, painfully, he knelt before her. "Khalidah Khanum, I am sorry, sorrier than words can ever express for abandoning you and the Jinn. I have no right to ask this, but if you could find it in your heart to let me stay…"

He trailed off, looking at her. In his face she saw all the hell of the years he had lived since they parted, and the greater torment of his regret.

"Stand, Sulayman," she said sternly.

He stood, trembling. She looked at him for a long moment. And then she took him in her arms.

"Welcome back," she said.

ACKNOWLEDGEMENTS

Many people have helped in many ways to bring this book to light, but I'd particularly like to mention Elaine Thompson and Jeanie Goddard for their enthusiasm and their meticulous reading of the manuscript at various stages of completion; Professor Peter Jackson of Keele University for patiently answering all of my obscure Crusade questions; Fiona Walling of Cumbria Arabians for sharing her horses (and their Bedouin tack); Dr. Maktoba Omar, Latifa Mohamed and Asim Shehzad for help with Arabic language and Muslim culture; Lubna Asim for checking the Pashto; Abdullah Chhadeh for the recordings of his qanun playing (amazing!); Colin for his ability to untangle the most horrific plot problems and for generally picking up the slack; and last but far from least, Gilly & crew at Snowbooks for their continuing support and belief in my writing. Any mistakes or diversions from historical fact are mine, and not theirs!

SELECTED BIBLIOGRAPHY

Though there isn't space to list all of the resources I used in researching this novel, listed below are a few books which provide interesting further reading about some of the subjects involved in *The Sand Daughter*. For those interested in the Battle of Hattin, there are numerous first-hand accounts from both the Muslim and Christian perspective. The Jinn, their military tactics, culture and religion are based on traditional Pashtun, Kalash, Mongolian and Tibetan culture and mythology, all of which make fascinating reading material.

By kind permission of Saqi books, English translation of "The Crusades Through Arab Eyes" © 1984, 2004. from original edition by Amin Maalouf 1983

"A Vanished World" by Wilfred Thesiger

"An Arab-Syrian Gentleman in the Period of the Crusades" by Usamah Ibn-Munqidh

"The Book of Saladin" by Tariq Ali

"Desert Tracings: Six Classic Arabian Odes" translated by Michael A. Sells

"Arabia of the Bedouins" by Marcel Kurpershoek

"Veiled Sentiments" by Lila Abu-Lughod

"Before Homosexuality in the Arab-Islamic World" by Khaled el-Rouayheb

"A Traveller on Horseback" by Christina Dodwell

"A Short Walk in the Hindu Kush" by Eric Newby

"Afghanistan: A Companion Guide" by Bijan Omrani and Matthew Leeming

(The publishers have made every effort to contact the copyright holders for content quoted in this edition and would be delighted to acknowledge any further references in future editions)

GLOSSARY

Abatah – father

Ahdath – city militia

Akhah – brother

Akhd – part of Bedouin marriage ceremony, where the marriage contract is negotiated

'Alif – the first letter of the Arabic alphabet

Amir (pl. Umara) – any of several types of leader, including military commander and prince

Amir al-Hajj – leader of the pilgrimage

Ammah – uncle

Atabeg – governor of a nation or province, subordinate to a monarch

Ba'a – second letter in the Arabic alphabet

Banj – a medieval version of hashish

Bedu – Bedouin

Darwish – dervish; a Muslim ascetic/mystic

Farsakh – ancient Arabic unit of distance, about 6 km

Franj – literally, 'Franks'; medieval Arabic term for any Europeans in Palestine, regardless of their country of origin

Ghata – the front flap of a Bedouin tent

Ghazi (pl. Ghuzat) – warrior; raider

Ghazw (pl. Ghazawat) – raid

Ghusul – Muslim ritual bath

Habibti – darling, directed at a female

Hadith – traditional sayings attributed to Muhammad

Hajj – pilgrimage to Mecca

Imam – prayer leader

Irta – woody plant, whose roots the Bedouin use as fuel

Jihaz – new clothing for a girl to take with her when she is married

Kafan – shroud, generally a plain white sheet

Kafir (pl. Kuffar) – infidel, non-believer (in Islam)

Koutha – official marriage proposal

Kufiyya – man's head-scarf

Laylat al-Henna – henna night, part of an Islamic a wedding

Ma'dan – Marsh Arabs (from Iraq)

Maharama – women's section of a Bedouin tent

Majlis – men's section of a Bedouin tent

Mamluk (pl. Mamalik) – elite slave-recruited Muslim soldiers, later a ruling dynasty

Mudhif – Iraqi marsh Arabs' reed house

Muharram – first month of the Muslim year

Mujahid (pl. Mujahiddin) – Muslim holy warrior

Muttawiyah – unskilled Muslim religious volunteer soldiers

Na'ay – reed flute

Nafathin – fire-troops

Oud – instrument like a lute

Pullani – mixed-blood Frankish soldiers, offspring of Frankish-Arab unions

Qanun – instrument like a zither

Al-Quds – Jerusalem

Rajjalah – low-ranking Muslim infantry soldier

Sajjadah – flat-woven rug

Salatu-l-Fajr – Islamic dawn prayer

Saqa – small division of Muslim cavalry

Sayyid/Sayyida – Sir/Lady

Sharbush – a type of peaked hat, worn by the Sultan's mamluk guards

Sidi – "my master"

Suq – commercial quarter of an Arab city

Sultan – Muslim leader, beneath the caliph in hierarchy

Tabla – drum

Tal – hill
Tawashiyah – Muslim heavy cavalry, generally noblemen
Thoub – traditional Bedouin double-dress
Ummah – mother
Wadi – river bed or valley, generally dry
Al-Zuhra – Venus, the planet

ARABIC PHRASES

Alhamdulillah – Praise be to Allah
Allahu Akbar – God is the greatest
As-Salaamu 'alaikum – Peace be upon you (equivalent of hello)
Bismillah ar-Rahman, ar-Raheem – In the name of Allah, Most Gracious, Most Merciful
Insha'Allah – If God wills it
Ma'as Salaama – Go with peace (equivalent of good-bye)
Wa 'alaikum as-salaam [wa rahmatu Allah] – And upon you is the peace [together with God's mercy]; the response to "as-salaamu 'alaikum"

PERSIAN/PASHTO WORDS

Aghundem – to dress, to put on
Amesha Spentas – one of seven divine beings in Zoroastrianism
Aylaq – shepherd's hut
Betaan – shaman; prophet
Bibi – female title of respect; "lady"
Dadaji – grandfather
Ghar – mountain
Harquus – facial tattoos

Hewad – homeland
Husay – falcon
Jan – dear; term of affection when added to a name
Kavir – salt desert
Khan (f. Khanum) – title for a leader
Mateledal – to wait for
Meerre – literally, warrior; colloquially, husband
Mor – mother
Pakol – traditional Nuristani hat
Psarlay – spring
Qanat – underground canal, used to carry water to dry places
Setar – stringed instrument like a lute
Turcoman – people from modern Turkmenistan
Tut – mulberry
Wradz de shode – Milk Day

OTHER

Saracens –medieval Europeans' term for Arabs
League – 2.2 km; medieval European unit of distance